They'll pay him a fortune to find a violent tornado for their movie. He knows the risks all too well, but he never imagined just how complicated the perfect storm could be.

Chuck Rittenburg was one of the most successful storm chasers in history until a bad decision resulted in the death of a young couple who'd paid to ride along. A decade later, broke, divorced, and estranged from his college-age children, he's got nothing left to lose. When a film producer offers Chuck one-million dollars to help find and photograph an extreme tornado in Oklahoma, Chuck sees a chance to earn his kids' respect again—and maybe his own.

The situation quickly becomes about more than tracking a monster storm for Hollywood. FBI Agent Gabi Medeiros insists on joining his crew. A burglary ring is targeting tornado-ravaged neighborhoods, and their tactics now include murder.

With the stage set for a major heist, a deadly twister, and a confrontation between Man and Nature on an epic scale, Chuck and his crew will be lucky to escape in one piece.

Praise for Buzz Bernard's Previous Novels

Plague

"A page-turning thriller rooted in today's world of political unrest. This all too realistic fiction will suspend your belief in the safety of home and the assurance of government protection. *PLAGUE* will keep you up at night long after you've finished it."
—John House, MD, author of *So Shall You Reap*

"If you love thrillers and haven't read Buzz Bernard yet, I suggest you stop what you're doing and rectify that right now. *PLAGUE* grabs you around the throat and squeezes, with believable characters, a realistic plot, and non-stop action. One of the best thrillers of 2012."
—Al Leverone, author of *The Lonely Mile*

"An all-too-believable nightmare tale about the horrors of biological terrorism. Buzz Bernard will keep you up at night wondering *What if?*"
—Tom Young, author of *The Mullah's Storm*, *Silent Enemy*, and *The Renegades*

"Fans of the late Michael Crichton should check out Buzz Bernard's PLAGUE. This bioterrorism thriller is a real page-turner."
—Cheryl Norman, author of *Rebuild My World*

"A delight for thriller readers. Intense, edgy, full of twists and scary plausibilities. A totally unexpected protagonist and a brilliant cast of characters. Fans of Michael Crichton, Robin Cook and Stephen Coonts will want to pick up H.W. "Buzz" Bernard's PLAGUE, but not before clearing all decks and fastening their seat belts."
—Donnell Ann Bell, bestselling author, *The Past Came Hunting*

Eyewall

"Buzz Bernard bursts on the scene with EYEWALL, a compelling and suspenseful tale told with the insight and authenticity of one who has walked in the world of the famed Hurricane Hunters and endured the harsh realities of a major, devastating storm. Great characters combine with razor-sharp suspense and leave you breathless. A one-sitting, white-knuckle read."
—Vicki Hinze, award-winning author of *Deadly Ties*

"A well-crafted tale you can't put down; characters you care about; a spot-on insiders look at hurricane forecasting and flying."
—Jack Williams, author and founding USA TODAY Weather Editor

"A dramatic and frenzied story of how an angry hurricane collides with the frailty and heroism of human nature. After reading the exciting and emotional EYEWALL, I admire even more those who work to protect us from the next category five."
—Michael Buchanan, co-author and screenwriter, *The Fat Boy Chronicles* and *Micah's Child.*

"Riveting . . . Intrigue, power struggles . . . Frightening reality from several perspectives . . . EYEWALL will keep you more than interested. Having been on location interviewing survivors of a Cat 4/5 hurricane that hit Charleston SC in 1989 (Hugo) and witnessing the destruction left in its wake I fully understand how a Cat 5 might impact a barrier island along the southeast coast of the United States. The author takes us there and describes in frightening detail the impact of this scary scenario."
—Marshall Seese, retired anchorman and meteorologist, The Weather Channel

Other Novels by
Buzz Bernard
from Bell Bridge Books

EYEWALL

PLAGUE

SUPERCELL

Supercell

by

H.W. "Buzz" Bernard

Buzz Bernard
11/2/13

B

Bell Bridge Books

Bell Bridge Books
PO BOX 300921
Memphis, TN 38130
Print ISBN: 978-1-61194-339-9

Bell Bridge Books is an Imprint of BelleBooks, Inc.

We at BelleBooks enjoy hearing from readers.
Visit our websites – www.BelleBooks.com and www.BellBridgeBooks.com.

10 9 8 7 6 5 4 3 2 1

Cover design: Debra Dixon
Interior design: Hank Smith
Photo credits:
Tornado photo (manipulated) © Solarseven | Dreamstime.com

:Lsaz:01:

Supercell:

At once the most beautiful (visually) and violent of all thunderstorms, it also is the least common. A supercell is characterized by a deep, persistent, rotating updraft called a mesocyclone. In a favorable environment, a supercell can last for many hours, unleashing violent weather—tornadoes, damaging wind gusts and very large hail—all along its track.

The Enhanced Fujita (Ef) Scale of Tornado Intensity

Rating	Winds (mph)	Damage
EF-0	65–85	MINOR - chimneys damaged; tree branches broken; shallow-rooted trees toppled
EF-1	86–110	MODERATE - roofs stripped of shingles; windows broken; some tree trunks snapped; unanchored mobile homes overturned
EF-2	111–135	CONSIDERABLE - roofs torn off; frame houses shifted on foundations; mobile homes destroyed; large trees snapped or uprooted; cars lifted off ground; debris becomes airborne (missiles generated)
EF-3	136–165	SEVERE - roofs and some walls torn from structures; some small buildings destroyed; forests flattened; SUVs picked up and thrown; trains overturned
EF-4	166–200	DEVASTATING - well-constructed houses completely leveled; vehicles hurled great distances; large debris becomes airborne
EF-5	>200	INCREDIBLE - strong frame houses lifted from foundations; reinforced concrete structures critically damaged; high-rise buildings deformed; trees completely debarked

NOTES:

Only 0.1 percent of tornadoes attain an EF-5 rating.

The vast majority (95 percent) are EF-0, EF-1, or EF-2.

Tornado ratings are determined by careful analyses of structural damage during post-storm surveys. The strength of a twister can't be gauged accurately by its appearance, nor can its intensity be measured, since anemometers suffering direct hits are destroyed.

Dedication

For my brother Rick,
who's not a storm chaser,
but who's weathered
more than his share
of storms in life

Chapter One

SATURDAY, APRIL 13

CHUCK RITTENBURG, slump-shouldered, unshaven, stood on the concrete walkway in front of his dingy row-apartment in Norman, Oklahoma, sipping a Coors Light. It hadn't always been like this, a beer for breakfast. But now . . . what the hell.

Pulses of warm, humid wind from the Gulf of Mexico via the Piney Woods of east Texas whipped over him, bearing away the odors of cleaning solvent and insecticide that leaked from his cheap efficiency like aerosols of despair. Something else rode the wind, too; something at once ominous and exhilarating. He'd sensed it before, many times: the threat of monstrous thunderstorms, the kind that give birth to the Grim Reapers of the Great Plains—tornadoes.

The day that had heralded the unraveling of his life had begun like this . . . a decade ago. The image of what happened that day was seared into his memory like a psychic scar, one that would never heal, never stop hurting, never allow him to raise an emotional white flag and say *I surrender,* let this be the end of it. Instead, it clung to him like psychological leg irons, reminding him constantly of all he once had but had no more.

HE'D BEEN DRIVING the lead van of two belonging to Thunder Road Tours, his eminently successful tornado chasing operation. The vans had stopped on a shelf of high ground in Oklahoma's Glass Mountains, a rugged, semiarid landscape of mesas and buttes in the western part of the state. A line of thunderstorms, like slow-motion, alabaster napalm explosions, billowed along a dryline advancing out of the Texas and Oklahoma Panhandles.

A dozen chasers, tourists really, each having shelled out over two grand for the privilege of getting intimate with a tornado, piled out of the vans to watch the closest cell a few miles to their west. A visibly imposing, low-hanging bulwark of blackness, the wall cloud, rotated counterclockwise beneath the towering storm.

"Looks like it's about to drop a funnel," Chuck's partner, Mac Beauchamp yelled, his gaze on the right rear flank of the thunderstorm. A wind-borne rumble of thunder almost blotted out his words.

A bolt of lightning lanced out of the storm onto a nearby mesa, immolating a scrubby pine and simultaneously launching an artillery-like explosion of sound.

"Back in the vans," Chuck screamed. "Now!"

The chasers scrambled back into the vehicles. All except for two: a young man and his girlfriend. The man, from the West Coast and perhaps unfamiliar with the dangers of lightning, didn't heed Chuck's command. Instead, he pointed a digital camera at the cauldron of clouds and snapped a series of photographs. His lady friend stood beside him, her head dipped into the wind, her blond hair whipping around her face.

Chuck waited a moment, then stepped from the driver's seat of the van onto its running board and yelled at the two stragglers. But he was a heartbeat too slow.

The man turned and looked at Chuck. It was that image that Chuck knew he would carry with him the rest of his days: the man's electrically-charged hair standing on end, his eyes pleading, his mouth wide with unspoken thoughts—secrets only a man who knows he has a millisecond to live can harbor. The brilliant stroke hit him square, knocking him out of his shoes and throwing him yards away as if he were no more than a stuffed toy.

His girlfriend passed to the next realm with him. She didn't even have time to look up. She jerked spasmodically as the dart of lightning struck, then crumpled into a heap, dead before she hit the ground.

In tandem with the fatal harpoon of electricity, thunder erupted in an ear-splitting barrage and rolled across the barren landscape for several seconds, like tympani for a dirge.

Between the two bodies, a shallow, smoking crevasse lay in zig-zag repose across the gravelly surface, a final, eternal link between the young man and his lady friend.

CHUCK TOOK A SWIG of his Coors and stared across the parking lot in front of his apartment. The lot remained filled with cars—Saturday morning. Not too many people going to work, transporting their kids to school, or setting out for classes at the nearby University of Oklahoma.

He didn't realize at the time, on that day ten years ago, but the deadly lightning bolt claimed not only the lives of the young man and his lady, but his as well. Not in a physical sense, of course, but in all aspects of his life that mattered. Even though his company was covered by liability insurance and waiver forms, slick, predatory personal injury lawyers and the spiraling cost of mounting a defense forced Thunder

Road Tours into bankruptcy. Chuck lost not just his company but, in quick succession, his savings, home, and wife.

Suzanne, his wife, had been unable to adapt to their new status as "have nots," and after a brief affair with a former boyfriend, she and Chuck divorced.

His nineteen-year-old son, Ty, with whom he'd always had an arm's-length and contentious relationship—undoubtedly a contributing factor to the animus in his marriage—had stormed out of his life accusing Chuck of "blowing my college money chasing clouds."

His daughter, Arlene, seventeen, had moved with her mother back to her mother's native Virginia. There was no doubt in Chuck's mind he would have been helpless attempting to raise a teenage daughter with his life in shambles. He'd kept in close touch with her, however, talking on the phone with her at least once a week during her high school and college years. Until she was 21, he'd dutifully delivered what little child support he could muster by working as head custodian at a local middle school and at various odd jobs, all of them menial. Even now he and Arlene remained in touch, though less frequently, as she busied her life carving out a career in public relations and attempting to find "the right guy."

Chuck turned as the man who lived in the apartment next to him stuck his head out the door, stooped to retrieve the morning newspaper, and said, *"Buenos días, amigo."*

Chuck nodded. He didn't know the guy's name, nor those of his wife and three kids. Probably illegals. He seated himself on the steps leading to his apartment and placed the beer beside him. Empty paper cups and styrofoam hamburger containers tumbled across the parking lot, driven by the fitful wind. A small whirl of dust chased a mangy-looking dog toward the main street.

A black SUV, a Lincoln Navigator, turned into the lot and eased along the row of apartments where Chuck lived. Looking for a specific unit, he guessed. The Lincoln coasted to a stop behind the vehicles jammed into the narrow parking slots directly in front of where Chuck sat. He watched as the front driver-side window of the SUV opened. A well-groomed man with a broad face and full black beard, wearing a white Greek fisherman's cap, leaned his head out.

"Looking for apartment 3A," he said.

"Guess you found it," Chuck answered. He remained seated.

"Charles Rittenburg?" the man asked.

Shit, not another fucking lawyer. "Who wants to know?"

The man scratched his nose, perhaps buying time to formulate a response, then laughed softly. "I come in peace, Mr. Rittenburg. With an offer of employment."

"I've got a job."

The man looked down at something on the passenger seat, then moved his gaze back to Chuck.

"Pushing a broom at Kiowa Trails Middle School?" he said.

Chuck didn't answer.

"Oh. Almost forgot. You've got a summer gig ushering at RedHawks Field. Big-time stuff. The team must draw what, four, five thousand per game? You gotta be raking in the dough from that."

Chuck fingered his beer. "Who are you?"

"Jerry Metcalf," the man said. "How about I buy you breakfast?"

Chuck held up the Coors Light. "Got it," he said.

The man shut off the Navigator's engine. "Not exactly the Breakfast of Champions."

"Then I guess it fits."

"I passed a Waffle House when I got off the Interstate. How about it?"

The dog shooed away by the dust devil earlier returned and crept toward Chuck, stalking the beer can but probably hoping there were some accompaniments nearby—pretzels or chips or popcorn.

Chuck stood and, carrying the Coors, turned to go into his apartment. "Not interested," he said.

The Lincoln's door opened, then slammed shut.

"Hear me out," Metcalf said. "I'm from Global-American Cinema. I'd like to hire you as a consultant for a film."

Chuck pivoted to face Metcalf, a large man, overweight, with an odd sense of style: In addition to the fisherman's cap, he wore a white dress shirt with epaulets, cargo shorts and Timberland hiking boots.

"Don't know anything about movies," Chuck said.

Metcalf stood on the short walkway leading to Chuck's apartment. "Yes," he countered, "but you know about tornadoes."

"Not anymore."

"Bullshit, if you'll pardon my French, sir. You were the best chaser in the business. Charles Rittenburg: The Great White Hunter of Tornadoes. That's what you were called, wasn't it? You were a guest on 'The Today Show,' 'Good Morning America,' '60 Minutes,' and The Weather Channel. You were featured in *USA Today* and *People* magazine. Don't blow smoke up my ass. Chasing storms isn't a skill you lose overnight or even in the depths of a beer can. Hell, I know you've kept up with stuff because I saw you as a talking head on CNN and Fox after the Joplin disaster, in the wake of the Dixie tornado swarm in 2011, and then Moore in 2013. Jesus, that was close to home wasn't it?" He paused, seemingly thoughtfully, then shook his head. "Ya know, Charlie, I don't understand why anybody would want to live in a place like this."

"A place like this," Chuck responded, a hard frost on his words, "is where a lot of people *choose* to live. It's good country with good people. As far as keeping my hand in the business, I did that as a hobby until my laptop went tits-up last year. I haven't been able to afford a new one. Look, I can't help you, Mr. Metcalf. And something else, just for the record. I like to kick off my day with a Coors, you know, smooth the rough edges. It's my first and last of the day. I'm not a boozer. By the way, it's Chuck, not Charlie."

"Sorry," Metcalf said. "Look, I know some heavy-duty shit came down on you. Life's unfair and all that crap. But I'm offering you a chance to even the score."

Chuck opened the door to his apartment. "Life only works out like that in the movies," he said.

"Exactly." Metcalf paused. "Did I mention I represent a film company?" He smiled broadly. Chuck could have sworn the man's teeth sparkled in the low-angled morning sunlight.

The mangy dog, some sort of terrier-Lab mix, settled onto its stomach and watched the exchange between the two men.

Chuck glanced at the mutt, then at Metcalf. "Like I said, I can't help you."

"Help yourself then."

"I've never been good at that."

"You've given up?"

Chuck shook his head. "I'm just tired. Tired of fighting lawyers. Tired of arguing with bill collectors. Tired of explaining to others how my life got so fucked up." He stepped into his unit and slammed the door.

Metcalf's voice carried into the apartment. "I'm going to tape an envelope to your door, Chuck. The envelope contains a proposal from Global-American Cinema. Take a look at it, then decide how tired you are."

Metcalf paused as if waiting for a response. But Chuck said nothing. Metcalf continued. "I'm staying at the Colcord Hotel in Oklahoma City. I've attached my business card to the proposal and put my room number on it. Give me a call after you've read what we're offering. I think you'll change your mind."

Chuck still didn't respond.

"Okay. I know you can hear me," Metcalf said. "I'm leaving now. But I'll be in the area for a couple of days."

Chuck stood near the door, gripping his beer can, waiting for Metcalf to depart.

"Two weeks' work, Chuck. And an opportunity to make more money than you probably ever netted in a year from Thunder Road Tours." Metcalf fell silent briefly, then added, "A chance at redemption, too, my friend, if you're interested."

Metcalf's footfalls retreated from the door. Chuck stepped to the front window of his unit, parted the stained venetian blinds, and watched as Metcalf climbed into his Navigator and drove off.

Chuck drained the rest of his Coors from the can, tossed the empty container into the trash, and settled into a tattered, faded armchair, Goodwill-issue, in front of his TV set. He clicked it on with his remote and watched a meteorologist with a manufactured grim-faced expression explain there was a threat of severe thunderstorms and tornadoes later in the day.

Chuck switched the channel to ESPN to check out how the Royals had done in their first home stand of the season. He'd become a Royals fan when he lived in Kansas City from the mid-'80s to the mid-'90s working at the National Severe Storms Forecast Center, now called the Storm Prediction Center.

He'd moved to the Oklahoma City area in 1996 and started Thunder Road Tours. Success came rapidly and he spun off a subsidiary, Cat Five Tours, to pursue hurricanes. But his life and business and everything else had imploded with the lightning strike in the Glass Mountains.

Some things, apparently, were never meant to be.

He stood, retrieved another beer from the refrigerator, and plopped back into the ratty chair. Normally, as he'd told Metcalf, a single beer was his limit, but today . . . too much melancholia. He changed channels again and found an old Tarzan movie. He watched the film disinterestedly and sipped his beer until he dozed off, his chin resting on his chest, like a geezer in a retirement home.

He awoke with a start, realizing it was almost noon. The Coors can, half empty, sat on the floor beside him. The Tarzan film had morphed into an old Western, something starring Randolph Scott.

Chuck rose unsteadily, stretched, and poured the remaining beer into a soiled sink cluttered with unwashed dishes and a deceased cockroach. He exhumed his wallet from beneath a pile of dirty clothes in his bedroom. He opened it. Eight bucks. At least enough for lunch at McDonald's.

He opened the front door. A gust of wind darted into his apartment like a refugee seeking asylum. A piece of Scotch tape, nothing fastened to it, clung forlornly to the exterior of the door. The proposal. He'd forgotten about it. Well, it didn't matter now. The wind had taken it. The story of his life. Some things never change. *Que sera, sera.*

He shrugged, shut the door and headed toward McDonalds, dodging a dozen kids on trikes and skateboards monopolizing the sidewalk. He headed west, noting with a meteorologist's practiced eye towering cumulus clouds in the middle distance, billowing skyward.

Something brushed against his leg. He looked down. The mutt that had been hanging around the apartments earlier trotted beside him, a white business envelope clamped in its mouth.

The dog stopped, dropped the envelope at Chuck's feet, and waited expectantly, its head tilted to one side, probably hoping for a game of toss and fetch.

"Not today, doggy," Chuck said. "Beat it."

He continued walking.

The dog did, too, envelope again in its slobbery mouth.

"Hit the road, Jack. If you're counting on lunch, I can barely afford to feed myself."

Once more, the mutt dropped the envelope. This time, Chuck saw a name embossed on its upper-left hand corner: Global-American Cinema. He picked it up. The dog yapped and ran off a short distance, waiting for Chuck to lob the thing.

Instead, Chuck opened it and extracted three sheets of paper pitted with teeth marks, the proposal that Metcalf had taped to his door. He looked down at the dog, who stared back with big brown eyes almost hidden behind a tangle of matted fur.

"Whaddaya think, pooch, worth looking at?"

The dog cocked its head in a quizzical pose.

"Well, *que sera, sera*," Chuck said, and began to read.

When he came to the paragraph spelling out the amount of money being offered, he jerked his head up and glanced around, certain he was being set up as the butt of a TV gag show.

Chapter Two

SATURDAY, APRIL 13

CHUCK SAT AT his kitchen table, a battle-scarred throwback to the 1950s, munched on the grilled chicken sandwich and fries he'd picked up at McDonalds, and reviewed, for the third time, Metcalf's stunning proposal.

Finished, he picked up the business card the man had left and dialed the number of the Colcord Hotel. He asked for Metcalf's room. The film company rep picked up almost immediately.

"I knew you'd call," he said. Chatter from a TV program filled the background.

"I wouldn't have, if it hadn't been for Jack."

"Who?"

"My new best friend."

The dog, the one that Chuck had told earlier to "Hit the road Jack," crawled from beneath the table. Bits of chicken clung to the knotted fur beneath its chin.

"Well, good for Jack, whoever he is," Metcalf said. "Look, when can we start? The producers are anxious to get going on this."

"I'm not starting," Chuck said. "I'm not signing on. The stipulations you laid out are ridiculous—"

"What's ridiculous about $500,000, Charlie . . . Chuck?"

"Nothing. I said the stipulations are absurd."

"Finding us a violent, photogenic tornado within two weeks? From what I've heard, you ought to be able to do that in your sleep."

"Yes, that's what I do . . . or did, find tornadoes. But the proposal specifically states I have to find an *EF-4 or -5* within two weeks or I don't collect the commission. Bottom line: There's a 99 percent probability I don't get shit. Actually, less than that, since you're giving me only fourteen days."

Metcalf started to speak, but Chuck ignored him and continued talking.

"We're not hunting deer, Mr. Metcalf. Deer are always out there somewhere. It's just a matter of locating them. Not so with tornadoes. It's possible we could select a two-week period and come up empty. If atmospheric conditions aren't right, there aren't any tornadoes. Let alone an EF-4 or -5, which represent less than one percent of all twisters. That means out of every 100-plus tornadoes, only one is going to meet your criterion."

"I know what it means, Chuckie. But here's the one-time good deal for you: You select the time frame."

"Not really. The proposal states completion by mid-May. So you're really offering me just a four-week window to pick from."

Metcalf expelled a long breath. Exasperation. "Jesus. You act like you don't need the money."

"What I don't need is the frustration, the hassle."

"Come on, man—"

"And besides," Chuck interrupted, "you never know what you're dealing with until after the fact. Contrary to what's been depicted in movies, you can't judge the category of a tornado just by looking at it. The biggest, blackest wedge in the world can look like the Tornado that Ate Toledo and turns out be an EF-2. Tornadoes are classified by the damage they do, not their appearance. Categorization requires a post-storm survey."

Jack rested his chin on Chuck's shoe.

"Don't forget about your consultant's fee," Metcalf said. "A thousand bucks a day. That's $14,000 even if Mother Nature screws us."

"Screws me, you mean. It'd be penny wise and pound foolish. If I'm MIA from my job at the school for two weeks, I've lost it. Nope, count me out. Find yourself another chaser. There are plenty out there."

"My instructions were to get you."

"Yeah," Chuck said, "but you don't want someone with my reputation." He hung up.

Immediately, the phone rang back. Chuck waited seven rings, then picked up.

"Leave me alone," he said.

"No," Metcalf said. "I won't. I'm going to sweeten the pot. A million bucks. You find me and my film crew what we want and you get a check for more money than you've ever seen."

Silence ensued on both ends of the line. Chuck sucked in a deep lungful of air, not quite sure he'd heard right.

Finally he asked, "How much?"

"One million dollars."

"You toss that figure around like it was Monopoly money."

"This is Hollywood, Chuck. Everything is make-believe and fantasy. Only the money is real. Hop on board."

"The odds are still against me."

"The odds are always against everyone."

"Let me think about it. I'll call you back."

"No. Don't think about it. Don't convince yourself this isn't your due, that fate is stacked against you, that bad karma is part of your genetic make-up. You're the once and future king, man. You can do it. And even if you somehow feel you're 'unworthy,' that you aren't among the chosen, that there is no pot of Benjamin Franklins at the end of a rainbow, then maybe there's someone else in your past you could carry the flag for.

"Look, I know a lot about you, Chuck. I know the jackals, the lawyers, got to you; bankrupted your business—chapter 7, forced you into personal bankruptcy. Your house was foreclosed; your wife couldn't take it, had an affair with an old flame; you got divorced and in the process had to let your daughter go, too. Then there's your son . . . well, things were never good there, were they?

"Whaddaya say, partner? Unto the breach?"

Chuck moved his gaze to a row of framed photographs hanging on the living room wall. Dust coated the frames. A compound fracture, like forked lightning, split the piece of glass covering his wife's picture. *Appropriate.*

And appropriate, too, that all the portraits were layered in dust, as though lost in the dry haze of time. Ancient history. Hieroglyphics on a caveman's wall.

"Yeah," Chuck said. "Unto the breach."

"I'll bring the contract by this afternoon," Metcalf said.

METCALF SHOWED UP at three o'clock with the documents.

Chuck leafed through them, making a cursory examination.

"Do I need a lawyer?" he asked.

Metcalf rocked back in his chair and rumbled with laughter, sending Jack scurrying into a far corner of the room.

"Who do you think will screw you worse, my friend," Metcalf said after his guffawing subsided into winded gasps, "me or some shark who

10

has 'Esquire' appended to his name?"

"I'll take my chances with you," Chuck said. "Where do I sign?"

Metcalf pointed out all the places. Chuck pushed the papers back to Metcalf when he was finished.

"When do we start?" he asked.

"As I said earlier, that's up to you, Chuck. We did our research and learned that mid-April through mid-May is prime time for the biggest, baddest twisters in Oklahoma—"

"That's where the film is set, in Oklahoma?"

"More or less. On the Great Plains. Anyhow, we figure you can narrow down the best time to go hunting to a two-week block."

Chuck shrugged. "We'll see. But why two weeks? Why the mid-May deadline? The nastiest storms might not show up until after that."

Metcalf flipped through the contract documents, stuffed most of them into his briefcase, and slid several sheets of paper back across the table to Chuck.

"Your copies," he said. "And to answer your question, we're on a tight schedule. Blow it and we're blowing money. The producers get really pissy if we start flushing dollars down the dumper."

"Why not just use some stock footage of tornadoes? Lots of that around."

"We want 35-millimeter, high-def digital imagery shot by experienced cinematographers. Not some grainy crap captured by amateurs on a cell phone. We'll be using three Panavision Genesis cameras, gold-standard systems. Two of 'em will be truck-mounted, the third available for Steadicam use. And by the way, for logistical purposes, we'll need about a five-day heads-up."

"What?"

"We'll need five days to get the equipment mounted, secured, and staged."

"Staged?"

"From Southern Cal to Ok City."

"Shit. You didn't tell me that. Now you're asking me to make a three-week outlook instead of a two-week prediction. Half the time we can't even get it right at five days."

Metcalf raked his fingers through his thick beard, as though pondering the statement. "Maybe you *should* have hired a lawyer," he said. He tapped the briefcase containing the signed contract. "Too late. But that's why we hired you, Charlie—"

"Chuck."

"Chuck. Because we think you can beat the odds and get us into position to get the best damn footage of tornadoes ever shot."

Jack stood, passed gas, sat, and scratched at something behind his ear.

"Nice pet you've got there," Metcalf said. "Maybe you should send him to charm school."

"He's the reason you're sitting here," Chuck said, and told Metcalf the story about how Jack had rescued the proposal.

When he finished, Metcalf stood and lumbered over to where Jack dozed.

"Good pooch," he said and bent to stroke his head. "You saved me from getting skewered by my bosses."

Jack rolled over and spread his legs, perhaps waiting for a tummy rub.

"Find yourself a boyfriend," Metcalf muttered. He turned to Chuck. "I don't think she's a 'Jack'."

He walked back to the table and sat. "Let's go over some details," he said.

They spent the next hour discussing the logistics of the chase, including communications, chains of command, and safety, a subject Chuck insisted be covered thoroughly.

"I know you guys won't sue me if something goes wrong," Chuck said, "blood-from-a-stone and all that. But I don't want to witness ever again what I did ten years ago."

Metcalf nodded. "I understand."

He handed Chuck a card with five telephone numbers on it. "When you see the day for the Great Hunt looming, give me a call. Start with the first number and work your way down the list. Sooner or later you'll reach me, or someone who knows how, and I'll have my crew here in five days."

"Yeah," Chuck said without enthusiasm.

"Oh, come on, Chuck. This will be the greatest adventure of your life."

"I've already had that, thanks."

Jack, who'd been sleeping in the kitchen, suddenly awakened and stalked toward the front door, growling, ears pinned back. The low rumbling from her throat seemed more a warning than a threat.

"What's wrong with him . . . her?" Metcalf said.

"How would I know? I didn't even know he's a she."

Chuck cracked open the door and looked out. The wind, stronger now, moaned through the apartment complex. Far to the west, pulses of lightning danced through the tops of clouds that lined the distant horizon like dusky mountain peaks

Chuck opened the door wider and looked up. Overhead, a milky gauze—cirrus from thunderstorm anvils—veiled the sky. He studied the motion of the high, thin clouds for several moments.

"What is it?" Metcalf asked, coming up behind Chuck.

Chuck pointed west. "What we're going to be pursuing. Supercells. The big-boy thunderstorms that drop tornadoes."

Metcalf looked down at Jack, who stood by Chuck's leg, nose held high as if sniffing the wind for danger. She let loose a series of short, sharp barks.

"Well, she's either Jackie or . . . hey, how about Stormy? Like some North Hollywood stripper?"

Chuck looked askance at Metcalf.

"Not me," he said. He clapped his hand over his heart as if offended. "I don't hang out at bazonga bars. I just hear stuff."

"Okay. Stormy. Sure. Stormy the Weather Wonder Dog."

"She looks like she's been living in a garbage dump," Metcalf said. "You'd better get her cleaned up."

"I can't afford it."

"Now you can. Here's an advance on your consultant's fee." Metcalf fished three one-hundred dollar bills from his wallet.

Chuck shook his head, declining the offer.

"You don't want my money?"

"I don't want your condescension."

Metcalf cocked his head at him.

"I don't need money to get some stray mutt a bath," Chuck said. "I need money to help me get back on my professional feet."

"Okay. How much?"

"My consultant's fee up front. All of it."

Metalf stared at him, a hard-eyed squint.

"I can't go tornado chasing without technology," Chuck said. "I'll need a couple of high-end laptops, a GPS navigation system, a whizbang iPhone—"

Metcalf attempted to interrupt, but Chuck ignored him.

"—plus subscriptions to meteorological forecast models and real-time weather radar feeds."

"Wasn't in the contract," Metcalf snapped.

"Well, fine, Mr. Hollywood. We'll just tootle aimlessly around the

High Plains for two weeks searching for nymphocumulus."

"Nympho-what?"

"Big fucking clouds. That'll be the best I'll be able to do flying blind."

Stormy, formerly Jack, turned away from the door and sniffed Metcalf's shoes.

"So, you want $14,000 just like that?" He looked down at Stormy. "She's not gonna piss on me, is she?"

"Only if you don't come up with the money. Look, I'm not gonna skip town and take up with some Mexican honey in Acapulco on a measly fourteen thousand dollars. It'll be money well spent, believe me."

Metcalf eyed Stormy who stared back.

"Consider the check in the mail," Metcalf said.

Stormy stalked off.

"I'll get busy," Chuck said.

Metcalf extended his hand. "Nice to know you've still got some moxie left," he said.

The men shook on the deal.

"One final thing," Metcalf said. "Just curious. What changed your mind about the deal? Most people would pee in their pants from excitement if they were offered a chance at a million bucks. Not you. You were kicking and screaming to stay away from it. Then you grabbed at it. I have a feeling it wasn't my persuasive argument. What was it?"

Chuck studied the tops of the distant supercells for a while before answering. Then he said, "My son."

"Your son? A guy you haven't seen in eight years?" The words came out as if Metcalf were issuing an indictment.

Chuck nodded, but didn't turn to face Metcalf.

Chapter Three

SATURDAY, APRIL 13

SEVENTY-FIVE MILES west-southwest of Norman, the late afternoon had turned evening dark as though the sun were being swallowed by the gaping maw of a bottomless pit. Dirt and grit, riding the stiff inflow wind of a strengthening supercell, filled the air.

Clarence and Raleigh Jarrell, brothers, monitored the growing thunderstorm from within their GMC Terrain, a mid-sized black SUV sporting a steel grill guard. Parked on a dirt road, the men maintained a safe distance between them and the billowing storm less than a half mile to their northeast.

"Won't be long now," Clarence said to his younger sibling, Raleigh, in the passenger seat.

Raleigh nodded, but looked away from the storm to the east.

Clarence followed his gaze. "Yeah, I know," he said.

"That son of a bitch," Raleigh responded, his voice low but sharp.

Clarence knew who he meant. The old bastard had lived not far from here, in Windsock, a town Clarence described as being "fifty miles from Nowhere and thirty miles south of Despair." Clarence and Raleigh had lived there, too, as foster children of the old bastard—he could think of the man in no other terms—and his timorous, withdrawn wife.

The boys had been placed in the home after their mother's death. Their mom, Rita, had been a rodeo groupie and boozer who'd died of acute alcohol poisoning when Clarence was seven and Raleigh four. Each had a different father, and they knew their dads' names, rodeo cowboys, only by virtue of their birth certificates.

The old bastard had been kind to them at first, occasionally giving them "softball" jobs around the down-at-the-heels Sinclair station where he worked, or taking them to Oklahoma City to see a baseball game or Norman for football. But as the boys grew older, he began to make . . . demands.

Clarence's stomach churned as he recalled. The old bastard crawling into bed with him at night, his breath reeking of whiskey and cigarettes, his skin stinking of gasoline and motor oil, and demanding Clarence perform acts that even Satan must have found despicable—acts that would leave no physical evidence and could be readily denied by the old bastard, charming and soft-spoken when he was sober.

Initially, it was only "hand jobs," but later . . .

Clarence rolled down the window and spit, as if attempting to purge himself of the vileness and filth he'd been forced to endure. A futile effort. The abomination would always be with him. His stomach heaved again.

The great irony was that it was during this time, his "time in Hell" as he came to call it, that his passion for storm chasing was born. It began after a tornado leveled most of the buildings in Windsock, but not the old bastard's, a sign, Clarence divined, that "God didn't give a damn about me or Raleigh." His fascination with nature's violence grew. With Raleigh riding shotgun, he began chasing. Driving mostly pickup trucks "borrowed" from local farmers and ranchers, the boys learned the craft by shadowing more experienced chasers.

After a couple of years, they struck out on their own. As soon as he was eighteen, Clarence had taken Raleigh and fled their repulsive keeper. They supported themselves with a variety of construction jobs and petty thievery. Clarence took a few "distance learning" classes in meteorology from Mississippi State, and both boys signed up for on-line paramedic courses. The combination of meteorology and paramedic curricula led them to a new and fruitful career. Which was why they now sat watching vivid forks of lightning shoot like electric lizard tongues from the mass of blackness just ahead of them.

Their gazes fastened on the underbelly of the boiling storm. There, spinning like an immense, inverted whirlpool, hung a classic wall cloud.

"Look!" Raleigh said. He pointed at the edge of a field where winter wheat was just beginning to green. A slender, spinning column of dirt and debris skipped across the field. In tandem with and above it, a gray-white condensation funnel dipped from the wall cloud. Seconds later, the funnel appeared to drop even lower, joining forces with the debris column and morphing to black.

"Tornado," Clarence said. He slipped the GMC into gear. "Here we go."

The funnel threaded its way over the field, flinging chunks of soil and stalks of wheat outward like an uncapped food blender. The twister bounced and weaved along a zig-zag track, growing in girth and fierceness. It filled the air with an atavistic roar, perhaps something akin to what a charging T-Rex might have sounded like in a primeval world.

The SUV jounced along the rutted road, Clarence allowing the strengthening storm to remain a respectable distance ahead. He reached a paved road and turned left, north, still trailing the tornado.

"Anything in its path?" he asked his brother.

Raleigh, stocky, muscular and broad-faced, gazed at his laptop computer, examining a digital roadmap overlaid with detailed radar imagery of the storm. He looked up, peering at Clarence through thick glasses. "Yeah, it's heading northeast right toward a little burg called Honeybee."

Clarence slowed the vehicle and studied the whirling monster for several moments. A farm truck coming from the opposite direction blinked its headlights in warning.

"Stay on this road?" Clarence asked Raleigh.

"For about four miles, then take a right on Thirteen Hundred."

The tornado, now a seething ink-black cauldron, careened across the road in front of them, leaving the pavement strewn in dirt and shattered vegetation. Wounded utility poles, their wires drooping precariously near the surface, leaned over the road at extreme angles. One or two had been snapped in half.

Clarence slowed the Terrain and eased around the dangling wires, careful not to make contact. The twister, now a mature funnel, churned over a low rocky ridge. Once clear of the road debris, Clarence sped up, closing the gap between the storm and the SUV.

He turned east where his brother had indicated and slowed again, once more allowing the tornado, grinding northeastward, to transit the road in front of them. Its path, marked by downed poles, flattened fences, and a scattering of snapped scrub oaks and cottonwoods, appeared to be several hundred yards wide.

Clarence eased the vehicle to the side of the road and stopped. He rolled down the front windows. Gusts of wind whipped through the interior. The distant thrashing roar of the twister reverberated through the semidarkness.

Raleigh checked the map and radar overlay. "The town should be about to get hit," he said.

Virtually on cue, the eerie wail of warning sirens cut through the air, as if trumpeting the ride of modern-day Valkyries come to claim their dead. The two men waited, their gazes fixed on the obsidian buzz saw barreling toward tiny Honeybee. After several minutes, they saw what they were waiting for: brilliant explosions of blue-white light, electrical transformers falling victim to the twister's violence.

"That's it, bro'," Clarence said. He and Raleigh bumped fists.

Clarence reached into the back seat, grabbed a light bar with warning flashers, and handed it to Raleigh. "Hook it up," he said. "I'll get the signs."

He exited the SUV, lifted the tailgate, and pulled out three magnetic signs. He checked the road behind him to make certain there were no other chasers or emergency vehicles coming. Satisfied none was, he affixed a sign to each of the front doors and one to the tailgate: *EMT-Rescue.*

By the time he got back into the vehicle, Raleigh had mounted the light bar on the dash, plugged it into the cigarette lighter and set the flash pattern for the bank of red LEDs.

"Let's go," Clarence said.

Now, as paramedics and not storm chasers, the brothers continued east on the county road. Raleigh instructed Clarence to make one last turn, north onto Main Street, and they accelerated toward Honeybee.

They reached the edge of the small town that now lay in the deep dusk of evening, the township's lights having fallen victim to the storm. Clarence guided the SUV, its emergency lights strobing the gathering darkness, cautiously around fractured branches and fallen trees. Their investment in a heavy-duty grill guard for the GMC seemed well worth it in situations like these. Raleigh moved the beam of a roof-mounted halogen spotlight in a search pattern, looking for the more severe damage that would mark the exact track of the tornado.

Here and there, people had already stepped from the safety of their homes and stood gazing at the evidence of the twister's near miss in their once-tranquil neighborhood: splintered trees, missing shingles, dangling power lines.

A frightened cat darted in front of the Terrain. Clarence braked the vehicle. "Poor thing," he said.

Raleigh continued sweeping the spotlight beam along the row of neat homes that lined Main Street.

"Anything look promising?" Clarence asked.

"Not yet. Maybe the funnel lifted before it got here."

"Don't think so. Too many power flashes. Someplace got clocked."

The brothers entered the business district of Honeybee, which wasn't much: two or three blocks of shops, restaurants, and a couple of banks.

"More damage here," Raleigh said.

Shards of glass, pieces of aluminum, chunks of masonry, and broken bricks coated the street. The walls of several buildings had collapsed, leaving the structures looking like victims of a bomb blast. A step van, compressed to the height of a flatbed by a heap of fallen bricks, hemorrhaged gas and oil into a curbside gutter. A dozen parked automobiles and pickups, reduced to junkyard status by flying debris and massive chunks of destroyed buildings, gave testament to the tornado's path.

EMTs from the town's fire department surged into a shattered restaurant filled with thick smoke. A fire truck, siren spooling down to a throaty gurgle, pulled up to the scene. Other sirens, more distant, told of additional help racing toward Honeybee.

The brothers continued along Main Street, Raleigh playing the spotlight back and forth from one side of the street to the other, examining the broken buildings.

There was just enough ambient light for Clarence to see ahead, but not clearly. "Shine the light down the block there," he said. He pointed to the right side of the road.

Raleigh aimed the beam where Clarence suggested, at the corner of the next block where two of four walls of a brick structure had collapsed. Amidst the rubble, a fallen sign rested ankle-deep in the detritus covering the sidewalk. Raleigh ran the beam over the sign: KELLER BROS. JEWELRY, WATCHES, ELECTRONICS.

"Dontcha just love it?" Clarence said. "Small towns and their—"

"—catch-all stores," Raleigh interjected, finishing his brother's sentence.

"Let's take a look. Grab the trauma kit."

Clarence pulled the SUV to the curb, leaving the emergency flashers on. The two men exited the vehicle, Raleigh lugging a large red bag stuffed with splints, a BP cuff, Mylar blankets, and a variety of other first aid supplies.

Blue lights flashing, an Oklahoma Highway Patrol car pulled alongside the Terrain and stopped. A trooper stuck his head out the window.

"You guys need assistance?" he asked.

"Nah, we got it, sir," Clarence answered. "Thought we heard someone calling for help in here."

"Okay. Good. We're spread pretty thin right now. Ya'll be careful in there."

Clarence gave the trooper a thumbs-up as the cruiser pulled away. The yowl of sirens, some sounding closer now, continued to fill the evening. From down the street, where emergency workers had entered the damaged restaurant, shouts and screams added to the growing cacophony.

Clarence and Raleigh clambered over a pile of bricks and masonry into the destroyed business. It was darker in the interior—former interior—and Clarence played a powerful Maglite beam over the wreckage as Raleigh struggled behind him with the medical bag.

Dust hung in the air, mingling with the electric smell of ozone and the faint stench of rotten eggs. Sheet lightning from the departing storm painted the sky a pulsating neon purple.

"Careful, no sparks or anything," Clarence said. "There's a gas leak someplace. Not here, but nearby. Let's work fast."

They moved through the rubble, Clarence probing the dimness with the flashlight's gleam. Broken glass from shattered display cases blanketed the floor, sparkling like morning hoarfrost in the beam's brightness. Lying among the shards were gold and diamond rings, silver bracelets, expensive wristwatches, and digital cameras.

"Welcome to Shangri-La," Clarence said, his words breathy.

Raleigh set down the trauma kit and withdrew his own flashlight from a pocket in his cargo pants. He swept the beam over the debris, then stopped it abruptly.

"Hey," he said.

Clarence moved his own beam to where Raleigh's had stopped.

A pair of legs clad in gray slacks protruded from a stack of broken bricks.

"Let's take a look," Clarence said.

The brothers worked quickly, removing the debris from the half-buried victim. Their efforts revealed a man, perhaps in his 60s, who, judging by his finely-tailored suit, probably was the proprietor. Blood streamed from a gash on his head. He moaned softly as Clarence examined the wound.

"Get the bag," he said to Raleigh. To the man he said, "Can you hear me, sir?"

The man opened his eyes. "What happened?" he said, his words slurred.

"Tornado. Are there others in here?"

"Feel sick," the man said.

"Okay, relax. We'll take care of you. Listen, are there other people in here?"

The sound of sirens, very loud now, warbled through the destroyed building, signaling that additional help had arrived in Honeybee.

"Where am I? What happened?" the man asked.

"You're in a business, a store. I assume it's yours. It was hit by a tornado. Are there others here who might be hurt?"

"No others," the man said, then lapsed into unconsciousness.

Raleigh arrived with the trauma kit.

"Flush out his wound," Clarence said. "Get a bandage on it. And a cold pack. He's probably got a concussion. Keep him still, too, since he might have a neck or back injury."

"I know what to do," Raleigh snapped.

"I know you do." Clarence patted his kid brother on his shoulder. "Do your thing. I'll do mine."

Raleigh nodded.

Clarence pulled a folded canvas bag from the trauma kit and set off through the store, sweeping his light beam through the suspended dust, searching first for intact display cases. Most were indeed smashed, their glass tops shattered, their wooden frames fractured. But several were not.

One held a treasure trove of high-end wristwatches: a handful of Rolexes, Tag Heuers, and Breitlings, along with a couple of Raymond Weils and half-a-dozen Citizens. *Probably not a lot of demand for expensive chronometers in a small town.* He picked up a heavy chunk of masonry and hammered it down on the glass. It exploded in a crystalline spray.

He stared at the watches for several seconds. A Rolex or Breitling would be nice, but too easily missed. He withdrew several Eco-Drive Citizens instead and dropped them into the bag. Then, second thoughts. He reached into the case and grabbed a Rolex Daytona. A nice memento.

He scanned the already-destroyed cases and the rubble on the floor, being careful to remove only a few retail items here and there: a diamond engagement ring, a bracelet of tricolored gold, and a fistful of cell phones.

Raleigh called to him: "I've got the old fart—"

"Elderly gentleman," Clarence corrected.

"Elderly gentleman stabilized," Raleigh said, an edge to his words.

"Good. Almost done here. Pack up."

Behind where the display cases had stood, several wall racks had toppled, spilling their contents of laptop computers and digital cameras into the dreck that layered the floor. Clarence bent and fished out a Nikon Coolpix and a Canon PowerShot. Then he added a Dell Inspiron and an Apple MacBook Air to the loot in his canvas bag.

Raleigh joined him. "Ready," he said. "Get some good stuff?"

"Lots." He held the bag aloft, like an equatorial headhunter displaying a trophy or a Native American exhibiting the scalp of an enemy. "Should get us a several thousand bucks from a fence or pawn shop."

The clatter of shifting debris drew their attention.

"Shit," Clarence muttered.

The injured man apparently was not so badly hurt as first thought. He had pushed himself into a sitting position and now, through the dim light and floating particulates that filled the destroyed store, he stared at the bulging canvas sack.

"What are ya doin'?" he asked, the words sounding as if his mouth were stuffed with a wet rag. "Thought you guys were medics?"

Clarence lowered the bag. "We are, sir. This is just our back-up med kit."

"Don't think so," the man said. "Saw ya helpin' yourself to a couple a laptops." He attempted to push himself up.

"Hold it, sir," Clarence said. "Don't do that. You're hurt."

He turned to his brother and whispered, "Okay, you know the drill."

"Do we have to?" Raleigh asked, his voice low, a bit quivery.

"Of course not, brother," Clarence hissed, "as long as you're okay giving blow jobs to some 300-pound greaser and his Mexican Mafia *amigos* in McAlester."

Raleigh sucked in a deep breath, expelled it, then aimed the beam of his MagLite into the injured man's face.

The man raised his hand to shield his eyes from the blinding brilliance. Clarence, attempting to move quickly and silently through the debris, positioned himself behind the man, then fished through the rubble until he found the broken leg of a display case.

The man twisted around, trying to see what was happening.

Clarence knelt and placed his hand on the man's shoulder. "Just look straight ahead, sir. Watch the light. I'm sorry about this. But I promise it will be over in a fraction of a second."

"Jesus Christ." The man made a feeble effort to rise.

"Please," Clarence said, his command harsh and sharp, "don't." He pushed the man down, stood, stepped back, and swung the broken leg like a baseball bat at the man's head.

Chapter Four

SATURDAY, APRIL 13

THE MAN TURNED and lifted his hand into a defensive position, but the piece of wood wielded by Clarence knocked it away like a wind rush flattening grass and caught him full on the side of his face. A sound like a two-by-four thunking into a watermelon reverberated through the ruins of the store.

The victim toppled. Raleigh stepped forward and checked the man's pulse, then nodded at his brother.

"Get the dressings off him," Clarence said, "then let's get out of here."

"Poor guy," Raleigh said as they scrambled from the wrecked building.

"Yeah," Clarence said without emotion, "the storm took its toll."

A short distance outside of town, Clarence pulled the SUV to the side of the road and stopped. "This is the end of the gig, you know," he said.

"The cop?" Raleigh asked.

"Yeah. Even though nothing can tie us to the guy's death, if someone from the store realizes there's stuff missing and the patrolman remembers two paramedics entering the place, it's going to create a lot of curiosity. More than we need."

Raleigh was already pulling off his EMT jacket. Clarence stepped from the Terrain into the now-dark evening and removed the magnetic signs from the SUV. Crickets in an adjacent field chirped a lively greeting to the night while a brisk, cool wind whipped over the toneless landscape. Occasional bursts from distant sirens, emergency vehicles in Honeybee, flailed through the deepening darkness.

Clarence climbed back into the Terrain. "We'll ditch all this stuff later," he said, gesturing at the signs, the jackets, and the medical bag.

"And then?"

Clarence shrugged. "Just ordinary storm chasers, I guess. At least for a while. We'll figure something out."

He slipped the GMC into gear and drove off into the Oklahoma night.

AFTER METCALF departed, Chuck walked three blocks to his frequent nightly haunt, a sprawling bar and grill called The Cowboy Corral. Lightning flickered in the darkening sky to the west, and the rumble of distant thunder rolled over the landscape in alternating waves of pianissimo and forte.

He took a seat at his customary table near the front window, underneath a neon sign advertising BEEF, BEER, and BANJOS. The Banjos, a bluegrass band, wouldn't start until later, well after he was home. The aroma of grilled meat and barbecue sauce filled the restaurant.

Daisy, a waitress of a certain age with a cute face, curly red hair, and a stick figure greeted him warmly. "Hey, hon, right on time I see." She patted his hand in a motherly fashion. "Ya have a good day?"

"Pretty good."

"Reckon ya want the usual? Cheeseburger—Swiss—fries and a whiskey?"

He nodded.

Daisy turned to go, but he remembered the advance pledged by Metcalf and called her back.

"It *was* a good day," he said. "Start a tab for me and bring me a Porterhouse, medium rare, and a Black Jack on the rocks, not the cheap stuff."

"Good for you," she said, and walked off humming to herself. She returned shortly with his drink. "A little fuller than usual," she pointed out, "to celebrate." In truth, she probably was just lobbying for a healthy tip, a share of the fruits of "having a good day."

As he waited for his steak, Chuck nursed the Jack Daniel's and reviewed the contentious relationship that existed between him and his son, Tyler.

He'd lost track of Ty after Ty had stormed out of his life, angry over the bankruptcy, angry over the loss of his college funds, and angry over Chuck's "failure" to accept him.

But he was a difficult kid to accept. He challenged the norms of society and the Bible, choosing his own life style despite the admonitions of his family and counselors, and was adamant there was nothing wrong with his behavior. Anyone who wanted to change him was accused of having a "narrow-minded agenda." Chuck indicted him as a "pig-headed teenager."

They'd never had a knock-down-drag-out argument; instead, they merely threw verbal barbs and insults at one another and allowed a low-grade animosity to hover over their tenuous kinship.

Chuck's steak arrived, still sizzling, accompanied by Daisy singing along with country music wafting from overhead speakers. She smiled sadly as she vocalized with George Strait that "All My Ex's Live in Texas," and did a little shuffle to Toby Keith's "Beer for My Horses" when she left.

As Chuck cut into his Porterhouse, his musings drifted back to his son. Perhaps it was time to try again, to reach out to Ty, to extend an olive branch, to offer him a chance to ride shotgun for his father as dear old Dad went on a hunt for a million bucks—more than enough to replenish the lost college savings. Or, if Ty had completed college on his own, enough to cover the cost of an advanced degree. He owed his son that much, even if it turned out they were unable to abolish the familial DMZ that divided them. That would be his way, he decided, as the lyrics of the Toby Keith piece went, of raising up a glass "against evil forces, singing whisky for my men, beer for my horses."

He tried to envision what Ty might look like now, but couldn't. The last time he'd seen his son he'd been a gangly 19-year-old with unkempt shoulder-length hair, a bad complexion, and an addiction to The Smashing Pumpkins and their grunge-heavy metal-gothic rock music. Surely he wasn't the same person now, as a man.

Chuck resolved to call him as soon as he got back to his apartment. His ex-wife had given him Ty's number several years ago, but he'd never bothered to phone, wasn't even sure where his son lived. Who knows, maybe the number was no longer valid.

Still, he'd try, knowing his call would likely be greeted by Ty with all the warmth a member of Hamas might get from a rabbi.

He finished his meal, signed the chit brought by Daisy, added a ten-dollar tip, and headed home.

SUNDAY, APRIL 14

ON SUNDAY, Chuck made a trip to the Storm Prediction Center. The center had moved to Norman from Kansas City a number of years earlier and set up residence on the University of Oklahoma's campus. He still had friends there, and they allowed him to pore over data looking for telltale signs of future atmospheric turmoil, the sort that triggers the monster supercells of the Great Plains, the breeders of the Grim Reapers of spring: violent tornadoes.

But there was none. No prediction of the classic upper-air pattern that gets the hearts of chasers and forecasters racing. No southward undulation of the jet stream winds over the Rockies that create the warring air masses on which supercells thrive: warm, humid conditions over the Plains and a cold, dry environment in the Mountain West. It wasn't that simple, of course, but Chuck knew the upper-air signature, the large-scale initiator, had to be there before he worried about smaller-scale details, parameters such as vorticity and helicity, instability and inhibition, theta-Es and LFCs.

He called Metcalf to tell him there was nothing on the meteorological horizon to get excited over.

"Let me remind you, Chuckie," Metcalf said, "mid-May. That's when the clock strikes midnight and you either turn into a frog or Prince Charming."

"I don't think that's a strictly accurate interpretation of the fairy tale."

"Close enough for Hollywood work."

"I can't change what I can't change," Chuck snapped.

"But you can change where we go hunting . . . just so it's someplace that looks like frigging Oklahoma."

"Right," Chuck said, resignation threading his voice.

TUESDAY, APRIL 16

ON TUESDAY, he returned to the Cowboy Corral for dinner, Ty still on his mind. He'd tried several times over the past three days to reach his son by phone, but never got an answer. He was reluctant to leave a voice mail, deeming that an inappropriate way to make initial contact after almost a decade of estrangement. He wanted to have a conversation with Ty, not leave a recorded message.

Daisy arrived at his table.

"Good to see ya again, hon. Another steak this evening? Got some good lookin' T-bones back there." She inclined her head toward the kitchen.

"No," Chuck said, his voice soft. "Better make it a cheeseburger.

And no Black Jack, either. Back to the bar stock, I'm afraid." Although the promised check from Metcalf had arrived via FedEx on Monday, Chuck realized the money wouldn't last long if he insisted on living a Rolls-Royce lifestyle on a roller-skate budget.

Daisy nodded, looking a bit downcast, likely realizing there wouldn't be another ten-dollar gratuity this evening.

On the stage near the dance floor, a man sipped a beer and plunked on a banjo, apparently just practicing. The band wasn't scheduled to perform tonight.

Daisy delivered the burger and whiskey, and Chuck worked his way slowly through both. As he drained the last smidgen of liquor from his glass, a woman approached the table where he sat.

"Good evening," she said. "Mr. Rittenburg?"

Chuck studied her. Dark-complected, hazel eyes, short black hair—attractive but not classically beautiful. A tan business suit and white blouse suggested she was something other than a "working girl."

"And you are?" he asked.

She fished into a black leather purse hanging over her left shoulder and pulled out an ID case. She flipped it open.

"Special Agent Medeiros, FBI," she said.

Chuck examined her ID. "Shit. Now what? Cuz I missed my alimony payment last month? Cuz I was late with my rent?" *Well why not?* He remembered an old joke from somewhere in the past: "Cheer up," my friend told me, "things could be worse." So I cheered up and sure enough, things got worse.

"I'm not *after* you, Mr. Rittenburg. I just want to talk with you."

"Talk?"

"I have a proposal, a job offer."

Chuck fiddled with his empty whiskey glass and stared at the woman. *Bizarre. Two offers in one week?*

"Can I buy you another one?" she asked, pointing at the glass.

Daisy stood at a distance, eyeing the exchange and frowning a bit. She reminded Chuck of a protective, but skinny, mama bear watching over her cub.

"No, one's my limit . . . ah, screw it. Why not? Sure. Have a seat and enlighten me." He gestured at a chair on the other side of the table.

She sat. "Mind if I grab something to eat?" she asked. "Maybe a sandwich. I skipped lunch. Kinda hungry."

He motioned Daisy over, but she took her time.

"Something for Ms. Medeiros," he said when Daisy finally arrived.

"And a Black Jack for me."

Medeiros ordered a turkey burger—no mayo—and a green salad. "Gotta watch what I eat," she said, "or I get a little heavy in the ass and start looking like a female Michelin Man." She laughed lightly, helping ease the tension that had tightened across Chuck's shoulders.

"So, have you been staking me out, Agent Medeiros?" he asked.

"No. And call me Gabi, please. My full name is Gabriela Galina Medeiros. Gabi's a lot easier. I considered phoning you, but I really wanted to make my pitch face-to-face. I thought maybe I could catch you at your apartment after work—my work—but you were gone by the time I got there. Neighbors told me they thought you ate supper 'down the street someplace,' so that pretty much narrowed it to this place or Mickey D's. And this place seemed a better fit for supper. Since it's early, you were pretty easy to spot."

Daisy delivered the Jack Daniel's, burger, and salad, then hovered nearby, perhaps making sure there was no hanky panky going on, until Chuck cast a steely-eyed glare at her.

"So, Agent Gabi, what is this job offer you have? It's hard to believe I have any skills the Feds would be interested in. I'm not a lawyer. Never worked in law enforcement. I don't have any forensic meteorology skills. You probably got the wrong guy."

He took a sip of his upgraded whiskey and swilled it around in his mouth, savoring its bite.

"You accusing the FBI of screwing up, not knowing what they're doing?"

"No. I guess that's never happened, huh?"

She dropped a smidgen of dressing onto her salad, then tossed it with her fork.

"Never," she said. A hint of a smile snuck across her face then quickly dissipated. "Charles Rittenburg. Born Emporia, Kansas, 1963. BS and MS in meteorology from the University of Oklahoma. Worked at the National Severe Storms Forecast Center, later the Storm Prediction Center, from 1986 to 1996. Started Thunder Road Tours in—"

"Okay," Chuck interrupted, "you got your man." He raised his arms over his head in mock surrender.

Gabi nodded, then took a bite of her turkey burger.

"So that brings me back to my original question," Chuck said. "Why does the FBI want a broken down, bankrupt, under-employed weatherman?"

Gabi continued to chew her burger before answering.

"Because," she finally said, "I want to go on a tornado chase."

Chuck laughed, reached for his Jack Daniel's, and took a good pull. "In case you missed it, I don't do that anymore."

"Oh, I didn't miss it, Mr. Rittenburg. Do you read the newspaper?"

"Can't afford a subscription."

"Sunday *Oklahoman*," she said. "A little article noting that Charles Rittenburg, former owner and president of Thunder Road Tours, has signed a contract with Global-American Cinema to lead cinematographers for the upcoming movie, *The Okies*, on a tornado chase. Specifically, in pursuit of an EF-4 or EF-5, if I have my terminology correct."

"You do," he said.

He downed the remainder of his whiskey in one swallow. A pleasant hum surged through his head, disconnecting him from the reality of the conversation he was having.

"Look, I just want to tag along on your storm safari," Gabi responded. "The government will pay for your services. Maybe not what a Hollywood film company dishes out, but we'll ante up a fair consulting fee."

"So this isn't personal? It's a federal thing?"

"Yes."

"Something to do with Global-American Cinema?"

"No."

"If it's government business, why not use a government worker as your guide, someone from the Storm Prediction Center or National Severe Storms Laboratory?"

The banjo player had stepped up his pace, tapping his foot and picking out a tune that sounded like the dueling banjo music from *Deliverance*.

"Guy's good," Gabi said, finishing her salad. "But to answer your question, I thought about getting a NOAA employee, then decided against it."

"Why?"

"Several reasons. One, I wanted the best chaser on the Plains, even if he's no longer active. But, thanks to Global-American, it turns out he is—I've researched you thoroughly, Mr. Rittenburg. Two, since you've already got an expedition set up, it seemed logical just to piggyback on it and carry a low profile. And three, I'm stalking the same thing you are."

"For what reason, if I may ask?"

"If we're partners, I'll tell you." Gabi rested her chin in her hands and gazed directly at him.

The buzzing swirling through his head increased, picked his thoughts and flung them around the room like a dust devil in a drought. Against his better judgment, which apparently had taken shelter in a storm cellar, he smiled and extended his hand to Gabi.

"Deal," he said.

They shook on it.

"So?" he asked.

"Why do I want to find an EF-4 or -5?"

Chuck nodded.

She pursed her lips, then blew out a soft breath. "Bait," she said.

Chapter Five

TUESDAY, APRIL 16

"BAIT?" CHUCK said. "Bait for what?"

Gabi pondered for a moment how much to tell him, but decided since he was granting her a favor, she should be up front with what she was looking for. She glanced around the restaurant to make certain no one was close enough to eavesdrop. Then she leaned toward Chuck and spoke in a low voice. "I think the more correct question is 'Bait for *whom*?'"

"A person?" Chuck said, surprise registering in his voice, his words vaguely slurred.

She gazed more closely at him: auburn hair flecked with gray, thinning a bit; green eyes that registered something camouflaged—a modicum of sadness perhaps? When he smiled it was with a degree of wistfulness. Though he appeared a bit underweight, she judged him a once-handsome man, but now . . . she understood what he had been through and could see it had taken its measure. Still, she wondered if his ex hadn't let something of value slip from her grasp.

"Yes, a person or maybe persons," she said.

He fingered his empty whiskey glass.

"Another one?" she asked. Testing him.

"No." He removed his hand from the tumbler. "Tell me what you're trolling for."

She massaged her right temple, feeling the first foreshadowing throb of the bane of her existence, a migraine headache.

"About eight years ago," she said, "a scattering of expensive wristwatches, like Rolexes and Movados, and few pieces of top-dollar jewelry, and one or two gem-grade diamonds, that had been reported 'missing' in the aftermath of destructive tornadoes, began to show up in pawn shops.

"The first discovery was accidental, by a homeowner in Kansas

City. After his house had been leveled by a violent twister, he realized his Breitling watch was missing, but curiously, none of his other jewelry. Well, he was visiting a pawn shop in Omaha several months later when he spotted a Breitling that looked just like his. Sure enough, it was. He was able to produce documentation with the serial number."

The banjo player packed up his instrument, nodded to Daisy, and exited the restaurant. Daisy approached the table where Chuck and Gabi sat.

"Anything else?" she asked.

"Only the check," Chuck said.

Gabi handed a credit card to Daisy. "Put it on that," she said.

Daisy, in her mama bear mode again, cocked her head at Chuck.

"Business," he explained.

Daisy shrugged and left.

Gabi continued. "A notice went out to law enforcement agencies from Bismarck to Houston. Local authorities visited more pawn shops and turned up additional high-end items originally thought to have been lost in bad storms. Not many, but enough to raise suspicions."

Chuck dabbed at his mouth with a napkin. "Couldn't it have been the work of random looters who just happened to find targets of opportunity?" he said.

Another pulse of pain, this one sharper, knifed behind Gabi's right eye. She tried to ignore it.

"No," she said. "The selected high quality of the items and the fact there wasn't any wholesale pillaging, you know, like armloads of stuff being carried off, suggested something carefully orchestrated."

Chuck considered her words, then said, "So you think there might be a connection to the storm-chasing community?"

"The thefts have occurred only in the wake of tornadoes that produced an immense amount of damage, so it's someone—or *someones*—who's Johnny-on-the-Spot; who manages to arrive in devastated areas in the immediate aftermath of really violent twisters."

"Yeah. Sounds like it could be a chaser, or somebody shadowing chasers. But why is the FBI interested in this?"

"Because it involves similar crimes in a number of states and because . . ." she hesitated, wondering if she had already told Chuck too much.

Daisy returned with the tab for Gabi to sign.

"Thanks, hon'," Daisy said to her. She turned and patted Chuck on the cheek before leaving. "Ya'll behave yourself now." She winked at him, then trotted off.

Gabi found some humor in her comment. "She's afraid you'll try to put the make on an FBI agent?"

"She doesn't know you're an FBI agent."

"You must have a reputation then."

Chuck smiled. "Daisy only hopes. You're safe. Now tell me about the 'and because'."

Gabi closed her eyes, as if she could squeeze the nascent pain from her head. She opened them and found Chuck staring at her.

"Are you okay?" he asked.

"Been a long day. Just a little tension headache," she lied.

"Maybe Daisy could bring you some aspirin."

Gabi waved off the suggestion. "I'll be fine."

"Okay then. Tell me the rest of the story."

"Last Saturday," she said, "a tornado, an EF-3 I think is what news reports called it, hit Honeybee—"

"I saw it on TV," Chuck interjected. "A lot of damage."

"Yes. Including a family-run jewelry and electronics store."

"Let me guess," Chuck said. "Some expensive watches and computers were missing after the storm."

"Worse," Gabi answered. "One of the co-owners, a 68-year-old man, was found dead in the rubble."

"EF-3s kill people."

"People kill people, too. The gentleman's wristwatch had stopped 20 minutes *after* the tornado hit."

Chuck rested his chin on his knuckles and appeared to consider her statement.

"Well," he said after a moment, "maybe he was a guy who set his watch fast. A lot of people do that so they're never late for anything."

"The police asked his family about that. His family said he was diligent to a fault about keeping the correct time on his watches—almost to the nearest second."

Gabi caught Daisy giving them the evil eye as the dinner crowd streamed into the restaurant. She probably wanted the table.

"That doesn't seem like much to go on," Chuck said.

"The coroner said the man appeared to have defensive wounds on his hand and forearm, and that the side of his head was caved in. Usually people killed by collapsing walls don't have damage to the *side* of their head."

"Could have been flying debris."

"Maybe. But there's something else. About five minutes after the tornado struck, an Oklahoma State Trooper remembers seeing two EMTs enter the store. He doesn't recall any ID on their vehicle, a black GMC Terrain, that suggested they were local. He asked them if they needed help, but they said no. He was busy and forgot about them until later when the suggestion of foul play came up."

"I dunno," Chuck said, "it all sounds pretty flimsy, pretty circumstantial to me. But I'm not a cop."

"Yeah, but you're smart and analytical . . . and right. It's supposition piled upon supposition, which is why law enforcement never went public with it. Still, I think there's something to it."

An invisible vise beneath her scalp snapped tight and she winced involuntarily as a wave of pain swept through her head, then relented. She knew the reprieve was only temporary.

"Okay," Chuck said, "assuming you're right about the thefts, why turn to murder?"

"The victim probably caught them in the act, could've identified them."

"So again, assuming, we might not be looking for chasers but EMTs."

Gabi shrugged. "Maybe. But if these are the same guys who have been working the Plains for a decade now, they always seem to be in the right spot at the right time as far as violent tornadoes go."

"Any other suspicious storm deaths?" Chuck asked.

"We've just started looking at that, but it probably will be difficult to determine so long after the fact. There was one case, however, in eastern Nebraska about five years ago. A man and his wife were found dead in the wreckage of their house after a huge tornado sliced through town. The house had a storm cellar. The door to it was open. Why would they come out of or not be in the cellar during a vicious storm?"

"Was stuff missing from the house?"

The buzz of conversation in the restaurant had increased, and Gabi leaned closer to Chuck so she wouldn't have to raise her voice. "The wife's five-carat diamond wedding ring," she said. "Her children said she always wore it."

"Did it turn up in a pawn shop?"

"Never found it. But it might have been fenced."

"So the working hypothesis is they were killed—murdered—after the storm, and the ring taken from the wife's finger?"

Gabi nodded. "And unfortunately, it's *just* a hypothesis."

"Which leads to your hunting expedition. You figure since I'm going in search of an EF-4 or -5, you'll ride along and see if you can get lucky, maybe catch your will-o'-the-wisp crooks in the act?"

"That's about it."

"It sounds like a long shot to me. And you'll understand, of course, that whatever happens, my movie client will take precedent."

"Absolutely. When do we start?"

Chuck explained to her the contingencies of the chase and the arrangement he'd made with Global-American Cinema. After he finished, he said, "I'll call you with a launch date the same day I call the film company."

Another explosion of agony erupted deep in Gabi's head. The Cowboy Corral seemed infused with flashes of light. She stood.

"I need to go," she said. She dropped her business card on the table. "My phone numbers are on there."

She hurried from the restaurant.

CHUCK RETURNED TO his apartment and found Stormy snoring softly in the threadbare armchair that seemed to have become community property, a piece of raggedy-ass furniture shared by man and dog.

"Good thing I didn't bring you on as a watchdog," Chuck said.

Stormy yawned and rolled over.

Chuck attempted to analyze the somewhat bizarre turn his life had taken over the last several days—job offers from a film company *and* the FBI—but found the two shots of whisky working against any sort of intellectual assessment. The developments were what they were. And maybe Metcalf was right. He, Chuck, could be about to embark on the greatest adventure of his life, or more recently, his so-called life.

Not that it would be high adventure in the sense of facing great danger—experienced storm chasers knew how to stalk storms without putting themselves in jeopardy—but it would be a ticking time-bomb escapade in terms of racing the clock to find a violent tornado and secure a million-dollar prize. A million dollars. Had he heard that right? Was that really in the contract he'd signed?

He shuffled to the kitchen table where the documents lay and studied them again. Yes, even through his liquor-fuzzed vision, there it was: $1,000.000. For the first time since hearing the proposition, his heart beat a little faster. Reality coming home to roost.

Oh, there was also the reality of perhaps confronting a thief and murderer—a long shot, of course—but that was Agent Medeiros' reality, not his.

His phone rang. Probably a solicitor or bill collector, but he didn't have caller ID. Maybe Metcalf. Chuck elected to answer.

"Hello," he said.

"Who is this?" a voice responded. "You've called my number several times recently."

"Charles Rittenburg," Chuck said. He tried to place the voice of the caller, but couldn't. The connection fell silent.

"Hello?" Chuck repeated.

Stormy lifted her head to see who Chuck was talking to.

"Charles Rittenburg?" the caller said. "The Charles Rittenburg who lost his business, drove his wife off, and turned his back on his kids?"

"I didn't drive my wife off and I didn't turn my back on—" It abruptly dawned on Chuck who was calling. His son. "Tyler?"

"Yeah, it's me. I'm surprised you remembered." Anger threaded his words. Hardly a surprise. But there was more than that. Hurt and loss, too. Chuck acknowledged that his son probably had every right to stick a knife into him and twist.

"I handled the situation poorly—"

"Is that all I was to you, a *situation?*" The word came out venom tipped.

"Ty, listen, let's not try to undo a decade of animosity over the phone. I called because I'd like to see you."

"Let me guess. You're broke and need a place to crash?"

Chuck expelled a long breath. The conversation wasn't going well. But perhaps he shouldn't have expected it to.

"No. I want you to come here."

"I can't afford it. In case you couldn't figure it out from the area code, I live in Oregon. It's not exactly an overnighter to Oklahoma."

"I'll pay."

"Really?" Ty coated the word in skepticism.

"Yes. Really. I want you to ride shotgun for me on a hunting expedition."

Chuck explained. He finished by telling Ty there was a substantial amount of money involved and that if the venture were successful he'd like to share with him "to make up for past shortcomings."

Ty didn't speak for a long time after Chuck had finished, and the most prominent sound in the room became the beat of Chuck's heart.

Stormy stood, shifted in the armchair, then lay down and positioned her head on the edge of the chair so she could keep an eye on Chuck.

Finally Ty said, "Money cures all, right?"

"No, of course not. I just—I really—I want to see you, son."

"You'll understand if the feeling isn't mutual."

"Give me a chance, Ty."

Again, Ty remained silent before responding, perhaps gauging the pros and cons of the request and his reply. Eventually he spoke. "I suppose everyone deserves a second chance, even if they don't. Or maybe I just have a perverse desire to see you get flushed down the crapper again. Okay, I'll show. Call me when you're ready. Five days notice you said?"

"Yes."

"One more thing."

Chuck waited.

"I am who I am. Don't expect somebody different, somebody changed." He hung up.

Chuck, still gripping the phone, gazed blankly at the ceiling. "Why should I have expected that?" he asked softly.

Chapter Six

WEDNESDAY, APRIL 17

CHUCK FOUND A reasonable price on a short-term lease of a pre-owned Ford Expedition at a dealership in nearby Moore. The SUV appeared to be in excellent condition, and—a huge plus—sported virtually new Michelins and a full-sized spare. The Ford, with the addition of some electronics, would make a great chase vehicle. Chuck haggled briefly over the contract details, signed an agreement, shelled out the upfront money—a small portion of the advance from Metcalf—and had the SUV back at his apartment by late afternoon.

The following day, he bought a number of items he would need to support his chase. The purchases included an AC to DC power inverter, cell phones, signal boosters, and a high-end laptop computer. His final acquisition: a sophisticated hardware/software package that integrated meteorological, radar, and GPS data broadcast via XM Satellite Radio. Perfect for storm chasers on the move.

Several days later, he found an independent mechanic who made several modifications to the Ford to accommodate his purchases. First, the serviceman wired the inverter to the vehicle's battery, thus providing a way to convert its 12-volt DC output to a standard 110-volt AC supply. The inverter came with standard household outlets that would allow Chuck to keep his laptop powered and cell phone charged.

Second, over the center console, the mechanic installed a computer mounting bracket on a swivel arm that would allow Chuck to view his laptop from either the driver's or passenger's seat.

Finally, the mechanic affixed three antennae to the Expedition's roof that would facilitate extended cell phone, XM, and GPS data reception.

Except for a few minor additions—a first aid kit, flashlights, and jumper cables—Chuck was ready to chase. All he needed was for the weather to play ball.

MONDAY, APRIL 22

AFTER A WEEK of daily trips—long, generally pleasant walks through the warming Oklahoma spring—to the Storm Prediction Center to review the weather situation, Chuck struck pay dirt. Or at least thought he had. Numerical models, he well knew, could be notoriously fickle the further into the future you attempted to apply them.

But five days down the road, a deep trough was forecast to pivot from the Rockies out over the Great Plains, setting up the requisite clash of air masses and winds that trigger the monster supercells of meteorological legend. There appeared to be enough support for the scenario, from different models and their ensemble variations, that Chuck felt emboldened to summon the troops.

He first called Metcalf, letting him know the Great Hunt would be ready to launch by the end of the week.

"Hey, that's great, Chaz," Metcalf bellowed. "I'll have my little convoy rolling along I-40 by Wednesday. Should be there Saturday."

So now it's Chaz?

"Call me when you guys get into town and settled," Chuck said. "If things look good, we'll launch on Sunday."

Next, he phoned Agent Medeiros, Gabi. He told her to be ready to depart on Sunday and promised to call her later in the week with more details.

"If the meteorological parameters don't fall into place, we may have to delay," he cautioned. "But Metcalf and his cinematographers will be here by Saturday and probably rarin' to go."

Finally, he called Ty and explained that the weather conditions appeared ready to come together. "Looks like great tornado-hunting weather next week, son," he said. "Are you ready to go?"

"Careful how you toss that word around."

Chuck didn't understand. "What word?"

"Son," Ty snapped.

The barb drove deep into Chuck's being.

"Look, can we raise a white flag for a while . . . Ty? See if we can attain a modicum of civility for at least a couple of weeks?"

"You mean like never existed when we lived under the same roof?"

Chuck counted silently to ten before answering. "Yes. Like that."

"Yeah, fine. I can suck it up for a while. The big question is, Can you?"

Chuck let the comment pass. "I'll purchase an electronic ticket for you. Best you fly in on Saturday. What's the nearest airport to you?"

"Portland. I live outside the city in a small town called McMinnville. You didn't know that, of course."

Again, Chuck didn't respond to the needle. "I'll need an email address, too," he said.

Ty gave it to him.

"I'll pick you up at Will Rogers," Chuck said.

Ty gave a sharp, derisive laugh. "How will you recognize me?"

Eight years. It had been eight years since he'd seen his son. A teenager then. Now a man. It was a fair question.

Chuck stumbled over the answer. "I . . . I don't—"

"Not to worry," Ty said, "the disembarking flaming fairy shouldn't be hard to spot, right? The guy levitating in his loafers? Giving a limp-wristed wave."

"Stop it, Ty."

"Tell you what. I won't squeeze your nuts any more than I already have. I'll find you. Easier that way. See you Saturday in Oklahoma City."

After they hung up, Chuck reflected on the call and the one a week prior. What bothered him most was not Ty's antagonism or sarcasm or bitterness. Perhaps he'd earned that, although it certainly was a two-way street. No, what bothered him most was that not once had his son referred to him as *Dad* or *Pop* or *Father*.

For the first time, a tiny acorn of doubt about the wisdom of inviting Ty on the expedition rattled around somewhere in the back of Chuck's brain.

SATURDAY, APRIL 27

ON SATURDAY, Chuck drove the Expedition to Will Rogers World Airport on the southwest edge of Oklahoma City. He parked, then waited for Ty's flight from Portland to land.

After the arrival was posted, Chuck paced the lower level of the terminal, keeping watch on the area around baggage carousel number four, where Ty would claim his luggage. He attempted to picture what his son might look like now, but couldn't conjure up an image. Ty had been only 19 when he'd last seen him, an unkempt, withdrawn boy trying to beat his way out of the thick underbrush of adolescence. Now he was a man, well into his 20s, creeping up on 30. At least in appearance, he would be a different person

In hindsight, it was easy to see that Ty had borne a heavier psychological backpack than most teenagers. Not only had he had to deal with the normal angst of growing up, but with his homosexuality, the loss of financial means to attend college and a disintegrating family.

Chuck had always harbored the hope that Ty would change his sexual orientation, perhaps through counseling or religion, and abandon his deviant lifestyle. Or maybe just realize that being what he was, was abhorrent; he could think of no other way to put it. But Ty had already shot down that hope a week and a half earlier when he'd warned Chuck in their phone conversation: "I am who I am. Don't expect somebody different, somebody changed."

Passengers from Ty's flight began to descend the stairs and escalator connecting the upper level of the terminal to the baggage claim area. A harried-looking young mother with three small kids in uneven, rapid orbit around her led the pack. Following her came a handful of men, a few in business suits, others decked out in cowboy hats and Western boots. None seemed interested in searching for someone waiting for them.

Next down the escalator, a girls' sports team of some sort, probably golf, judging by the proliferation of golf bags littering the carousel.

After a brief break, a crowd of young men and women in military camo uniforms flooded into the lower terminal and spilled toward the baggage carousel as duffel bags began to appear. They probably were bound for sprawling Tinker Air Force Base, 12 miles east.

Tinker Air Force Base. Chuck's thoughts drifted from Ty for a moment. He wondered how many people were aware of the role Tinker had played in the birth of tornado forecasting. In 1948, in the wake of a devastating twister that smashed into the base, two young Air Force officers tackled the virtually impossible task, as it was then deemed, of predicting tornadoes.

Against overwhelming odds, a second twister thundered over Tinker just five days later. This time, however, a warning—based on the officers' hurried research—was issued, and the feasibility of tornado forecasting, however crude at the time, thus validated.

Chuck paid homage to that forecast. Decades later, at the Storm Prediction Center, the modern-day legacy of the "Tinker warning," he'd earned his spurs in severe weather forecasting.

But today he was spurless . . . and clueless: looking for a son he might not, it had been suggested, recognize.

A light tap on the back of his shoulder caused him to turn abruptly. He found himself staring into a vaguely familiar face, freckled and round but not fleshy, slightly sunburned, unsmiling. Ty? But no. It couldn't be. This individual had an almost military bearing and appearance with a hard, muscular body and short, brush-cut hair. Yet . . .

"Ty?" Chuck failed to hide his surprise.

"I'll grab my bag," his son responded. No salutation. No handshake. No hug. Ty merely wheeled and strode toward the luggage carousel.

He returned shortly with a large polycarbonate spinner in tow. "Lead on," he said.

They took the escalator to the terminal's main level. "I'm in short-term parking," Chuck said. He pointed outside, across the curving multi-laned roadway and plaza that fronted the terminal.

"Let's go." Ty headed out.

As they walked, Chuck attempted to initiate a conversation. "When I first saw you in there, I thought I was looking at a soldier."

"Yeah. A year ago, you would have been. I spent seven years in the army. Out now, though."

"And doing what?"

"Taking college courses on-line."

"Working toward a degree?"

"Yeah."

"In?"

"Criminal justice. My partner is a cop."

"Oh."

"A little too much info?"

"No . . . it's just that . . . I don't know."

"Don't worry. I'll try not to embarrass you. You know, like running around with my flopper hanging out or leering at young boys."

"I didn't think that would be a problem," Chuck responded, his voice a bit more acidic than he'd intended.

They reached the Expedition and Ty tossed his bag into the rear.

Their conversation, such as it was, remained strained as Chuck drove back to Norman. Small talk. Trite questions. Clipped answers. "How's Mom and Arlene?" "Good." "What school are you taking courses from?" "Western Oregon University." "Do you work?" "Part time. Construction." "How's it feel to be back in Oklahoma?" "Awkward."

LATER, THEY SAT in silence as they waited for their dinners at the

Cowboy Corral. The silence, however, was only between them. The restaurant was otherwise filled with country music, laughter, the clatter of dinnerware and shouted exchanges between the wait staff and kitchen workers. A bustling Saturday night. Daisy, apparently sensing the tension between Chuck and Ty, kept her distance and busied herself with other customers.

Chuck agonized over how to begin reparation with his son, how to reach him after so many years of animus, how to reconnect after such an extended period of dissociation. He came up with no good solutions, so merely launched into another attempt at initiating a conversation.

"Ty, it's good to see you. It really is."

Ty nodded without saying anything. He reached for one of the cheese biscuits Daisy had provided.

Chuck continued. "I'm proud of what you've accomplished. I mean, seven years in the army. Wow, who would have thought. And now working on a degree in Criminal Justice. I'm impressed."

Ty took a bite of the biscuit. He swallowed, then forced a wan smile.

"In the army, what did you do?" Chuck asked, attempting to draw his son into an exchange of some sort. He studied Ty more closely now than when they'd met at the airport. His son was no longer the spindly, pimply teenager he'd known. Far from it. He'd grown into a mature adult—red hair like his mother's, green eyes like his father's. And in those eyes—this was surprising—there seemed a hint of merriment despite the hostility that emanated from him.

"Special Operations," Ty said.

"You mean like the Green Berets?"

"Not like. I *was* a Green Beret. In Afghanistan."

The answer prompted Chuck to look more analytically into his son's eyes, and he saw something else, something beyond the subdued sparkle of buoyancy he'd first noticed: the gaze of a keen observer, a thoughtful examiner, an experienced soldier.

"Surprised?" Ty asked

"Well—"

"I mean, a gay Green Beret. Doesn't quite fit the mold, does it?" Ty took a drink of water.

"No."

"Don't ask, don't tell. At least that's the way it was then. Life goes on."

"I suppose. But I guess that gets us to the crux of the matter."

"Which is?"

Chuck wished he'd ordered a whiskey when Daisy had first come to their table. Now she was nowhere to be seen.

"Your lifestyle," Chuck said, swallowing hard, "I couldn't accept your lifestyle, your refusal to change."

"Life*style*? How is what you *are* a life*style*? Is your heterosexuality a lifestyle? When did you *choose* to be straight?" Ty fixed his father in a piercing stare.

"I . . . I never chose to be straight. I just . . . was."

Ty thumped the table with his forefinger. "That's my point. You just *were*. Do you think it was any different for me?"

"I think you could have changed if you'd wanted."

Ty leaned across the table and spoke in sharp, low tones, almost a hiss. "But of course, I didn't want to. I was much more comfortable *choosing* a way of life in which I would be reviled, scorned, taunted, and bullied. Much more at ease with a *decision* that would lead me to be rejected by my own father. Happy to lead a life in the closet, hiding what I was, pretending to be what I wasn't. It's just Mayberry RFD for us gays every day, *Dad*." The last word he pronounced with particular contempt.

Chuck remained silent, unable to formulate a response, stunned by the vehemence of his son's words, yet realizing they represented a controlled explosion of pent-up emotion and long-considered introspection. He sorted through Ty's mini-diatribe, actually finding some validity in his arguments. Yet so many questions remained, particularly those springing from the Bible's vilification of homosexuality.

He pondered again the wisdom of inviting Ty on the chase. Would he and Ty find some common ground, mutual respect, a modicum of understanding that would allow a father to find his son; a son, his father? Or would their time together ratchet up the tension that already existed between them to the point it would fracture into an abyss so wide and deep it could never be bridged?

Chuck hoped for the former, wished for the former, but feared the latter.

Chapter Seven

SUNDAY, APRIL 28

EARLY SUNDAY morning, Chuck met Ty at the motel where he'd stayed overnight. Ty merely nodded to his father—no "good morning" or "great day, huh?"—as he approached the Expedition, tossed his suitcase into the rear and climbed into the passenger seat.

Stormy, from the back seat, stretched forward and rested a paw on Ty's shoulder in greeting. Ty turned and petted her. "Hey, boy," he said.

"Girl," Chuck corrected.

"My mistake," Ty said. "But that was always my problem, wasn't it? Not having an eye for the ladies."

Chuck gritted his teeth and held his gaze straight ahead, through the windshield. From that point on, except for strained, mumbled, one-sentence exchanges, they rode in silence to the assembly location for the chase team, the parking lot of a suburban shopping mall on the south side of Oklahoma City. Since the mall didn't open until noon, the team had the lot to itself. An unusually warm wind for late April gusted in fits and starts over the nearly deserted asphalt. The vague odors of breakfast, probably from a nearby Denny's or Waffle House, rode the breeze.

Metcalf was there already, dressed as he had been when Chuck first met him: hiking boots, cargo shorts, white shirt, and a Greek fisherman's cap. He stood near his Lincoln Navigator chatting with members of what Chuck presumed was his crew.

Behind the Lincoln, the slanting rays of the rising sun glinted off two more vehicles, one silver, one white. Chuck studied them closely, suddenly impressed by the little expedition he was tasked to lead. The vehicles, moderate-sized crew-cab flatbed trucks, sported exoskeletons of metal scaffolding and platforms. Large compartments snugged flush against the rear of each cab housed what appeared to be high-amperage electric generators. Tarps, firmly secured, obscured whatever the beds of

46

the trucks carried.

The trucks seemed a hybrid of what a commercial painter might drive to ferry his ladders and scaffoldings around, and something Mel Gibson might have raced about in one his old *Mad Max* movies.

"Hey, Chaz, great to see ya," Metcalf boomed as Chuck, Ty trailing, walked toward him. "Who's your best boy?"

"My what?"

"Movie lingo. Best boy—like an apprentice or helper. Who's the dude behind you? Long-lost son I'll bet."

Chuck didn't care for Metcalf's public proclamation, but realized it was just the man's uninhibited nature. He turned to introduce Ty. "This is Tyler—Ty—Rittenberg. He, as you say, is my 'best boy.' Ty, this is Jerry Metcalf from Global-American Cinema."

Metcalf and Ty shook hands. Ty inclined his head toward the trucks. "Impressive rigs you've got there."

"Camera trucks," Metcalf answered. "There's a retractable 15-foot crane in the bed of the white truck, a 22-footer in the silver one. We can hang a Panavision camera on the end of a crane, extend it, then operate the camera with a joystick. Pretty neat. Gives us nice elevation and great panning capabilities." He turned to Chuck. "Let me introduce my crew."

One by one the team, four men and two women, stepped forward and shook hands with Chuck and Ty as Metcalf rattled off their names and titles. Chuck knew he wouldn't remember, at least immediately, all of the names—Ziggy, Nosher, and Boomie were in the mix—but counted three cinematographers, a key grip, a best boy, and a second-unit director.

Willie Weston, the second-unit director, Metcalf pointed out, would be looking for shots not only of tornadoes—"the big, nasty ones," Metcalf reminded Chuck—but scenery and landscape footage as well. "Find us some good stuff, Chuckie," Metcalf said.

Chuckie? Chuck shook his head.

At the far end of the parking lot, a Chevy Camaro appeared and drove toward the group. The car stopped next to Chuck's Expedition. Gabi exited the Camaro and strode toward the gathering. In white shorts and a lightweight khaki blouse, fit and tanned, she looked good—not at all like an FBI agent, Chuck noted.

Metcalf nudged Chuck and said in a stage whisper, "You dog you. Back in the game again. Who's the chick?"

Chuck answered according to an agreement he and Gabi had reached earlier. "She's a feature writer for a local magazine. She wanted to do an article on storm chasing, so I invited her along."

Metcalf stroked his beard and held his gaze on her. "She probably didn't miss the redemption angle either. Good story there: Down and out storm chaser gets a chance to rebuild his life."

"That, too," Chuck said.

"Well, she won't get in the way, will she?"

"She knows how to take care of herself."

Gabi reached the assemblage and introduced herself. "Hi, I'm Gabi Mederios from *The Sooner, the Better* magazine. Gosh, this should be so fun. Going on a tornado chase with a movie company. Our readers will absolutely devour it. Neat, neat, neat."

Chuck marveled at Gabi's ability to transform herself from an FBI Special Agent to a slightly ditzy magazine writer. The men in the group certainly bought into her act, although Metcalf gave Chuck a quick glance from beneath a furrowed brow that suggested he sensed there was something just a bit off kilter about Gabi's story. But he welcomed her with a hearty handshake and a bear hug that seemed to last just a second too long.

"Ohhh," Gabi squealed. "You're strong!"

Chuck almost laughed. Gabi could probably flip the guy upside down and stuff him into a bag if she wanted to.

Instead he said, "Okay, listen up folks. Let's get started." He pulled three cell phones from his pocket and handed them to Metcalf. "One for you and one for each of your trucks. They have Direct Connect or what most people call walkie-talkie capability. That's how we'll communicate when we're on the road." He explained how to use the feature.

"Next," Chuck said, "let me lay out a few ground rules before we launch. First, safety. What we're attempting to do is inherently dangerous: get close enough to tornadoes to get some great shots, but not so close as to be in jeopardy. I've been doing . . . well, did . . . this for a number of years. I know how to maneuver around supercells. I know how to get up close and personal with the greatest storms on earth without getting dismembered. Believe it or not, these things are predictable. Predictable but at times erratic. They can surprise me. Not often, but it happens.

"So you gotta listen to me. You gotta pay attention. Do what I tell you when I tell you. If I tell you to pull out, pull out. No questions. If I tell you to run, run like the wind. If I tell you to dive in a ditch, bury your face in it."

He found himself staring at the camera trucks again. He tossed a question at Metcalf. "How long does it take you to set one of those things up? To be ready to shoot?"

"We can do it pretty fuckin' fast—oops, sorry, missy." Metcalf nodded at Gabi.

Gabi placed both hands over her ears and grinned. Ever the innocent young writer.

"We're pretty damn fast," Metcalf continued. "Been practicing. Got the drill down pat. Like marines storming a beach. The camera will be preassembled. So it's a matter of attaching it, cranking up the generator, and extending the crane. We can do it in about 15 minutes, maybe less."

Chuck hung his head in mock dismay. "Fifteen minutes? Fifteen minutes! Do you realize the average lifespan of a tornado is less than *ten* minutes?"

"Then find us tornadoes that aren't average, Chaz. That's why we hired you."

Chuck drew a deep breath. Ignoring Metcalf's gibe, he continued his briefing. "Despite what you may have seen in the movies or on TV, most chasers aren't reckless. We'll be abiding by speed limits, not using warning lights or flashing our headlights and honking to part traffic, even though chasing can get really congested at times."

"Chuckie, Chuckie, Chuckie," Metcalf said, as though admonishing a child. "We're talking a million bucks here. I'll bet you'll move like you had a bottle rocket strapped to your ass if you have to."

Chuck had to concede, at least silently, the guy from Hollywood might have a point. He concluded his briefing by addressing the plan for the first day's chase. He spread out a roadmap on the hood of the Navigator. "It looks like there'll be a well-defined dry line in western Kansas and the Oklahoma and Texas Panhandles tomorrow," he said. He traced his finger southward from near Garden City, Kansas, to just west of Lubbock, Texas.

"Ahead of it—" he swept his hand northward from San Antonio to Wichita "—strong moisture advection. Now, a couple of terms you'll hear me use a lot are CAPE and CIN." He pronounced the last word "sin."

"Whoa, hold on there, Chaz," Metcalf interrupted, "the only sin I wanna hear about is from hardcore porno flicks. Spare me the eye-of-newt, toe-of-frog meteorological shit. Just tell me where the tornadoes are gonna be."

Chuck squeezed his lips together and looked away from Metcalf. He tracked some birds in flight as they dipped and turned in the morning wind. He felt more comfortable talking about weather parameters, the elements that go into a forecast, than he did merely presenting what comes out: the prediction. At least a discussion of parameters gives visibility to the uncertainties that plague any and all weather forecasts.

But he understood the Golden Rule applied here. He who has the gold . . . "Sure," he said, "tomorrow there's a good chance there'll be some supercells and a few tornadoes, maybe even a big boy or two, in western Kansas. So we'll head north today toward Wichita and stage out there for day one of the chase."

"Excuse me," Metcalf said, "day one?"

"Tomorrow."

"Today is day one, my friend. Tomorrow is two."

"But—"

"Our corporate lawyers will back me up on this," Metcalf snapped.

"Yeah. I know all about lawyers," Chuck responded. He glared at Metcalf, but couldn't think of a viable counterargument, just invective. He'd been out-finagled.

"Let's get moving," he said, and stalked toward the Expedition. *Not off to a good start. Screwed out of a day right off the bat. And it's going to take these clowns 15 minutes just to set up the cameras. A twister can come and go in that time.* Yes, he conceded, he'd been blinded by the chance at a million bucks. Like or not, he was probably on a fool's errand.

He reached the SUV and motioned for Gabi to get into the passenger seat. She hesitated, glanced at Ty.

"It's okay," Chuck said, "my son doesn't talk to me."

Ty nodded at Gabi and opened the door for her. "There's a void in our relationship," he explained, and shut the door after she was in. He climbed into the rear seat with Stormy.

"Oh, who's this?" Gabi said, reaching for Stormy.

"That's Stormy, the Weather Wonder Dog," Chuck responded.

"She's a she," Ty said. "Just so there's no confusion."

Gabi glanced at Ty, a questioning look in her eyes, then ruffled Stormy's fur. "So, are you a bomb sniffer or just a mascot?"

Chuck recalled Stormy's actions the first night at the apartment. "Not a bomb sniffer," he said, "but I think she might have some pointer blood in her . . . for storms."

"Well, I can see why you're on the trip then." She scratched Stormy's head, then turned and faced forward.

Chuck exited the parking lot and headed toward I-35 north. Metcalf's team followed.

"Well, I'm interested," Gabi said. "What're cape and sin?"

"Ever the curious writer," Chuck noted.

Gabi smiled and turned toward Ty. "I don't have anything to do with a magazine," she said, "I'm an FBI agent. But that's just between you and me your dad. Not for public dissemination."

Ty leaned forward. "I can keep a secret. Army. Special Ops. Seven years."

"Iraq?" Gabi asked.

"Afghanistan. A couple of tours."

"I'm impressed. Thanks for your service, Ty." She turned toward Chuck. "You must be proud as hell."

Chuck nodded, but didn't say anything. He held his eyes on the road. *How do I explain my ambivalence about my son to a virtual stranger? Yes, I'm proud, but I'm not proud.*

"Okay," Gabi said. She drew out the word and settled back into her seat.

"Tell me why we have an FBI agent, undercover, on a tornado chase," Ty said.

Gabi explained.

"So *your* hunt could be a lot more dangerous than stalking tornadoes," Ty said after Gabi had finished.

"Probably not. It's a long shot."

"No longer than mine," Chuck interjected.

"We're probably both pissing into the wind," Gabi said.

"How does that work for a female, anyhow?" Ty asked.

Both Gabi and Ty laughed. Chuck flashed a smile at Gabi, but wondered if Ty's riposte had really been meant for her. *Or for me? Ty trying to make a connection? Probably not. He's been hostile toward me from the get-go.*

"Now then, back to cape and sin," Gabi said. "Lay it on me."

"It's CAPE and CIN," Chuck said, and spelled out the acronyms. "CAPE stands for Convective Available Potential Energy. It's a measure of how much energy—fuel—there is in the atmosphere for thunderstorm development. The more energy there is, the bigger and nastier the storms are likely to be."

"Energy? How do you calculate something like that?"

Gabi sounded interested, but Chuck wasn't sure. A lot of people feigned interest in these things, but their eyes glazed over if you went into too much detail. He decided to keep it simple.

"Easy. We examine vertical temperature and moisture profiles and from those determine how buoyant the atmosphere is, that is, how much energy or 'lift' is available. The greater the lift, the bigger any thunderstorms can get."

Gabi appeared to dwell on the statement before speaking again. "You said 'any storms,' so I guess that means just because there's a lot of CAPE, as you call it, doesn't necessarily mean thunderstorms will form?"

Chuck took a quick peek in the rearview mirror to see if Ty was listening. Ty caught his glance and turned away to stare out the window at the flat landscape flashing by.

"That's where CIN comes in," Chuck said, responding to Gabi's question. "Convective Inhibition. In laymen's terms, it's a warm layer, or lid, in the atmosphere that inhibits convection—thunderstorm development. Sometimes you'll hear guys on TV refer to it as a 'cap'."

"So, if the atmosphere is capped, no thunderstorms, even if there's a lot of that other stuff?"

"CAPE?"

"Yeah, CAPE." Chuck could see why Gabi might be a good FBI agent. She paid attention, thought things through.

"And tomorrow?"

"A lot of CAPE, a lot of CIN."

Ty spoke from the backseat. "So which wins, O Meteorological Maestro?"

So he had been listening. Still miffed by his son's attitude, however, Chuck addressed his answer to Gabi. "I think there'll be enough energy—surface heating—to bust through the cap by late afternoon. We should see a few supercells before sunset. I'll just have to figure out *where*—but that's always the challenge. Where."

"And tornadoes," Gabi said, "how do we get from supercells to tornadoes?"

"First the resident professor-driver-tour guide introduces another term: helicity," Chuck responded.

"Should I be taking notes?" Gabi asked.

"I don't know. Should you? You're the magazine writer."

Gabi chuckled. "Yes I am. And I have perfect recall. Tell me about helicity."

"Allow me to use a football analogy. When a quarterback throws a pass, he's usually got a tight spiral on the ball. That's basically helicity. A twisting motion."

"No quarterbacks in the outback," Ty said, gesturing at the featureless farmland through which they drove.

"The helicity comes from wind shear, winds blowing in different directions, close to the ground. A parcel of air caught in the shear will start spinning like a thrown football. Helicity. But it's horizontal helicity. If, however, the parcel gets lifted into a supercell, it becomes vertical helicity. And it's that that provides the initial spin for a tornado. It's a hell of a lot more complicated than that, but those are the CliffsNotes."

"Helicity," Chuck muttered, "So that's what I felt going out the front door eight years ago. A nice tight spiral speeding my departure."

After that, they rode in silence.

Chapter Eight

MONDAY, APRIL 29

CHUCK, UP BEFORE sunrise, sat at a desk in his room at the Digg Inn motel in Dodge City, Kansas. A desk lamp cast a dim circle of light over his computer while he studied the latest weather models and Stormy snoozed at his feet.

The models depicted an upper-air disturbance sweeping northeastward out of New Mexico over the High Plains. Chuck envisioned the disturbance, a little ripple in the wind flow aloft, as a tripwire that would ignite scattered supercells along a dryline running from western Kansas southward through the Texas Panhandle.

While the atmosphere appeared likely to remain capped much of the day, putting a lid on the strong upward air motion needed for storm development, Chuck judged the afternoon heating would take care of that. Then, boom! It would be like yanking the top off a pressure cooker. Only, it wouldn't be steam and superheated water that erupt, but massive thunderstorms. Maybe not many, but all it takes is one. One fire-breathing, roaring, chest-thumping monster supercell to unleash a tornado.

Chuck drew his finger along the computer screen, tracing the dryline from near Colby, Kansas, to Plainview, Texas. Four hundred miles. The trick would be to strategically position the team in the right place along that 400-mile stretch. Once storms start to pop, you can make a tactical run of 50 or 60 miles, but not much more than that before the window of opportunity slams shut.

Two staging targets presented themselves: western Kansas, where the stronger helicity, the atmospheric twisting motion required for tornadoes, would be present; and West Texas, where the greater instability would be likely to occur, leading to more certain thunderstorm development. Pick the wrong place in which to wait and he could blow an early shot at his million-dollar payday. Chuck drummed his fingers on the desk. He looked down at Stormy. "What do I do, Storms?" he said. "Where do I position our team?"

Stormy sat up and cocked her head. She issued a soft doggy fart and flopped back down on her belly.

Chuck fanned the air with his hand. "Stormy the Wonder Dog. Yeah. I wonder why I kept you."

He clicked through the array of models on his computer again. CAPE, CIN, helicity, wind shear, vorticity, cloud cover, surface pressures. After 45 minutes he stood. "I need a beer," he announced. He walked to the door, opened it, and looked back at Stormy, who was still lying on the carpet. "If you're interested, I'm following your lead—we're staying put today. And yeah, I know I can't get a beer at this time of morning, but it's the thought that counts."

He shut the door and walked down the hallway toward the lobby and the advertised continental breakfast. *I may want a hell of a lot more than a beer by tonight if things go to crap today.*

Metcalf, working on five hardboiled eggs, each with the yolk removed, greeted Chuck as he entered the breakfast area. "Grab some eggs, Chuckie. Great protein. Scoop out the yellow stuff, though. Too much cholesterol."

I want a beer, not eggs. He said good morning to Metcalf and walked to the coffee dispenser. He drew a cup and sat down across from Metcalf.

"So," Metcalf said, "think we can end this game in the first inning? I go home a hero, you go home a millionaire."

Chuck sipped his coffee before responding. "You a gambling man, Mr. Metcalf?"

Metcalf popped an egg white into his mouth, chewed, swallowed, and then answered, "Vegas is my second home."

"Well, good. Cuz we're gonna gamble today. If I'm right, we win. And yeah, we could end the game early. If I'm wrong, we lose and—"

"I get pissed off when I lose, Chaz. When I lose, the dealers don't get tipped. The hookers don't get laid. And I kick puppies if they walk in front of me. Don't piss me off."

Chuck studied the man, trying to take his measure. Was there really a streak of meanness interred beneath his gruff, teddy bear appearance and hail-fellow-well-met bonhomie, or were his words part of an act, a Hollywood shtick? "Maybe you shouldn't gamble."

"Maybe *you* shouldn't gamble." Metcalf crammed two more egg whites into his mouth.

"It's a team effort."

"You mean I can override your decision?" A piece of egg tumbled from Metcalf's lower lip as he spoke.

"We can discuss it."

"Tell me about it."

Chuck explained the basis of his decision. In the meantime, more members of the expedition straggled into the eating area—Ziggy and Boomie and one of the women, Chuck thought her name was Dakota.

Metcalf, polishing off his eggs and downing a glass of cranberry juice, listened quietly to Chuck. After Chuck had finished, Metcalf said, "Well, quite the dilemma, bwana. Either our safari sits on its ass here and hopes for a big score. Or we beat south and catch some storms for sure, but maybe not the beast we're after."

"So?"

"So nothing. You're the leader." Metcalf wiped his mouth, arose from his chair and walked to where Ziggy, Boomie, and Dakota sat.

Chuck looked after him. *I guess that was our discussion.*

By 4 p.m., the team, assembled in the parking lot, stood ready to move out. A few of Metcalf's crew, smoking cigarettes and looking bored, leaned against the camera trucks. Metcalf paced up and down the lot carrying on a vociferous conversation with someone over his cell phone. Ty played with Stormy on a grassy medium strip. Gabi maintained a vigil near Chuck as he sat in the Expedition monitoring weather developments on his laptop.

"Shit," he muttered silently. He stepped from the SUV and gazed west, toward the dryline. A few towering cumulus clouds had billowed skyward, but none of them looked remotely like an embryonic thunderstorm. They would blossom vertically, looking like little cauliflower explosions, then abruptly collapse and disappear. *Cumulus collapsus* in chaser vernacular.

"Trouble in paradise?" Gabi asked.

"Trouble in Kansas, at least."

"Yes?"

"It looks like the cap isn't breaking."

"The models lied?"

"That's one way of looking at it."

"What's the other?"

"P-cubed."

"What's that?"

"Piss Poor Prognosticator Performance."

She laughed.

"In the end," Chuck said, "it's up to the forecaster to make the call, to evaluate the models and know how much faith, if any, to invest in them. Sometimes, I think, we put too much credence in computers and mathematics at the expense of personal experience and old-fashioned manual analysis. It's a lesson I obviously need to relearn." He pointed at a map displayed on his laptop. "See that, all those little squares and circles with identifiers next to them?"

"Looks like they're clustered in West Texas. What are they?"

"They represent other chasers, those with transponders. They've gathered near Lubbock. That's where things are beginning to pop." He clicked a key on his computer keyboard and overlaid a radar display on the map. "Couple of big cells down there. It's just us and handful of other chasers stuck here in the Kansas outback—outta storms, outta hope, and shit outta luck." The words came out edgy and brittle.

Metcalf, finished with his phone conversation, joined Chuck and Gabi. "So, great white hunter, where's our prey?"

Chuck tapped the computer screen. "Down there."

"Texas?"

Chuck nodded.

"Perhaps we should be tear-assing south then?" Metcalf leaned close to Chuck. His words seemed more of a command than a question. Overhead, a fleeting cloudlet from a decaying cumulus briefly dimmed the sun.

"It's too far. By the time we got there, the show would be over."

"Well, that's just fine and Jim fucking Dandy, fearless leader." Metcalf looked at Gabi. "Sorry, miss. But, I'm a little torqued. Here we sit with our thumbs up our butt, a couple of million bucks of equipment idle, and the clock ticking while things go wild in West Texas." He turned to go, but then looked back and glared at Chuck. "Strike one, Chuckie!" He snapped his right arm into the air like a home plate umpire. "You managed to piss me off on our first day out."

"Second," corrected Chuck.

"Yeah, smart ass, second." Metcalf stalked off. Sotto voce he said, "Lesson learned. Don't hire over-the-hill chasers working as janitors and living in Third World apartments."

Gabi studied the radar imagery on Chuck's laptop. "Nasty storms?" she asked.

He pointed at one west of Lubbock. "That one has a tornado signature."

"You think my bad guys could be down there?"

He shrugged. "From what you told me, they always seem to be in the right position at the right time."

Gabi expelled a long, slow breath.

"Look, I know, I know," Chuck said. "I blew it. We shoulda been in Texas. But even if a twister forms, if it doesn't smack a ranch or a farm or a town, then, well, it's like it never happened, right?" *Pathetic. Now I'm groping for the silver lining of a shitty forecast.*

"Right." The word came out flat, emotionless.

Chuck looked away, studying the limp-dick cumulus. *Unbelievable. Right out of the blocks, I've managed to piss off the guy with the money and lose credibility with an FBI agent.*

AT FIRST, THE STORM appeared as if it would be something less than a godlike Zeus, relegated to coughing up sporadic bolts of lightning and spittles of rain. Run-of-the-mill for the High Plains of West Texas. But now, as Clarence and Raleigh stood monitoring the tempest near the small town of Levelland, west of Lubbock, Clarence realized they were about to witness something special: the transformation of an ordinary thunderstorm into a full blown supercell. It was as if they were voyeurs, watching the innermost—almost miraculous—workings of life developing within a woman's womb.

A ragged snippet of scud, like an orphaned spermatozoon, materialized beneath the base of the storm. Then, other clouds, larger, blacker, joined the tiny tatter of grayness and pirouetted counterclockwise beneath the base of the cell but remained separate from it. But not for long. In a quick umbilical effort, they attached themselves to the parent, assembling into a spinning, circular wall, dark and angry.

The storm's inflow strengthened, making it difficult for the brothers to stand. Gale-force gusts slammed into their backs. Marking the powerful inflow, a "tail cloud" materialized, a dark appendage on the rotating wall.

Abruptly, the gusts ceased. "Holy shit," Clarence said, "this thing's going right over us." He and Raleigh found themselves directly beneath the storm's powerful updraft. In essence, the winds had switched from horizontal to vertical. The spinning, low-hanging cloud deck lumbered overhead.

Seconds later, dirt and dust whipped across the khaki landscape near the rear flank of the storm. Raleigh saw it first and pointed.

"Downdraft," he said.

"Yeah, this thing's crankin' up," Clarence responded.

A spear of lightning and a simultaneous explosion ripped over them.

"Car," Clarence yelled.

They dived into the GMC as more bolts lanced into the ground around them. Raleigh slammed the Terrain into gear just as a downdraft-driven pall of grit and debris swirled over the vehicle, obscuring the road on whose shoulder it was parked. Raleigh held his foot on the brake, waiting for the localized *haboob* to pass. Once it had, he accelerated southward, away from the strengthening supercell. At Clarence's command, he turned east and ran parallel to the obsidian darkness barreling toward Lubbock.

They stalked the storm from a mile or so south, Clarence monitoring the radar imagery of the storm on his laptop computer. "This thing's got a hell of a hail core," he said. "Somebody's getting hammered with softball-sized stones."

"How fast is it moving?" Raleigh asked.

"About 30 mph."

"*We* aren't," Raleigh noted. A traffic jam of sightseers and other chasers packed the highway leading toward Lubbock.

"Friggin' chasers," Clarence said. "Too damn many amateurs out here. We gotta get off this road."

"Tell me what to do. You're navigating."

Clarence bent to his laptop. "There's a county road coming up. Take a left in about a tenth of a mile."

Raleigh looked at his brother. "That'll put us right in the storm's path."

"I know. But there's a cross road we can turn right on and get ahead of the storm and this mob of idiots. Then we'll duck back south to the main highway and be in position to make our move if there's a tornado."

"We'll have to break speed limits."

"The cops aren't gonna be looking for speeders with a supercell bearing down on Lubbock."

Raleigh turned left and pointed the vehicle into the roiling blackness churning toward the city. He stepped on the accelerator and the SUV leapt forward, racing toward the maw of a monster.

Lightning, like a myriad of lizard tongues, licked from the storm and sent crescendos of thunder tumbling over the flat land. A powerful wind, the cell's inflow, shook the vehicle as though it were a toy car in the grip of a hyperactive child. Raleigh fought the steering wheel to hold the SUV on the road.

"Gotta turn, bro'," Raleigh said, "gotta turn. We're too damn close to the storm."

"Coming up." Clarence fell silent and squinted through the dust being kicked up by the powerful gusts. "There, there." He pointed at an intersection a hundred yards ahead. "Turn right."

Raleigh whipped the SUV through the turn and pushed the accelerator to the floor. Clarence tensed, hoping there were no other cars on the narrow lane. The vehicle hit a bump and went briefly airborne. Focusing on the computer became next to impossible as the laptop jiggled and jumped in Clarence's hands. He barely had a grip on it.

He thought he glimpsed something on the display, but wasn't sure: a tiny circular icon, a rotating whirl on the radar overlay, indicating the possible presence of a tornado. Clarence twisted in his seat and looked behind the vehicle at the pursuing storm. Visual confirmation was always best. "Oh shit, it's there."

Raleigh glanced into the rearview mirror, saw what his brother saw—a black funnel on the ground a quarter mile behind them—and leaned forward against the steering wheel, grasping it in a white-knuckle strangulation hold. "How far to the next intersection?" he yelled, his voice edged in panic.

Clarence tried to focus on the computer display. "Maybe a half mile. We'll make it." *I hope.*

Raleigh braked hard as the vehicle blasted into a T-intersection. The GMC slewed sideways and slid into the crossroad narrowly missing a mail delivery truck racing southward, away from the storm. Raleigh got on the truck's tail, passed it, and tore back toward the main highway.

There he turned east again, ahead of the main phalanx of chasers and TV trucks pursuing the massive supercell. He sped past the southern end of the shuttered Reese AFB.

"Okay, slow down, pull off here," Clarence said. "This is a good spot to wait."

Raleigh steered onto a quiet side road leading to a small mobile home development. He parked the vehicle facing north, toward the storm, and he and Clarence watched as the tornado, broader and blacker now, twisted across dryland farms and ranches. Suddenly, it lifted, skipping over the northern end of Reese's old runway. Past Reese, it dropped once more and resumed its scorched-earth assault on the outskirts of Lubbock. Shards of sheet metal, shingles, and shredded insulation tumbled from the sky, confetti from the storm's violence.

Clarence studied the map overlay. "Get ready to move," he said. "There're some residential areas in its path. It's gonna rip into one of them. Maybe more."

Raleigh, without being commanded, stepped from the SUV and once again retrieved several magnetic signs from its rear. Not *EMT-Rescue* this time—they'd overplayed their hand on that masquerade—but *Interagency Disaster Response Team*. Phony, like their counterfeit IDs and embroidered names on their white denim shirts.

Checking to make certain no one was watching, Raleigh placed a sign on each front door and the rear lift gate. The banshee yowl of tornado warning sirens—an eerie counterpoint to the low roar of the tornado—filled the late afternoon.

The brothers waited until the tornado swept past, then accelerated into its wake, a path marked by downed power poles, fallen utility lines, and severed trees. They entered what appeared to have been a small subdivision of neat brick ranches. Now, along one street, only shattered sections of walls remained standing. Broken bits of furniture, parts of roofs, and battered automobiles littered yards and driveways. Residents stood dazed, trying to gauge why some homes had survived and others hadn't. The area looked as though a suicide bomber had hit it.

A woman, her dress in tatters, blood streaming from a scalp wound, tried to flag down the brothers, but they kept going, ignoring her need, intent only on their own: finding a target of opportunity. Prey.

Clarence saw it at the end of a cul-de-sac. A house, its roof ripped away, tattered curtains flapping in glassless frames, and a partially collapsed brick wall. "Pull up here," he said.

Raleigh steered the SUV into the home's driveway and stopped. The brothers waited. The wind quieted but continued to gust fitfully, sending bits of paper and pieces of debris tumbling through the shell-shocked residential area. A discordant chorus of sirens, first responders—EMTs, firemen, police—replaced the rolling thunder of the departing storm.

The brothers watched the home for almost five minutes. No one emerged from it. No neighbors approached. No cars sat in the driveway. Clarence nodded at Raleigh. Raleigh exited the GMC and walked to the home's relatively undamaged garage and peered in. "No vehicles," he announced. No one home.

Clarence joined Raleigh and together they entered the home by clambering over the partially destroyed brick wall. They moved down a hallway, well lit since the roof had disappeared, and pushed open a bent door, entering what they assumed was a bedroom. "Always jewelry boxes," Clarence said.

Raleigh pointed at a dresser that had fallen over, littering the floor with carved wooden boxes of various sizes, photographs, and perfume bottles. Clarence knelt and sorted through the boxes, opening and closing lids. Raleigh rifled through the dresser drawers. "Hey," he said. He reached into one of the drawers, pulled out a small leather bag, and tossed it to his brother.

Clarence opened it, whistled softly, and poured its contents onto the bedroom rug. Dozens of gold coins rattled onto the carpet. "The real deal," Clarence said, and scooped the treasure back into the bag.

"Yes, may I help you?"

Clarence stood and whirled. A middle-aged woman—brunette, slightly overweight, designer glasses, business suit—hands on hips, stood at the entrance to the bedroom.

Raleigh stepped beside Clarence and smiled at the lady.

"I'm sorry, ma'am," Clarence said. "We didn't mean to startle you. I'm Carl McDeel. This is Ralph Lederson." He gestured at Raleigh. "We're with the Interagency Disaster Response Team. We've been dispatched by your insurance company to survey the damage to your home." He extended his ID badge to the woman. Raleigh did the same. "We climbed in over the broken bricks. We thought there might be someone hurt in here."

"And hiding in the dresser drawers?" the lady said, an edge to her words. She examined their IDs.

"The coins had spilled out. We were just picking them up," Clarence explained. He handed the bag of coins to the lady. *Where was this bitch when we arrived?*

"Interagency Disaster Response," the woman said. "Never heard of it."

"It's something new. An effort to get help to home and business owners faster in the wake of disasters. If you'd rather, we could come back later." Clarence edged toward the door. Raleigh followed. *Come on, bitch. Drop it. Let it go. We walk. You walk.*

"You were sent by my insurance company?" the lady asked. "Funny they didn't call me. I've had my cell on ever since I left work after I heard about the tornado."

"I'm sure they'll be in touch with you shortly, ma'am." He flicked his head toward the bedroom door as he looked at his brother. *Let's get out of here.*

"Then you know the name of my insurance company," the woman said, blocking their way. "And my name. And the address here."

Neither brother answered.

"No?" she said. She reached into her purse and withdrew a cell phone.

Raleigh swatted it from her hands.

Chapter Nine

TUESDAY, APRIL 30

AFTER MONDAY'S defeat, Chuck had moved the team east to position it for what he saw as a future threat. They ended up in a cheap motel in the small town of Niren, west of Wichita. The fiasco of the previous day—*his* failure, quite frankly—nagged at him like an annoying puppy nipping at his heels. He tossed and turned in a too-soft bed into the wee hours of the morning.

Finally, he surrendered to his sleeplessness, arose, and walked a quarter of a mile through a chilly dawn to a weather-beaten roadside diner. He sat there now sipping slightly burnt coffee as a handful of regular customers—farmhands mostly, it appeared—drifted in for breakfast.

The aroma of scrambled eggs, grilled breakfast steaks, and baked biscuits filled the small establishment. An ancient radio sitting on a shelf behind the counter, where most of the clientele perched, crackled with static-infused farm and weather reports.

Chuck stared out the dusty front window of the diner into the brightness of a rising sun. It didn't take a meteorologist to figure out there would be no storms to chase today and probably tomorrow, too.

He'd blown it yesterday, positioned the team too far north. Big thunderstorms had erupted in West Texas, well south of where his team had maintained a vigil in Kansas. A supercell had blossomed near Levelland and dropped a brief, violent tornado on the outskirts of Lubbock. Preliminary guess: an EF-3 or maybe even a four. Early reports indicated two residents had been killed. Plenty of chasers had been in the area. But not Chuck's team.

What had happened was easy to see in hindsight. The Texas storms had interdicted a rich stream of moisture flowing northward over the Plains, in essence gobbling up the energy needed for thunderstorm development farther north where the Global-American crew had sat and waited . . . and waited . . . and waited. He should have recognized what was going to happen *before* the fact, not after. When he was on top of his game, a decade ago, he would have.

Had he lost his groove, his mojo, his touch, whatever it is people lose when they're out of the loop? He had to admit that was a possibility. He'd gambled on placing the team where he thought the greatest wind shear and instability would set up. He was right about that, but hadn't counted on the moisture-robbing storms in Texas. Half right in this game doesn't cut it. He'd squandered not only yesterday's opportunity but now two more days in which the team would have to stand down. That left only ten days in which to grab the million-dollar ring off the supercell merry-go-round. He figured his odds might be better playing Powerball.

More so than on previous mornings, he craved a beer to kick-start his day, to erase the defeat of the previous afternoon, to shatter the hope-numbing miasma that had retreated but now returned. But this being a small-town diner, a family place, alcohol was verboten.

Chuck opened his laptop computer and studied the meteorological models—the numerically-driven depictions of weather patterns—for the coming days. It looked as though there might be a chance of a few tornadoes on Thursday in the eastern portions of Kansas and Oklahoma. Maybe not the EF-4 or -5 monsters he was hunting, but he had learned over the years that nature's supply of surprises is endless. He confirmed his analysis by clicking onto the Storm Prediction Center's Website. The forecasters there had outlined a threat area very similar to the one he envisioned.

Gabi straggled into the diner. Chuck motioned to her and she walked toward him, unsmiling. She settled into the booth where he sat. He signaled for the waitress.

"Bad news," Gabi said, her voice raspy and low.

Chuck had a pretty good idea what was coming.

"Another apparent robbery-homicide yesterday where the twister hit. A woman in her home. They're doing an autopsy tomorrow."

Chuck stared into his half-empty coffee mug as Gabi gave her order to the waitress.

"Anything for you, sir?" the waitress asked.

"No, not hungry," Chuck said without looking up.

The waitress departed.

Gabi reached over and patted Chuck's hand. "I've heard it said that Babe Ruth struck out almost twice as many times as he hit home runs."

Chuck looked up. "Babe Ruth didn't have a two-week season."

"I'll bet he never went two weeks without hitting a home run."

"Something you've researched?"

"Naw, it's total bullshit. How would I know? All I know is you can't afford to go around for the next ten days dragging your ass behind you and looking like a Bassett Hound who can't find his bone."

"Were you ever a coach?"

"No. I hate team sports. It's just that someone has to boot you in the butt to keep you going and stop feeling sorry for yourself. Look, you aren't the only one around here with something at stake. As a female agent, there are more than a few guys in the Bureau who'd like to see my tits get caught in a ringer."

In spite of himself, Chuck smiled. He had to admit he liked this down-to-earth, slightly profane FBI agent. For the first time, he allowed his gaze to fall on her left hand. No wedding ring.

"I overheard one agent say just before I left," Gabi continued, "that 'She'll probably end up in the Land of Oz and we'll have to send in a SWAT team to rescue her.' The next day there was a package addressed to Dorothy on my desk. Little red slippers."

To Chuck it sounded as if Gabi were describing good-natured ribbing as opposed to harassment, but he understood she was trying to make a point.

The waitress returned with Gabi's breakfast order—scrambled eggs, toast, and sausage—and placed it on the table. Chuck eyed it for a moment, then said, "Changed my mind. Same thing for me."

"Good for you, Fearless Leader," Gabi said. "So what's next?"

Chuck stared out at the flat Kansas landscape while gathering his thoughts, then said, "The Land of Oz."

Gabi was about to stuff a forkful of eggs into her mouth, but stopped short. She held her gaze on Chuck, waiting for him to continue.

"We need to reposition for Thursday. We're going somewhere that's become a legendary gathering place for storm chasers."

Gabi put the eggs into her mouth and chewed. She motioned with her left hand for Chuck to go on.

"It's in northeast Oklahoma west of Bartlesville. A motel and restaurant complex called the Gust Front Grill."

Gabi finished chewing. "The Land of Oz?"

"You'll see when we get there."

AFTER LUNCH, Chuck had the team on the road again, pushing east through Wichita, then south on I-35, and finally rolling east on US 166 across Kansas. Gabi sat in the passenger seat of the Expedition, dozing on and off. Ty, as usual, rode silently in the rear with Stormy resting her head on his lap.

Chuck turned south on a secondary road and they soon entered Oklahoma. Gabi stared out the window at the endless, rolling grasslands. Flat-based cumulus, cotton-ball tops alabaster in brilliant sunshine, dotted the sky. Their shadows, like animated spots on a Dalmatian, raced alongside the SUV, riding a stiff northwest breeze.

"Not much here," Gabi noted. A scattering of cattle and orphaned stands of trees, thicker along creek beds, seemed the primary features.

"It's an Indian reservation," Chuck said.

"The Osage?"

"Yes."

"I've heard of it, seen it on a map. Never been here."

"Not much reason to come."

"Unless you're storm chasing?"

"It's a good launching point in certain situations."

Gabi studied Chuck as they drove. He'd been handsome once, that was obvious. But now, perhaps beaten down by the events of life, he appeared older than he really was. His receding auburn hair, flecked with gray, couldn't hide the fact he was no longer young. Not old, but past his prime. Square-jawed and sad-eyed, he was given to smiling wistfully at times, as though remembering something in his past he didn't wish to share.

He seemed a decent man, self-contained and introspective, but largely resigned to his own fate. Gabi wished he were a bit angrier, a little more willing to fight back, claw his way out of the professional dungeon into which he had thrown himself. But maybe he was just tired, as though the cross he was bearing were made out of mahogany and had forced him to his knees. She supposed that could happen to a man, and that perhaps there's less pain in merely surrendering.

Oddly, she found herself reviewing the lovers she'd had—the few, anyhow—and comparing them to Chuck. He certainly didn't fit the mold of the self-assured, smooth-talking, slightly sexually aggressive males she'd found attractive in the past. Yet, there was something appealing about him. Perhaps it was just his vulnerability. No, something more. *Stop it.* She squirmed in her seat and turned to gaze out the passenger-side window.

A half-hour and several turns later, they passed through a small town that time had left behind, a few blocks of yesterday. Not down-and-out by any means, but a place locked in a freeze-frame of the 1950s. On the other side of the hamlet, they approached a cluster of single-story log buildings perched on a low knoll and surrounded by a windbreak of oak and hickory trees. A weathered, barely readable sign announced the GUST FRONT GRILL AND LODGING.

Smoke spiraled from a chimney of the largest building, presumably the grill. It featured a covered wooden porch spanning perhaps 75 feet either side of a double-doored front entrance. To the right of the grill, a long, narrow, rough-hewn structure—a fugitive from over a half-century ago, Gabi judged—offered lodging. A single, tiny window and a door opening directly onto a parking lot defined each room, of which there were about two dozen.

"The Ritz in the Wild?" Gabi said.

"No concierge service," Chuck answered. "But it's clean and comfortable."

"It must have something going." She gestured at the parking area in front of the grill. Scores of vehicles—cars, SUVs, pickups, vans, motorcycles, and even a satellite TV truck—jammed the lot.

"Think of it as an ad hoc convention of tornado chasers," Chuck said. He parked next to a heavy-duty auxiliary generator bolted to a concrete pad at the far end of the lot. Adjacent to the generator, sited in a compact mound of earth, sat a slope-front storm shelter.

An exhaust vent poked vertically from the shelter. Capping the vent, an aluminum turbine spun lazily in the breeze. Ty eyed it. "They take this tornado shit seriously around here, don't they?"

"Kinda," Chuck answered without looking at his son.

He exited the Expedition and walked toward the grill. Ty, Gabi, and Stormy followed. "I suppose, on second thought," Chuck said as they walked, "it's not so much a convention as it is something akin to a bunch of hunters sitting around a campfire after a long day. You know, swapping lies, telling tall tales about 'the one they just missed,' and speculating where the hunting is going to be best tomorrow or the day after that."

They entered the building.

"Wow, time warp," Gabi said. Flashes from psychedelic strobe lights—red, green, blue—bounced off the log walls while the throaty, soaring voice of Grace Slick spilling from banks of overhead speakers filled the sprawling interior—*Somebody to Love*.

Gabi moved her head from side to side in time with the music. "I remember that from classic rock stations. The Jefferson Starship. Something from the '70s."

"The '60s," corrected a gruff male voice from behind her. "And it was the Airplane then. By the end of the decade, we were all looking from somebody, or something, to love."

She turned to see who had spoken and involuntarily shuffled back a half step. She found herself looking into a deeply-tanned face folded with age and memories. Rheumy eyes appeared focused on her but seemed to be appraising something more distant. A thick, graying handlebar mustache, once black, drooped over the speaker's jowls.

Heavyset but not overweight, he wore a white cotton shirt, a scarred leather vest, tattered jeans, and battle-tested cowboy boots. Most notable, a black stovepipe hat with a feather jammed into the hatband perched on his head.

He smiled slightly and extended his hand. "Sam Townsend," he said. "Proprietor."

"Gabi Mederios," she responded, "magazine writer." They shook hands.

His smile grew broader as he released his grip and stepped toward Chuck. "God damn," he said, "I'd heard you were back in the game. It's great to see you again, old friend." Sam wrapped Chuck in a bone-crushing bear hug, then stepped back and looked him up and down. "None the worse for wear, I'd say."

"What a blatant bullshitter," Chuck said. "You haven't lost your touch."

Sam moved his eyes to Ty, then to Chuck, then back to Ty. "I know who this is," he said.

"Tyler Rittenberg," Ty said.

"I've heard about you," Sam responded, as they shook hands. "I'm glad to see you with your dad."

Ty nodded. No smile.

Sam maintained his grip on Ty's hand and held his gaze for what seemed an instant too long to Gabi. Something passed between them. Not anything sexual, but certainly something unique, as though they were members of the same fraternity.

Sam's gaze fell on the dog.

"That's Stormy," Chuck said.

Sam squatted and ruffled Stormy's fur. "You may have to wait outside, buddy. This is a people-food place."

Sam stood and asked, "What's he do?"

"She," Chuck corrected. "Mostly sleeps and farts. But I think she has a sixth sense for storms."

Sam smiled, revealing a missing incisor, and nodded. "A service dog, then. Good. Welcome, Stormy. Come on in, all of you. Take a load off. Find yourself a booth. I'll grab some beers. On the house." Sam moved off, limping almost imperceptibly.

The Jefferson Airplane faded away and Buffalo Springfield filled the void. Something about a man with a shotgun. The '60s again.

They found an empty booth in a corner of the grill. Gabi looked around. "All these people," she said, "they're storm chasers?" She had to raise her voice slightly to be heard over the din of the music and babble of conversation.

Chuck examined the crowd. "Mostly," he said. "There's a TV crew, from a Tulsa station I guess, according to the truck outside. A couple of tour groups—"

"Like what you used to have?" Gabi said.

"Yeah, there's about a dozen or so outfits that offer commercial tornado 'tours' now. That's Silver Lining Tours over there." He pointed to the center of the room, where a group of men and women clustered around a large, circular table. "And in the far corner there, that's Tempest Tours. Cloud 9 Tours used to drop in here once in a while, but I don't see them today."

Chuck continued to scan the restaurant. "The rest are independents. Onesies and twosies chasing for the thrill, the excitement, the spectacle. A few make money by selling storm videos to television stations. If they can get a network to upload their stuff, that's a pretty good payday. And see those guys with the map spread out on the table?" He pointed. "That's a university research team. I recognize their leader. They try to snuggle up to twisters, get all touchy-feely with high-tech instrumentation to see if they can figure out what makes them tick."

"Who's the dame with the tattoos plastered all over her arms, the one who looks like she could bench press 300 pounds?" Gabi asked.

"I don't know her real name. She goes by Harley. Chases on a Fat Boy. Oh, and those guys next to her. They drive something that looks like an armadillo on wheels, a battle tank that they think they can punch into the center of a tornado with."

"Right," Gabi said.

Sam returned with the beers and plopped into the booth beside Chuck. "Some guy just came in, said he's with you. A movie company or something. Needs some rooms for tonight. Legit?"

"Jerry Metcalf, Global-American Cinema. Yeah, he's legit. At least as much as guys from Hollywood can be. I'm trying track down an EF-4 or -5 for his cinematographers."

"Ummm. Tall order." Sam knocked back half his beer in one swallow. "Maybe you need an Indian guide."

Chuck smiled. "Sam's half Osage," he explained.

Sam nodded. "You guys gonna need rooms, too, I guess?"

"Three," Chuck said.

"I'm full up, but I'll make space for you and your movie buds. I think several of my rooms are about to develop plumbing problems." He winked. "Good excuse for booting a few people and shipping them off with the rest of the diaspora. You're always welcome on the rez." He downed the rest of his beer. "Give your dinner order to the waitress. Take your time. I'll be back when things quiet down."

The Grateful Dead replaced Buffalo Springfield. The strobes grew brighter as the ambient light from outside faded. The room continued to reverberate with music from another era, *Zeitgeist* from a time when America had changed.

"So what's his story?" Gabi asked.

"Well, there's a story and there's a legend. Which would you like to hear first?"

Chapter Ten

TUESDAY, APRIL 30

"I WANT TO HEAR the legend, of course, but let's start with the story, the facts," Gabi said.

Chuck held his beer, a COOP Porter, up to the dwindling light as if to examine the beverage's pedigree. Apparently it passed; he took a long quaff.

"Here's what I know," he said. "White father, Osage mother. Grew up off the rez in Kansas. Drafted by the army in the early '60s, served in Vietnam. Silver Star and Purple Heart. After his stint in the military he kicked around in the Texas oil fields for the next two decades. In the late '90s he showed up on the rez and started building what you see now."

"Curious," Gabi said. "He didn't grow up here, yet he came back, so to speak. To his mother's family home, I assume."

"So it would seem."

"How in the hell does he make any money?" Ty said, entering the conversation. "I mean, after the tornado-chasing season is over, who comes here? In the middle of frigging nowhere? A handful of tourists maybe? People trying to get lost forever? We're in the middle of a prairie-grass desert." He swept his arm at a nearby window.

"All I can tell you," Chuck said, "is that he loves storms and he loves chasers."

"But to Ty's point," Gabi said, "how does he survive?"

"That's where we get to the legend part," Chuck said. He tipped the beer bottle to his lips before continuing. "In the late 19th century, huge oil deposits were discovered on the reservation. Fortunately for the Osage, they, unlike many tribes, actually owned their land. Eventually, many of them—those who weren't murdered or swindled—became quite wealthy. I seem to recall reading someplace that when petroleum royalties peaked in the mid-1920s, the Osage were the 'richest people in the world'."

"Hyperbole?" Gabi asked.

"Probably. But the point is, many of the folks who lived here were extremely well off."

"So how does all this relate to Sam?" Ty said. "He certainly wasn't around in the 1920s."

"But his grandparents, his mother's parents, were," Chuck said. "And they evidently were restrained in their spending and avoided the white man's banks."

"Ah, so they probably made it through the Great Depression with their fortune intact," Gabi suggested.

Chuck nodded. "Leaving a large amount of money to Sam's mother. And when she passed, Sam got it."

"I know it's impolite to ask," Ty said, "but how much?"

"Rumor has it—and I emphasize *rumor*—millions," Chuck said.

"So that's the legend?" Gabi asked.

"Only part of it," Chuck said.

Gabi took a swill of her beer, which she hadn't yet touched, and leaned forward. "So what's the rest of it?"

A waitress, a plump, middle-aged Osage with a happy face and bright eyes, arrived to take their order.

"We haven't had a chance to look at the menu yet," Chuck said.

"No problem," the waitress said. "It's on Sam. Big filets, he said. Best in Oklahoma. You'll love 'em. How ya want 'em grilled?"

"Any seafood?" Ty asked.

The Osage woman smiled solicitously, as if Ty were a learning-challenged youth. Using her thumb like a hitchhiker, she pointed outside. "Sea of grass here, not water."

Ty laughed. "Medium rare," he said.

The trio completed its order. The waitress looked down at Stormy, who lay quietly beneath the booth's table. "Small steak for him, okay? Maybe not a filet."

"Okay," Chuck said.

The waitress left and Chuck resumed his story. "There's long been a tale floating around within the storm chaser community that Sam indeed is a multimillionaire, and that his money is stashed right here, someplace in the Gust Front Grill. Like his grandparents, he doesn't trust banks."

"That doesn't sound too smart," Ty said.

"Ah, but here's the rest of the story . . . the legend. And maybe it's just a tall tale, but the money is supposedly guarded by a mysterious roommate of Sam's named Monty."

"Ever met him, this Monty?" Gabi asked.

"No one has."

"So it's just a myth, then?"

Sam returned and seated himself next to Chuck. "Things have quieted down a little," he said. He looked at Gabi. "What's a myth?"

"Your friend, Monty."

"Oh, no, not at all. Monty is . . . well, he's a loner. Keeps to himself. Sleeps a lot. Doesn't eat much. But loves chicken."

"And he guards your money?" Chuck said. He drained the last of the COOP Porter from the bottle.

Sam allowed a smile to creep over his face. "What money?"

"Your mythical fortune."

"Yes, he guards my *mythical* fortune." Sam laughed, a hearty rumble burbling forth from deep within him. He signaled the waitress for a beer.

"So how'd the rumor of your mythical millions and the mysterious Monty get started?" Gabi asked.

Sam shrugged. "How does any rumor begin? An anecdote here, an anecdote there, a couple of iterations and pretty soon the stories get strung together into a legend that takes on a life of its own."

"Perhaps your roommate, Monty, is kind of a rough character. Could that be what triggered the tale?" Gabi said.

Sam shook his head, a negative answer. "Monty's a gentle soul," he said, and paused briefly before continuing. "Still, I wouldn't want to tangle with him."

"Why's that?"

"He can be a tenacious son of a bitch. He's not aggressive, but he can be fierce."

"You've known him for a while?"

"Twenty years maybe. I knew one of his relatives—a cousin or uncle or something—in Vietnam."

Ty, who'd been following the conversation in silence, sat up from where he'd slumped into a corner of the booth and joined in. "When were you in 'Nam?" he asked.

"Sixty-seven, sixty-eight. First Air Cav."

"You saw some heavy-duty shit then?"

Sam nodded and fixed his gaze on Ty. "You were a soldier, too, weren't you, son? I could tell from the instant I first saw you. The way you carried yourself. The memories hidden behind your eyes."

"Fifth Special Forces," Ty said. "Afghanistan."

"Welcome home, brother," Sam said. He leaned across the table and laid a hand on Ty's shoulder.

"Thanks," Ty said, "but maybe *I* should be welcoming *you* home."

"It was a long time ago."

"Do you ever get over it? The war, I mean."

The music changed again. The Stones now. *Gimme Shelter.* Sam's gaze wandered and seemed to focus on something far away, invisible to others. "Just a shot away," he said, his voice soft, barely audible over the edgy rock number. "Lyrics for a poisoned era."

Chuck, Gabi, and Ty remained silent, watching Sam.

"Sometimes," he said, his stare blank, "when the wind flattens the prairie grass just before a storm, I hear the whop-whop-whop of chopper blades, see Hueys flaring, coming in for landings through a curtain of automatic weapons fire." He paused and looked around, though Gabi doubted he saw anything but what was locked inside his reminiscence.

"The Gooks," Sam said, speaking again, "sometimes they even shot up the Dustoffs. Red crosses and all—just come to ferry some poor kid home." He squeezed his eyes shut. "Some poor kid holding his intestines in with his hands, screaming for his mother cuz there wasn't enough goddamn morphine to stem the pain. And he's lying there in the mud, dying, 10,000 miles from home in a country we didn't give a flying fuck about."

He flicked his eyes open and looked at Ty. "Not like your war," he said. "At least you guys were volunteers, professional, older. That doesn't mitigate the horror and brutality of what you went through, the sacrifices you made, but I think it was worse in 'Nam."

The Stones gave way to The Animals. "We Gotta Get out of This Place."

Sam smiled sadly and looked up at the speakers. "That was a theme for my generation," he said. "That's all we wanted, outta this place, outta 'Nam, outta the army." He brought his gaze back to those in the booth. "Most of the grunts were just teenagers, you know—draftees barely out of high school. Shit, all they wanted was to be back in Wyoming or South Carolina or Pennsylvania or wherever the hell they came from, copping a feel at a drive-in movie, sneaking a fifth with the guys, dreaming of their first car. Not slogging through a stinking tropical jungle in Chinkland, fighting off malaria, wondering if a Bouncing Betty was going to blow their balls off." He paused, then went on. "Just kids . . ." His voice trailed off. He removed his stovepipe hat and worked an indentation out of its brim, then slapped it back on his head.

"Just kids," he said again softly, "just lookin' for somebody to love."

No one spoke for a while after Sam completed his emotional soliloquy. Even the music and background chatter seemed muted.

Finally Ty said "Don't you think that's all anyone is ever looking for, even now?" The words came out subdued, but they carried a biting edge. Gabi wondered if they might be designed for his father.

"You're right, my friend, even now." Sam sat up more erectly and looked around, as if suddenly discovering the bustling, noisy environment that surrounded him. His dark reverie fled into the present. Upbeat and robust once more, he clapped his hands together. "So, hi ho, hi ho, it's off on the chase we go, is it?"

Ty, seemingly lost in his own thoughts now, perhaps memories of something broken between him and his father, abruptly said, "Excuse me." He stood and slipped from the booth, apologizing to Gabi for making her move.

"Dinner's on the way," Sam reminded him.

"Stormy's hungry," Ty responded, and stalked away.

Sam, his face etched in puzzlement, looked at Chuck.

Chuck flushed in what seemed a mixture of anger and embarrassment. "It's a long frigging story," he said.

THE SETTING SUN, in broad strokes of gold, salmon, and rouge, tinted the evening sky in psychedelic pastels, as though the throwback lighting from within the Gust Front Grill had fled the outdoors.

Chuck and Gabi strolled toward the rooms Sam had assigned them.

"Well, you were right about the Land of Oz," Gabi said. "That was a bit weird in there: the '60s ambience, Sam's Vietnam flashbacks, his maybe/maybe-not fortune, a mysterious roommate, Ty's hissy fit." When she said "Ty's hissy fit," she looked directly at Chuck, as though expecting an explanation.

"Yeah," was Chuck's only response. He didn't want to talk about Ty with Gabi—someone he barely knew—especially when he had no idea what to do about the situation. He did know he didn't want the tension with Ty bubbling over into the open, staining the chase team. Perhaps he should just offer his son a bus ticket back to Ok City and write off the attempt to reconnect with him as a really bad idea. He kicked at an empty Coke can that lay crumpled on the walkway and changed the subject.

"I was wondering," he said, "when you were tossing questions at

Sam in the restaurant, whether you thought he might somehow be involved in the killings?"

"You aren't going to talk about Ty, then?"

"No. It's a private matter."

"Fine. I'll respect that. But if you ever need, shall we say, some feminine perspective or advice on the issue, I'm your gal."

"So noted."

"But to answer your question about Sam," Gabi continued, "no. His plumb line is a bit off vertical, but he's too much of a character to go unnoticed. I suspect the killer probably isn't among the mainstream chasers. It would be someone who hangs around the periphery of the main corps. Someone who operates independently, who wouldn't be noticed if he or she suddenly morphed into an EMT or some other persona and dashed into the middle of a wrecked town."

"So you probably won't be eyeing any of the folks we saw today?" Chuck said. The long, melancholy hoot of a locomotive's horn carried across the prairie and faded into the growing dusk. Bats, in determined pursuit of bugs, darted and dipped through the yellow-orange glow cast by a row of sodium vapor lamps.

"No," Gabi said. "Even though you pointed out a few people who might be considered points-off-the-curve: the chick chasing on a Harley Fat Boy, the guys driving an armadillo—they're not exactly carrying low profiles. Whoever the hyena is that's preying on storm victims doesn't want that kind of attention. We'll find him, or them, lurking somewhere in the shadows."

"Ah, then what about the enigmatic Monty? Any interest in him?"

Gabi shrugged. "Do you think he's even real?"

"No. Considering I've never met him, I suspect he's a manufactured boogeyman. People are afraid of boogeymen. What better way to ward off anyone interested in a hidden fortune."

"Alleged fortune."

"Good point. And more support for the theory that ol' Monty may be just as mythical as the money."

Gabi stopped and pointed at a number on a door. "My room," she said, then addressed Chuck's comment. "I don't know. There was real emotion, genuine anger in Sam's little trip back into Vietnam at dinner in there." She inclined her head toward the grill. "And the story about knowing Monty's relatives in 'Nam. I sensed something dark, or maybe even malignant, if that's the right word, connected to that."

"FBI intuition?"

"No. More like a woman's intuition, I think." She fished for the room key in her purse.

"So you think Monty exists?"

"I believe it's a good bet. But I also believe, if he does, he probably has nothing to do with the robbery-homicides. Sam never mentioned the guy was a chaser. He sounds more like a recluse. That doesn't quite fit the ad hoc profile of who we're looking for." She twisted the key to open the door of her room.

"And I'll tell you one more thing," she said. "I wouldn't want to meet Monty in a dark alley."

"Woman's intuition again?"

"No, more law enforcement instinct this time."

"Then it's a good thing our chase doesn't lead into dark alleys."

"You never know," Gabi responded evenly. "Good night." She stepped into her room and shut the door.

Chuck stared after her briefly, then moved out of the glow cast by the sodium lamps and gazed out over the prairie. Only the pinpoint twinkle of stars pierced the utter blackness that cloaked the landscape. *You never know.*

Chapter Eleven

WEDNESDAY, MAY 1

CHUCK STOOD beside the Expedition, its engine idling, and waited while Metcalf herded his crew into the two camera trucks.

Sam, his stovepipe hat tipped down over his forehead to shield against the morning sun, walked up to Chuck. The old man's worn countenance folded into a gentle smile. "Should be a good day for hunting," he said.

"Native American wisdom?" Chuck asked.

"Naw, I checked the models on the Internet when I got up this morning. Lots of instability, lots of wind shear."

"Modern Indian," Chuck acknowledged.

"Halfbreed."

"Whatever. Well, we're headed north into eastern Kansas. You goin' out today?"

"No. Not today. Hate to miss the opportunity, but I got a lot of work to do around here." Sam stepped closer to Chuck and rested a hand on his shoulder. "Be careful."

"Always."

"No, I mean . . . well, the Osage half of me had a dream last night." He removed his hand from Chuck's shoulder.

Out on the prairie, a humid wind rippled through the grass, choreographing a sweeping ballet of swaying green stalks.

Chuck dipped his head, squinted at Sam, a tacit question.

"I was back in 'Nam," Sam said. "A line of Hueys was dropping into an LZ in a rice paddy. No Charlie. Just water buffalo. It looked safe. We dismounted, fanned out. No fire. Quiet. Suddenly, thunder all around us. Boom, boom, boom. Continuous. Like a mortar barrage. But no explosions. You and your little film caravan were right in the middle of it. Then you were gone. Swallowed in a cloud of dust. Just like that."

"We're not filming a war movie, Sam. We're after tornadoes."

"I know. Just made me uneasy."

"Nightmares do that. I'll be fine, partner. I think that wasn't the Osage half of you dreaming, that was whatever part of you you left in 'Nam." He stepped to Sam and embraced him. His old friend felt less substantial than he looked. A bit frail. The faint odor of liquor and old cigarette smoke leaked from his skin.

"I'll be careful," Chuck said.

"Sometimes the greatest danger comes from the threats we least expect."

Chuck stepped back from Sam. "Old Indian wisdom?"

"Old soldier wisdom. See ya."

Chuck climbed into the Expedition and slipped it into gear. He rolled down the window and called to Sam. "Regards to Monty."

Sam smiled and tipped his hat. "Beware the thunder," he said.

CHUCK AND METCALF stood side by side on a deserted farm road in southeast Kansas near the town of Fall River. Sporadic rumbles of thunder rolled across the pastureland that stretched for miles in all directions. On the opposite side of the road, a few head of cattle, munching idly on whatever cattle munch on, watched the two men with seeming disinterest. A few yards away, the chase vehicles rested on a grassy shoulder while Ziggy and Boomie played with Stormy, and Gabi and Ty snapped photographs of the windswept landscape.

Despite the fact a tornado watch had been issued, the afternoon so far had been devoid of anything remotely threatening. Although storm after storm had bubbled to life in the vast, flowing fields of towering cumulus, none had even scratched on the door of supercell status. They'd pop up, shoot out an anvil, and then collapse as though suffering from erectile dysfunction.

Metcalf checked his watch. "Shit. Almost six. Damn, Charlie, you never told me chasin' involved so much waitin'. We gonna get a twister, or are we gonna putz around here until the cows come home?"

Chuck nodded at their watchers across the road. "A few apparently already have."

"Yeah, I know. Bad friggin' sign."

Chuck scanned the horizon through a 360-degree arc, searching for a fragment of hope. Oddly, and suddenly, it was there, but a long way off. Far to the south, the corrugated crown of a massive cumulonimbus billowed heavenward like a mini-nuclear explosion. He stuck his head into the Expedition and checked the radar imagery on his computer.

"We're moving," he said, more a command than a declaration. "Get the guys into the trucks." He whistled for Stormy and motioned for Gabi and Ty to get into the SUV.

"What's up, bwana?" Metcalf asked.

"Big storm." He pointed at the mass of billowing clouds. "Down over Oklahoma. If we hustle, we can be there before dark."

"Tornado?"

"No guarantees," Chuck said. "But conditions are ripe and that thing's the only game in town." He performed another quick scan of the radar imagery and confirmed the storm, 60 miles distant, was already a supercell.

Chuck, knowing nightfall was his enemy, broke speed limits barreling south out of Kansas, back into the Osage land of Oklahoma. Metcalf's Navigator and the two camera trucks held tight on his tail. He silently and somewhat reluctantly had to acknowledge that Metcalf had been right when he'd said a few days earlier "I'll bet you'll move like you had a bottle rocket strapped to your ass if you have to."

The target supercell dominated the southern skyscape. The cell's anvil, flattened against the underbelly of the stratosphere, fanned out toward Kansas. The mammoth torso of the storm, bulbous with towers of cumulus and illuminated by the setting sun, shimmered ivory in sharp contrast to the dead-of-night blackness cloaking its base.

Lightning, still so distant from the chase team that individual strokes could not be discerned, sheeted from the lower half of the storm. It coursed through the growing dusk in brilliant waves that lent a strobe-light stop-motion to the wind-whipped grass of the prairie.

Chuck's cell phone rang, a Direct Connect call from Metcalf.

"Answer it," Chuck said to Gabi. "Put it on speaker."

She nodded, pressed the Talk button, and told Metcalf to go ahead.

"Hey, Chaz," Metcalf yelled, "what the fuck? These camera rigs weren't designed to be raced. There's a lot of expensive shit on them."

Gabi held the phone for Chuck to respond.

"Put a sock in it, Jerry. You're the one who told me about bottle rockets. So suck it up." He secretly reveled at the chance to verbally jump on Metcalf for a change. "We gotta get around the backside of this storm and approach it from the south before dark. That doesn't leave a lotta time."

"Why the south?"

"If a tornado is gonna spin up in a supercell, it'll be near its right rear flank. That's the southwest side of a storm moving toward the northeast, like this one."

"So why not just tear-ass straight through the damn thing and pop out on its southern edge? That'd be a hell of a lot quicker than playing 'Ring Around the Rosie' with it."

Three white-tailed deer bounded parallel to the speeding caravan for a few moments, then veered away from the road and knifed through knee-high grass flecked with vivid wildflowers.

Chuck ducked his head to get a better view of the upper reaches of the storm through the SUV's windshield. A huge, bubbling cloud, like an ascending white cauliflower, punched vertically through the cell's flat anvil and jabbed into the stratosphere.

"Look," he said, "an overshooting top!"

Gabi looked to where Chuck pointed. "Yeah?" she said, lifting an eyebrow. "What's it overshooting?"

Chuck had momentarily forgotten he wasn't chasing with meteorologists. "The updrafts in big thunderstorms," he answered, "get so powerful they force the cloud tops thousands of feet above where they normally would fizzle and flatten out in the anvil. If we see repeated overshooting tops, it's pretty much money in the bank a storm's gone tornadic."

"Hey, Chuckie," Metcalf's voice crackled through the phone Gabi still held, "you there? Quit feeling up the magazine chick and answer my question. Why can't we just make a bee line through the storm to the other side?"

Chuck shook his head in apology to Gabi for Metcalf's crudeness. "Because," he said to Metcalf, "as much as you're a loud-mouthed pain in the ass, I'd like to keep you alive until I get my pay check." *If I get my paycheck.* "You don't wanna drive through a supercell because the rain and hail in the thing could be hiding a tornado. And you wouldn't know it until you're ass-over-teakettle in low-earth orbit."

"Point taken, Chuckie. Nice imagery."

Chuck slowed the Expedition and examined the GPS mapping system he'd mounted on the dash. "There should be a county road running westward coming up shortly," he said.

Ty, suddenly engaged in the chase, leaned forward from the rear seat. "There," he said, pointing at a barely readable sign a hundred yards ahead on the right.

Chuck braked and flipped on the turn signal. He steered onto the county road and accelerated, the SUV's tires hammering over some sort of grating separating pavement from hard-packed gravel.

"What was that?" Gabi asked.

"Cattle guard," Chuck said.

"There was a warning sign back there," Ty said. "We went by it a little fast for me to read."

"Probably just telling us to watch out for livestock. Don't want to go one-on-one with a Texas Longhorn out here."

"How long will it take us to get around the backside of the storm?" Ty asked. Stormy stood on the seat beside him, bristling at the storm that continued to launch broadsides of lightning.

"Maybe twenty minutes," Chuck said.

"Be dark in thirty."

"I know, I know." Chuck pressed the accelerator to the floor. "Maybe we can make it in fifteen."

The storm was now to their left. Another overshooting battlement popped from its top. "Thing's gonna drop a tornado any time now," Chuck said, unable to hide the excitement rippling through his gut. "We're gonna be on it this time."

It felt almost like old times, back in the heyday of Thunder Road Tours, back when all he had to worry about was the adrenalin rush of the chase. Better than sex, some chasers used to say. Not really, but he had to admit the heart-pounding rush of a pursuit lasted longer. And you could do it more than once in a short time.

He held the Expedition at 60 mph on the narrow road. If he did hit a Longhorn, there'd be ground beef as far west as New Mexico.

Gabi peered out the driver side window at the storm. "We're almost abeam of the rear of it," she said.

"Okay, we gotta get south then," Chuck responded. "Look for a road. Anything. Even if it's not paved."

They raced westward for several more minutes until Chuck spotted a track, loose gravel and dirt, running south through the grassland. He whipped the SUV onto it and slowed, allowing the Lincoln and two camera rigs to make the turn and catch up.

Again he accelerated. The Expedition bounced and weaved over the rough road spewing a long rooster tail of dust in its wake. The running lights of the pursing trucks dimmed to small yellow orbs, like iridescent wolves' eyes looming through dense fog.

Metcalf called again. "Christ-on-a-crutch, Chuckie, what are you doing?" he bellowed. "Slow the fuck down. We aren't driving demolition derby vehicles."

"For shit sake," Chuck shot back. "Quit whining and put the pedal to the metal. We aren't gonna get many opportunities, but this is one. If one of your rigs gets a paint chip we'll find a MAACO. And one more thing, see if you can figure out a way to get your cameras up and running in less than 15 minutes. Out here the special effects won't wait for us."

The small caravan pulled within earshot of the seething black supercell. Thunder rolled over the prairie in a continuous crescendo. Discrete spears of lightning, clearly visible now, jumped in jagged bolts from cloud to ground and cloud to cloud in a relentless electric barrage.

They crossed in back of the storm, careening through grassland that had been pummeled flat by rain, hail, and wind. The odor of damp vegetation, mud, and ozone permeated the air. The vehicles slewed back and forth on the wet gravel now littered with melting hailstones. Shallow drainage ditches on either side of the road ran full with fresh rainwater.

Once south of the storm's swath, Chuck turned eastward, again paralleling the storm. Beneath the supercell, several pendants hung from the rotating wall cloud—low, black, menacing.

"Get Metcalf on the walkie-talkie," he said to Gabi.

She made contact and again held the phone for Chuck. "Get ready to act fast," he said, his voice loud with excitement. "Once we gain a little ground on the storm, we'll stop, set up, and hope for the best—or worst. Can't guarantee an EF-4 or -5, but we'll get something. This thing's ready to spit out a tornado."

"Leaning forward in the foxhole, Sarge," Metcalf responded.

"Keep the link open."

"Roger that," Metcalf said.

Chuck shook his head in mock dismay. "He must work a lot of war movies."

Gabi smiled, nodded, and placed the phone in her lap, angling it toward Chuck. Lips pinched together, she gazed intently out the window. "We're running out of light," she said.

"Yeah, yeah. I know." Back on dry gravel and dirt now, he mashed the gas pedal to the floor and pulled ahead of the supercell. The camera trucks hung doggedly on his tail, easier now that a stiff wind feeding into the storm cleared the slipstreams of dust off the road.

He spotted, in the gloaming, what appeared to be nothing more than a footpath through the grass leading toward a hillock. "Follow me," he yelled at Metcalf through the phone-cum-walkie-talkie. "I think I see a spot we can shoot from. If you guys can hump it and get your cranes up in ten minutes, we got a chance."

He whipped the SUV onto the path and plowed through the grass. He glanced at the wall cloud again, could see grass and dirt being sucked toward its base by a dagger-like funnel, white with condensate. The embryo of a twister. It would pass about a half-mile north of them.

The Expedition dove into a gully thick with grass and spring wildflowers. Chuck felt the vehicle slip sideways near the base of the depression before its tires found purchase and climbed toward the top of the low hill. He glanced in his review mirror and saw Metcalf's SUV swerve, too, before regaining its forward momentum and following Chuck up the hill. The silver camera truck followed.

Chuck stopped his SUV at the crest and leapt out. Metcalf and the camera rig pulled in behind him. Two men bolted from the camera truck's cab and clambered onto its bed.

The headlight beams of the fourth vehicle swept up the hill, then arced sharply off to the right and canted downward at an awkward angle.

"What the hell happened?" Metcalf, now beside Chuck, said. The roar of the increasing wind whipped his words into the maw of the storm.

"Dunno," Chuck said, his optimism suddenly deflated like a balloon jabbed with a pin. "Let's get down there."

He took off in bounding deer-like strides down the hill, trying to follow the track the vehicles had carved through the sea of grass. Metcalf lumbered behind him, followed by Ty, Gabi, and Stormy.

The white camera truck, its Diesel thudding at idle, titled at a precarious 40-degree angle on the edge of a damp swale. Scrawny, isolated oak trees marked the perimeter of the depression.

"Hidden side-slope in the grass," the driver of the truck, Ziggy, explained. "Didn't see it." He squatted down and examined the position of the vehicle. "I think I can get it out," he said. "I'll put it in four-wheel and try to ease it up the slope. Hopefully it won't lose traction and slip farther down."

Chuck glanced at the top of the hillock. The crewman from the silver truck appeared to be mounting the Panavision on the crane. Lightning from within the bowels of the supercell backlit them in almost continuous white and blue brilliance.

"Tornado!" one of the men yelled. He pointed off into the distance. "We're gonna miss it."

"Get the friggin' camera up," Metcalf screamed in return.

One of the men cranked the generator and the crane began to lift.

"Shit," Metcalf said. "It'll be too damn dark by the time they can shoot." He turned his attention to the listing truck and Ziggy. "Get this piece of crap outta the ditch."

Ziggy, a tall black man with dreads and tattooed biceps, glared at Metcalf but didn't say anything; he merely nodded, then after Metcalf had turned away, snapped off a mocking salute.

Stormy growled, a low, menacing rumble. She stopped and cocked her head as if listening for something hidden in the wind or camouflaged within the rumbles of thunder.

"Jesus," Metcalf said. "Now what? She gotta take a dump or something?"

Stormy ceased growling, walked toward Chuck, and let loose a series of short, sharp barks as she stared into the gathering darkness. The fur on her hackles bristled. A warning.

Chapter Twelve

WEDNESDAY, MAY 1

IN RESPONSE TO Stormy's warning growl, Chuck scanned the sky above and to the west. Had he missed something? Another storm? Nothing but the evening star met his gaze. The sky behind the supercell remained clear. He looked up the hill again. Had the tornado changed course? No, the men in the camera truck would have warned them. Well, maybe Stormy just didn't like being in the dark in open country.

A faint vibration from the ground rippled up through Chuck's legs. He looked around to see if anyone else had felt it. Apparently not. Ziggy, in the truck, eased the vehicle forward; Metcalf, outside the cab, shouted useless instructions. Ty and Gabi watched in rapt attention.

Stormy, growling again, her tail tucked between her legs, moved away from Chuck and sniffed the air. She paused, then backpedaled toward Chuck.

Chuck squatted, put his hand on her head. "What is it girl? Something out there?"

The vibration came again. A little stronger, a bit more persistent.

Ty removed his gaze from the truck and looked at Chuck. He'd felt it, too. The solider in him sensing something. He walked toward Chuck. "What's that?" he asked when he reached his father.

Chuck shrugged. "Hey, Jerry," he yelled at Metcalf. Have Ziggy turn off the engine a minute."

"Turn it off?"

"Yes."

"Why?"

"I'm just exercising my authority, that's all." *Dipshit.*

The Diesel clattered to a stop. Now the only sounds were the thrum of the generator on the other truck, the occasional rumble of distant thunder, and the rush of wind through the prairie grass.

One of the men from the truck on the hill called down to Metcalf.

"Got about 60 seconds of the twister, but it was pretty damn dark. Nice effect with the lightning illuminating it, though."

"Was it a monster?" Metcalf yelled back.

"Don't think so."

Metcalf walked toward Chuck. "Strike two, Chuckie. Now what's with interrupting our effort here? Okay if I get my truck outta the wallow?"

"Just hold on a minute, will you. And listen."

"For what?"

Chuck placed his forefinger over his lips.

Metcalf muttered something, then fell silent.

Stormy paced in circles around the group, which was now clustered together. Except for the headlight beams of the white truck, and the lighting from the truck on top of the rise, darkness had taken over. Not total. Shapes and forms remained visible, but not detail.

Stormy ceased barking and in slow, measured steps, tail still between her legs, head lowered, ears flattened, crept away from the damp swale, toward the east. A low rumble, not thunder, more like a low-pitched, steady hammering, drifted through the deepening blackness.

Chuck tensed. The others heard it, too, looked to him for answers.

Certainly not a storm. He tried to process the sound, identify it. Nothing he was familiar with.

He looked at Ty, Ty at him. "Don't like it," Ty mouthed.

Now, something else. Snorts, grunts. Faint.

"Oh, Jesus," Chuck said. "Up the hill. Now."

"What the fuck is going on?" Metcalf demanded.

"Up the hill. Run."

Sam had warned him this morning. *Beware the thunder,* but neither of them had really known what it meant. Native American folklore? A throwaway line? No, not out here on the Oklahoma prairie. He understood now. The cattle guard. The warning sign. Not for Longhorns.

The group sprinted through the grass, toward the crest of the rise. Gabi stumbled. Chuck lifted her. Got her moving again. Halfway up. Chuck stopped. Turned. Where was Stormy? There. In the depression, holding her ground in front of the truck, ready to challenge whatever was coming. He knew she didn't stand a chance. He whistled. Then bellowed: "Stormy, come!"

She didn't move.

"Stormy!"

She took a step toward him.

The ground shook in a steady, rolling beat now, like a low-grade earthquake growing in intensity.

Explosive, guttural exhalations and drumming reverberations filled the darkness with a netherworld sense of danger and fear. Chuck struggled to breathe, to get his words out.

"Stormy!" he called again. More pleading than demanding. He looked to his left, toward the source of the approaching cacophony. Just enough light to see the grass rippling, parting, flattening.

The first of the beasts burst from the grass. Massive and dark with great shaggy heads and short horns. Dozens upon dozens more followed, dust rising from their hooves like black mist. Snorting, bellowing, grunting.

The lead wave of animals was almost upon Stormy before she realized her folly. She pivoted and dashed toward Chuck.

The stampede, a throwback to a time when millions of American bison roamed the Great Plains, thundered into the swale. The living flood widened, filling the shallow gully, flowing over the lower reaches of its slopes, almost to where Chuck stood riveted to the ground by the stunning sight.

Stormy, in a desperate uphill run, knifed through the tall grass toward him, avoiding the sharp hooves of the lead animals by mere inches. Panting, she dropped to her stomach near Chuck's feet and issued a series of pro forma, winded barks at the invaders.

The nearest of the bison—nearly a ton apiece, Chuck judged—swept by within yards of him. He could smell the dirt and dung that clung to their tangled fur, hear their heavy expulsions of breath, sense the herd instinct of fear that propelled them forward.

As an entity, the stampede flowed into, around, and eventually over the camera truck, sending it tumbling deeper into the swale. Over the din of the charge, Chuck heard Metcalf screaming. Suddenly the man was beside him, bellowing in his ear. "Do something, do something!"

"Okay." Chuck turned and walked toward the summit of the hillock where the rest of the group waited.

"Chaz, goddamnit, this is your fault," Metcalf called after him. "That's about two mil worth of hardware that just got turned into scrap metal by Ted Turner's pets." He dashed after Chuck, stepped in front of him, whipped off his fisherman's cap, and threw it on the ground. "Whaddaya think, dimwit, we came out here to do a fucking remake of *Dances with Wolves?*" Spittle flew from his mouth and clung like dew drops to his thick beard.

Chuck lowered his head. Metcalf's anger was not misplaced. He, Chuck, had screwed up. In the excitement of the chase, he hadn't realized, at least until after the fact, that he'd led the team onto the Tallgrass Prairie Preserve, located in the center of the Osage Nation, home to 2500 American bison.

"We'll get a tow truck out here in the morning," Chuck said, his voice barely above a whisper. He continued up the hill, Stormy trotting behind him.

When he reached the top, Gabi walked over and laid a hand on his shoulder. "It wasn't your fault," she said. "Who could have foreseen something like this?"

"Sam Townsend," he whispered. He held Gabi in his gaze. "Remember? The last thing he said on the rez this morning before we left was "Beware the thunder." And his dream. He told us about his dream, seeing us swallowed in a cloud of dust. That's not possible is it? Dreams can't really foretell—"

Metcalf interrupted, verbally pouncing on Chuck once more. "How in the hell am I gonna explain this to our insurance company?" he yelled. "They gonna believe some Bozo led us into the middle of Buffalo Bill's Wild West Show and Bison Stampede?" He stalked away grumbling, "This is just unbefuckinglievable, just unbefuckinglievable."

"Come on, Metcalf," Gabi said. "How could he have known—"

"He's our fearless leader," Metcalf snapped. "He's supposed to know!"

Chuck shuffled toward the Expedition. "Let's get out of here."

"Leave it to me to pick a loser," Metcalf called after him.

Ty fired a verbal volley at Metcalf. "Okay, give it a rest, buddy."

Chuck, a bit surprised, looked in the direction of his son, but Ty chose to ignore him. He opened the rear door of the SUV and herded Stormy into the vehicle without speaking further.

Chuck settled into the driver's seat, glanced in the rearview mirror at Ty, and started to say something but decided against it. *What the hell.* It had been that kind of a day.

Distant lightning, the last hurrah of the departing supercell, flickered across the prairie, painting the swaying grass in dissipating neon whiteness. A chorus of coyotes yelped in counterpoint to the final echoes of thunder.

The rumble and quake of the stampeding bison faded, too, like a BNSF fast freight hurtling down the rails and disappearing into the night. A metaphor, perhaps, for the likelihood of ever realizing a million-dollar payday.

Chapter Thirteen

THURSDAY, MAY 2

THE OWNER OF the Tulsa body shop where the damaged camera truck had been towed came out of the garage area shaking his head. "Buffalo stampede, you said?"

"Yeah," Chuck answered. He could read in the guy's acne-scarred face that he wasn't the bearer of good news.

"Never heard of that happening before. Anyhow, it's gonna be about a week before we can get that rig patched up and aligned and everything else."

Metcalf, who had accompanied Chuck to the repair shop, expelled a long breath, then whispered in Chuck's ear: "Strike three, Chuckie. You oughta be back on the bench, except then I'd look like dog poo to my bosses. So, you're still in the game. Just barely."

Chuck let the put-down pass and addressed the repairman. "Can't you get it done any quicker?" He sounded like a teenager pleading to use Dad's car on a Saturday night.

"Sorry. Lotta damage. Have to order some parts. And that crane is gonna be a bitch to fix."

"Isn't there some way you could expedite—"

"Forget it, Chuckie," Metcalf interjected, "the Genesis is history anyhow. It'll be at least a week before we can get a replacement. In the meantime, we'll press on without it. We still got one good rig with its camera, and a Steadicam."

"A what?"

"Steadicam. It's a stabilizing system, like a harness, that a cameraman can wear and hand-carry a camera. It minimizes shake. It's not the way I'd like to film a tornado, but if you keep busting our equipment, maybe that's all I'll end up with."

And if you keep busting my balls, maybe you'll end up with nothing. Chuck gave his cell phone number to the owner of the shop and requested he stay in touch.

As Chuck and Metcalf headed back to their motel, a Hampton Inn, Metcalf continued with his slings and arrows. "So, any more opportunities in the near future of getting caught in a buffalo stampede or setting up 300 miles out of position?"

Chuck answered through clinched teeth. "Not until next Monday."

THAT NIGHT, THE stymied entourage journeyed to a nearby restaurant for a leisurely dinner. Chuck and Gabi settled into a booth near the rear of the establishment, a reasonably up-scale eatery with a large, softly-lit dining area, several smaller satellite rooms, and a long mahogany bar set against a far wall. Metcalf held court at the bar, regaling his cronies and Ty with a seemingly endless string of anecdotes and gossip from the exotic world of movie making.

Chuck had asked him once, right after they'd first met, what his job title was—there'd been nothing on his business card—and Metcalf had merely shrugged. "I just make sure stuff gets done and things happen," he said. "I kick ass and take names. Think of me as a chief of staff. Or, if I'm really pissed, a first sergeant." Chuck knew him primarily as a first sergeant.

Chuck and Gabi studied their menus, but Chuck's thoughts were not on food; they were on the Great Hunt. So far, however, it had been far less than great. He'd fired two large-caliber blanks. He'd positioned the team poorly on its first day out, then managed to get them into the middle of a buffalo stampede a few days later. *A fucking buffalo stampede. How on earth could something like that happen?*

"What's the matter?" Gabi asked. "Nothing on the menu suit your fancy?"

"What?"

"What are you ordering?

Chuck stared at the menu. "A BLT, I guess."

"It's dinnertime."

"I'm not hungry."

"I am. You think they have swordfish here?"

"We're on the Great Plains, Gabi, not the Grand Banks. Try something from a cow."

"I'm lactose intolerant."

Chuck laughed in spite of the bluesy malaise gripping him. "I was thinking more along the lines of a top sirloin, not milk."

Gabi peeked over the top of her menu at him. He caught a brief glint of mischievousness in her greenish-brown eyes, but it quickly disappeared, replaced by a more practiced neutral look, the gaze of a federal law officer. Yet there was something beckoning in her stare, not in a sexual sense, but in the more veiled suggestion of something waiting to be discovered.

He placed his menu on the table. "Where are you from?" he asked. "I mean originally."

She hesitated before replying, perhaps weighing how much of their relationship was professional as a opposed to personal. "New Bedford, Mass," she said. "My dad was Portuguese, a fisherman. My mother, Russian. And yes, I speak both languages."

"Probably something the FBI liked."

"It helped get my foot in the door."

Peals of laughter exploded from the crowd at the bar. Metcalf, red-faced and grinning, stood in the middle of the group and appeared to be reveling in the accolades for yet another story well told. Probably one about a buffalo stampede.

"Bit of a blowhard," Gabi said, inclining her head toward the racket.

"I guess he has to be, in his business," Chuck said. "But we were talking about you. Where'd you get started?"

"Before I joined the Bureau, I was an interpreter for the Federal District Court in Massachusetts. Five years. Then into the Bureau. First in Mobile, then back north to New Haven, then to Ok City and criminal investigations."

"Family?"

The waitress arrived to take their orders. After she left, Chuck repeated his question.

Gabi narrowed her eyes and looked at Chuck as though he'd stepped into *verboten* territory.

"Oh, come on," he said. "You know *me* like a book. I'm just trying to level the social playing field here."

"There is no social 'playing field' here. I'm a working FBI agent. Let's just leave it at that."

Chuck stared at her, a bit taken aback by her curt rebuff. "Just making conversation," he offered.

"I understand," she responded, but didn't follow up with any further explanation. Instead, she changed the subject. "Oh, I probably should tell you, the autopsy results came back from the woman found dead after the tornado in Lubbock Monday. Blunt force trauma. It was an injury that could have been caused by the tornado. Except, neighbors remember the woman arriving home *after* the storm. They also recall seeing a black SUV with a grill guard and some kind of signage on the doors being parked in her driveway."

"Didn't you mention a black GMC was spotted by a state trooper at the scene of the murder in Oklahoma?"

She nodded. "Good memory. At the time, he thought it was an EMT vehicle."

"But the one in Lubbock wasn't?"

"Apparently not. The only common thread is 'a black SUV'."

"How about the signs?"

"No one paid any attention to them. Too busy with other things."

Gabi seemed reluctant to provide any additional information, and since she'd staked out her personal life with a NO TRESPASSING sign, they fell silent. Chuck leaned back in the booth, inhaling the aromas of wood-grilled beef, fresh baked bread, and steamed vegetables. Soft chatter from others and the clink of bottles and glasses from the bar filled the conversation void.

A server arrived with the dinner orders for Chuck and Gabi. Chuck nibbled at his BLT, which seemed to have more L than B or T, and watched Gabi attack a T-bone, a house specialty called The Ranchers Delight. She tackled the job with a mix of feminine grace and masculine determination.

Chuck, much to his surprise, had a difficult time pulling his gaze from her. As he'd noted in their initial meeting, she wasn't classically beautiful, but her dark complexion and ebony hair, coupled with her clear, unblinking hazel eyes, drew him in. Sure, she might be fighting a weight battle, as she herself had suggested, but she obviously was winning the fight; her well-toned body and subtly sculptured muscles gave testimony to that. She seemed the kind of woman who could grow on a man. But he wondered about her reluctance to discuss her life beyond the professional details. He decided on a different approach.

"Gabi," he said.

She looked up from carving another bite-size piece from her T-bone.

"You suffer from migraines, don't you?"

She put the chunk of meat into her mouth and chewed, her stare fixed on him. She swallowed the bite and said, "You like to pry, don't you?"

"No—"

"What I suffer from or don't and what my personal history is, isn't a topic for discussion. Just leave it."

"I wasn't prying, damn it. My mother suffered from migraines. I know the precursors, the symptoms, the aftermath. I know how debilitating they can be. She could be laid up for days at time, moaning, throwing up, unable to function. Once or twice she ended up in the hospital. But all they could do was knock her out with drugs. I just wanted to say I understand. If there's any way I can help—"

"You can help by being a little less inquisitive about me and maybe dealing with the weeds in your own backyard." She squeezed her eyes shut tightly and tilted her head back.

"What weeds?"

She opened her eyes. "The tension between you and your son hasn't gone unnoticed by me or anyone else on this expedition. I don't know what the issue is between you two, and I don't need to know. It's obviously lost on you in all the smoke from the verbal gunfire you guys trade, but he's reaching out to you—like the other day when he told Metcalf to put a sock in it—and all you do is slap him down."

"That's your viewpoint," Chuck snapped.

"No. That's a woman's viewpoint. Call it female insight. If you can show compassion to me, a virtual stranger, you sure as shit can do it for your son, too." She placed her knife and fork on her plate, folded her napkin, tossed a 20-dollar bill on the table, and stood. "I feel a headache coming on. See you in the morning." She walked away.

Chuck stared after her. "Well, that went well," he said to no one.

The waitress arrived to see if everything was okay.

"What the hell did I do wrong?" Chuck said to her.

She backed away.

BACK IN HER ROOM at the Hampton Inn, Gabi fumbled in her purse for her bottle of Treximet. She downed a tablet without the benefit of water and flopped onto her bed, hoping the combination of sumatriptan and naproxen sodium would stave off the worst of the agony aborning. If she interdicted it early enough, maybe she'd sleep through the night and be reasonably pain free by sunrise. Maybe.

She stared at the ceiling, otherwise dark except for intermittent flickers of blue and white brilliance. Sheet lightning boring through the window from a distant storm? Or the strobing aura from an incipient migraine? She didn't know.

She did know she'd probably been too hard on Chuck. The guy most likely had just been trying to find a way to connect with her, to climb over the business barrier that existed between them.

The barrier, however, existed not only for professional reasons, it protected her personally, too. For one thing, her migraines were something the Bureau knew nothing of. She didn't want them on her official record. She dealt with them on her own by consulting doctors who knew nothing of her real profession.

Further, she knew in the wake of her first marriage she wasn't cut out to be a typical—whatever that was—soccer mom. But she also came to realize there was a scarcity of men who wanted to settle down with a "woman who shoots guns, curses in Russian, and can't cook worth a shit," as one of her lovers once told her. That hurt.

She was hurt a few more times before the obvious became obvious to *her*. She was merely a target. Screw an FBI chick and you've got bragging rights at the bar for perpetuity. Hence the barrier. But couple the barrier with the hormonal cyclone that accompanies an onrushing migraine, and an apparently decent guy like Chuck gets steamrollered.

A shadow passed between her and the pulsing, fluorescent ceiling. Chuck leaned over her, brushed her forehead with his hand.

"Thank you," she said. "I'm sorry." But she knew she was asleep. Dreaming.

Chapter Fourteen

FRIDAY, MAY 3

"I APOLOGIZE," Gabi said.

Chuck looked up from the *USA Today* he'd been reading in the lobby of the motel.

"For last night," Gabi explained, her voice hoarse. "I was a bitch. A little too defensive, a little too hurting . . . you were right about the migraines. I had a doozy last night."

Chuck stood. Gabi appeared pale, drained. Redness tinted the whites of her eyes. She seemed strangely vulnerable this morning—almost little girlish in her white blouse and blue jeans—not at all like the confident, professional, and yes, defensive woman he'd had dinner with last night. He fought back an urge to give her a comforting hug. Instead he asked, "Had breakfast yet? It's late."

"No. Not hungry." She seemed to reconsider. "Well, maybe some juice and toast."

"This way." He offered her his arm.

She took it and leaned against him ever so lightly. "So, am I given absolution?"

Her touch, almost like low-voltage electricity, rendered him temporarily speechless. He realized how long he'd been without a woman in his life.

"Hey," she said, "you okay?"

"Fine. I just need another cup of coffee. And yes, you're forgiven. Like I told you, I know about migraines."

She leaned closer to him—a sort of silent thanks, he decided—triggering another tiny jolt of sexual energy. When they reached the breakfast room, she released his arm and stepped away. "What do you take in your coffee?"

He watched her walk toward the pots. Not a little girl now. A woman in tight jeans and a form-revealing blouse. "Better make it decaf," he called after her. He drew a deep breath and reminded himself she was an FBI agent and they were in a business relationship and nothing more.

She returned with a cup of coffee for him and they seated themselves at a small table. Only one other person populated the room, a man dressed in a business suit who slathered cream cheese on a bagel while he watched Fox News. A cowboy hat rested on the table beside him.

Chuck took a swallow of the decaf. "Thanks," he said to Gabi. "What about you? Some toast now?"

She squeezed her eyes shut and leaned back in her chair. "Give me a minute. Still recovering. By the way, just between you and me, the FBI doesn't know anything about my migraines."

"Should they?"

"If they did, it could preclude me getting certain assignments."

"Then my lips are sealed."

After a moment, she arose, dropped a couple of slices of wheat bread into a toaster, and poured herself a glass of cranberry juice.

Toast and juice in hand, she seated herself at the table again. She brushed a loose strand of hair from in front of her eyes and bit into the toast. As she ate, a subdued rosy glow gradually crept back into her cheeks. When she finished, she dabbed a napkin against her mouth.

"Well," she said, "don't let the bastards get you down."

"What?"

"You seem to have a lot working against you. I mean over and above the professional scarlet letter you started out with. Metcalf acts like a first-class prick. Your son and you bond like water and oil; why, I don't know. And me, your phony magazine reporter gal, goes off on you like a harpy on a broomstick."

"I haven't exactly performed up to expectations."

"We've got over a week to go. Things'll work out."

"Thanks, Mom."

The businessman-cowboy stood, retrieved his hat, and nodded at Chuck and Gabi as he left the breakfast area.

Gabi gave Chuck a fleeting smile. "Do I remind you of your mother?"

"Mom never wore blue jeans. But she was good at giving pep talks."

"Do you object to jeans?"

"Not on you." *Shit.* Heat swarmed through his cheeks and he felt himself color what must have been fifty shades of red. "Damn. I'm sorry. Inappropriate remark."

Gabi laughed. "Oh, come on. I'm a ditzy freelance writer who revels in remarks like that. Feel free to boost my ego any time."

"No. It was—"

"Not inappropriate," she finished his sentence for him and reached across the table to rest her hand on his. She spoke in a soft voice. "Don't get wrapped around the axle over the fact I'm an FBI agent. I'm a woman, too, and I'm glad you noticed."

The warmth in Chuck's cheeks receded . . . but not completely. A degree of awkwardness lingered. *Idiot.* "I wasn't trying to put a move on you. I just blurted out something sexist without thinking."

"*Now* you're hurting my feelings. You mean I don't look that good in jeans?"

"That's not what I meant."

"What did you mean?"

"I think I'll get another cup of coffee."

Gabi laughed. "Sorry. Just yanking your chain."

"You're feeling better?"

"I am. And I appreciate your being concerned . . . even if you don't care for the way I look."

Chuck issued an exaggerated sigh. "I'd never win an argument with you, would I?"

"I'm a highly trained FBI agent."

"So highly trained you took a chance on a broken down, virtually destitute storm chaser to help you catch a killer." He drained the last of the coffee from his cup.

"I know what I'm doing. You do, too. You'll find your magic again and we'll get the son-of-a-bitch. When's the next round of storms coming up?"

"Not until early next week. But . . ."

"But what?"

"There was something I saw in the models this morning." He leaned toward her and lowered his voice. "How'd you like to be a co-conspirator in a little plot to rattle the cage of our loud-mouthed movie mogul?"

"I'm all in and all ears," Gabi said.

After detailing his "fun and games" scheme to Gabi, Chuck called Metcalf on his cell.

"Hey, Jerry," Chuck said, "how'd you like to get out of town for a bit while we're waiting for the next storm threat to materialize?"

"Anything's better than hanging around in Oral Robertsville. Whaddaya got in mind?"

"How about as a complement to your tornado shots—"

"Which we haven't got yet."

"Which we haven't got yet—thank you for reminding me—we film some really large hail?"

"What're talkin' here, Chuckie, like D-cup sized stuff?'

It dawned on Chuck he might need to come up with a totally new hail-size comparison paradigm for Metcalf. *Jesus, does everybody from Hollywood think like this?* He decided it might be unique to Metcalf. "I was thinking more along the lines of apple or grapefruit."

"Doesn't sound that big to me."

"It would if you got whacked in the head by one."

"Got whacked in the face by a 44 triple-D once. That hurt."

"Spare me the details. You interested or not?"

"Like I said, anything to get out of Tulsa. Where're we headed?"

"How about to the site of a little film nostalgia, the Red River?"

"Ah, yes. The great John Wayne. And not that it's germane, but *Red River* was filmed mostly in Arizona. What time do we boogie?"

BY NOON, THEY were on the road, heading southwest on I-44 toward Oklahoma City. Metcalf had elected to leave his Navigator in Tulsa and ride in the camera truck, so the caravan consisted only of Chuck's Expedition and the rig with the 22-foot camera crane. Gabi and Stormy rode with Chuck. Ty had remained behind, choosing instead to visit the Tulsa Air and Space Museum.

Late afternoon brought the ad hoc chase team to Wichita Falls, Texas, just south of the Red River. There, Chuck turned west, following US 287. At a truck stop outside of Harrold, they took a break.

While the rest of the team piled into the facility to use the restrooms and raid a Subway for footlongs, and Stormy trotted off on her own to do her thing, Chuck examined the latest radar imagery on his laptop. "Got a target," he yelled to Metcalf when he returned.

"Can I finish my hoagie?"

"Not here. Eat on the run. We're heading south. There's a big hailer near Crowell moving southeast. We're gonna intercept it." Chuck pointed southwest. "You can see its anvil." The feathering cirrus, tinted orange and salmon by the low-angle sun, radiated outward from the distant storm like the bill of a ball cap.

"And when we catch it?"

"Your cinematographers will get some super shots—close-ups of stones the size of baseballs."

"I've known some guys in Hollywood that had stones that big," Metcalf said as he scrambled into the truck.

Gabi took over driving the Expedition while Chuck navigated, monitoring the storm on his computer.

"You think this is going to work?" Gabi asked.

"It should. But let's make sure. There's a little town, Barrington, about 10 miles ahead of us. We'll mosey through it kind of slow and make sure it has what we need. It's been a while since I've been there, so I need to confirm my memory."

"This could be fun."

"Yeah, as long as Metcalf doesn't stroke out first."

They reached Barrington 15 minutes later.

"God, this is depressing," Gabi said, surveying the hamlet. Half the buildings appeared abandoned or boarded up, many homes seemed below the threshold of ramshackle, and dozens of trucks and autos—those that had not yet descended to rusted-out hulk status—rested on blocks.

"Yeah, I know," Chuck responded. "It looks like some photographs I've seen that were taken during the Dust Bowl days."

Yet there were signs of viability: a Wendy's that appeared fairly new, a service station with two pumps, a small supermarket with signs in both English and Spanish, and a bar and grill that had more vehicles in the parking lot than did the grocery store. Next to the bar and grill Chuck spotted what they needed. He pointed it out to Gabi, who nodded.

"Okay," he said. "Go about a mile out of town and stop. That should set us up just right. Then—oh, wow!"

"What?"

"This thing's spitting out grapefruit-sized hail now."

"That oughta kill a few cows."

"Not to mention people if they get caught outside. Hail that big can punch holes in houses."

"You sure you wanna try this?"

"No problem. I'm a trained professional."

"How's that worked for you so far?" She looked at him and raised one eyebrow.

"Just drive," he said.

After two minutes, Chuck told Gabi to make a U-turn and stop. As she made her turn on the quiet highway, Chuck signaled the driver of the camera truck to do the same. Both vehicles halted along the shoulder, an area thick with dry, short grass.

Chuck and Gabi joined Metcalf, Boomie, and Dakota between the two vehicles for a quick conference. Stormy, nose to ground, cruised up and down the roadside until she flushed a quail from the grass adjacent to a wire fence. Peals of thunder from the approaching supercell tumbled over the dusty prairie in intermittent bursts.

Metcalf studied the storm. "How big ya say the hail is?"

"At last check, four inches. Grapefruits."

"Uh, we're kinda exposed out here, aren't we? I mean, ya already lost one rig for me." Metcalf looked around as though expecting shelter to materialize from the darkening sky.

"You're right, boss." Chuck made a show of evaluating Metcalf's concern. "The main hail core will probably just miss us. But—" he rubbed his chin feigning thought "—we probably shouldn't deploy the crane. It would take us too long to get it down if we have to run for it."

"If we have to run for it? Shit. Where we gonna run, to? We're a mile outside East Bumfuck with its two-pump gas station. You might be able to hide your Ford under the overhang there, but where am I gonna put this rig?" He pointed at the silver truck.

"Could be a problem, all right. Well, let's not worry about it. Couldn't you use that Steadicam thing you were telling me about."

"Hey, excellent idea, Numb Nuts." Metcalf's face tightened, turned a light shade of red. "Hey, Boomie," he called out. "Come here. Ya wanna get the Steadicam vest on and stand out in a hailstorm with ice balls the size of Rhode Island?"

"No."

"Oh, come on. Be a sport. You'd get some great shots. Probably a raise, too."

"Posthumously."

Metcalf spread his hands, palms up, in front of Chuck. "Well, another wasted trip. What the hell were you thinkin', Chuckie?"

Chuck held up his right hand, signaled for silence. "Listen," he said.

"What?" Metcalf responded, the word edged in snippiness.

"Hear that?"

"Thunder?"

"No. A thrumming sound. Like distant jet engines."

"It's thunder, weather boy."

"No, it's not. It's not rumbling. It's steady."

"So?"

"That's a hail roar."

"Hail roar? Bullshit."

"In hailstorms, the stones ride vertical air currents up and down. If the stones are large enough, like in this storm, they ram into one another—bumper cars in the sky. That's what you're hearing."

"Are you pullin' my pud, Chaz?"

"Google it. It's for real. Not many people have ever heard it, though. Or didn't know what they were hearing if they did."

Gabi stepped close to Chuck and whispered in his ear. "This isn't part of the game, is it?"

He shook his head. "Real deal."

Metcalf stood with his hands on his hips, staring at the storm. Without looking away from it, he called to the lady in his crew. "Dakota, grab the boom mike and see if you can get this. If Fearless Leader is right, this might be great stuff for the film." He turned to Chuck. "Maybe you finally done somethin' right."

Dakota and Boomie wrestled to get the boom mike from the rear of the truck, but it was too late. A huge rain drop splatted down on the road, then another and another. Within a matter of seconds, a monsoonal downpour ensued, turning the landscape into liquid gray.

Chuck and the rest dove back into their vehicles. The first hailstones, pea-sized, pinged down, mixing with the downpour. The rain abruptly relented, but was replaced by even bigger hail that thudded into the vehicles like large-caliber bullets.

"Fast as you can, back to town," Chuck told Gabi. He called Metcalf on his cell. "Follow us, Jerry. And get Boomie ready to use the Steadicam."

"Forget about the Steadicam, Bozo," Metcalf yelled. "If you don't get us out of this hail, we're gonna have another rig turned into junk yard fodder."

"In my business," Chuck responded, his voice calm and steady, "what I'm about to do is known as 'core punching.' I'm taking us right into the center of the hail storm."

"You're fired, Chaz, you hear me? You're fired! You're fucking incompetent!"

Chuck imagined if Metcalf were wearing a blood pressure monitor it would have red-lined.

Now it was golfball-sized chunks of ice that ricocheted off the windshield and exploded like shotgun blasts on the roof. "This is gonna be close, Gabi," Chuck said. "Any bigger and we're gonna lose the windshield." He swallowed hard. *Not another damn miscalculation.*

Behind him, the driver of the camera truck, Dakota, flashed the headlights and lay on the horn . . . as though that would deliver them for the storm's wrath.

Hail continued to thunder down. In a pasture adjacent to the road, cattle, seeking shelter, huddled humpbacked, like Halloween cats, under scattered trees. But even the trees offered scant protection as the hailstones stripped away leaves and branches as if they were but *papier-mâché.*

In the rear seat of the Expedition, Stormy, whining, paced from one side to the other.

They entered the edge of Barrington. "Almost there," Chuck said. None too soon, he knew. The epicenter of the hail core was almost upon them. *Had he cut this too close?* The stones had become weaponized, hammering into the SUV like rocket-propelled grenades. Gabi screamed as a concentric crack blossomed on the windshield.

Chapter Fifteen

FRIDAY, MAY 3

"TURN NOW," Chuck yelled over the din of the storm's assault.

Gabi whipped the steering wheel hard right and hurled the Expedition into one of two bays in a ratty-looking carwash. The camera rig followed, barreling into the second bay but tearing away part of the building's structure as the scaffolding on top of the truck's cab scraped through the entrance.

Metcalf, out of the truck instantly, leveled a string of profanities at Chuck that included words Chuck had no idea existed. It seemed fortunate a cinder block wall separated him from Metcalf.

When the tirade ceased, Chuck yelled back. "Are you filming this, Jerry? If not, you're missing one of the greatest opportunities ever in cinematography." Probably hyperbole, but he didn't care. It had been worth it just to drag Metcalf to the edge, leading him to believe his one remaining camera rig was about to be pulverized by an artillery barrage of hailstones.

Gabi stood next to Chuck in the bay. As close as she was to him, she had to raise her voice to be heard over the din of the storm as huge chunks of ice banged off the flimsy roof of the carwash. "We're sick, aren't we?" She stifled a laugh.

"Absolutely," Chuck responded. "Totally adolescent."

Stormy, tail between her legs, crouched at the edge of the bay, watching the landscape morph to transient winter. Enormous hailstones, some approaching the size of softballs, exploded off the asphalt outside the carwash. Smaller stones bounced into the air as if springing from a trampoline. Across the street, a tree, severed by the icy onslaught, took out a power line in a brilliant blue-white flash.

Several giant stones battered holes in the roof of the carwash; cascades of water and ice gushed into the improvised shelter. Gabi and Chuck scurried back into the Expedition. Chuck heard Metcalf, in the adjacent bay, screaming at Boomie to get "some fucking film."

The blitz of massive hail seemed to go on forever, though Chuck knew it was only minutes. The fusillade of stones echoed like small arms fire. And indeed, after the attack waned, the small town looked as though it been raked by gunfire: shattered windows and windshields, dented cars and trucks, fractured roofs, split trees, broken picket fences. A cacophonous chorus of vehicle alarms, triggered by the storm, replaced the thunder of the hail.

After the storm abated, Metcalf stalked into the bay where Chuck and Gabi waited. "What the hell was that all about?" he yelled. "You had this all planned ahead of time, didn't you? Ducking into a car wash and all. Just rattling my cage. Fun and games. Good fodder for a magazine story. What a bunch of dipshits. I swear, I'm gonna claim PTSD after all this is over. And who's gonna pay for the damage my rig did to the carwash?" Metcalf, gasping for breath, ceased his harangue.

"Well, it was *your* truck that tore away the superstructure, not mine," Chuck said. "Besides, you probably got some of the greatest shots ever of large hail. The return on that oughta cover the damage."

"I didn't hire you to lead me into a frigging hail storm, you clown. I hired you to find me a fire-breathin' twister. So far you've failed miserably. Hope you enjoyed your little laugh, because it appears to me that's all you're ever gonna earn out here. Let's get the fuck back to Tulsa now."

"METCALF DIDN'T TAKE that well," Gabi said as they headed back to the city.

"He'll change his tune when he sees the film," Chuck said. "Besides, the trip was worth it just to see Foghorn Leghorn get his feathers ruffled. Like he said, that may be the only reward I'll get."

"You're raising the white flag already?"

He slowed down as they eased into heavier traffic on I-44 in Oklahoma City. "Let's say I've run it part way up the pole. It's half time and we haven't scored yet. Our next shot at putting points on the board won't be until Monday. If we can't do it then, that may be the end game for us. I don't see any other threats until the following week."

"And the clock runs out next Saturday?"

"That's about it."

"So bye-bye million bucks unless we hit it big on Monday," she said softly.

He glanced over at her and found her staring at him, her face streaked in neon as the lights of the city, flickering to life in the growing darkness, flashed past. Far to the south, behind them, lightning painted the horizon in broad, explosive sheets of electric whiteness.

He shrugged. "Well, I can't lose what I never had. I feel worse about not being able to help you. If only I'd had us in Texas that first day . . ."

She reached over and squeezed his hand. "So, ya wanna just call it quits and go bowling or something?"

He laughed out loud. "No, it's just that—"

"Then quit kvetching and find us a tornado, O Great White Hunter. The Fat Lady isn't even humming yet." She gave his hand a little extra pump and released it.

"THANKS, SIS."

"Is that how you think of me, as a sister?" The words slipped out of Gabi's mouth unchecked. Without meaning to, she'd verbalized a thought. She hoped Chuck couldn't see the blush she felt rushing into her cheeks.

"How do you want me to think of you?"

She cracked the window open. *How do I answer that? In truth, I don't know.* Sister *is certainly not the right answer. Neither is* FBI agent. *Jesus, why am I even thinking about this?* She put the window up and said, "Just a dizzy broad who writes fluff for magazines."

"Really?"

"Really," she said. *Time to change the subject.* She placed an open palm on top of her head. "See? Feature writer's hat on. And with it, a question: Why do you—why does anybody—chase tornadoes? I'm not sure I get it. I mean, you're pursuing things that kill people, things you can't kill in return."

"So how is that any different from what you're doing, Agent Mederios?"

"It's my job."

"Once upon a time, I had a job chasing storms."

"I know. But give me a more 'from-the-gut' answer. What's the attraction in chasing?"

"It's different for different people, I suppose. For some, it's just the thrill of the chase, Belling the Cat—being able to look into the eyes, so to speak, of one of the most powerful forces on earth. For others, it's seeing beauty in fury, like a perfectly symmetric supercell with a wall cloud that looks like an alien spacecraft. Chasers call it a 'mothership'." He glanced at Gabi. "Maybe you've seen photos. So flawless and spectacular they looked like they've been photoshopped."

She shook her head. She'd never really been attracted to severe weather.

"There are a few people," Chuck continued, "from universities, for instance, who pursue storms for research purposes. Trying to position radars to look into the bowels of a tornado, or attempting to place instrument packages in the direct path of a twister . . . like Mountain Men setting trap lines."

"Anybody actually make a living chasing storms?" Gabi asked, then, considering Chuck's legacy, wished she hadn't. "I mean, you know, besides leading tours?"

Stormy, from the rear seat, stuck her nose over the center console and licked Chuck's elbow. He petted her and answered Gabi's question.

"Beyond the tour business? No, probably not. There are guys who supplement their income by selling videos and photos to TV stations and stock agencies, but with the exception of one or two, it probably doesn't pay the freight."

"There was a movie about tornado chasing a while back—"

"*Twister.* 1996. Flying cows and all that bullshit."

"Yeah. Did that do much for the tour business?" She hoped she wasn't rubbing salt into an open wound.

Chuck didn't seem to mind. "Initially it did. But people, except for hard core chasers—those really enamored by big storms—soon discovered that reality and Hollywood's take on it didn't mesh. Chasing, as you've found out, is mostly sitting on your butt in a vehicle for hours on end, gagging down fast food, and then standing around like lost souls in purgatory waiting for something to happen."

"Amen, brother."

"But the payoff can be spectacular."

Gabi wondered if he was referencing the million bucks or something more esoteric. "So what motivated you, in the beginning, to chase twisters? Certainly it wasn't money, at least initially."

"With me, I guess it's a combination of the chase and being able to poke a finger in the eye of something akin to the Grim Reaper."

He sped up as they left Oklahoma City, heading northeast on the Turner Turnpike, then continued with his answer to Gabi's question. "I love the chase, and I'm not talking about just the tactical pursuit. I crave the strategic challenge, too, trying to figure out where to lie in wait for the prey, the supercells. It's a cat and mouse game against Mother Nature, or maybe God."

"God?"

Chuck, in a stentorian voice said, "Who cuts a channel for the torrents of rain, and a path for the thunderstorm . . . ?"

"Bible?"

"Job 38:25. So yes, God, if you're a fundamentalist. I'm not. I don't see God's directing hand in every storm. To me, it's more like standing in His test tube and watching His laws of physics and thermodynamics at work. It's at once humbling and awe-inspiring." He moved his gaze off the highway for a moment and looked at Gabi, a light of excitement in his eyes, as though he were a child again.

He turned his attention back to road. "Just imagine," he said, "watching a puff of fluffy cumulus grow into a monster. It starts as a thermal, an invisible updraft rising in the afternoon heat but cooling as it rises, eventually squeezing out whatever moisture it bears into a cloud.

"The cloud grows, billowing upward, expanding, churning, responding to its environment, sucking more heat and moisture into what's become an engine, an atmospheric motor of immense horsepower." Chuck stared straight ahead, appearing to become lost in his words.

He went on: "It seems suddenly alive: fierce, majestic, potentially deadly, yet with a structure—a personality, if you will—that's understandable and approachable. It allows you to stand next to it until it morphs into something more violent, something that chases you away with blasts of wind and spears of lightning . . ." His voice trailed off and Gabi sensed he was somewhere else.

She waited a while and then asked, "You still with us?"

He answered her, almost in a whisper. "I've seen 'the storehouses of the hail' and 'the place where the lightning is dispersed'."

"Job again?" she ventured.

He nodded, almost imperceptibly. "From a story 4000 years old." He seemed to drift away again. "No. No. It's only ten years old. I know. I was there."

Chapter Sixteen

SUNDAY, MAY 5

THE CHASE TEAM had spent Saturday in Tulsa and used the time for personal pursuits. Ziggy, Nosher, Boomie, and Willie Weston rented clubs at a nearby golf course and played eighteen, Gabi and the two women working with Global-American toured the Tulsa Garden Center, while Ty and Chuck hung around the motel. Metcalf mostly bitched, proclaiming Tulsa the tedium capital of the world.

After discovering the city was originally part of Indian Territory, he suggested giving it back to them and letting them turn the town into a giant casino. "At least there'd be something to do," he groused, "and it might even attract some decent pussy."

Now, on Sunday, Chuck vectored the team northward into eastern Nebraska, leading the small caravan through green rolling farm country speckled with evergreens and oaks. Tidy small towns, the kind that once might have graced Norman Rockwell paintings, greeted them at regular intervals. Homes with front porches and rocking chairs, small churches advertising potluck suppers, and Dairy Queens with full parking lots proclaimed Middle America.

Chuck took only cursory notice, however. His mind was on the following two days. Even though the chase was only at its halfway point, he knew full well Monday and Tuesday probably would present the last viable opportunities to catch what Metcalf and his cinematographers were after. Beyond that, it appeared the next chance wouldn't materialize until the following Sunday at the earliest. By then, Chuck's coach would have turned into a pumpkin, his dreams of a million dollars into the unrequited fantasy of a middle-aged loser.

The Storm Prediction Center had already defined an area of "moderate risk" for tomorrow, meaning there would be a good chance of seeing tornadoes, though being in the right place at the right time would be, as always, the real challenge. The region outlined encompassed central and eastern Nebraska and eastern South Dakota. Chuck planned on overnighting near Lincoln, Nebraska, then launching from there in the morning.

MONDAY, MAY 6

THOUGH EARLY, pillars of clouds towering into a hazy morning sky suggested extreme instability and the promise of thunderstorms to come. A busy southerly breeze, clammy with humidity, bore a strange amalgam of odors: spring wildflowers and *ordure de cow*. Stormy, nose to the ground and running a zig-zag course in a field adjacent to the motel where the team had spent the night, appeared in hot pursuit of a good spot to deposit her own *ordure*.

In the motel's parking lot, Chuck placed his laptop on the hood of his SUV and pulled up a roadmap of Nebraska. Metcalf and his crew gathered around it along with Ty and Gabi.

"We're here," Chuck said, pointing to Lincoln. "A squall line is expected to form later today west of here—" he moved his finger over the map until it reached the town of Lexington near the Platte River "—and punch eastward."

A gust of wind deposited a sheen of dust on the computer's screen. Chuck brushed it off and continued. "Our best chance to corner a supercell with a tornado will be just after the line starts to develop, when the cells are still discrete."

"Discreet cells, Chuckie?" Metcalf said, his eyes red and clothes rumpled, perhaps from a late night of partying, "Who woulda thunk. I was led to believe we were after storms behaving badly." He laughed, burbled really, at his own lame play on words.

"As a matter of fact, my bleary-eyed friend," Chuck responded, "that's the optimal time to catch 'storms behaving badly,' when they're still discrete, spelled with an e-t-e. For those of you interested in the science—"

"I'm interested in the cinematography, not the science," Metcalf interjected, his words muffled by a soft burp.

"Go on about the science," the cameraman, Boomie, said, ignoring his boss. "Maybe it'll help me when we're filming." Squat and powerfully built, Boomie sported the incongruence of a buzz cut in combination with a short, pointed goatee. Both bleached blond.

Chuck nodded, glad to have an ally within Metcalf's ranks. He made a mental note to ask Boomie about his name sometime. He wondered if the guy had been a boom operator of some sort in the past.

"So here's the deal," Chuck said, "when a line of storms is just beginning to form and the cells are relatively isolated, that is, before they merge into a more or less solid line and don't have to compete with other storms for the nourishment they need to grow—you know, things like heat, moisture, spin—"

"Helicity!" Gabi said, raising her hand like a kid in school and simultaneously playing the ever-energized magazine reporter.

"Yes, helicity. Gold star for you," Chuck responded. "Anyhow, discrete cells—" he glared at Metcalf "—have all that stuff to themselves without having to share it with a bunch of wannabes. Bingo! That's when they have that magic moment when they can explode into real monsters, the things we're hunting, tornadic supercells."

"So," Boomie said, "we wanna keep our eyes on the lone wolves, the outsiders, so to speak?"

"Maybe you should be boss-man," Chuck said, folding his laptop.

Metcalf stomped away. "Maybe you should pontificate a little less and actually *do* a little more, like finding us a goddamn tornado."

MID-AFTERNOON. The small caravan paused on the shoulder of a road just north of Holdrege in the Platte River Valley. Thunder from a storm about 25 miles southwest grumbled over the square-gridded farm country, much of it freshly planted in what Chuck assumed to be corn or soybeans.

Chuck studied the radar image of the storm on his laptop. Gabi, from the passenger seat, leaned over the computer. Ty scooted forward in the back seat to peer at the image.

"See this?" Chuck said. His finger rested on an appendage protruding from the lower left corner of the storm's brightly-colored radar return. "That, my friends, could be the beginning of what's called a hook echo. When you see one of those form, it's a classic sign of a tornado. Doesn't always verify, but it's a big, fat canary gasping for breath in a coal mine."

The screen refreshed and an electronically generated white line appeared, extending from the appendage toward a position on the computer map near where the vehicles waited. Several short bars, evenly spaced along the longer line, crossed it at right angles. Chuck moved the laptop's cursor over the white line and clicked on it. Times appeared near each cross bar. He studied them for a moment, then stepped from the SUV and walked to where Metcalf and his crew waited. His heart rate accelerated ever so slightly.

"We're going to move about a mile north," he said. "That'll put us just south of the supercell that's headed this way, ETA 40 minutes. That should give you guys time to get the crane and camera deployed. Then we'll hope for the best . . . or worst."

Metcalf studied the southwest horizon, now obsidian in roiling clouds. "Looks nasty," he said. "Death and destruction. I love it." He turned to Boomie. "Let's get truckin'. Get the Genesis up as fast as you can when bwana gets us in position. Maybe we can get what we need and get off these Godforsaken plains back to civilization before I lose my mind."

Boomie nodded and clambered into the camera truck's cab.

A pair of vans, antennae sprouting from their roofs—and on one, an anemometer—raced past heading north. The driver of the lead van waved and gave a friendly toot on his horn as he shot by.

"Chasers," Chuck said. "Let's get going before the roads get clogged."

"Out here?" Metcalf said, unable to hide his amazement.

"You'd be surprised. Supercells attract chasers like moths to a candle."

Metcalf rolled his eyes and climbed into the Navigator, a vehicle Chuck had begun to think of as the "Blustermobile."

They drove north for about five minutes and halted on a low rise, pulling off the road next to the gated entrance of a freshly cultivated field. Boomie and Ziggy went to work as soon as the camera truck rolled to a stop. With help from Nosher, they secured the Genesis to the end of the crane, then elevated the crane above the truck to a point where the camera, its sweep unencumbered by utility poles and wires, had a panoramic view of the approaching storm.

Ziggy maneuvered the crane using controls mounted on the truck bed. Boomie, seated in a chair affixed to the base of the crane, operated the camera remotely, his gaze locked on a small monitor mounted next to him.

Metcalf and his second unit director, Willie Weston, stood on a platform over the cab. Willie scanned the darkening sky with a pair of binoculars, tracking the approach of the supercell. Metcalf, trying to appear officious, shouted orders to Boomie, who largely ignored them. Chuck guessed that Boomie probably had a lot more experience operating cameras than Metcalf and didn't need any "guidance." Finally,

Metcalf gave up trying to direct Boomie and turned his attention to Chuck.

"How much longer, Chaz? Is this thing still comin'?"

"It's almost on top of us. We may have to pursue it if it doesn't drop a tornado right away."

The wind, blowing toward the storm, had grown noticeably stronger, lifting dirt from surrounding fields and stirring it into a ground blizzard of dust. Overhead, an arc of ragged clouds, black as death, marked the leading edge of the supercell's wall cloud. It came on steadily, almost touching the earth, spinning over the flat plain of the valley on a gyroscopic track toward the Platte River.

Chuck searched the base of the inky, low hanging mass for the telltale pendant that would announce the birth of a funnel aloft, the embryo of a tornado. "Come on, come on," he muttered out loud, his words lost in the howl of the wind.

Stormy, standing at his feet, growled.

Then it was there. A tiny wedge of darkness hanging from the base of the wall cloud. Seconds later it morphed into a distinct funnel, its tail whipping back and forth like a demented sting ray's. Chuck spun to look at the camera; Boomie had it pointed at the funnel, tracking the incipient twister with a steady hand.

The whirling blackness, a mere two or three hundred yards distant, edged lower and lower. A twisting spiral of dirt appeared beneath the funnel. "Go, go, go," Chuck yelled at the melee. It did, blossoming into a full-fledged tornado as the fertile Nebraska soil exploded around it

Metcalf, on top of the cab, held onto his cap with one hand while clapping Willie on the back with the other. Yet Willie seemed less than excited. Chuck knew why. Yes, they had a tornado. Up close and personal. But not exactly an EF-4 or -5. The twister churned past, heading toward the river.

Willie called to Chuck: "We goin' after it?"

Chuck held his gaze on the twister, wishing it toward adulthood as it spun by. Like a stubborn child, however, it refused to mature, clinging to its ropy adolescence. He ducked back into the Expedition, checked the radar, didn't see any other immediate targets.

"Okay," he yelled back to Willie, "let's go. We'll try to jump ahead of the storm, reposition and redeploy." He studied the track of the storm against the map on his computer, doing calculations in his head, while Boomie and Ziggy retracted the crane, dismounted the Genesis, and made certain everything was stowed securely. Chuck glanced up to find Metcalf standing next to the SUV.

"Ya know, Buffalo Bill," Metcalf said, "this would have been a whole lot easier if we'd had two trucks. We could've leapfrogged ahead of the storm with one truck moving while the other filmed. But noooo . . ." He walked away.

Chuck resisted the urge to give him the finger. Mainly because Metcalf was right. Two trucks would have made a difference. With only one, every time they wanted to move they'd lose time, breaking down the equipment, stowing it, driving, then setting everything up again.

Boomie signaled he was ready to go. Chuck called him on his cell phone. "We'll drive north until we find an east-west road that intersects a route that'll take us across the Platte. There're only a few highways that have bridges. Then we'll jump on I-80, east to Gibbon, turn north again and try to interdict the cell somewhere west of Grand Island."

"Roger that," Boomie said. Military lingo. "How's the storm lookin'?"

"It's holding together. Hook echo disappeared, but the cell's probably just cycling. I think it'll come back. Still tracking northeast."

"Let's light the afterburners."

"We're off," Chuck responded.

Forty-five minutes later they again pulled off the road on a low rise, but this time in dry grassland about 30 miles west of Grand Island.

Chuck quickly scanned the radar image of the storm before getting out of the Expedition. He walked back to where Boomie and his cohorts were already preparing to redeploy the crane and camera. "You've got about 15 minutes," Chuck said.

"No sweat," Boomie said. "We'll be ready."

A battered pickup truck stopped on the road next to the camera truck. The driver, a wrinkled, sun-reddened farmer, rolled down his window and surveyed the scene. "Guys makin' a movie?" he asked.

"Hoping to get some footage of a tornado," Boomie said.

"Yeah?"

"Yeah."

"Well, probably will." The rancher studied the darkening, lowering clouds, the wind-flattened grass, the lightning pulsing in the blackness layering the horizon. "But not a big one." He nodded, rolled up his window and proceeded along the road.

Chuck, hands on hips, watched him depart. *Thanks for the encouragement.*

"Not a big one, huh?" Metcalf said as he walked toward the camera rig. He didn't wait for an answer.

"So what's a farmer know anyhow?" Gabi asked. Stormy stood next to her, nose jabbed into the wind.

"Sometimes, I hate to admit, quite a bit," Chuck responded. "I've learned a few of these old codgers, guys who've spent their entire life on the Plains, are strangely savvy when it comes to storms. They've lived and died, financially speaking, by the weather for decades."

"So Farmer-Boy Bob can out-forecast the Great White Tornado Hunter?" Ty, who'd joined the conversation, said. He grinned, suggesting it was a lighthearted throwaway line but Chuck knew it was also meant as just another little needle for dear ol' Dad.

Chuck smiled. "We'll see." What else could he say?

Gabi started to speak to Ty, but he raised his hand as if to ward off her words and walked away.

"Don't let the bastards get you down," she whispered to Chuck.

"Too late," he said. He needed a victory, a smash-mouth tornado, to fill the hollow spots that Metcalf and Ty, and even himself, had carved out of his psyche.

"Wall cloud," Boomie called from the camera rig.

Chuck looked to where he pointed. "Yeah, you got it. Track it." Black scud raced beneath the angry-looking cloud rotating a mere step-ladder's reach above the rolling fields. Darkness enveloped the land as if a burial shroud had been drawn over it, or a vengeful pagan god had swallowed the sun. The wind howled, filling the air with loess of glacial ages past.

Boomie panned the Genesis with a steady hand as the spinning bulwark of clouds approached. Still, no funnel appeared.

"There!" Metcalf yelled from his position atop the truck's cab. "Tornado!"

Dirt exploded from a field across the road, filling the gap between earth and cloud. It expanded, yanking a wheeled pivot-irrigation rig into the air. Metcalf's cap flew off, disappearing into the airborne whirlpool. The twister, in an eardrum-shattering roar, churned across the road in front of the parked caravan.

Chuck and Gabi struggled to remain upright in the wind. Stormy, issuing throaty growls, paced a nervous circle around their feet.

Boomie continued to follow the tornado with the boom-mounted camera while Ziggy operated the hydraulic lift for the crane.

Metcalf called out to Chuck, but Chuck couldn't make out the words over the bellow of the wind. He, Gabi, and Stormy crouched near the hood of the Expedition, watching the twister. Ty remained with the cinematography team, huddled near the camera rig.

Then, as quickly as the tornado had materialized, it disappeared, retreating into the parent wall cloud as if lifted by an unseen hand. An alien snatched home by a mothership. For a few brief moments, the only evidence it had existed was a thin ebony tail hanging from the sky. Shortly, even that was gone.

Chuck and Gabi stood.

"Well?" she said.

He shook his head. "Not good enough. Damn. Nowhere near even a four." A long, low-decibel rumble of thunder bounced across the plain.

Metcalf appeared beside them. "Nice try, Chuckie. But it looks like the old farmer guy bested you in that round. 'Not a big one,' he said. It wasn't, was it?"

"No."

"Must feel good to have a Nebraska redneck shit all over your *CV*."

"Maybe you should've hired a farmer," Chuck snapped.

"Maybe. But somebody told me you were the best. Lesson learned: don't believe everything you hear."

"You knew going in there were no guarantees. That the odds were against us finding a violent tornado from the get-go."

"I'm from Hollywood. I believe in magic. Movie magic. I just didn't know I was going to end up with Dumbo."

"Dumbo could fly," Gabi interjected.

"Yeah, I know," Metcalf responded. "But my Dumbo crashes and burns. He needs flying lessons." Metcalf patted the top of his head. "You don't suppose I can find a Greek fisherman's cap in Nebraska, do you?"

Chuck inhaled slowly, deeply, and watched the departing supercell. After a moment, he stuck his head into the SUV and studied the radar imagery. "The storm's collapsing," he announced. "And I don't see anything else worth pursuing." A glint of sunshine broke through the clouds to the west.

Metcalf, arms folded across his chest, focused his gaze on Chuck. "Well, at least you found us a tornado today. My hat's off to you for that." He paused, as though waiting for a chuckle. None came.

He shrugged and continued. "But I still want, Godzilla . . . I still *need* Godzilla—an on-screen twister that's so damn terrifying theaters will have to offer movie goers new underwear and deodorant after they've viewed it. That's why I'm dangling that million-dollar carrot in front of you. Giddy-up, Chuckie."

"Yeah, giddy-up," he responded, knowing full well that the hopelessness he harbored within himself resonated in his voice. Regardless of the fact there was almost a week of contractual time remaining, the opportunity clock, for all practical purposes, was one tick from midnight.

Tomorrow would be the make or break day.

Chapter Seventeen

TUESDAY, MAY 7

THE TEAM overnighted near Lincoln again. But sleep eluded Chuck. He finally surrendered to his insomnia and arose shortly after 4 a.m. Stormy lifted her head from where she slept at the foot of the bed, stared briefly at Chuck, then plopped her head back on the floor and closed her eyes.

Chuck flipped open his laptop computer and went to work studying the meteorological setup for the day's chase. The Storm Prediction Center has posted another moderate risk for severe storms, similar to yesterday, but this time for the eastern Dakotas and western Minnesota. The discussion from SPC even suggested the possibility of a long-track tornado or two. Chuck examined the forecast parameters and concurred with that assessment.

A long-lived supercell was what he needed: a thermodynamic brute that could be pursued for miles across the open prairies of the Great Plains. A storm whose very nature would dictate it would eventually spit out a twister, maybe two or three or a dozen, over its life span. Not only that, but such cells were often the ones that ended up harboring the most violent of tornadoes, the EF-4s and -5s.

He hadn't been chasing during that awful year of 2011, but he remembered well the tales of those stalking what became known later as the Joplin Supercell. The storm blew up over southeast Kansas. For three hours, chasers tracked it toward Joplin, until it finally dropped a twister along the Kansas-Missouri border just southwest of the city. Within five minutes, the tornado had morphed into a killer, a coal-black, mile-wide wedge devouring both buildings and people.

More than a few chasers broke traffic laws that day, running red lights and making illegal U-turns over traffic medians, to escape the violence that was in the process of leveling a modern American city. Others, as though tracking the bloody spoor of a wounded animal, followed in its wake, pulling wounded souls from debris, tallying the dead and breaking down in tears of emotion. They had become part and parcel of the single deadliest tornado in over half a century.

Earlier that year, a multi-day tornado outbreak claimed more lives than any siege since the 1930s as swarms of twisters raked through the South. One supercell, Chuck recalled, traveled over 400 miles from Mississippi to western North Carolina. During its eight-hour search-and- destroy life span, it spit out at least a half-dozen tornadoes. One of them, a massive EF-4, churned through both Tuscaloosa and Birmingham on an 80-mile-long blitzkrieg.

He didn't wish death and destruction on anyone, but he needed to corner a supercell with the DNA of the beast that had churned through the Deep South. But he wanted it to be on the Great Plains in a non-target-rich environment.

Chuck stood, walked to the window and pulled back the curtains. Still dark outside. Dense fog hung in the air, creating fuzzy yellow-orange coronae around the security lights in the parking lot. He shuffled into the bathroom, read the instructions on the Keurig coffeemaker, and brewed himself a cup of Paul Newman Something or Other. Cup in hand, he sat back down at the table and noodled on the laptop, letting his thoughts run.

There was, of course, the notion of scoring a million bucks. At the outset, it had seemed remotely possible. The pot of gold at the end of a rainbow. But, like rainbows in nature, his retreated with each step he seemed to draw nearer to it. Now, it had almost faded away. A sunshine daydream. Somehow, it never had seemed real. And he found solace in the notion you can't lose what you never had.

The opportunity he dreaded losing even more—even more than raking in the chips for a once-in-a-lifetime payday—was being able to poke a hole in that Hindenburg of a gasbag from Hollywood, Jerry Metcalf. Just to be able stuff a sock in the guy's mouth if they were able to actually film an EF-4 or -5 would be worth a million dollars.

Well, not really. But at least metaphorically.

And then there was Ty. Nothing on this expedition appeared to be working out like Chuck, had envisioned. He had to admit, though, his visions were probably Pollyannaish. The troubled waters between him and his son were wider and deeper than he'd imagined. *A Bridge Over Troubled Waters?* So far he'd been unable to erect even the piers for a bridge, let alone the superstructure of one. In truth, he probably shouldn't even be thinking of a bridge. He'd likely be better off planning some sort of sneaky, amphibious assault, just to establish a beachhead in Ty's life, recapture a tiny bit of lost territory. He hadn't a clue how to do that, however. *Why does everything have to be so fucking difficult?*

He tipped the coffee cup to his lips, hoping to drain the last quarter-inch of Paul Newman from it. Instead of channeling into his mouth, however, the now-lukewarm coffee dribbled onto his laptop. "Shit!"

Stormy bounced up, whimpered, looked around.

"Sorry, girl," Chuck said. He wiped the computer dry with a T-shirt. "Let me get dressed and I'll take you out."

Stormy, stiff legged and stretching, made her way to the door and sat and waited.

GABI, YAWNING, found a pot of fresh coffee in the motel lobby. She filled a cup and walked outside. Mist blanketed the dawning day. At the far end of the parking lot she spotted a figure walking a dog along a grassy fringe. Chuck and Stormy, more than likely.

She moved toward them. The dog stopped, raised its head and yipped as she approached, a friendly greeting.

"Hey, Storms, what's up?" she said.

Chuck turned toward her and spotted the coffee in her hand. "Oh, hi. I thought maybe you were room service come to the rescue," he said. His lightheartedness seemed forced.

"I can get you a cup if you'd like." She petted Stormy with her free hand.

"Already brewed some in my room."

"So, are you always an early riser, or just worried about today?"

"Among other things, there's a million dollars at stake."

"And you really think this will be your last hurrah?"

A diesel engine rattled to life somewhere in the morning murk.

"Not only mine," Chuck said, "yours, too. If we don't find our dragon today, then we've both lost. There won't be another major threat until early next week. After that, the game is over."

There seemed a note of resignation in his voice, as though a shutout were a *fait accompli.*

"Don't worry about me," she said, "my hunt isn't on the clock. Look, enough of this oh-woe-is-me shit. You did a good job getting us in position yesterday. It wasn't the big score we needed, but you did your part—"

"That's the problem. I can do just so much, then it's up to luck. And I haven't exactly been walking through fields of four-leaf clovers lately."

Gabi drew a deep breath, drawing in the moisture-laden air, the faint odor of pancakes on a griddle somewhere nearby, the smell of damp earth. She stepped closer to Chuck. "Luck, someone wise once said, is the residue of design."

"I'll bet it wasn't Wile E. Coyote."

"Will you stop it," Gabi said, maybe a bit too sharply. She immediately regretted her tone.

"Can't help it. I've had too many damn Acme safes fall on my head."

She grabbed Chuck's wrist, a move that surprised herself. "Well BFD. So have a lot of people. I know you've had a ton of shit dumped on you. I know you've been beat down. I know the chase got off to a rocky start. But what the hell, Chuck, it isn't over. And in case you've forgotten, you weren't picked for this job because you're a loser."

They stood face to face, inches apart. He merely stared at her, not responding, not offering a defense. Her heart hammered. She'd overstepped her bounds. Gotten too personal. But there was something about him, beyond his maddening passivity, that incited her to challenge him—to, in cruder terms, jam a firecracker up his ass. Why? For a fleeting moment, she was terrified. Not of Chuck. Of herself, of what she'd let happen. Of what she was afraid to admit. That she saw within him a decent man who'd been trampled by life, who deep down was strong, who at his core possessed integrity. In other words, a man worth making a commitment to. She released his wrist.

Neither, however, backed away from the other. His gaze remained fixed on hers. She attempted to read what lay behind his eyes—what he thought, what his emotions were . . . how he *felt* about her. Her breathing became slightly spastic. Did he notice?

She stepped back. "Sorry," she mumbled. "That was out of line." She looked away from him, into the fog.

He remained silent.

Stormy sat at their feet, her gaze moving from Chuck to Gabi, from Gabi to Chuck.

Well, this is awkward. "So," she asked, electing to alter the course of the conversation, or at least her monologue, "have you ever played 'what if' with the million dollars? I mean, thought about what would you do with it if you actually got it?"

Chuck cleared his throat. "No, not really." He paused. "Well, some obvious things. Get a car. Upgrade my digs." Again, he paused. "Help Ty."

The morning had brightened, the mist morphing from a wooly gray to burnished platinum. Gabi and Chuck headed back toward the motel.

"What happened between you two," she asked, "between you and your son?" *Careful*, she admonished herself.

He walked several steps before answering. "I guess we just view the world differently."

"What the hell does that mean?"

"Let's not go there. It's something between me and him."

"It might help to talk about it. Air some things out. I'm a good listener. Maybe I could find some common—"

"You can't," he snapped. "What's with this camp counselor routine anyhow? First you're giving me the 'old college try' pep talk. Then you come up with some cockamamie notion you can fix a relationship that's not just broken, it's been shattered by a head-on collision."

"I didn't say I could *fix* anything. All I said was it might help to talk about it." The words came out snippy, like she meant them to.

"It hasn't helped yet."

She looked away from Chuck and rolled her eyes. "That's because you're talking directly to each other. You need a mediator. A neutral party."

"No, I need a son who will admit he's wrong. Who will change his act." A sheen of anger coated his voice.

"What act?"

"Jesus. Let it go." They reached the entrance to the motel. He opened the door for her. "How about some breakfast?"

"No," she said. "What time do we push off?"

"Ten."

"See you at ten." She walked toward the elevator, then stopped and pivoted. "You want Ty to, as you put, change his act. He pisses you off. I understand that. Yet at the same time, you feel you owe him something. I don't get it." The elevator door slid open. Gabi stepped in. The door began to shut. She extended her arm to stop it. "I don't think you do, either."

METCALF, STANDING beside his SUV with Chuck and Gabi, took stock of the surrounding landscape. "This is flatter than fu—friggin'—Kansas," he said, then grinned sheepishly at Gabi. "Where in the hell are we?"

"About 50 miles northwest of Yankton," Chuck said.

"Jesus. We're in Canada?"

"South Dakota."

"Wherever. At least it still looks like Oklahoma. Without trees."

"There're trees," Gabi said.

"They look like accidents," Metcalf countered.

"Let's get moving," Chuck said. He pointed at a towering mass of clouds, a burgeoning supercell, to the north. "We're going after that."

Metcalf looked around. Another huge supercell, its cauliflowered top anviled out toward Minnesota, bubbled skyward to their southwest. "What about that one?" he asked.

"I checked them both," Chuck said. "The one to the north is showing better rotation right now. And it's moving into an environment that's rich in helicity, CAPE and—"

"Mumbo jumbo," Metcalf interrupted. "It's all witchcraft to me. But I gotta trust ya, Chaz." He motioned for the camera truck to start up. "Okay, the native beaters are ready, let's go."

With the country roads partitioning the ironing-board-flat farmland into neat squares, staying out in front of the supercell proved easy. Chuck led the short caravan on a zig-zag course, east then north, east then north, repeated over and over as the storm churned toward the northeast. The team shared the roads with a least a dozen other chase vehicles in pursuit of the same cell.

Metcalf called Chuck on his cell phone. "Gettin' crowded out here," Metcalf said.

"Everybody thinks this is the Big Kahuna."

"Yeah, but is it gonna drop a tornado?"

Chuck wouldn't admit it to Metcalf, but he was beginning to harbor doubts. The wall cloud had spun out a couple of nice-looking funnels, but nothing touching the ground. Meanwhile, the southern cell appeared to be growing healthier, at least on the radar returns. "Let's stick with it," Chuck said. "It's still got a lot going for it."

"Yo da boss-man," Metcalf responded, and killed the call.

Several of the other chasers suddenly raced past Chuck's contingent, heading in the opposite direction, toward the southern supercell.

"Where are they going?" Gabi asked.

"They've thrown in the towel on this one," Chuck answered. "They're betting on the big boy down south now."

"So what are you gonna do, fearless leader?" Ty asked from the back seat.

Another chase vehicle sped by, barreling south.

Chuck slowed the Expedition, pulled to the side of the road. He studied the radar imagery of the two storms. The northern supercell still showed good rotation, but the southern one now seemed on the verge of developing a hook, the classic radar signature of a tornado. He ran the pros and cons in his mind. They were on the northern cell, glued to it like a Pointer on a pheasant. He hated to abandon it, knowing if he did, Murphy's Law would undoubtedly come into play.

While the southern storm now appeared the more robust of the two, it would take them at least an hour to get into position to safely interdict it, and there were no guarantees it would still be a viable target then. *A bird in hand . . .*

Chuck turned toward Ty. "We're gonna dance with the one what brung us," he said.

Ty sighed theatrically and sat back. "Nothing like a little corn-fed wisdom to make a million-dollar decision," he said.

"What would *you* do?" Gabi asked, her tone less than conversational.

Chuck reached over and touched her arm. A friendly "back off" gesture. He didn't need Gabi rushing to his defense.

"I'm not the one bearing the load," Ty said. "But sometimes—" he nodded toward the SUV's window as two more chase cars zoomed by, southward bound "—it makes sense to go with the preponderance of evidence. Or in this case, actions."

Chuck glanced in his rearview mirror. Metcalf's SUV and the camera truck had pulled off the road behind him. He saw Metcalf talking animatedly on his cell phone, obviously not to him. To Metcalf's bosses in Hollywood? To Boomie in the camera rig? Chuck stepped out of the Expedition and walked toward Metcalf.

Metcalf waved him off, pulled the Navigator onto the road, made a U-turn and signaled for Boomie to follow.

Chucked dashed back to his vehicle.

"What the hell is going on?" Gabi asked.

Ty, looking at the departing vehicles through the rear window, answered, "Insurrection."

Chapter Eighteen

TUESDAY, MAY 7

BY THE TIME Chuck got the Expedition turned around, Metcalf's Lincoln and the camera rig had a good half-mile lead on him. "Call Metcalf," Chuck said, handing his cell phone to Gabi. She punched in the number and gave the phone back to him.

"What in the hell are you doing, Jerry?" Chuck barked when Metcalf answered.

"Finding us a tornado. Something you haven't delivered on, *jefe*."

"We had a really nice supercell in our crosshairs."

"Yeah? Well maybe it was too nice. We tracked it for two friggin' hours and it didn't do a damn thing. Now you wanna beat a dead horse while the rest of the chasers gallop off to greener pastures."

"You don't know that."

"Know what?"

"That they're heading for greener pastures." Chuck put a bit more pressure on the accelerator pedal.

"I'm sticking with the majority, Charlie. Somebody in this 'Land That Time Left Behind' must know what they're doing."

"In case you missed it, Mr. Hollywood, the majority, as you call it, cast its lot with the northern supercell just like us. Now you're gonna follow the lemmings over a cliff?"

"You're assuming it's a cliff."

"I'm not assuming anything. I'm telling you it's a bone-headed idea. Even if the southern storm drops a tornado, you're out of position to catch it." The Expedition hit a pot hole and jounced hard. Chuck fought the steering wheel to hold the vehicle on a straight course.

"I've got the radio on, Chuckie. A tornado warning's just been issued for the next county south. We're gonna get that sucker."

Chuck called up the warning overlay on his computer. Metcalf was right. A tornado warning had been posted for the cell to the south, its radar echo now displaying a prominent hook. He muted the phone. "Deliver me from drunks and movie people," he said, shaking his head.

Gabi chuckled. She seemed to be enjoying Chuck's sudden display of ire. Even Ty issued a brief snort, though Chuck didn't know how to interpret it. Support for him, or Metcalf's rebellion?

Chuck un-muted the phone. "Jerry, damn you. Wait for me. Don't try to intercept that storm on your own."

"We'll follow the other chasers."

"You won't be able to keep up with them." Chuck cast a glance at the radar image again. No question the cell had morphed into a nasty storm. The hook echo, hard evidence of a twister, appeared to be arcing toward the center of the storm. Metcalf had no idea how much danger he was about to blunder into.

"Listen to me," Chuck yelled into the phone. "The twister's becoming rain-wrapped. You'll never see it 'til it's on you. It's too damn dangerous to chase without radar. Wait—"

"Look out!" Gabi screamed.

Chuck hadn't seen it, hadn't been alert. A tractor pulling onto the road in his lane. He jerked the SUV's steering wheel to the left. Stood on the brakes. The tractor veered right. The Expedition shot past it, crossed the center line, careened onto the opposite shoulder, smacked into a barbed wire fence post.

Chuck, Gabi, and Ty, uninjured, scrambled from the SUV and examined the damage: a crumpled left front fender. The tractor driver, a sunburnt farmer wearing a John Deere ball cap, ran to where they stood. "Everyone okay?" he asked, breathless.

"We're fine," Chuck said. "Sorry, my fault. Didn't see you."

The farmer surveyed the situation. His gaze fell on the Expedition's antennae, the darkening sky to the south. "Tornado chasers?" he asked.

"Yeah."

The farmer shook his head, a barely perceptible movement. Tacit disapproval. "Well," he said, "let's see if we can get you back on the road."

The bent metal of the fender rested against the tire. "Need to pull that away," the farmer noted. "I've got some gloves on the tractor. Hold on." He retrieved them and returned. Ty found a towel in the Expedition and wrapped it around his hands. Together, he and the tractor operator pulled the metal off the Michelin.

After they finished, the farmer placed his hands on his hips and took stock of the result. "Still looks ugly," he proclaimed, "but you'll be able to drive without shredding the tire."

Chuck thanked him profusely.

The farmer nodded, slapped his gloves together, and jammed them into the back pocket of his jeans. "You folks be safe now. Lotta tractors, combines, and pokey pickups use these roads." A friendly warning, a stern undertone. He smiled, touched the brim of his cap, and walked back to his tractor.

Chuck cranked up the Expedition and took off in pursuit of the renegade chasers. "Call Metcalf again," he said to Gabi. She made the call and handed the phone to Chuck.

"Hey, what happened to you guys?" Metcalf asked. "We were talking, I heard someone yell, then nothing."

"Almost hit a Deere," Chuck said.

"In broad daylight? Well, shit. Better than a buffalo, I guess. You all right?"

"We're fine. Where are you?"

"How in the hell should I know. Everyplace out here looks the same."

"There must be something around. A sign. A crossroads. A landmark of some sort."

"No—wait, hold on. We're coming into some kind of a little hick town."

"What's it called?"

"Hicksville."

"Come on, Jerry."

"There aren't any signs."

"Ask someone."

"Don't see anybody. I'm guessin' no one lives here."

"Jerry!"

"It's South Dakota. Nobody lives anyplace here."

"Look for a water tower. There's usually a water tower in these little towns. It'll have a name on it."

Chuck heard Metcalf conversing with someone in his Lincoln, one of the women on the Global-American crew, Julie or Jolie or something like that.

"We got it, Chuckie," Metcalf said, "a water tower. We're in, well, just passed through, Rippington."

Chuck glanced at the map on his computer. "Wait for us," he said.

"No can do, Charlie. We're gonna bag this baby."

"Wait, damn it!"

Metcalf broke the connection.

"Shit. He's got a ten-mile lead on us now and he's on a collision course with a supercell. Only, he doesn't know it." Then under his breath, but not quite, "Fucking moron."

"Yea, verily," Gabi said. "What do we do?"

Ty leaned forward and rested his arm on the back of Chuck's seat. He didn't say anything, just hung there, apparently waiting for Chuck to come up with a brilliant Plan B. Stormy, oblivious to all, snoozed on the seat beside Ty.

"Head 'em off at the pass," Chuck said. At the next intersection he turned left, pressed the accelerator to the floor, and swept eastward.

Gabi tensed. "Please let there be no more tractors," she muttered.

Ty seemed unfazed. "So what's the plan, John Wayne?"

Chuck focused on the road, shifting his gaze from one shoulder to the other, watching for cross traffic . . . for combines and tractors. He didn't even glance at the speedometer. He knew he was breaking the speed limit—one of those "yahoo" chasers the storm-chasing community abhors. But this could be a matter of life or death.

"I-29 is just a few miles east of here. We'll jump on it, head south, probably twice as fast as Metcalf can, and when I think we've gone far enough, get off, barrel west, and try to intercept 'em."

"Might work," Ty acknowledged, "if we really knew where he was."

"There'll be some Kentucky windage and dead reckoning involved."

"Anything I can do?" Gabi asked.

"Call Metcalf again in a little while, see if you can find out where he is."

Chuck reached the Interstate several minutes later, accelerated, and watched the speedometer climb to between 80 and 90 mph. Northbound vehicles, headlights on, appeared like fireflies emerging from a dark cave as they fled the blackness cloaking the distant southern horizon—the supercell.

"Keep an eye out for cops," Chuck said.

Gabi gazed at the midnight sky ahead. "I have a feeling most of them are otherwise occupied."

Ty turned to peer out the rear window. "Not much traffic behind us."

Stormy sat up, looked around, woofed softly, then lay down again.

"Try Metcalf now," Chuck said to Gabi.

She did, but got no answer.

"Ty," Chuck said, "how are you at reading maps and calculating intercept courses? Was that part of your Special Forces training?" An opportunity to engage his son.

"What do you need?" Ty asked, neither enthusiastic nor disinterested.

"I can't drive, track the storm, and guess where Metcalf is all at the same time. If you could take a WAG at where we should get off the Interstate, run west, and try to reach him before he gets himself and crew into big trouble, it'd take a load off me." Chuck spun the computer around so Ty could read it from the rear seat.

"Metcalf should be pressing south on that road roughly five miles west of the Interstate," Chuck said. He pointed at the route. "Metcalf mentioned he passed through Rippington about ten minutes ago. Let's assume he's doing 45 mph. We're moving twice that speed. The storm is that big red and purple splotch in the lower left of the screen. It's heading northeast around 35 mph."

"Crap," Ty said. "If Jane has six apples and gives four to Dick, and he sells them for ten cents each, what color is Jane's dress?"

"It's not a trick question." But Chuck could see his son already had attacked the problem, tracing his finger across the screen and plotting the projected track of the supercell toward the Interstate.

Gabi tried again to reach Metcalf on his cell phone. Still no response.

"Exit 94," Ty said. "Best guess. Should be in just a couple of minutes. Jump off there and tear ass west. If Metcalf has stayed on the same highway he took through Rippington, we should be able to find him around a little town called—" he consulted the map again "—Colton." He paused. "Maybe."

Chuck exited where Ty suggested. The sky, now seething black and filled with crooked forks of lightning, seemed a warning in and of itself. Large raindrops splattered against the windshield of the Expedition. Chuck pulled the vehicle to the side of the road, stopped, and swiveled the computer back to where he could see it.

"Oh, boy," he said. "This thing's got a rain-wrapped tornado for sure." The hook, no longer an appendage, had curled into the core of the storm. Hard to discern, even on radar. Chuck switched the image to velocity mode. The juxtaposition of red and green colors, velocity differentials, pinpointed the twister . . . at least to his experienced eye.

He wheeled the SUV back onto the road and barreled west. "Got ten minutes, at most. This is the most dangerous kind of tornado there is. Visually, you can't spot it. Too much rain and hail. If Metcalf isn't south of the storm by now, he's gonna drive right into it."

"I'll bet he isn't south of it, not yet," Ty said, tightness in his voice.

"Then we'd damn well better find him in the next few minutes. Cuz after that, I'm gonna make like a sheep herder—we're right in the twister's bulls-eye."

"Sheep herder?" Gabi said.

"Get the flock outta here," Ty responded.

"Oh." She didn't seem to find it humorous.

The rain, without any preamble, increased to Niagara Falls intensity. Explosive bolts of electricity speared into the surrounding farmland as though the SUV were transiting some sort of vast, outdoor shooting gallery.

Chuck slowed the Expedition to a crawl. He leaned over the steering wheel trying to see through the translucent sheets of water coating the windshield. The wipers, even on full speed, proved no match for the cloudburst. Thunder reverberated almost continuously, an ear-splitting counterpoint to the tympanic crescendo of the downpour.

Suddenly, the shotgun detonation of hail intermingled with the rattle of the rain.

"Don't like this," Chuck said. "Time to go. Film-boy is on his own." He rolled to a stop at a crossroad, preparing to turn and run. Maybe he'd waited too long already. He nosed the Expedition into the intersection. Headlights loomed out of the blackness to his right. He braked. Metcalf's Lincoln and the camera rig rolled by in front of him heading due south, into the jaws of the storm.

Chuck laid on the horn as they passed. To no avail. He went after them, flashing his headlights. Hail thundered onto the roof of his vehicle. A crack spider-webbed across the windshield, joining the one incurred a few days earlier.

"Call 'em," Chuck yelled over the din of the storm.

Gabi did. "He's not answering," she said, raising her voice.

He hung on the tail of the camera truck. Not exactly a high-speed pursuit. The rain and hail had slowed it to the pace of an O. J. Simpson chase. He risked a glance at the radar image. A minute or two to go—a minute or two before the tornado would cross the road they were on. He had to decide now. Let Metcalf discover his own fate? Or save him from his folly?

There are others besides Metcalf. This isn't going to be the Glass Mountains again. He pulled out to pass the camera rig. Surely there wouldn't be any traffic coming from the direction of the twister. The Expedition slewed from side to side, fighting for a grip on the watery-icy road. He drew alongside the cab of the truck. Almost slid into it. Laid on his horn again. Gabi signaled the driver, probably Boomie, to stop. He did.

Chuck drew abeam of Metcalf. Passed him. Snapped the steering wheel to the right, cutting in front of the Navigator. Metcalf swerved, sending the Lincoln into a sideways slide along the muddy shoulder of the road.

The rain and hail suddenly ceased, replaced by a deafening roar. Wind. Leveling the grassy fields. Snapping branches from a tiny copse of hardwoods. Propelling dirt and debris horizontally through the air.

Then the funnel. Black upon black. Wide. A wrecking machine churning across the prairie, devouring it, sweeping it clean of structures, topsoil, even life.

Chapter Nineteen

TUESDAY, MAY 7

CHUCK LEAPT FROM the Expedition and yelled at Gabi and Ty to get out. "Get Stormy. Get away from the car. Into the ditch." He pointed at a shallow, water-soaked depression bordering the road.

Metcalf, Willie, and the two women riding with them exited the Lincoln. Metcalf screamed at Chuck. "What the fuck—" He saw the massive tornado and stopped, wide-eyed, his mouth open.

"In the ditch," Chuck bellowed.

Metcalf and his companions didn't hesitate. He belly-flopped into the water, a walrus in a water circus, followed by Willie and the ladies.

Boomie and his riders were already out of the camera truck, dashing for cover. Chuck swung his arms, motioning them to stay away from the truck, away from what could become—he didn't know—a ten-ton missile?

A blast of wind smashed into him from the rear. He staggered and fell face down. He crawled toward the ditch, a jet-engine howl filling his ears. When he reached the depression, he buried his face in the damp grass. Then gunfire, rapid reports riding the wind. No, not gunfire. Trees rent by powerful gusts.

He turned his head, trying to get a view. Power flashes illuminated the blackness. Sheets of aluminum tumbled by, some getting briefly airborne. Shingles, like asphalt shrapnel, shot past. A tree toppled onto the camera rig. A branch from a pine, like a giant, errant javelin, lanced into a side window of Metcalf's SUV.

As suddenly as it began, it was over. The wedge of blackness, disappearing into the rain again, swept away to the east. Only a fitful wind lingered in its wake. An electric odor, mixed with the essence of freshly split wood and muddy earth, filled the air.

A tornado warning siren wailed somewhere in the distance.

Chuck, followed by Ty and Gabi, their clothes soaked, arose from the trench. Stormy scrambled out, too, and shook herself, spraying water outward like a 360-degree sprinkler head.

"Holy shit," Metcalf said, rising like a sludge-encrusted specter from the ditch, "we got hit by a tornado."

"No we didn't, you asshole," Chuck screamed. "Another 500 yards down the road and we would have. And we'd probably all be dead. What the hell were you thinking, you ignoramus? Driving into a rain-wrapped tornado. Nobody does that, at least not intentionally."

"I thought we could beat it, get out in front of it," Metcalf responded, subdued for the first time since Chuck had met him.

"It wouldn't have made any difference," Chuck yelled. *Blood pressure. Take it easy.* "It was hidden in the core of the storm. No way you could have filmed it."

Metcalf stalked toward him, brushing mud off his clothes, wiping it from his face. Fresh fire burned in his eyes. "Then we should have gone after the storm earlier, like the other chasers. Caught it before it got shrink wrapped or whatever in the hell it did." Anger threaded his voice, his own transgressions forgotten.

"Yeah, no astigmatism in hindsight is there?" Chuck said, firing his words like bullets.

"I'm paying you for 20/20 *foresight*." Metcalf stood face to face with Chuck.

"You aren't paying me a goddamn thing unless you film a tornado, and you sure as shit can't film a tornado with a tree stuck in your truck. I'm supposed to be running this expedition, not you. Great job, Jerry." Chuck gestured at the camera rig buried in the crown of a fallen oak tree. "Now I'm out my money, you're out your tornado. Game over."

Metcalf walked toward the truck. "It's not that bad, Chuckie. The tree's resting on the cab, not the crane. And the Panavision didn't get hurt. It's stored safely. We'll get this thing back on the road tomorrow and resume the chase. We've still got a few days."

"No we don't, dick head." Chuck pursued Metcalf. "You just don't get it, do you? Today was our last hurrah. This weather system will be in Wisconsin tomorrow. So, number one, we'd never be able to catch up to it. Number two, with more trees and traffic and hills, chasing east of the Mississippi sucks. And number three, Wisconsin doesn't look like frigging Oklahoma anyhow." Chuck's voice rose with each sentence. He felt a hand on his shoulder and turned to see Gabi.

"Let it go," she said as Metcalf continued to walk away.

"How can I let it go?" Chuck hissed. "I knew the odds were against me from the beginning, but when the guy you're supposed to be working with works against you . . ." His voice trailed off as the anger inflaming him began to dissipate like a summer storm surrendering its virility to the coolness of an evening.

"I don't know," he said, then faltered again. He tilted his head back to look at the sky, at the gray scud racing after the blackness of the departing supercell. "I sometimes wonder if there isn't some sort of cosmic balance scale at work in our lives, measuring the good times against the bad. Making certain that success never exceeds failure. That you're never up more than you're down. That happiness and security and comfort are held in check."

"That sounds rather defeatist," Gabi said.

"It's just my perspective."

"You were king of the road once. As far as I know, there's no prohibition against a second coronation."

"That's just it. I think there might be."

CLARENCE, TRAVELING north with his brother Raleigh, pulled their GMC Terrain to the side of the road. He reached into the back seat and retrieved a pair of Nikon binoculars. He brought them to his eyes and scanned the route ahead.

"Lot of poles and trees down," he said. "The tornado crossed the highway here. This is as far as we can go."

Several cars and trucks came up behind them, stopped, and turned around, their drivers spotting the impassable road beyond.

"Looks like vehicles stopped on the far side of the damage swath," Clarence said. He twisted the focus knob on the binoculars. "Hey, take a look." He handed the field glasses to Raleigh.

Raleigh removed his thick spectacles and lifted the binoculars to his eyes. "Oh, yeah, it looks like that movie crew we heard was out here chasing. Got a tree down on one of the trucks. Didn't we hear they were being led by that guy who ran Thunder Road Tours once upon a time, what was his name?'

"Charles Rittenburg. Used to be a star. 'Til he got a couple of tourists killed, then there was a feeding frenzy by lawyers and they pretty much ate him alive."

Raleigh handed the binoculars back to his brother.

"Well, let's see if we've got any opportunities around here," Clarence said. He glassed the farmland surrounding them, moving the binoculars slowly over the wet, wind-flattened fields. He stopped and refocused on a farm house set well back from the road. "Got a place with part of its roof gone, lotta broken windows." He watched the house for several minutes. "No movement. Probably nothing worth grabbing there, but why don't we take a look?"

Raleigh grunted his assent.

Clarence backtracked a short distance, then turned onto a puddled gravel road lined on both sides by a split rail fence that appeared more decorative than functional. He drove the SUV slowly, constantly monitoring the partially destroyed home. He pulled up near a side entrance, waited a few moments, and then he and Raleigh got out of the Terrain.

Except for the sigh of wind through the now gathering dusk, an eerie silence cloaked the area.

"Anybody here?" Clarence yelled.

No response.

"Let's go around back," he said.

A small shed, largely undamaged, sat about 100 yards behind the house. "I'll go," Raleigh said. He peeked through a window. "Couple of nice ATVs in here. Whaddaya think?"

"Nope, forget it. Too big. Not the kind of stuff that would disappear in a storm. Besides, the shed's intact. Even if there were something in there worth taking, it would look like an obvious robbery. Let's check out the house."

They walked to the house and entered through the side door, which was unlocked. Clarence called out again. "Anybody home?" This time, a prolonged groan answered him.

"Where are you?"

No answer.

They stood in the kitchen. To their left, a small dining room, empty. Straight ahead, a hallway running into the interior of the house. The kitchen, neat but dated, appeared relatively unused, almost *pro forma* as opposed to a place used to prepare meals regularly.

Clarence motioned for Raleigh to follow and they moved down the hallway. A moan came from the first door on the right, from what appeared to be a den with collapsed rafters resting on the floor. Near one of the fallen beams, an elderly woman lay on her back, blood streaming from her head. Overhead, the room opened to the sky.

Clarence knelt by the lady and examined her wound. He turned to Raleigh. "Get the first aid kit. We need to stop the bleeding and patch her up. She's got a nasty cut that'll probably need stitches."

Raleigh didn't respond immediately.

"Raleigh, go."

He trotted off.

"Ma'am, can you hear me?" Clarence asked.

"Yes," she mumbled.

"What's your name?"

"Evelyn."

"Do you know what happened?"

"Tornado."

"Do you know what day this is?"

"Monday. No, Tuesday."

He continued asking her questions until Raleigh returned with the first aid supplies.

"Evelyn," Clarence said, "I don't think you've got a concussion, but you'll certainly need some stitches in your scalp. And I'm guessing you'll need some x-rays, too. You're pretty banged up. I'll call 9-1-1 and get some help out here."

"Thank you," she said, hoarseness in her voice. "Who are you?"

"We're helping a university do tornado damage research. We saw your place had been clipped by the twister and decided to check it out. Lucky for you, we did. We've had a little medical training, so we can patch you up and make you comfortable until the real EMTs get here. Okay?"

"Okay."

Clarence swabbed Evelyn's wound with antiseptic while Raleigh unfolded some bandages.

"Do you live here alone, Evelyn?" Clarence asked while he worked on her.

"My husband died several years ago, so it's just me and Lewis now."

"Lewis?"

"My dog, a big Irish setter. You didn't see him outside, did you?"

"No."

"He doesn't like storms." Her voice sounded stronger.

Raleigh covered Evelyn with a blanket and slipped a small pillow under her head, careful not to move her too much.

"Don't you get frightened, living here by yourself?" Clarence asked.

"Lewis, remember?"

"Right. But if he blows town every time a storm comes along, what good—"

"Well, then, there's my husband's collection."

"Collection?"

"In the case against the wall."

Clarence hadn't noticed it before, hidden behind the fallen rafters, but a large, glass-fronted gun case stood adjacent to the wall on his left.

Raleigh walked to it, surveyed the contents, and whistled in admiration. "You got a whole arsenal here, ma'am."

Clarence finished securing a bandage around Evelyn's head. "Something to protect all your other valuables with, huh?"

Evelyn snorted softly. "I live on Social Security. Just barely live. Sometimes, when the end of the month gets here, I have to visit the food bank." Her voice cracked.

"Okay. Take it easy now. Close your eyes and relax." He arose, walked to the gun case, and stood next to his brother. The case held a cornucopia of weapons—hunting rifles, shotguns, handguns. Among them, a few antiques and a handful of custom-made pieces.

"Well?" whispered Raleigh, his eyes wide, sparkling, apparently in anticipation of becoming better armed than most small town police departments.

Hand on chin, Clarence studied the domestic armory. It appealed to him, something Western and independent and masculine about it. He looked back at Evelyn. "This is worth a small fortune," he said.

"It's all I've got."

"It's a really nice collection." Clarence ran his gaze over the weaponry again, feeling the power it represented, allowing it to embrace him, beckon him to a different level. He squeezed his eyes shut and backed away. "Let's go, 'bro," he said softly.

"Clarence," Raleigh hissed. He grasped his brother by the arm.

"It's not us." Clarence pulled away from Raleigh and walked toward the hallway. "We'll call 9-1-1 now, Evelyn. Help will be here shortly."

"Thank you, boys."

"What the fuck?" Clarence said, not quite loud enough for Evelyn to hear. He tugged on his brother's shirtsleeve.

"We don't need guns, to use or fence," Clarence said, his voice harsh but barely audible. He laid a $20 bill on the kitchen counter and walked out, a silent scream filling his head, a poltergeist with evil intent urging him to return.

He stared at the sheet lightning painting the eastern horizon and kept walking.

Chapter Twenty

WEDNESDAY, MAY 8

WITH THE HELP of a friendly utility crew—"Wow, you guys shootin' a movie, really?"—and a wrecker out of Sioux Falls, the camera rig was freed from the embrace of the toppled oak. The truck proved still drivable, validating Metcalf's initial damage assessment. A large dent in its cab and bent and broken scaffolding on its roof lent a battle-scarred aspect to it, but it remained functional. A quick test proved the crane still worked, and the Panavision Genesis, stored securely, had survived unscathed. Little matter. The chase was over.

The crew spent the night in Sioux Falls. Metcalf and a couple of his cronies went in search of a "titty bar." Chuck collapsed into bed. Tired. Defeated. Angry.

He arose early, at an hour when the day's first light glowed low in the east, a mere sliver of silver strung along the horizon, and walked to his SUV. Overhead, night dawdled, the sky blue-black and pinpricked with dimming stars. Heavy dew coated the SUV, the condensate glistening like hoarfrost in the false dawn. Using his hand, Chuck brushed at the moisture on the driver's side window. A scree of droplets, like falling tears, slid down the glass.

"Going for breakfast?" a voice asked from the unlit dawn. Gabi.

"And a beer."

"You want company?"

"No."

"Good. I'll join you."

"I'll be fine."

"Probably. But you need somebody to talk to."

"I'll bet you were a hostage negotiator for the Bureau."

"I'll bet you couldn't recognize a friend if she kicked you in the ass."

She stood next to Chuck now, her breath warm on his cheek, her exhalations creating fleeting puffs of steam in the morning coolness.

He stared at Gabi, frozen in place as she tilted her face to his and kissed him on the lips. "There," she said. "I'm glad we're past that. Let's get some food."

Fifteen minutes later, they sat in a disreputable-looking roadhouse that advertised breakfast. Chuck asked the waitress, a haggard-looking woman whose hair suggested she might have been caught out in yesterday's storm, if he could get a beer.

"At this hour?" she asked, a smoky rasp in her voice.

"I suppose I could sit here until noon."

"It's breakfast time."

He opened his wallet, plucked a $10 bill from it and slid it across the table toward her. "Just bring me something that looks like an extremely large apple juice."

She snatched the bill from the table and flounced off.

"You sure you need a beer?" Gabi asked.

"No, I don't need it. I want it." He paused, changed gears. "Gabi, what was that, back there in the parking lot?" He still felt the press of her lips against his. A sugariness that refused to fade.

"I figured a kiss might be better than a kick in the ass. I'm sorry if I was out of bounds. I guess it was an overstated way of saying I'm your friend."

He reached across the table and took her hand. "You weren't out of bounds. You just . . . you took me by surprise, that's all. I want your friendship. But, you know, it's a little weird. One minute you're an FBI agent, then you're . . . I don't know."

"A girlfriend?"

"It's funny to have a girlfriend at my age."

"Why do you say that?"

"I mean, it's like I was back in high school or something." He released her hand.

She smiled. "Some of us have good memories from high school."

She had a point. Good memories—days of exploration, coming of age, testosterone at the boiling point. In truth, Gabi had brought to life within him a *zeitgeist* of those days, albeit a *zeitgeist* tempered by middle age.

He enjoyed being around Gabi—enjoyed her intellect, her sense of humor, her directness. She exuded a mature sexiness, not a cover girl or movie star sexiness, not a physical sexiness, but an allure born of self-confidence, compassion, and knowing—he was pretty sure—her physical assets were, well, certainly competitive. For an unguarded moment, he imagined what forbidden, hedonistic pleasures she might harbor.

"You're blushing," she said.

Jesus. "It's hot in here."

She smiled again. Nailed him dead to rights. No more unguarded moments.

The waitress returned and plunked down a large mug of amber liquid. "Your apple juice, sir. First one I've ever seen with a head."

Without hesitation, he lifted the container to his mouth and took a swallow. "Yes," he said, when he'd finished, "very good. Washington apples, I'd guess. Golden Delicious, probably."

"Ya betcha," she answered. "I'll be back to take your orders shortly." She ambled away.

Gabi watched in silence as Chuck took another long swill from the mug and wiped his hand across his mouth.

"What?" he said.

"So you're just gonna run up a white flag, suck down a defeatist beer, and slink back to Oklahoma City?"

"That's about it."

Gabi leaned toward Chuck and in a sharp whisper said, "I thought you had bigger balls than that."

"Enormous nuts aren't the issue here, girlfriend. Numb nuts, maybe, like that idiot Metcalf. Runs off like a scalded cat, chasing a storm on his own, and wrecks his truck *and* our chances of catching a twister. I mean, I was swimming upstream from the start, but when that jerk won't even play by the rules—"

"Maybe we take the game into overtime," Gabi interjected.

Chuck tipped the mug to his lips again, drank, set it down. "What do you mean?"

"You were right, I did do a little hostage negotiation with the Bureau. One of the things you always look for in a negotiation is something both of you, the good guy and the bad guy, want. Then you work from there. At first, you barter little items to build trust. Then you gradually escalate the stakes until you reach a point where you know you can't afford to give away the farm to the hostage holder. But the issue with Metcalf isn't that thorny, isn't that complicated. It's pretty simple, in fact. He wants a violent tornado on film, you want a million bucks."

Chuck nodded, waving away the waitress as she approached. The smell of burnt toast wafted through the eatery, followed by a loud verbal exchange exploding from the kitchen. Spanish.

Gabi ignored it and continued, "I know contractually the hunt is over on Saturday. But that's not the end of tornadoes for the season, is it?"

"Of course not."

"So when's the next threat?"

"Probably Sunday."

"A significant threat?"

"I'd have to take a closer look." He fiddled with the beer mug on the table, rotating it in a slow circle.

"Do it. Then go to Metcalf and ask for an extension, one more day. Tell him you'll guarantee him a tornado. Tell him you'll get him his twister."

"There's no way I could guarantee—"

"You think we tell the truth in hostage negotiations all the time?"

"No, but—"

"But nothing. A million bucks, Chuck. That's really what's at stake here. Besides, what's the down side? Say you don't get a tornado. So you don't get your million dollars. You weren't gonna get it anyhow. This way, there's at least a chance." She reached out and laid her hand over his. "Give it a shot, boyfriend."

The waitress loomed over them, unsmiling. "You two love birds ready to order? Got a special on crunchy toast."

BACK IN HIS MOTEL room, Chuck, with Stormy lying near his feet, studied the most recent weather models on his laptop. He scanned several different ones, each confirming the other. What he saw caused him to catch his breath. Even the Storm Prediction Center seemed excited at the prospects. Though SPC rarely outlined threat areas more than three days in advance, their graphics and accompanying discussion defined what they termed "a significant threat of a major outbreak" for Day Five—Sunday. The region at risk extended from the Red River along the Texas-Oklahoma border northward through eastern Kansas.

The setup appeared classic, with a powerful jet stream aloft forecast to dive from the central Rockies into the Southern Plains and there hook sharply northward. Beneath it, a deep stream of high-octane warmth and moisture was predicted to barrel northward from the Gulf of Mexico.

Chuck's initial analysis suggested eastern Oklahoma would be ground-zero for a violent atmospheric war.

"Armageddon?" he said out loud. Stormy looked up and cocked her head. "Okay, maybe too strong a word." He reached down and petted her. "But it's gonna be wild." *Maybe a million-bucks-worth of wild.*

A short time later he knocked on the door of Metcalf's room. No response. He knocked again. Silence. He tried once more, this time hammering. From within the room came muffled cursing. Something crashed to the floor. More cursing. Metcalf yanked open the door and stood glaring at Chuck.

Red-eyed and rumpled, Metcalf obviously had slept in his clothes. They reeked of stale liquor and cigarette smoke. A funk of dead air fled the room through the open door.

"Jesus, Chuckie," Metcalf growled, "cantcha fuckin' let a guy sleep in."

"It's almost noon."

"Shit. That's what I mean. Whaddaya want?"

"Can I come in?"

"At your peril." Metcalf stumbled back to his bed and sat on the edge of it. A table lamp lay sprawled on the floor next to the bed. He bent to pick it up, belched and farted simultaneously, and decided against retrieving it. He put his hands on the bed to steady himself. "Tough night."

"No shit."

"Don't pass judgment on me, man. This is Sioux Fucking Falls. It's not exactly the entertainment Mecca of the world. Luckily we found a nice . . . uh . . . gentlemen's club."

"I'm sure."

"Gawd, the women here are built like brick shit houses. Must be that good Iowa corn—.

"We're in South Dakota."

"Whatever. Interesting dudes, too. Hey, could you make us some coffee?" He pointed at a Keurig on the dresser. "Yeah, met a guy with an ankle monitor who said he was on an undercover job for the CIA. Another weirdo, a black dude with a mohawk, claimed he was an alien from Pluto and looking for investors to help develop a tourist industry there."

Chuck busied himself with the Keurig. "Maybe you should shoot a movie here."

"Yeah," Metcalf snorted derisively. "Might have better luck with that than trying to film a tornado."

"That's what I wanted to talk to you about." The Keurig hissed as it jetted a stream of hot coffee into a cup. "How do you like it?"

"Like what?"

"Your coffee."

"Black." He burped softly as Chuck handed him the cup. He took a tentative sip. "Hot." He placed it on the night stand. "So what's up, Chazoroo?"

Chuck, thanks to Gabi's mentoring, convinced himself he wouldn't be groveling, which he detested, but that he would be opening "negotiations" with Metcalf. "I've got a deal for you. I'll get you your tornado." He couldn't quite bring himself to say "guarantee."

"What's the catch?"

"Why does there have to be a catch?"

"There always is."

"No. No catch, as you call it. Just a contract extension."

"You had your chance. Saturday's the last day. No storm. No moolah." He reached for the coffee, dribbled a dozen drops onto the bed sheet.

"Sunday. One stinkin' day. Extend the deal one stinkin' day and I'll find you the most spectacular twister anyone has ever filmed." *Damn you, Gabi.*

"No." He drained the cup and wiped his mouth.

"No?"

"Is there an echo in here?"

"Why not?"

"Because I'm on a time clock, too, Chuckie. I'm bound by the film's production schedule. We need to press on regardless of whether or not you've delivered."

"I'll deliver. Give me one extra day."

Metcalf shook his head. "Negative."

"So, you'd rather go back to L.A. empty handed in order to stay on schedule rather than sacrifice 24 hours to get some blockbuster footage for your movie?" Chuck's gut churned. He really wanted this now but sensed the opportunity slipping away.

Metcalf extended the empty cup to Chuck. "Do you mind?"

Chuck took the cup and went back to the coffee maker. "Same kind?"

Metcalf nodded.

"Good. That's all they've got." He started another brew.

Metcalf stood and sauntered over to the window. He drew back the curtains. Daylight flooded into the room. Metcalf squeezed his eyes shut and pivoted away from the brightness. "So. Sunday. A slam dunk you say?"

Chuck knew it wasn't. Didn't want to say it was. But Gabi's words slithered into his head: *You think we tell the truth in hostage negotiations all the time?* "Slam dunk," Chuck said. *Double damn you, Gabi.*

A weasel-like smile creased Metcalf's face. He approached Chuck and extended his hand. "Sure, and you're an alien with property on Pluto." His stale breath smothered Chuck in an 80-proof smog. "Lord, I hate the thought of hanging around Yahooville another five days. But you've got yourself an extra 24 hours, bwana. Make it happen."

They shook hands, Metcalf's grip feeling weak and irresolute. Little matter, however. They'd made a deal. The fat lady had just swallowed a chicken bone.

THAT EVENING, sipping a beer, Chuck played a game of toss and fetch with Stormy. Chuck hurled an old sock around the motel room with Stormy darting after it in happy pursuit. A sharp rap on the door brought the activity to an end. Chuck peered through the peephole in the door, then opened it.

"I heard you got a stay of execution," Ty said.

Chuck nodded and motioned his son into the room.

"Seems so," Chuck answered. "Who told you?"

"Gabi."

Chuck placed his beer back into the room's tiny refrigerator. "How about some Scotch?"

Ty shrugged. "Yeah, fine."

"So, what brings you into enemy territory?"

Chuck wondered how many others in the chase group besides Gabi were aware of the deep rift between him and Ty. He wondered if any of them knew his son was gay. Certainly Gabi must have some inkling. Nothing much got past her. But it really didn't matter. He didn't care what she or the others knew or thought. It wasn't their issue. It was his. But within him churned a conflict that seemed virtually unresolvable.

He harbored a huge amount of admiration for Ty, how he had

turned out, his accomplishments, his goals, his . . . manhood. Yet, he was gay. *How do I come to grips with that? How do I reconcile the inherent goodness of my son with the pejorative language and warnings in the Bible?* Had his son made a reprehensible choice, or had the choice been made for him and he was simply damned by genetics? He wished he could reach out and embrace Ty, but he sensed an almost palpable restraint against doing so. The dichotomy gnawed at him with surprising fierceness.

"Just curious," Ty said, "wondering if you really think you can pull this off? Believe that you can find the Atmospheric Holy Grail on Sunday? A magician pulling a tornado from a smoke-filled jar. A conjurer of storms. Thor, god of thunder." He jammed his fist toward the ceiling, a mocking gesture, but then seemed to reconsider. "Sorry." He lowered his arm. "That was uncalled for."

Chuck nodded and handed Ty a plastic cup half filled with Scotch. Ty l took the drink.

"Why do you care?" Chuck asked.

"Remember, I have a vested interest in this crazy-ass chase. I've pissed away two weeks out here on a gamble you might actually be able to deliver on your promise—well, sort of promise—of financial restitution. So far, it's been nothing but a flashback of my life: getting rugs yanked out from underneath me." He stared into his Scotch. "God, I don't know why I thought things might be different this time."

Because you hoped *they would, Son, just like I did.* "To answer your question," Chuck said, "yes. I think I can pull this off. Whether I will or not is another matter, but if ever there was going to be a chance, Sunday is it." A sourness crept into his gut, squeezings from a knot in his stomach formed from the pressure of the high-stakes game on which he'd embarked. He'd pretty much laid everything on the line to take this job. Now he'd gone beyond that.

The conversation lapsed into one-sentence exchanges . . . not much in common between father and son.

Ty sat in a chair near the room's window, swirling the Scotch in his cup and staring out into the evening darkness. Stormy lay on her side near the foot of the bed, snoring softly and occasionally uttering a brief whimper as if dreaming. The sounds from a TV in an adjacent room leaked through the cardboard-thin wall.

Chuck, who'd been pacing, stopped. "Ty?" he said.

Ty took a sip from his cup, then gazed at Chuck. "What?"

"Something's been bothering me."

"Now there's a revelation."

Chuck knocked back his own Scotch, tossed the empty cup into a waste basket, and wiped his lips. "Just for a minute, lose the attitude, if you can."

Ty took another swig of his drink and set the cup on a table near him. "I've been working on it. But it's hard to do after a decade of being kicked in the ass."

Chuck closed his eyes and let the brickbat fly past before speaking. "I like you, Ty. I admire what you've done with your life . . . in spite of me . . . without me. You're not what I expected—"

"Which was?"

"I don't know. Someone a bit more overtly gay."

"A stereotype?"

"Yes, I suppose. But that's not my hang-up. I get wrapped around the axle when it comes to the Bible and homosexuality."

"I don't." Ty polished off his remaining Scotch.

"I know. I could never get you to go to church after you were in high school."

"I go to church every Sunday now."

Chuck stared at Ty.

"I probably couldn't articulate it when I was younger," Ty said, "but I always believed in God. I felt trapped between religion and who I was. Not what I was, *who* I was. I didn't want to have to make an either-or choice, didn't want to have to choose between God and my sexuality. But with you hammering me for being a queer and the church damning me as a sinner, I saw no way out. I knew I was doomed. But as I grew older, I realized I wasn't, and that what I thought would be an excruciatingly difficult decision was really a false dilemma."

"The Bible's pretty specific about homosexuality."

"Not really," Ty said. "The word isn't in the Bible. It was your fire-breathing, Bible-thumping, Southern Baptist father, my grandfather, who was specific about us 'fairies.' He was certain we were destined to a fiery eternity in hell. Zealous about condemning our 'bestiality.' Convinced we were synonymous with pedophiles."

"Ty, stop." But Chuck spoke without conviction. His son, in fact, wasn't that far off base. Ty's grandfather had indeed been an archly conservative member of the church, a fundamentalist deacon. He'd put the fear of God into Chuck as a youngster and cultivated that fear even after Chuck had matured and had a family of own. Ty, in particular, had become a high-visibility target for his grandfather's fiery proselytizing and damnation.

Chuck eventually came to question the ultra-conservative Southern Baptist doctrine and drifted away from the church. But the teachings of his father stuck in his head, indelible ink that refused to fade even under the harsh illumination of 21st century science. *Was that good or bad?*

Ty continued speaking, ignoring Chuck's request. "Without belaboring the point, there are different interpretations of the Biblical passages traditionally employed to condemn people like me." His words seemed more challenging than angry.

Chuck resumed pacing. "Yeah, yeah. Liberal interpretations. I've heard them. That God's decision to destroy Sodom was made well before the men of the city were pounding on Lot's door demanding he turn out his male guests 'so we can have sex with them.' That Paul's writings are cloaked in first-century prejudices."

Ty remained seated, his gaze tracking his father around the room. "And?" he said, the word sharp.

"And what?"

"What makes those interpretations, liberal ones as you call them, any less valid than the more traditional ones?"

Chuck stopped and turned to face his son.

"What makes them any *more* valid?" Chuck fired back.

"Yes," Ty said, "that's always the impasse we reach, isn't it? You're really no different than Grandpop." He stood. "Well, I guess that's enough enlightened repartee for tonight. I need some fresh air." He moved toward the door.

Chuck stood, arms dangling at this sides, and watched his son walk away.

Ty stopped when he reached the door. Resting his hand on the handle, he turned toward his father. "Just for the record," he said, his voice even and controlled, "I actually have a conservative view of the Bible, at least when it comes to love, the unconditional agape type. When I was searching for a church, I looked for that, and found it in the one I finally joined. There was no hypocrisy, none of those 'love the sinner, hate the sin' platitudes thrown my way followed by attempts to 'convert' me."

Stormy lifted her head and eyed the two men as if wondering why they had disturbed her slumber. She issued a muted half-bark and sat up.

Ty continued speaking. "I was accepted because I was a follower of Jesus. I was accepted because I was Tyler Rittenberg, no questions asked, no labels attached. Most members of the church knew my orientation. And they understood and accepted that *what* I was, my sexuality, was integral to *who* I was." He paused a beat before adding, "Unlike some people I know."

Without allowing Chuck to respond, Ty opened the door, stepped out, and shut it firmly.

Chuck lowered himself to a sitting position on his bed and listened to Ty's retreating footfalls. He lowered his gaze, stared at the motel's faded carpet, and shook his head. The gulf between father and son loomed as dark and choppy and wide as ever.

Chapter Twenty-one

THURSDAY, MAY 9

GABI AND CHUCK strolled along a footpath adjacent to the Big Sioux River in the Mary Jo Wegner Arboretum just east of Sioux Falls. On the river side of the path, meadows rife with blossoming wildflowers blanketed a sun-blitzed floodplain. Farther from the water, stands of oak, elm, and Box elder, cloaked in the soft green of early spring, swayed in the gentle gusts of a warm wind. Overhead, riding the invisible up-elevator of a midday thermal, a pair of hawks orbited, perhaps performing recon for an opportunistic lunch. Some distance away and higher in the sky, a Bald Eagle, with languid flaps of its majestic wings, soared toward the spire of a White Spruce.

Gabi had awakened early that morning, the incipient pain of a migraine boring into her skull. Brilliant flashes, like sheet lightning exploding from a faraway storm, flickered behind her eyes. She'd fumbled with the coffee maker, got a cup brewing, and slammed a Treximet into her mouth. An hour and three cups of coffee later, she actually felt better.

Still a bit woozy from the medication, she didn't quite lean against Chuck as they walked, but the backs of their hands brushed. It was good to know he was there. Despite his defeatist attitude—understandable, considering what he'd been through both personally and professionally—he seemed a rock. Someone who could be relied upon. Someone who wanted to do right. Someone you could root for, the good guy, an underdog.

"I'm glad Metcalf granted you an extra day," she said.

"I had a good job-coach," he responded.

"You think it'll pay off?" She sidestepped a puddle.

He shrugged.

"But it looks good?"

"Yes. As good as any setup—okay, better than any setup—we've had in the past two weeks. It could be a big deal. But we still have to be in the right place at the right time."

She nodded. "You'll do it."

"You've got more faith in me than Metcalf the Magnificent does."

"Don't forget, I've got a vested interest in this hunt, too."

He bobbed his head up and down. Slowly, almost wistfully it seemed. "Yeah. Sunday will be pretty much an all-or-nothing day. I have no doubt the bad guys have seen the models, too. Probably licking their chops."

"We'll get 'em," she said. "And you'll get Metcalf his storm. Speaking of whom, where's the rest of the crew today?"

"Metcalf and his Merry Men, along with Ty, invaded a golf course again. I forget the name of it . . . somewhere near the airport. The two ladies schlepped off to the Great Plains Zoo."

"And here we are in an arboretum." She looked around. "You know, it's nice. Sioux Falls wouldn't be a bad place to raise a family."

Chuck stared at her.

"I meant that in a generic sense."

A Scarlet Tanager in low flight hurtled by in front of them.

"I know you did," Chuck said. "Not to pry, like you accused me of before, but did you ever—"

"Consider a family?" She gazed up into the cloudless sky, as though she might find a signal from on-high: Answer the question or evade it. Well, *his* life wasn't exactly hidden from *her*. *I guess it wouldn't hurt to level the playing field.* Especially, she had to admit, when their relationship had crept across that diaphanous boundary between professional and personal. She hadn't intended it to, but here they were, walking—well, not quite hand-in-hand, but almost—through the warm embrace of a spring day like a . . . couple. *Spring, when a young man's fancy turns to thoughts of? What? Gabriela Galina Mederios, a 40-something FBI agent? Or an EF-5 tornado?* She stifled a self-deprecating laugh.

"Too pointed a question?" Chuck asked.

"No. But I guess since we're . . . friends—"

He took her hand. She didn't resist.

"Since we're friends," she continued, "I can open a door to you."

He didn't respond, merely waited for her to go on. The piercing cry of a hawk mingled with the muted rustle of leaves from a nearby stand of oaks.

"I was married once. When I was in my mid-20s. But I discovered pretty quickly I wasn't cut out to be a stay-at-home wife. Fortunately, there were no kids. We divorced in less than two years."

"Where was this?"

"In Boston. I think I told you before, I was working as an interpreter for the Federal District Court of Massachusetts at the time. But I wanted more. Adventure, I guess. I applied to the Bureau, was accepted, aced the training, and was assigned to the Mobile Field Office in the late '90s."

"And then to New Haven, and then to Oklahoma City."

"You remembered."

"That's about all you ever told me."

A group of children darted past them, laughing, yelling, full of energy. Elementary school kids on a field trip. They raced up the path ahead of Gabi and Chuck.

"Maybe it's time to reassess what I want out of life," she said. *Or is it too late?*

"Meaning?"

She didn't answer, not sure herself.

He prodded her. "Second thoughts about not wanting kids?"

"No. I don't think it's that. I'm not Soccer Mom material."

"Something else then? A secret?" He thought of Ty.

She heard it in his voice, the standard accusation. If you're a single female, older, especially if you carry a gun, you must be a dyke. "To dispel that notion," she said, "let me tell you, I like men. I've had . . . affairs. I enjoy sex." She blurted it out, immediately regretted it. "Sorry, too much information." A surge of blood rushed to her head, her face undoubtedly flushing carmine.

"No. It's okay. We're friends, remember? I'm your confidant now."

"The lady is a tramp," she muttered.

"Really? Because you want affection, companionship, recognition? Like everybody else?" He stopped walking and made her turn and look directly at him. "You think I don't know what it's like to live on a deserted island?"

Deserted island. There it was. Easy to see now. Easy to understand what terrified her: living out her life alone.

"I don't want to be by myself," she whispered.

He pulled her to him.

"Mercy hug?" she said, her words almost smothered in the folds of his shirt.

"No. Don't you think we both harbor the same fears?"

A raucous conversation among a murder of crows interrupted the relative tranquility of the day, but the hubbub quickly subsided as the birds took flight on a low-level run to the opposite bank of the Big Sioux.

"Maybe we should run away together after this is all over," she said.

"I may be broke."

She pulled away from him. "I'll hire you as a gigolo."

"The equipment may not work."

"We need to find out."

He swiveled his head, scanning the area around him. Theatrically.

"Not here, bozo," she said. "And not until the Great Hunt is over."

They resumed walking. "Promise?" he said.

"Typical man."

FRIDAY, MAY 10

CHUCK GATHERED the chase team in a meeting room at the motel after breakfast.

"We're going to be moving," he said. "We'll head south today, spend tonight in Kansas City, then figure out tomorrow where to position ourselves for Sunday." He checked his wristwatch. "We'll shove off about ten-thirty."

"Still looking good?" Willie Weston, the second unit director, asked. An older man with a florid complexion and thinning hair, he seemed the only one of Metcalf's crew that paid the man little deference.

"Better than good," Chuck said. "The Storm Prediction Center has already issued a high risk for Sunday."

"Meaning?" Metcalf, who'd been pacing behind the rest of the group seated around a large conference table, stopped and stood with his hands on his hips.

"Meaning," Chuck responded, "they're virtually certain there's going to be a major tornado outbreak. So certain, in fact, that this is the first time *ever* they've issued a high-threat outlook three days in advance. As a point of comparison, a high-risk category wasn't posted until two days prior to the Dixie swarm of 2011."

"Was that when Alabama got clocked?" Willie asked.

"Yeah," Chuck said. "Most of the tornadoes, including four EF-5s, struck the Deep South, Alabama included, but there were reports of twisters from as far north as Upstate New York."

"I was in Tuscaloosa that day," Willie said. "I remember it well. Damn scary. A lot of people were killed."

"Over 40 in Tuscaloosa alone," Chuck said. "April 27th. All told, twisters claimed 316 lives that day, the greatest single-day toll on record since the mid-1920s."

Willie whistled softly. Stormy, who'd been lying near Chuck, lifted her head off her front paws and glanced around. Chuck petted her and she relaxed, laying her head back on her paws.

Gabi, doing her magazine reporter schtick, scribbled something on a notepad and looked up. "Was that the biggest outbreak in history? I mean, like for number of tornadoes?" She snapped a piece of gum she'd been chewing.

Chuck could barely keep from laughing. She snapped the gum again. *She could have been an actress.*

"Yes. There were 175 confirmed twisters. Prior to that, the record holder was the 'Super Outbreak' of April 1974 with, I think, 147 tornadoes. But seven of those were F-5s."

"Not EF-5s?" Gabi asked.

"The EF classification wasn't used until 2007. But an F-5 is roughly equivalent to an EF-5."

"Seven F-5s?" Metcalf asked. "Really?"

"Four in the Midwest, three in Alabama."

"Maybe we should be chasing in Alabama."

"Not this time. SPC has narrowed the target region to eastern Oklahoma and southeast Kansas."

"And you concur with SPC's outlook?" Willie asked.

Chuck nodded.

"Okay, a lot of tornadoes, but what about EF-4s and -5s?" Metcalf again. "That's all I'm interested in."

"High risk and violent tornadoes go pretty much hand-in-hand," Chuck answered.

"Will it be dangerous?" Gabi asked. Still the feature writer.

But maybe her question meant something else. At least to her and him. *Will we have a shot, one last chance, at catching the bad guys—whoever has been using tornado damage as a cover for robbery and murder?*

Metcalf snorted as Gabi finished her question. He walked over to her and placed a hand on her shoulder. She flinched, Chuck thought, ever so slightly. "Not with our Great White Hunter here, honey," Metcalf said. "He hasn't come close to putting us in peril yet. At least not from a twister. Buffalo stampedes, giant hail, hidden swales. Yeah, he can ferret those out. But an EF-5? No way."

Chuck looked at the ceiling. Held his tongue. *No, you Hollywood halfwit, only you can get us into trouble with a tornado.* The memory of three days ago remained vivid: lying in a muddy ditch as a black wedge roared overhead. Debris flying. Transformers exploding. Trees snapping. The remaining camera truck almost crushed.

He brought his gaze back to Gabi and Metcalf. "We'll find what we're looking for," he said. A different meaning for each.

But he hadn't really answered Gabi's question, Will it be dangerous? In truth, it would be. In any high-risk environment, especially one harboring the most violent storms on earth, there's inherent peril. Still, they had a couple of advantages: their ability to monitor the situation, to understand what and where any threats would be developing; and their mobility, their ability to move and reposition themselves, or even run for their lives if they had to.

The bad guys, of course, would have the same capabilities.

Perhaps that was the reason a certain unease gnawed at him, like a determined rat chewing at the exterior of a home, willing itself entry. There could well be danger from two sources: one natural, one human.

The natural one, the one spawned by nature, he could deal with.

The human one . . . ? That's where the real unpredictability lay.

Chapter Twenty-two

SUNDAY, MAY 11
EARLY MORNING

THE TEAM HAD traveled from Kansas City to Oklahoma City on Saturday, Chuck deciding Ok City would provide the best network of roads from which to launch the final hunt. They could move quickly north or south on I-35, east via I-40, or northeast on the Turner Turnpike.

Although the sun hadn't yet risen, Chuck had, several hours ago. With Stormy curled up in a corner and still sleeping, Chuck, using his laptop, reviewed the parameters for the impending tornado outbreak. He played devil's advocate, attempting to poke holes in his own analyses, find weak points in his prognoses, tweak input values to render the outputs impotent. But no matter how hard he tried to force conditions to seem less threatening, he couldn't.

Low-level jet, mid-level jet, instability, wind shear, moisture—the values for all sat on the upper end of the scale. As far as the area under the gun, a moveable feast: Any location east of I-35 to the Missouri and Arkansas borders and south of I-70 to the Red River had the potential to become a killing ground.

Already social media and television were ablaze with apocalyptic predictions: swarms of violent tornados, the greatest outbreak in history, maybe an EF-6. Bogus, of course. No one had any basis for such statements, but that didn't stop the doomsday proclamations from being promulgated as gospel. Not that the fear factor needed to be ramped up in this part of the country, the traditional Tornado Alley. But even for veterans of legendary outbreaks and storm cellars, the day would be explosive and filled with peril.

Chuck stood, his heart thumping like that of a marine about to storm a hostile beach. But was it danger or excitement that had released the floodgates of adrenalin that surged through his body? He certainly didn't need any coffee this morning. Or beer.

THE PAIN AWOKE her. Something loose inside her head and battering at her skull. A jackhammer trying to punch through bone. Gabi forced herself to sit up in bed. *No, not today. Not today of all days.* She staggered toward the bathroom in semi-darkness, gripping furniture, walls, anything to keep her upright as her world spun in a vicious kaleidoscope of painful lightning bolts arcing across her scalp. She dropped to her knees in front of the toilet bowl and vomited. It didn't relieve her agony, only left her throat seared and raw.

She crept back into the main room, groping for her purse, found it, and pawed through its contents until she felt the bottle of Treximet. She extracted a tablet and slammed it into her mouth. She lurched back to the bathroom, filled her hand with water, and downed the pill. But perhaps it was too late. The migraine might already be the victor, intent on holding her in agonizing imprisonment for the remainder of the day, if not longer.

She crashed backward into her bed, her right arm draped across her forehead as if to ward off additional assaults of pain. Knowing she would have to wait two hours to take another dose if this first one didn't do the job, she twisted her head to check the clock on the night stand. Just prior to six a.m.

She didn't like having to take the drug at all, especially when she was on the job. But without it, the pain would render her nonfunctional. She could only hope the medicine would work its magic. Experience had taught her that even with a single dose, however, because of Treximet's side effects, she would be off her game. Lethargic, a bit slow to react, unable to focus. Still, she'd have to *will* herself to overcome those liabilities. As Chuck had pointed out the previous night, they were going into overtime in the game, all or nothing, winner take all; loser, zero. Sudden death.

I want those bastards. I want . . . She drifted into blackness, a dark veil tugging her into a troubled sleep filled with flashes of light and dark shadows rippling over a barren landscape.

IN A RUN-DOWN motel north of Stillwater, Clarence and Raleigh, arose early and pored over maps and discussions. Their two-star lodging had been chosen deliberately, to keep them separated, unnoticed, from the hordes of chasers—professional, semi-professional, amateur and clueless—gathering on the southern Plains in anticipation of what could prove to be an historic day.

"I think," Clarence said, his angular face contoured with an incipient smile, "this could turn out to be a bonanza."

Raleigh nodded. "*Numerous* tornadoes, that's what the public statement out of SPC said."

"We just need to get lucky," Clarence responded, "hope some of them hit homes, businesses... in up-scale neighborhoods. Not goddamn trailer parks or Mexican ghettos with clapped-out shotgun houses."

"Just... just so we don't have to kill nobody," Raleigh said, his voice low and hesitant, his eyes appearing like chocolate-colored boulder marbles behind his thick glasses.

Clarence laid a hand on Raleigh's shoulder. "Listen, bro', I don't like having to do that any better than you. But sometimes, it's for the best. Sometimes you have to... neutralize a threat." He squeezed Raleigh's neck softly, almost lovingly. "Remember, nobody ever looked out for us. We gotta take care of ourselves. Each other. Right?" He cuffed Raleigh playfully on the head.

"Right." Raleigh sounded less than convinced.

"Look, a couple of big scores today, maybe we can stand down for a while. Take a vacation down on the Baja. Tequila. Mexican *senoritas*. Okay?"

"*Senoritas* with big casabas?"

"You bet, bro'. Casabas *grande*."

Raleigh cracked a smile. Good to go.

Clarence pulled up a map on his laptop. "We're here," he said, pointing. "SPC expects the initial supercells to develop here—" he pointed to an area just west of I-35 "—not too far from us."

Raleigh leaned in close, squinting, despite wearing glasses.

"The storms'll move east or east-northeast. There're some decent-sized towns that could get clocked: Stillwater, Ponca City, Arkansas City. That would be best for us. Anyhow, we'll sit tight right here until stuff starts to pop, probably mid-afternoon, then try to glom onto the biggest, baddest supercell and hope it spits out a wedge. If we get lucky, maybe a long-track tornado."

"Bonanza, you said?"

"Oh, yeah. A lot of storms, a lot of targets. Eventually, bigger cities on the target list, too. Emporia, in Kansas. Bartlesville and Tulsa in

Oklahoma."

Raleigh smiled, his pock-marked face looking like a happy moonscape.

"Yep," Clarence said, slapping his brother on the back, "somebody's misfortune will be our good fortune. If we're lucky, we'll get multiple opportunities."

A gust of wind smacked into the motel room's cheap door, rattling it like dry bones.

EARLY AFTERNOON. Chuck and the chase team killed time in a Walmart Supercenter parking lot in Stillwater. Most of the team had trekked off to a nearby Applebee's or Burger King for lunch, but now were back, wandering, gabbing, or talking and tweeting on their iPhones. Ty tossed a Frisbee for Stormy to chase. Metcalf paced around the lot by himself, now and then stopping by Chuck's Expedition for a status update or mumbling about the fact they were still short a camera truck. "Thanks to you, it's still in the Tulsa truck hospital," he pointed out to Chuck.

Chuck had stayed in the Expedition during lunch, munching on energy bars and sipping chocolate milk from Walmart while he studied the latest models on his laptop. Gabi, strangely silent, pale, and drained, had remained with Chuck. She'd barely acknowledged him earlier in the day; he had had little doubt what her problem was.

"Migraine?" he'd asked, a practiced softness in his voice he'd learned from being with his mother when she suffered the devastating headaches.

Gabi had merely nodded.

"Meds help?"

"A couple of Treximets. It's not so bad now. Just give me some space."

Now, eyes closed and her breathing soft and steady, she seemed almost asleep as she sat in the passenger seat with her head tipped back against the headrest.

Outside, dust and pieces of paper swirled around the lot, riding tiny whirlwinds kicked up by a stiff southerly breeze. The gusts bore a certain edginess, a hint of something Stygian despite the brightness of the sun in a sky dotted with only isolated tall-stacked cumulus.

Metcalf stuck his head into the Expedition and glanced at Gabi. "Magazine chick have too much to drink last night?" he asked Chuck, his voice almost a whisper. It seemed, perhaps, a compassion triggered by a familiarity with the throbbing headaches of hangovers.

"Migraine," Chuck answered.

"Oh. Well, being around you . . ." Metcalf winked, trying to make light of the comment. He looked up, squinting against the sun. "I gotta say, Chuckie, this doesn't look much like tornado weather."

Not wanting to disturb Gabi, Chuck exited the Expedition. "That model I've been looking at, the High-Resolution Rapid Refresh—"

"Just the no-bullshit bottom line, please."

Willie Weston appeared. "Disregard," he said, "tell me about the model."

Metcalf glared at Willie.

Chuck ignored the tacit put-down and responded to Willie. "The High-Resolution Rapid Refresh model or HRRR—" he pronounced it 'hur' "—is new and pretty damn sophisticated. It's run every hour with fresh data on a scale of resolution small enough to deal with individual thunderstorms." He reached into the vehicle and swiveled the laptop so Willie could see it.

"It cranks out extremely detailed forecasts through about 15 hours, but I'm usually looking at only the first six or eight. It's not a perfect model, no model is, but it's often a really good guide to thunderstorm development, evolution, and movement." He pointed at a map on the computer screen. "For instance, here's the output for three hours from now."

Willie stuck his head into the Expedition to get a better look. "You sure you got the right map? That looks like a radar image to me." He indicated a line of purple- and red-colored thunderstorm cells scattered across northeast Oklahoma. Sculpted and detailed, they appeared exactly like what might be seen on a radar scan.

"Nope, that's actually a forecast, a display of precipitation in the future. Here, I can put it into motion." Willie stepped out of the way, and Chuck reached into the SUV and tapped the computer's touch pad. The images on the screen sprang into motion with the smoothness of a looping radar presentation.

"So, bwana, what's it all mean?" Metcalf asked. "Am I gonna get my EF-5?" He looked again, with skepticism, at the relatively benign skyscape draped over Stillwater.

"For the last few runs, the model's been suggesting that the initial storms should erupt somewhere south of Wellington, Kansas, and north of Edmond, Oklahoma. When we see the first cells go up, we'll be in a good position to go after them." But on a day like this, they'd hardly be alone. "Along with a few million other chasers," he added. He knew from experience that on a Sunday around Oklahoma City a tornado traffic jam was a high probability. Anyone with a day off and even a casual interest in severe storms would be on the hunt.

"Focus, Charlie-O, focus. An EF-5?"

"The model won't tell us that. That'll be a real-time deal. Minute-to-minute radar monitoring. See a tornado signature. Plot its course. Hope it holds together. Calculate an intercept trajectory. Go after it. Set up. Shoot. Yeah, we'll get our EF-5. Today's the day. I feel it." New found confidence. *Where'd that come from?*

"Yeah, just like you felt that fuckin' buffalo riot." Metcalf, huffy, stomped off toward Ziggy and Boomie.

Willie remained. "I'll make sure we get the Panavision up and running in record time," he said. "Just get us into position."

A muted but piercing alarm sounded on a weather radio in the SUV. Gabi stirred and issued a soft moan, but didn't open her eyes. Chuck reached into the vehicle, switched off the radio, and tapped the computer's keyboard. A new image appeared on the screen.

"Yeeesss!" Chuck said. He pointed at the image. "A PDS box."

"A what?"

"A tornado watch, PDS. Particularly Dangerous Situation. Storm Prediction Center's words, not mine. In storm chasers' vernacular, Pretty Damn Serious."

Willie examined the map on the computer and the red-shaded rectangle outlined over northeast Oklahoma and southeast Kansas. "We're right here, correct?" He pointed at Stillwater in the southwest corner of the tornado "watch box."

"Yes. A good place to launch our pursuit. Jerry said to give him something that looked like Oklahoma, so what better place than Oklahoma?"

"So now what?"

"No point in chasing phantoms. We hang tight just a bit longer, watch the radar, and be ready to jet at a moment's notice. Why don't you let everyone know what the situation is, that the countdown clock has started."

"On it," Willie said, and left to round up the team.

Stormy skidded to a stop at Chuck's feet, snatching up the Frisbee Ty had thrown. Ty trotted over immediately behind the dog.

"So," he said, "last day."

"This is it," Chuck responded.

He met his son's gaze. *Last day.* A meaning beyond that of pursuing tornadoes. Something between a father and a son—last day to rebuild a fractured connection. Last day to overcome what had so far been a lost opportunity. But whose fault was that? Neither's? Both of theirs? *Mine—my inflexibility? Ty's—his hardheadedness? Why is it so damn hard to embrace your own son?*

"Ty . . ." The words wouldn't come.

"We tried," Ty said, a certain wistfulness in his voice. Something that wasn't there before. The hard edge gone. "Let's just leave it, not make it any worse. It is what it is. You go your way, I go mine."

"I'm sorry."

Ty folded his arms across his chest. "No, I don't think you really are. Not for your attitudes anyhow. I understand now, those are genuine. We won't get past that. So there's no need to apologize."

Stormy dropped the Frisbee at Ty's feet.

Ty bent, scooped it up, and tossed it a short distance. Stormy darted after it.

"I think maybe you are sorry," Ty continued, "that we didn't, or don't, have a traditional father-son pal-sy relationship. But then, I'm not traditional, am I?"

But still my son. Chuck remained rooted to the ground, unable to reach out to Ty, physically or emotionally. A shattered connection.

Stormy retuned with the Frisbee, dropped it again. Ty picked it up and flung it toward the edge of the parking lot. Stormy dashed in pursuit, Ty on his tail.

Last day.

THE WORDS exchanged between Chuck and Ty penetrated Gabi's semi-stupor. Her head continued to throb, but the beating within it now seemed more like someone drumming fingers on a table than whacking a bass drum. She opened one eye, then the other. Slowly, carefully. Things slightly out of focus. Her concentration AWOL. It felt as though she were experiencing her surroundings at a distance rather than being embedded within them. *Concentrate.* A forced effort. Not natural.

Chuck stuck his head into the Expedition. "You alive?'

"Barely."

"Better?"

"A little. I feel like a space cadet."

"Can I get you anything?"

"A new head."

"I'll check Walmart."

She smiled. "Hey . . ."

"Hey what?"

"You and Ty. Come on. What's the deal?" She turned to look at Chuck, but a ribbon of pain tightened over her scalp. She went back to staring straight ahead.

Chuck slid into the driver's seat. "The deal?"

"Don't play dumb. Why all the drama and tension? Is he on the lam from the law or something?"

Chuck didn't answer.

"Immunity granted. Talk to me."

No response. A diesel engine clattered to life somewhere in the lot. A horn beeped. Stormy barked. A gust of wind propelled a spray of grit into the SUV.

"I'm guessing you could use a woman's perspective on this. A friend's." *Maybe a lover's.* But not ready to say *that* aloud.

"Ty's gay."

Despite the low-grade pain still burrowing its way through her head, she turned to look at Chuck. "Oh, shit," she said. "I thought it was something serious." She would have laughed, but knew it would hurt too much.

Chuck's expression remained impassive, maybe slightly puzzled.

"I mean," she said, "homosexuality. It's not a condition. It's a description. Your son. Your legacy. Look at what he's made of his life. A soldier. A student. A responsible citizen. Just because he isn't mainstream doesn't mean he's an anomaly." She leaned her head back against the seat, exhausted from her minimal effort.

"He's not normal."

"BFD. Ted Williams wasn't normal. Albert Einstein wasn't normal. Mother Teresa wasn't normal. So Ty likes guys instead of girls. So what?"

"So it contravenes traditional values," Chuck answered, a touch of anger tinting his words. "Traditional family values."

Gabi snorted. "Traditional family values? You mean like traditional marriage? Man and woman? That didn't exactly pan out for you, did it? Or me. Or about half the folks in this country who get married. If people are afraid of gays destroying traditional marriage, they shouldn't be. The heterosexuals beat them to it."

"Let's drop it, Gabi."

"Avoidance?"

"Is this our first lover's quarrel?"

"No. We aren't lovers yet."

"Good point." Still some latent anger evident in his voice.

"Okay, truce," she said. "Let's go catch an EF-5."

"And some bad guys."

In truth, that scared her, just a bit. Chasing bad guys. Not the greatest idea in the world with the vestiges of migraine clinging to her head and a double dose of Treximet jamming her nervous system. *Not exactly on top of my game today.*

Chapter Twenty-three

THREE OR FOUR other chase teams that had been biding their time in the Walmart parking lot pulled out just after two p.m. in pursuit of the first big supercell of the day. The storm had just churned across I-35 near the Kansas-Oklahoma border, 60 miles north of Stillwater.

"Great structure," Chuck said, pointing to an intense red- and orange-colored radar echo on his computer screen. "It'll drop a tornado for sure." He swiveled the monitor for Gabi to see.

"Shouldn't we be going after it?" she asked, her voice subdued, a degree of wooziness still apparent.

"No. The chasers that just left here will have to haul ass to catch it. It'll probably be halfway to Missouri before they can run an intercept. And who knows, it might crap out before then."

He turned the computer back toward himself.

"There'll be others. More intense and closer to us. Guarantee it."

Had he really said that? Guarantee it? Yes. Confidence reborn. Skills resharpened. Mojo back. But it wasn't just magic or voodoo; it wasn't a mere "feeling" or sixth sense. His confidence sprang from insight honed on years of experience and relentless study. His ability to predict when and where to be in the field, to cozy up to atmospheric violence, had never really abandoned him; it had merely grown rusty.

He looked west. The sky in the direction of I-35 had grown black, an inky curtain lit from beyond the horizon by sheet lightning.

Ty leaned forward from the back seat and pointed at the computer screen. "Looks like another cell about ready to cross I-35 near—" he bent closer, attempting to read the name of a town on the background map "—Blackwell."

"We'll take a pass on that one, too," Chuck responded. "The parameters are looking even more explosive south of there. We might as

166

well hang on for Moby Dick."

"Well, I'll say one thing for you," Ty said, "you aren't afraid to put your money where your mouth is."

"Potential money," Chuck corrected.

"Potential or not, it's a gamble, isn't it?"

"Would you believe me if I told you it wasn't?"

Ty shrugged and slid back into his seat.

The remaining chase teams pulled out of the lot.

Metcalf strode up to the Expedition. "You guys taking a nap or something?" He gestured at the western horizon. Obsidian. Ominous. "It looks like we got foxes poppin' up all over the place, the hounds have boogied, and we're sitting here in a Wally World parking lot in Deadwater, Oklahoma, like we were outta gas. What's with you, Chuckarino? You just love yankin' my chain, don't you? You think the storms are gonna come to us?"

"If we wait long enough."

Metcalf rolled his eyes. "Two weeks wasn't long enough?"

Ignoring Metcalf's dig, Chuck refreshed the image on his computer. He zoomed in on a brilliantly tinted cell, a core of red and magenta, that had blown up east of Enid. He clicked several keys, scrolled through maps displaying esoteric parameters: EHIs, lifted indices, Craven-Brooks. "This is the one," he said quietly.

"What?" Metcalf asked, his breath pungent with onions and salami, a dab of mustard clinging to his beard.

"Saddle up," Chuck said. "We're outta here."

"'Bout damn time." Metcalf hitched up his cargo shorts and headed back to his vehicles.

"Jerry's gonna love this," Chuck said after Metcalf departed.

"What?" Gabi asked, not moving much.

"You'll see."

CLARENCE AND RALEIGH sat in their GMC Terrain north of Stillwater just off route 177, Clarence monitoring the latest radar images on his laptop. Raleigh leaned over from the passenger seat to take a look.

"Couple of good cells moving into Kansas," he said.

"Yeah, but there's nothing much up there for them to hit. The southern storm might whack Sedan, but that's a long way to travel on a 'maybe'."

"There'll be others, right?" Raleigh fiddled with his glasses; they'd slipped down on his nose.

Clarence nodded and looked to the west where the sky had become a seething black witches' brew of storm clouds. He tapped his finger on the computer screen. "There's a big storm blowing up just east of Enid. That's the one to watch. It's on the verge of a supercell already."

"We goin' after it?"

"I dunno." On his computer, Clarence examined an image that displayed a projected track for the storm. "Looks like it's headed toward the Osage Rez. Nuthin' there but Injuns and grass." He spit out the window. "We need a twister that's gonna tear something apart. In a city or town someplace. Let's cool it for a while longer."

Raleigh remained silent. Clarence read the disappointment on his face.

"Don't worry, bro'. The outbreak's just getting started. Before the day is over, there'll be plenty of wreckage for us to clean up on."

Raleigh didn't respond. He removed his glasses and massaged the bridge of his nose. He placed the spectacles back on his face and stared out the window, looking in the general direction of the Osage land.

"Okay, Raleigh, out with it," Clarence said. "I been around ya enough to know ya got something on your mind."

Raleigh turned his gaze toward his brother. "I was thinking about the stories."

"What stories?"

"The ones about the old Indian dude who owns the Gust Front."

"Sam Townsend?"

"Yeah."

"You mean those tall tales about his hidden fortune?"

"You think they're just tall tales?"

"They're rumors, bro', myths."

Raleigh frowned. A scolded puppy.

"It's like the legend of the Lost Dutchman's Gold Mine in Arizona," Clarence continued, trying to pacify his brother. "A story that's been around for over a hundred years, but no one's ever found the mine. A fairy tale."

"But it's never been disproven, either. Right?"

"Well, the fact the mine has never been found kind of disproves its existence, don't you think?"

"Well, okay. But no one has ever really searched for the Gust Front fortune, have they? So how do we know it really isn't hidden around there someplace? Supposedly guarded by Sam's buddy, whatever his name is."

Clarence shrugged and sighed. *Get off it, Raleigh.*

But Raleigh persisted. "Millions, Clarence, millions. What if it isn't a rumor? What if it's real?"

The weather radio in the vehicle squealed an alert. Clarence turned up the volume and the brothers listened. A tornado warning had been issued for Noble County, immediately north of them, a portion of which borders the Osage Reservation. The wail of warning sirens, rising and falling—distant banshees—rode the stiffening and ever more insistent wind. Overhead, thick, lowering nimbus, racing toward the core of the storm, cast an evening pall of darkness over the afternoon.

"So, let's say the stories are true," Clarence said. "That there's money stashed away somewhere around the Grill. What are the odds of a tornado hitting that place?" He made a circle, a zero, with his thumb and forefinger.

Raleigh pushed his brother's hand aside and leaned in close to him. "Millions," he whispered, "millions. A gamble? You bet. But what if . . . ?" He let the words hang.

Clarence leaned his head against the steering wheel. *What if?*

"We wouldn't have to do nuthin' anymore," Raleigh said. "We wouldn't have to, you know . . ." His words faltered.

Clarence knew what he meant. Kill anyone. He didn't enjoy that, either. But expediency, survival, sometimes dictated otherwise. Not a big deal.

But what if? Millions. A long shot, yeah. But what if? He allowed the thought to linger for a moment, then cranked the Terrain's engine.

CHUCK'S CHASE TEAM pulled out of the Walmart parking lot and turned north, toward the now massive supercell knifing toward I-35 in the direction of the sprawling Osage Nation northwest of Tulsa. The vehicles in the tiny caravan bore the ravages of two weeks on the road and too-close encounters with previous storms: two cracks in the windshield of Chuck's Expedition, a bowed-in door on Metcalf's Navigator, a cratered roof on the camera rig.

Chuck monitored the supercell's progress on his computer and checked the in-coming reports. Law enforcement, Noble County: large tornado near Ceres. Chaser report: wedge tornado west of 177 just south of Marland.

Ty leaned over Chuck's shoulder. "What's a wedge tornado?"

"Big, broad, and nasty. A twister that looks like a massive black triangle with its apex on the ground. Wedge-shaped. Almost as wide as it is tall."

In an effort to get ahead of the tornado-producing supercell, Chuck jumped on the Cimarron Turnpike Spur north of Stillwater. The Spur connected with the main turnpike leading east. He followed the turnpike a short distance, exited at route 18, and ran north. By the time the team reached Pawnee, the pursuit slowed, the road jammed with chasers, TV sat trucks, and sightseers.

"Gotta get out of this mess," Chuck said over his cell phone to Metcalf. "Follow me."

"Where we goin', *sahib?*"

"Farm roads."

"No, I mean where are we headed?"

"Oh, give me a home . . ." Chuck sang.

"You gotta be kiddin'. Not back to where the friggin' buffalo roam?"

"I don't think 'friggin' was in the lyrics."

Chuck led them north on back roads paralleling route 18 until they intersected 18 again near Ralston. Their alternate course appeared to have put them ahead of most of the chasers.

"We gotta get back on 18 here," Chuck said to Gabi, who continued to doze on and off. "It's the only way across the Arkansas River." The team's vehicles rattled across a narrow, two-lane, steel-truss bridge spanning the stream.

Gabi sat up, looked around, eyes a little glassy. "Where are we?"

"Just entering the Rez." He wasn't quite sure Gabi remembered what they were doing. "The storm we're chasing is about ten miles northwest of us." He pointed to his left at a mass of roiling darkness that pulsed with almost continuous lightning, a plasma of high-voltage anger. He glanced at the radar display on his computer. "Uh, oh."

"What?" Ty asked.

"It's losing its tornado signature."

"It's dying?" Gabi asked.

"Not necessarily. Storms cycle. They strengthen, they weaken, they strengthen again. We'll stick with this one. It's already proven itself. I think it'll come back." But suddenly, as though a pebble had been tossed into a still pond, there it was: a ripple of doubt spreading through his psyche, challenging his new-found confidence.

Not wishing to dwell on negatives, he changed the subject, speaking to Gabi. "How are you feeling?"

"Like howitzers have been going off in my head." She managed a weak smile. "That's an improvement, in case you were wondering."

A strong gust of wind shook the SUV. "Good sign," Chuck said, acknowledging the gust. "Strong inflow. It's still a damn healthy storm."

He addressed Gabi again. "You'll make it through the day then?" He hoped the question sounded empathetic, not like he was concerned she'd screw up the chase.

"I'll be fine. Long as I don't have to wrestle bad guys." A little laugh.

The short caravan approached the small burg of Fairfax. "For your trivia files," Chuck said, "some of the scenes for *Twister* were filmed around here."

Once through Fairfax, the vehicles sped north through open farmland and grassy prairies until they reached U. S. 60, where they turned east. Chuck picked up his cell phone and spoke to Metcalf. "We're headed toward Bartlesville. We'll try to set up someplace west of there." *And pray this storm cycles.*

"Let's stay on the main roads, okay?" Metcalf said. "No herds of hairy beasts there."

It wasn't sudden, just a gentle pull of the Expedition to the right, toward the shoulder, and then clop-clop-clop.

Stormy stood up on the back seat and half-growled, half-whimpered.

"Unbelievable," Chuck said.

Gabi looked at him.

"Flat tire." *The incident with the tractor on Tuesday come home to roost?*

He pulled onto the shoulder, turned on the flashers, and set the parking brake. The weather radio blared another warning. This one for Pawnee County. A different supercell, not the one they'd been tracking. Chuck expanded the view of the radar on his computer. He turned the screen so Gabi and Ty could see.

"There's a monster supercell north of Stillwater now." He pointed it out.

"Not far from where we started," Ty noted.

"Yeah. And it's got a great TVS."

"Good for it," Ty said.

"TVS. Tornado Vortex Signature. It's a Doppler radar algorithm that suggests the presence of a strong mesocyclone. That doesn't mean there *is* a tornado, just that there's a high probability of one."

Ty nodded his understanding. "Want me to start working on the tire while you monitor the storms?" he said.

Ty pitching in. A bit of a surprise.

"Yeah. Thanks."

Ty got out of the SUV and began unloading the luggage from behind the rear seat so he could get at the tools in the floor compartment.

Metcalf rapped on the Expedition's window.

Chuck opened the door.

"How much more can go wrong, *jefe*?" Metcalf said, his face tinted in various shades of crimson. "Do you plan this shit ahead of time or does it just happen to you?" His jaw kept moving even after he'd finished speaking.

Chuck pressed his lips together and held his gut-reply in check: *For you, I plan.* Out loud: "This isn't the end of the road. There's another cell coming up behind us that might be an even better candidate. Give me some space to work. We'll be back on the road in fifteen minutes." *Maybe, maybe not.*

Ty wrestled to get the jack set properly near the right front fender. Several cars and vans swept past them on the road, most giving friendly toots. After two weeks in the field, Chuck and his team had become easily recognizable entities by other chasers.

Chuck focused on the radar images. The northern storm, the one they'd been racing to get ahead of, continued to weaken, losing its TVS. The new contender, however, looked increasingly robust. A hook echo. Strong rotation. *Gotta be a tornado.* Then something else. "Whoa," he exclaimed, startling Gabi, who'd been half-slumbering again.

"Debris ball," he said. He pointed at the core of the hook echo, now colored vividly, a dot of death. "That's airborne wreckage. A tornado. Probably hit a small town." He read the name on the map underlay. "Morrison."

He scrambled from the vehicle and knelt by Ty, who was now busy loosening the lug nuts on the wheel. "Much longer? We got a new target."

"Five minutes, ten at most." He didn't look at Chuck. Turbulent gusts, bearing the essence of plowed earth and cow manure, jiggled the SUV. Thunder rolled over the flat landscape in a nonstop barrage, more ominous than loud, as if emanating from a distant battle . . . but drawing nearer. The sky, black and ragged, pulsed with electricity. In the middle distance, a coyote slinking along a low ridge line, perhaps fleeing the storm, seemed to disappear into the prairie, given shelter by the vastness of which it was a part.

Chuck looked down the road; he could see the chasers that had passed him braking, halting on the shoulder, probably seeing the same thing he had. The new storm. He watched as they pulled out again and made a right at an intersection a few hundred yards beyond. Reversing course. Heading south. The fresh storm now the target *du jour*.

He jogged to the camera truck. Metcalf, Willie, Boomie, and Ziggy stood near the cab, scanning the sky.

"As soon as the tire is repaired, we're on our way," Chuck said. "We're going after the storm to the southwest."

"What happened to the other one?" Willie asked.

"Crapped out. At least temporarily. But this new one's really cranking. You know, a bird in hand and all that."

"Let's get on it then," Metcalf said.

Chuck pivoted to return to the Expedition. Another chaser vehicle, antennae sprouting from its roof, flew past him, eastbound. No wave, no horn, no acknowledgment. Maybe a newcomer to the storm chasing game.

He reached the Expedition, where he found Gabi standing outside and Ty finishing his work. Gabi, brushing wind-blown hair from her eyes, stared down the road after the vehicle that had just gone by. She turned to Chuck. "Did you see that?" she said, a hint of excitement in her voice.

"What? The chasers who just passed us?"

"A black GMC with a grill guard." She let the words hang.

Chapter Twenty-four

SUNDAY, MAY 11
MID-AFTERNOON

BLACK GMC, GRILL guard. Chuck let Gabi's observation sink it. "The SUV spotted at the crime scenes?"

"It fits the description," Gabi said.

"But hardly a unique vehicle. Lots of black GMCs around, quite a few with grill guards."

"Yeah, but how many others like it have we seen the past two weeks? Driven by chasers, I mean."

Gabi had a point. The answer was None.

Chuck watched the departing SUV's brake lights come on. He expected it to pull to the side of the road, or make a right turn, like the previous chase vehicles had. But it didn't. Instead, it turned left—going after the initial storm? The one that had weakened? Did they think it would cycle, become a potent supercell again? Not impossible. But why roll the dice? Why not follow the crowd and pursue the southern storm? Tornado warnings on it continued to be issued one after the other, as if rolling off an assembly line. It appeared to be one of those rare supercells that would live for hours, a carrier of death packing a long-lived, violent tornado.

Gabi placed a hand on Chuck's arm. "So, can we follow those guys?"

Ty, finished changing the tire, joined Chuck and Gabi. "What's up?" He followed their gazes to the black SUV, now speeding northward, away from the main road.

"Gabi thinks that might be the vehicle law enforcement is looking for," Chuck said.

"We need to follow it," Gabi responded, perhaps hoping for an ally in Ty.

Chuck weighed his options—only two, really. Go in pursuit of the black GMC and possibly miss a shot at accomplishing what he'd been hired to do: lead Metcalf and his film crew to an EF-4 or -5. Or go balls-to-the-wall after a supercell that probably harbored a million-dollar payday. Frankly, not a difficult choice.

The GMC disappeared over the flat horizon.

"I'm sorry, Gabi," Chuck said. "I—" He stopped abruptly.

"What?" she said.

He ducked into the Expedition and pulled up a computer display showing the locations of all the chasers, at least those with their transponders turned on.

"Sam's chasing," Chuck said.

Gabi shot him a quizzical look.

"Sam Townsend. You met him at the Gust Front Grill."

"The Vietnam vet," Ty reminded her.

"Yeah."

"What's that got to do with the price of tea in China?" Gabi asked.

"The road the black GMC turned on leads in the general direction of the Gust Front."

The statement didn't seem to resonate with Gabi immediately, as though her thoughts were mired in mud, likely the side effects of the meds she'd been taking.

Ty understood right away. "So, if those are the bad guys, maybe they're going after Sam's rumored fortune."

"Even then, a long shot," Chuck said. "The odds of any kind of storm hitting there, let alone a twister, are infinitesimally small."

"But," Ty said, "it might be the only chance they ever get. If they're who we think they might be."

Metcalf, in the Navigator, laid on his horn and leaned his head out the window. "What's the hold up, Chuckie?" he yelled, his words barely audible in the ripping wind and rolling thunder. "We need to get this circus train moving."

"A minute," Chuck yelled back. He understood his contractual duty was to Metcalf, but he wanted to help Gabi, too. Maybe for something beyond altruistic reasons, but all the same, he wanted to act the faithful lieutenant. But he couldn't. Too much at stake. It always came down to money, didn't it?

"I just can't do it, Gabi," Chuck said. "I told you the first night we met, my client would take precedent and you said you understood."

Grasping the roof of the Expedition for support, she offered a counter-suggestion. "Let me take the Expedition and follow those guys," she said. "You and Ty can go with Metcalf and find your tornado."

Her thought process, Chuck could see, remained addled.

"No," he said. "I can't run an intercept on the storm without the equipment in the Expedition. Besides, you're in no shape to be going off on your own chasing criminals."

"Let me decide what I'm capable of or not," she snapped. "As a federal agent, I've got a job to do, too."

"You don't even know how to get to the Gust Front from here, Gabi. Settle down."

"Don't tell me to goddamn settle down. I know better than you what the hell I'm doing." Argumentative. Irritable.

Ty stepped to her side. "Truce," he said. He made a "T" with his hands, like a referee signaling for time out. "Let's consider a Plan C."

"*Really?*" Gabi said. Still upset.

"I'm listening," Chuck said, ready to accept any solution that would get them moving and Gabi to drop her harpy act.

"How about you and Gabi take the Expedition and head for the Gust Front? I'll ride with Metcalf. Over the cell phone, you can keep in touch with me and get us in a position where we can film the tornado. We can kind of watch what the other chasers are up to, too."

Chuck considered the idea, but decided against it. "Too dangerous," he said. "I need to be there, in person, making sure there are escape routes and that there's time to bail if we need to."

"I've been paying attention," Ty said. "You do everything using radar imagery and roadmaps. On your computer. So, you can vector me remotely. Just tell me what to do, where to go. I can follow orders. Army, remember?"

"I don't know, Ty. I don't like the idea of being separated." Chuck wished now he'd purchased transponders, locator beacons, for the vehicles, but he'd never envisioned that his team members might have to operate independently.

"Your son has a good idea," Gabi interjected. "It could work."

Could being the operative word. Not *will*.

Metcalf appeared, his anger boiling over, his words uncontrolled. "What the hell is going on?" he screamed, pushing Gabi and Ty away from the Expedition and leaning into its interior, getting in Chuck's face. "Are we going to miss another opportunity? I give you a break, we get a tornado swarm, yet here we sit like cow pies on the prairie. Unbefuckinglievable."

Chuck shoved Metcalf away and got out of the car. "Button your mouth, Jerry, and listen to me. Here's what we're going to do."

He told him about Gabi being FBI, about her migraines, about why she was on the chase, about the black GMC and the Gust Front Grill, and finally about Ty's plan. Metcalf stood silent, shaking his head, his jaw slightly agape.

"A second," Chuck said after he'd finished. He ducked back into the SUV and pulled up the latest radar loop on his laptop. The northern storm appeared to be cycling, regenerating. Not dead.

He stepped back out of the vehicle. "Here's an addendum to Ty's plan," he said to Metcalf. "The southern supercell is still the Big Show. You, Ty, and the camera rig will go after it. But the northern storm looks like it's making a comeback. Let's hedge our bets."

"How?" Metcalf said.

"You've got two Panavisions left, correct?"

Metcalf nodded.

"Send one of them and a cinematographer with me and Gabi. Just in case. Your guy could use that Steady Camera thing to shoot, couldn't he?"

"Steadicam."

"Yeah, Steadicam."

"Anything to get us moving." Metcalf, his head tipped skyward as though beseeching unseen gods, trotted toward the camera truck.

Moments later, one the cinematographers, Boomie, joined Chuck, Gabi, and Ty.

A crack of thunder like an exploding artillery shell rent the clamor of the wind and tumbled across the grassland in a diminishing wave of sound. Soon, it melded into a low-decibel grumble, mingling with the residue of a thousand other explosions.

GABI, AT CHUCK'S request, but slightly unsure of herself, took the wheel of the Expedition so Chuck could track the storms and maintain contact with Ty. They sped northward on a narrow county road beneath a death-shroud sky, the prairie grass on either side of them pressed almost horizontal by the wind. The pounding in her head had ceased, but her thought processes seemed mired in quicksand and her reactions restrained by heavy chains. She forced herself to focus on driving.

"How long to the Gust Front?" she asked.

Chuck looked up from his computer. "About 15 minutes." He

picked up his cell and called Ty. "You should be coming up on Pawhuska soon. Out of there, head south on route 99. Hustle. The storm will be bearing down on you from the west. You want to get south of its track, then set up somewhere just west of Wynona."

Chuck paused, listening to Ty's response, and said, "Get back to me in few minutes."

He turned to Boomie in the back seat. "How ya doin'?"

"Okay," the goateed cameraman said, "considering I've never assembled a Panavision in a moving vehicle." Gabi could hear click-click-click as he snapped together parts from three metal carrying cases. "I'll have us a full-fledged Genesis in about five minutes."

He stopped to pet Stormy, who evidently was watching the operation with interest, perhaps anticipating the man might be building something that produced treats. "Good doggie," Boomie said. "We'll have to see if we can fit you into a few shots. Film audiences love to see pets . . . as long as they don't get hurt." He ruffled the fur on Stormy's head.

"Boomie," Chuck said reflectively. "Where'd you get that name? I'll bet you used to be a boom operator of some sort."

"Good guess. But no. I was in the navy. Served on nuclear-powered subs that carried ballistic missiles. The boats were known as 'Boomers.' Thus, 'Boomie'."

The Expedition hit a pothole and jounced into the air. Gabi gripped the steering wheel with determined fierceness, her knuckles growing bloodless. "Sorry," she said.

"Make that seven minutes for the Genesis," Boomie said. He bent to pick up a part that had tumbled into the foot well.

"Black as an iron skillet," Gabi said, studying the horizon ahead.

Chuck bent to his computer. "Beautiful," he said. "This thing's definitely cycling. Got a TVS again. Intense. We may have gotten lucky." He turned to Boomie. "You gonna be ready?"

"Yeah. It'll take a few minutes to get the Steadicam rig on and the Genesis secured, but I'll be set."

"What do you mean, Steadicam *rig*?" Chuck asked. "I thought that thing you're putting together is a Steadicam."

"No. A Steadicam is a harness, or vest. It supports a vertical armature with a camera on top and a counterbalance, usually a battery pack and monitor, on the bottom. With the rig in place, I can run while filming and the shot remains stable. It doesn't come out all jiggly and jumpy."

"Like a human dolly," Gabi said.

"Good description. Might come in handy if I'm chasing a tornado."

"Or vice versa," Chuck said.

Ahead of the Expedition, continuous lightning painted the sky in blue-white spiderwebs of electricity. A muscular gust of wind buffeted the SUV.

"No sign of a black GMC," Gabi said, leaning forward, squinting, as if it would help her see through the dirt and dust whipping over the road.

"Those guys got a pretty good jump on us," Chuck responded. "They're probably already at the Gust Front . . . *if* that's where they were headed."

Stormy sneezed.

"*Gesundheit,*" Boomie said. "Dusty in here, huh?" He continued to work on the Genesis.

Gabi didn't know how much, if any, of the Sam Townsend legend to believe. "So what's your take on the hidden money and mystical Monty story?" she asked Chuck. "Half true, half tall tale? Total fabrication? The real deal?"

"Your guess is as good as mine. But—"

His cell rang. He answered. Ty, Gabi assumed.

"Keep pressing south," Chuck said. "The reason you almost got blown off the road is from the inflow to the storm. You're okay. Where are you?" He listened to Ty's response, checked his monitor, and responded. "Another five minutes. Then there should be a farm road on your right just as you enter Wynona. Take it. Then call me back."

He ended the call and addressed Gabi. "What I was about to say, is that Sam sounded pretty convincing when it came to this guy Monty, so I'm thinking he's real. Real, but weird, I guess. The hidden fortune? Well, Sam has never directly denied it, just joked about it. But I guess that's something you'd never just come out and say: Yeah, I've got a few million bucks stashed away around here."

"So it might be worth it then," Gabi said, thinking out loud, "for these guys—assuming they are the killers—to run a little armed reconnaissance on Sam's place, storm or no storm, knowing he's off chasing. They'd know that, right? From the transponders?"

"They would." He paused. "Gabi?"

"Yeah?"

"You've got a gun, I trust."

"A Glock .40 caliber."

"You sure you're gonna be—"

She shot him a "back-off" glance. He didn't finish the sentence. *Let me be, please let me be. It's hard enough dealing with a head-banging migraine. I don't need all the solicitous questions.*

Chuck went back to studying his computer monitor.

Stormy, growled—a warning, not a threat—and stuck her nose over the backrest of the front seat into Chuck's neck.

"Yeah, girl, it's okay. I see it on radar." To Gabi he said, "Go fast. We're in a race."

Gabi snuck a peek at him and quickly read two emotions on his face. First, awe—perhaps something sought after on a tornado chase. Second, just a hint of fear—clearly a reaction that shouldn't be there.

Chapter Twenty-five

SUNDAY, MAY 11
LATE AFTERNOON

"WHAT IS IT?" Gabi asked. She pressed the accelerator pedal to the floor.

Chuck turned to Boomie. "The camera ready to go?"

"Just about."

"And the Steadicam harness?"

"Won't take long. What's up?"

"The supercell we've been tracking has intensified again, really blown up. It's damn sure got a tornado, and it's a right-turner."

Boomie looked up from his work. "A what?"

"Right-turner. Very intense supercells sometimes deviate to the right of where you think they should go if you just look at the steering winds. I thought this storm was gonna pass just north of the Gust Front. Now it's peeled off to the right. It's headed directly for the grill . . . and us."

Gabi switched on the Expedition's headlights. A blizzard of dust filled the air as she reached the small town adjacent to the Gust Front Grill. She slowed. The howl of tornado sirens challenged the galloping wind. Along the main street of the village, people, their heads lowered against the gale, dashed for cover.

Gabi looked at Chuck, seeking instructions.

"Go through town," he said. "We can make it to Sam's place." They weren't in a good situation, but he didn't want to convey his apprehension to Gabi and Boomie. Still, he knew he wasn't hiding it well. His breathing became labored; it felt as if a wrecking ball of dread were crushing his chest.

Boomie snapped a power cable into place on the Genesis. "Ready," he said. He reached behind him and retrieved the Steadicam vest. Stormy paced from side to side in the footwell, alternately growling and whining.

Ty called again.

"We're on the farm road," he said. "It's really black and really windy. Lotta chasers parked along the shoulder. We must be in the right spot."

On his monitor, Chuck shifted the radar imagery to center on the supercell Ty pursued. *Don't need this, not now. Too damn much going on.*

"The cell still has a great TVS," Chuck said. "It's gotta be packing a tornado." He studied the roadmap underlay. A quick scan. "Stay on the road you're on another minute or two. It'll intersect with County Road 5270. Take 5270 south—just a few hundred feet. That'll give you a clear view back north. Get the crane and camera up. You'll have about 10 or 12 minutes. The twister should pass just north of you, within a quarter of a mile."

"That's cutting it pretty thin."

Chuck considered the possibility Ty's storm could become a right-turner, too, similar to the one thundering toward Sam's. "Look, if things go to shit, if you see the twister coming right at you, get out. You'll be pointed south, so all you have to do is beat feet in that direction. Got it?"

"Got it. Hey, we're at the intersection." Chuck heard Ty ordering Metcalf to turn.

Ty came back on the phone. "A few hundred feet you said?"

"Yeah." *Hurry up.*

Several moments passed before Ty responded. Finally he said, "Okay, we're here. They're getting the camera up." A pause, then: "Oh, wow. I see a wall cloud. Four, maybe five miles away."

Chuck marveled that his son had the terminology down. "Tell Metcalf to start filming as soon as he's ready," he said.

"I hear tornado sirens," Ty said, his voice taught.

"From the town you just came through. Look, Ty, I gotta go. It's getting a little hairy here, too. I'll get back to you as soon as I can."

Gabi pulled into the parking lot of the Gust Front Grill. On the front entrance of the building, a sign—CLOSED, GONE CHASING—flapped in the wind. No black GMC.

"Let's take a look around back," she said.

"Not much time left," Chuck responded. His heartbeat, rapid before, ramped up even more.

A plastic trash can, riding a spearhead of wind, bounced off the

Expedition.

Gabi, ignoring Chuck's anxiety, circled the grill in the Expedition, but discovered no other vehicles.

"Well, maybe those weren't the bad guys," she said, a smidgen of disappointment in her voice.

"Might have been just a couple of amateurs out for the day," Chuck suggested, relieved he had only one problem to deal with now: the tornado bearing down on them. Gabi was in no shape to be confronting criminals anyhow.

"Damn," she said. She pounded the steering wheel in frustration.

"Look, there's an alternative explanation," Chuck said, wanting to keep her thoughts focused. "Maybe we *were* tracking the right vehicle. The guys in it would know a tornado's bearing down on this place; they have access to the same info we do. They aren't going to enter a building realizing it could become kindling in a few minutes. They'd seek shelter. Wait it out." He glanced at the lowering black scud racing across the sky and the debris tumbling through the parking lot. "Which is what we oughta be doing. Right now."

"Hey," Boomie interjected. "I didn't come all the way out here to hide in a storm cellar. I wanna film this thing."

Chuck had to admit, the cinematographer was right. That's why they all were here. To film a twister. But he hadn't counted on getting quite this close to one. This wasn't going to be like photographing African wildlife from a Land Rover. This was going to be like facing a charging lion, on foot, in the bush, with nowhere to run.

They needed somewhere to run.

"Stop here," Chuck said to Gabi as they reached the front of the grill again. "Boomie, I'm with you. But I don't want to get anyone killed just to film my million-dollar baby."

"Remember," Boomie said, exuding confidence, "I can run and film at the same time."

"Well, you may have to. We've only got a minute or two left before this thing is on top of us. Let's get out and take a look." *Only a minute or two? What am I thinking?* He didn't want to admit it, but he knew damn well what he was thinking: a million dollars.

They exited the Expedition. Stormy darted out, too, barking furiously and sprinting in circles around the SUV. Warning sirens from the nearby town continued to moan.

"Jesus, look at that," Boomie said, gazing skyward, interrupting his effort to prepare the Steadicam for action.

From an inverted black ocean of twisted and torn clouds, chunks of debris tumbled earthward in a slow-motion ballet. Aluminum sheets, asphalt shingles, fiberglass insulation, shards of paper, a plastic wading pool.

"From the tornado," Chuck said.

"I'm ready for it," Boomie announced, finished with his task. An odd sight: a squat, buzz-cut man in a "vest" holding a vertical armature with a motion picture camera on top, a monitor on the bottom, and the entire assembly secured to his vest by an articulated arm capable of pivoting up, down, and sideways.

"Listen!" Chuck said. A low-decibel roar, like the beating wings of a thousand angels of death, mingled with the relentless wind and banshee sirens. "It's coming."

He peered in the direction of the sound. No tornado, not yet, only black-on-black, end-of-the-world darkness. But he knew what hid in the blackness. Verging on panic, he swiveled his head, searching for shelter. Above ground, they wouldn't survive a direct hit. Did Sam have a storm cellar? He couldn't recall. Wait. Yes, he did. They'd parked by it the first day they'd visited here. Next to a generator.

At the far end of the parking lot, he spotted it: the auxiliary generator. Adjacent to it, the mound of earth containing the tornado shelter.

Boomie, already at work, tipped the Panavision Genesis skyward, capturing the debris circling overhead—effluent from the twister. Then he lowered the aim of the camera, pointing it at the dead-of-night horizon looming over the town. He gripped the armature with one hand and let the other swing freely, helping to maintain his balance in the howling wind. Oddly, the thunder had ceased. Then, even the wind seemed to falter.

"Hey," Boomie yelled, "Joseph Conrad should have seen this." *Heart of Darkness.*

Chuck, on his way to the shelter to open its door, turned and yelled back, "You're right. But who knows, maybe he did." He resumed his jog toward the refuge.

Then a roar, unlike anything he'd ever heard, could ever have imagined, rolled over the parking lot in a thunderous, deafening explosion. It was as if a squadron of fighter jets preparing for takeoff, afterburners lit, engines at full military power, had blown away their blast shields.

"Oh, my God," Boomie screamed. "Oh, my everlovin' God."

"Chuck!" Gabi yelled, the word a mixture of terror and awe.

Stormy, ears flattened against her head, shot past Chuck and scuttled toward the generator.

Chuck wheeled. Saw something he'd never expected to see. And—except for a half-century old newspaper photo—wasn't sure even existed.

Chapter Twenty-six

SUNDAY, MAY 11
LATE AFTERNOON

IMMENSE, TENEBROUS, swirling. Not one funnel. Two. Side by side—massive twin tornadoes, full-grown adults devouring the small town a half-mile distant and churning relentlessly toward the Gust Front Grill. Chuck stood for a moment, mesmerized. Not quite grasping or believing what he was seeing. But there was no mistaking it. Not a twister accompanied by a wispy suction vortex or a ropy funnel. No. Conjoined monsters.

He broke his hypnotic state and bellowed, "Come on," motioning frantically for Gabi and Boomie to follow him to the shelter. He bent and yanked open the heavy steel door.

Stormy, tongue lolled out in a heavy pant, burst from behind the generator and darted into the shelter.

Gabi sprinted toward Chuck, debris showering around her in a cloudburst of shingles and siding and glass.

Boomie, still in the Steadicam rig with the Panavision pointed at the approaching double twisters, backpedalled slowly, determined to capture the oncoming monster on video. A two-by-four plunged into the ground next to him. Had he been a foot to his right, his skull would have been shattered.

Chuck screamed at Boomie to turn and run, but his words were no match for the ear-splitting clamor of the wind. A haboob of dust and airborne flotsam swept over the parking lot. Chuck gasped for breath. Gabi stumbled into his arms; he grasped her firmly and guided her to the top of the short flight of stairs leading into the shelter.

Power flashes lit the huge tornadoes in a strobing blue-white counterpoint to their death-shroud blackness. A roof, as if launched by a Space Shuttle Booster Rocket, took leave of a building. An entire block of the small town seemed to explode, leveled not by a massive car bomb but by wind of incomprehensible violence. A mobile home, tumbling end-over-end through the air, disappeared into the maw of one of the funnels, swallowed by a whirlpool of obliteration. A car, disintegrating in slow motion, barrel-rolled down a street before being crushed by a volley of concrete and steel hurled into it at several hundred miles per hour.

A large chunk of metal slammed into Boomie's shoulder and he went down, losing control of the Panavision. Chuck sprinted from cover and grabbed Boomie's Steadicam vest, attempted to drag him to cover. To no avail. A powerful gust slammed him into the pavement beside Boomie. They both lay in the open, the rubble of a dead town swirling around them in a macabre dance.

Chuck struggled to his knees. A shard of glass buried itself in his cheek. He tugged on Boomie's vest again, dragging him toward the sanctuary. The closer of the twin tornadoes reached the edge of the Gust Front's parking lot, a couple of hundred yards away. Chuck swept his gaze toward the storm cellar—ten feet behind him. Ten feet to safety. Maybe.

His world, now reduced to blackness and noise so deafening he felt suspended in silence, closed in on him, hell bent on only one thing: ending his mortal life. He closed his eyes against the stinging dust and chunks of wood and metal that flew horizontally through the blackness, flaying his face into hamburger. He concentrated on tugging Boomie to safety, a seemingly interminable effort. Tug. Pause. Tug. Pause.

Then a hand grasping the top of his pants. Pulling . . . Gabi pulling him; he pulling Boomie. At last, bumping down the stairs into the concrete safe room. He released Boomie, reached up, and slammed the door of the shelter shut. A barrage of something—two-by-fours? slabs of asphalt? trees? chunks of a disintegrating Gust Front Grill?—whanged against the exterior of the reinforced door, the wreckage hammering out a discordant death knell. Something, probably a tree, crashed into the earth above them, landing with a reverberating thump. "Not on the door, please," Chuck muttered aloud.

Gabi found a switch for a set of battery-powered lights within the shelter and illuminated the blackness in which they'd been standing. The room appeared to be about ten-by-ten, probably big enough for the employees of the Gust Front . . . none of them around today.

Chuck glanced down at Boomie, who was unresponsive but at least breathing. He had no idea how badly the cameraman might be hurt. He stretched him out on the concrete floor and knelt beside him, huddling with Gabi and Stormy.

Somebody had once told him: You can't survive an EF-5 above ground. He knew without a shadow of doubt, without waiting for the required post-storm survey, that an EF-5—probably two—the most violent category of storm on earth, was passing overhead. The Lord striking down the first born. Chuck bowed his head in thanks. They were the Israelites, protected by blood on the doorframe. Exodus.

Had they been caught in the open, a few feet above where they now nestled, they would have become nothing more than meat in a tornadic blender.

Even in their insulted sanctuary, Chuck sensed the deafening bellow of the storm above, its savagery, its cruelness. Time evaporated. He closed his eyes and endured, clinging to Gabi and Stormy. Clutching. It seemed forever.

The fearsome noise retreated. He drew a breath. It hadn't been forever, only seconds. Gabi stirred. Stormy lifted her head. Boomie remained motionless.

"Okay," Chuck whispered, "we're okay."

He nudged Boomie. The cameraman moaned.

"Boomie," Chuck said, "can you hear me?" Boomie didn't respond. Chuck rose.

"You're bleeding," Gabi said, pushing herself up, too, and staring at Chuck's head. She reached for his face, ran her fingers over his cheek, brought them away bloody.

He patted his cheek, found a long gash and felt the embedded piece of glass. "I don't think it's deep." He wiped at the blood, but succeeded only in smearing it, mixing it with leakage from the other cuts in his face.

Gabi fumbled in the pockets of her jeans. "I've got some tissues." Chuck accepted them.

Boomie moaned again.

"Hey, buddy," Chuck said, "you with us?"

Boomie opened one eye, closed it. "Maybe, maybe not. Shoulder hurts like hell. How come we're still alive?"

Chuck shrugged. "We're in a storm cellar. Can you sit up?"

"If you tug me by my right arm. I think my left shoulder's broken."

Chuck crammed the tissues in his pants pocket, grasped Boomie's right arm, and pulled.

"Fuck! Shit, goddamn that hurts."

"Sorry," Chuck said. But at least Boomie, still in his Steadicam vest, now sat with his back against the wall of the shelter.

Chuck walked to the door and cracked it open. Since it had been angled to match the slope of the mound, it remained unblocked by fallen trees or debris. In the distance, the storm churned away, the roar fading, tumbling toward pianissimo. A steady rain pattered down, as if a balm to the extreme barbarity that had passed over the land.

"Just one twister now," Chuck announced as he pushed the door wide open and stepped out.

To his surprise, Boomie followed. "What happened to the second one?" he asked, then grimaced in pain.

"Jesus, buddy. Take it easy. Here, let me help you." He guided Boomie toward the generator. Gabi and Stormy clambered out of the shelter.

"The second twister. What happened to it?" Boomie asked again.

"Dissipated," Chuck said. "I'll explain later. But what you filmed was extremely rare. The only other photographic evidence I've ever seen of two mature tornadoes side-by-side was shot during the Palm Sunday outbreak of 1965. That was in the days before you could photoshop stuff, so it was the real deal." He seated Boomie against the generator.

"The Panavision is gone," Boomie said. With his right arm he gestured lamely at the debris layered over the parking lot. "It's somewhere out there. Well, at least parts of it. I lost my grip on it after something smashed into me."

Chuck, feeling as if he'd just been suckered punched in the gut, surveyed the wreckage strewn around him. His million dollars were somewhere out there, part of a garbage dump now. He turned slowly, making a 360-degree pivot. The Gust Front Grill had become a pile of rubble—timbers, support beams, sections of roof, all laying in a twisted heap.

Beyond the parking lot, the little town had ceased to exist. For all practical purposes, it had been leveled. Only the skeletal remains of a handful of buildings suggested a viable community had once stood there. Here and there, smoke drifted from the wreckage. A full-fledged fire raged at the far end of the former town, chewing through a head-high mound of debris. People, seeming to have no purpose, dazed and confused, wandered along the street. A strange silence, except for the occasional wail of stunned humans, permeated the scene. What had happened to the First Responders? Had they, too, fallen victim to the double dose of violence?

Chuck spotted his Expedition. It had been hurled from one end of the Gust Front's parking lot to the other. It lay on its roof, twisted and crumpled metal, embedded in the wreckage of what used to be a motel room. A two-by-four driven into one of its doors protruded like the handle of a dagger.

"Hey, Chuck," Boomie called, the words followed by a prolonged groan.

"Yeah?" Chuck continued to stare at the desolation encircling him.

"Look for the recorder, will ya?"

"You mean the camera?"

"No. The camera doesn't matter. The recorder is what counts. It has the tornado images."

Chuck shook his head; despair. "It could be in the next county."

"It could be three feet away. It's a unit about the size of a shoebox with a digital readout screen on one side. Has *Panavision SSR*—for solid state recorder—written across it. It was attached to the camera . . . but God knows if it still is." His voice faltered. "Look, I'd help you search, but I'm feeling . . . a little . . . you know . . . lightheaded." Boomie's head tipped forward, his chin coming to rest on top of the Steadicam vest.

"I'll help," Gabi said. "I know how much it means to you." She eyed Chuck's face again. "Hey, keep pressing the tissues against your cheek. You're a mess."

He removed the tissues from his pants pocket and jammed them against his bloody face. With his other hand he pulled his cell phone from his shirt pocket and tossed it to Gabi. "Call 911. Tell them the town's been leveled. There are injured people. Not only in town, but next to where the Gust Front used to be. We gotta get Boomie some help."

"You think we've still got cell service? After the storm?"

"Probably. The tornado—well, tornadoes—cut a relatively narrow swath. There should still be cell towers standing within range."

The smell of burning wood and plastic, despite the rain, wafted over the piles of debris that littered the vast parking lot and undoubtedly extended for miles beyond.

Gabi made the call and connected with the state police. After she'd finished, she told Chuck that authorities were already aware of the situation and that help had been dispatched, but that it might be 15 or 20 minutes away. There were other locations in need.

"Thanks," he said. "Better try Ty, too."

She nodded and punched in his number. Chuck took stock of Gabi as she waited for Ty to answer. She, to put it frankly, looked a mess: her hair in a rats' nest-tangle, her face splattered with mud, her blouse torn, a hole in the knee of her slacks. But he knew he looked worse.

He glanced at his shirt, ripped and bloodied, one sleeve completely missing. Had he caught it on a sharp object or has it been yanked away by the wind? He had no recollection. Both legs of his pants had been shredded and now hung on him as if he were some sort of modern-day Robinson Crusoe.

Stormy milled around his feet, not venturing far from familiar sights and smells.

"Ty," Gabi said, and handed the phone to Chuck.

"You okay?" Chuck asked.

"Fine," Ty answered, sounding almost exuberant. "We got some great footage of a tornado. It might be your breadwinner."

"Did it hit anything? I mean like buildings? Homes? Barns?"

"Luckily, it missed the town. I think it stayed in open country. Lots of trees and farmland ripped up."

"Here's the thing, Ty, unless a tornado hits a built-up area, there's no way to categorize it. EF ratings are determined by structural damage. There's no way to prove a twister was an EF-4 or -5 unless it wrecks buildings. Unfortunately."

Ty fell silent. Chuck sensed his disappointment seeping through the phone signal.

Chuck tipped his face into the rain, which now seemed not a balm after all, but a mocking accompaniment to a double whammy. A lost video recorder. And now footage of a tornado with no way to prove its intensity.

"Listen," Chuck said, "it's okay, we got some great shots here, but the place got leveled." He drew a deep breath. "There's nothing left."

"But you're fine?"

"We found a storm cellar. We're scratched up and bruised, but moving. Boomie, the camera guy is hurt, though. I don't know how badly, but he needs medical attention. Then there's this little problem of a missing camera and its video recorder. Boomie may have filmed something never shot before, something spectacular, but now it's gone."

"Gone?"

"Carried away by the tornado. Two of them actually."

"Two?" Incredulity threaded the word.

"Hard to explain. Work your way back here. We could use your help."

"We're on our way," Ty responded.

Gabi tapped Chuck on the arm and pointed in the direction of where the Gust Front Grill had stood.

Chuck stepped to peer around the side of the generator to where she pointed, but Gabi yanked him back.

"An SUV just pulled up to the front of the building," she said, "at least to where the front used to be." She spoke in a deliberate manner, as though still countering the effects of the migraine-fighting meds she'd consumed earlier. Her eyes appeared wide and alert, however.

"What kind of SUV?"

She smiled. "A black GMC with a grill guard." She pulled her Glock from where it had been tucked into the back of her jeans.

Chapter Twenty-seven

SUNDAY, MAY 11
LATE AFTERNOON

CLARENCE PULLED the GMC to a stop near the stack of debris that marked all that remained of the Gust Front Grill. The windshield wipers beat out a steady rhythm as he peered through the rain-speckled windshield at the wreckage.

"Christ on a crutch," Raleigh said, "never seen anything like this. And the town—you believe that? Flattened!"

"An EF-5 for sure, bro'. First one *I've* ever seen."

"First two," Raleigh corrected.

"Like Siamese twins. That was incredible, unbelievable. Good thing we decided to hang back a little south of town until that thing swept through."

"You always make the right call." Raleigh removed his glasses and massaged the bridge of his nose. "You ever heard of such a thing? Twin tornadoes, side-by-side? Big ones?"

"I saw an old black and white photograph of double funnels on the Internet once, shot back in the '60s, I think, someplace in Indiana. Never thought I'd see something like it for real." His heart rate had ratcheted way up when the storm had hit and only now had begun to settle down.

"So, whaddaya think?" Raleigh said. He replaced his spectacles and peered intently at the stack of broken lumber, fallen bricks, and bent metal that used to be the Gust Front.

"Well, I can tell you one thing," Clarence said.

Raleigh turned his head toward his brother.

"If there's anybody in there—" he nodded at the rubble "—like that guy Monty, if he exists, they're either dead or badly hurt. More likely anyone in there got the hell out when the sirens went off. Probably stowed away in a shelter someplace. We should have free run of the place. At least for a while."

Who knew what they'd find in there. At least they'd have a chance to explore for a bit without having to worry about interference. Monty, whether the product of a tall tale or not, obviously wouldn't be a factor. It would be dicey, poking around in fresh wreckage, but the payoff could be enormous. Worth the gamble. If they found nothing, then the myth would be laid to rest. But who knows, some fairy tales have happy endings.

"Okay, let's grab our jackets, a crowbar, and a couple of flashlights and see what we can find in there," Clarence said.

Minutes later, the brothers stood at the threshold of the mound of debris, the razed Gust Front Grill. Raleigh brushed raindrops from his glasses. At least the precipitation had settled the dust.

"What a mess," he said.

"Let's be careful," Clarence said. "Follow me."

He stepped into the tangle of wood and metal, played his Maglite beam into dark crevasses searching for a safe passageway through the wreckage.

"This way," he said. He ducked under a fallen support beam, moved broken electrical wires out of his path, and shoved a shattered strobe light to one side with his foot. His feet, clad in heavy work boots, crunched through thick layers of broken glass. He moved slowly, continuously sweeping his flashlight from side to side.

After ten minutes of cautious exploration, they reached the stone fireplace of the establishment. It had remained intact, but its brick chimney had tumbled into the amalgam of disintegrated building materials, a trash heap that constituted the burial mound of the Gust Front.

Clarence paused at the fireplace and ran his light beam over the wreckage surrounding it. "As I recall, the fireplace was on the back wall." He pointed the Maglite to his right. "So, if memory serves, that means the offices would have been back that way. Let's work our way in that direction. If there's a safe or lockbox or something, that's where we'll find it."

Their journey became tedious. They slithered on their bellies underneath fallen beams, squirmed through narrow gaps between piles of brick and twisted aluminum, and clambered awkwardly over broken furniture and smashed kitchen appliances. Water sprayed from broken pipes and, in spite of their jackets, soaked them thoroughly.

"Shit," Raleigh said, "you sure this is worth it?"

"Won't know 'til we know, bro'. Let's press on."

From outside, the distant wail of sirens announced the approach of help for the tiny, ruined town.

A wave of unease surged through Clarence. Their exploration had taken much longer than he'd anticipated, or least hoped, it would. He pushed through the rubble more determinedly. *Gotta be almost there.* Wherever there was.

"Hey," Raleigh said, his voice soft, "hear that?"

"The sirens?"

"No. Something else. Listen."

A faint hiss. Then it stopped. Then another short hiss.

A natural gas leak? Clarence sniffed the air. No telltale odor of rotten eggs.

"It's okay," he said. "It's not gas. Probably just compressed air leaking from something. Look, we'll give this five more minutes. If we don't find anything of interest, we're outta here."

Raleigh nodded. They moved on.

A minute later they reached a broken door frame. They ducked to get through it and entered what appeared to be the wreckage of an office. Shards of glass, splintered wood, and chunks of plaster covered a heavy mahogany desk. Next to it rested an upturned chair with broken legs. Sheets of paper, like the aftermath of a ticker-tape parade, littered the room.

Clarence switched off his Maglite and looked up into a brightening sky. The rain had ceased and rays of sunlight filtered through the roofless wreckage to where he and his brother stood.

"Look around," he said. "We might get lucky, find a safe or storage box of some sort." Collapsed book shelves and broken tables gave further testament to the suggestion this once had been an office.

"Hey, hey, hey," Raleigh said a moment later, his voice rising each time he pronounced the word. "Look at this."

Clarence went to where his brother knelt in the debris, brushing away pieces of plaster and glass from . . . a safe!

"Well, whattaya know," Clarence said. "Myth becomes reality." *Maybe.* He studied the safe, a small depository model with an electronic lock and weighing maybe a few hundred pounds. "It's a little more than you might need for keeping petty cash."

"Yeah," Raleigh mumbled, "how do we get it open?"

"We don't. Look, we're near the rear of the grill, or what used to be the rear. A few yards that way—" he pointed "—and we're clear of the wreckage. We'll bring the Terrain around, attach a tow rope to it, string the rope in here, secure it to the safe and drag the motherfucker out. Sound like a plan?"

Raleigh didn't answer. He remained frozen in place, his gaze fixed on something beyond the safe, his expression a mask of terror.

Clarence followed his brother's gaze, spotted what he saw, felt his bowels loosen.

"Back away," he whispered to Raleigh. "Slowly. Just ease into a standing position and back away." His words came out ragged and choked. His heart pounded in a fierce drumbeat. He shuffled backward, his legs feeling like stacks of Jello.

Monty.

GABI CHECKED THE clip in her Glock, crouched, and snuck a peek around the corner of the generator. The pounding in her head had ceased, but the after-effects of the Treximet lingered. It felt as if she were moving in an underwater ballet; still, she couldn't wait for her physical and mental functions to return to "normal." If those were the bad guys up there, she'd never have another chance at grabbing them.

Two figures—men, she was sure—exited the SUV. Flashlights in hand, they entered the wrecked Gust Front Grill.

"What happening?" From behind her, Chuck rested a hand on her shoulder.

"Two men just went into what's left of the grill." She pulled back into the cover provided by the generator, stood, and brushed her wet hair from her eyes.

"You aren't going to go after them, are you?" Chuck asked

She stared at him, incredulous he'd ask such a question.

"Look," he said, "you aren't in any shape—"

"Don't tell me what kind of shape I'm in," she snapped. Then more gently, "Please."

Stormy sat near her feet, staring up at her.

"Why not just wait 'til whoever went in there comes out? You don't have to go clambering around in the wreckage like some gung-ho marine in urban combat. Just cool it."

"And then when those guys leave, they'll claim they were just rescue workers doing their job. No. I wanna know what they're really doing in there. First responders would be in town, not prowling around in someplace most townies know is closed for the day."

"You're outnumbered."

"Not really. Those guys don't even know I'm here."

A long peal of thunder from the departing supercell rolled across the debris-littered parking lot.

"Wait 'til help comes."

"In case you haven't figured it out, 'help' is otherwise occupied."

"Then I'm coming with you."

She moved closer to him. "Don't be a moron. You can't help me. You'd be in the way. And I certainly wouldn't want to end up accidentally shooting my boyfriend." She pecked his cheek.

"You don't have to be so . . . so . . . damned macho, Gabi," he sputtered.

"Thanks for the positive reinforcement." She took another quick look around the corner of the generator.

"I'm coming with you," Chuck said, his words hard and determined.

"No, you're not, Mr. Rittenberg. You're not interfering with a federal investigation. Stay here and take care of Boomie and Stormy. And look for that recorder."

She broke cover and sprinted through the rain toward the mound of debris that used to be the grill. Truth be told, she wished she had backup. But untrained backup would be worse than none. It was nice though, to have a man concerned about her. More than nice, actually.

She reached the heaped-up rubble and paused, taking careful stock of the situation before entering the wreckage. Once inside, she halted again and listened carefully, seeing if she could detect any sounds: voices, scrapes, tinkles. But there was nothing.

She drew a long, deep breath, exhaling slowly to calm her heart rate, and then stepped deeper into the tangle of wood and metal. Arms extended, the Glock in a two-handed grip, she crept forward, sweeping the weapon from side to side as she advanced.

A rush of adrenaline hit, attempting to negate the drug-induced lethargy that enveloped her, but she knew the surge probably wasn't up to the job. She sensed her brain and body continuing to function as if they were on one-second delays from what her real-time reactions should be. Okay for everyday life. Potentially fatal in an armed confrontation, if indeed that was what she was headed into.

The rain had ceased and weak sunlight filtered into the ruined structure. She spotted what appeared to be a quasi-cleared path through the wreckage, something akin to a game trail through underbrush. Two sets of wet footprints in the dust layering the debris clearly indicated the individuals she'd seen earlier had pushed deep into the remains of the grill.

She moved carefully, trying to minimize noise and pausing intermittently to listen for any sounds that might give away the location of the men she pursued. But all that reached her ears was the gurgle of leakage from broken pipes and the drip of rainwater from above. She eased ahead, following the footprints, slithering and scrabbling through, around, and over the stacked and layered rubble, knowing full well she was being less than stealthy. The only thing she had working in her favor was that her prey might not be on full alert, never suspecting someone was tracking them.

Ahead, a scuffling sound. Transitory. She halted and listened. The noise didn't repeat. She crouched and, one measured shuffle at a time, moved forward. She reached what looked like a broken door frame. Again, she stopped, waited for some indication of movement—a footfall, a piece of debris skittering across the floor, maybe a whisper or sniffle. Nothing. Then a brief hiss. Air? Water? Gas? The sound ceased.

Heart pounding, still in a crouch, she sidestepped into what appeared to have been an office. Shafts of sunlight speared through the wreckage, creating a checkered montage of brilliance against deep shadow. The sharp contrast between light and dark made it virtually impossible to discern figures and forms. Yet she sensed something or someone—two someones?—shared the space with her.

Her heartbeat accelerated, reverberating through her head, thrumming in her ears. She should have waited for backup. A ripple of panic raced through her body, but she willed her training to take over. She crouched lower and brought the Glock up in front of her, curling her finger against its trigger. "FBI," she announced, forcing her voice to sound commanding. "Come out and show me your hands."

She caught only a glimpse of the thing, could only mutter, "Jesus," before a blow to the side of her head sent her reeling into the wreckage strewn at her feet, into blackness, probably—her last conscious, ephemeral thought suggested—into her grave.

Chapter Twenty-eight

SUNDAY, MAY 11
LATE AFTERNOON

CHUCK KNELT NEXT to Boomie, who remained in a sitting position with his back against the generator. He stared at Chuck with unfocused eyes.

"In a lotta pain," the cinematographer said. "Can't move my left arm. Ya find that SSR yet?"

"SSR? The video recorder?"

Boomie nodded.

"Haven't had a chance to look for it," Chuck said. For the time being, he remained more concerned about Boomie and Gabi than the film Boomie had shot. He touched Boomie's shoulder lightly. "Like you said, I think it's broken, partner. Wish I had some painkillers to give you, but I don't even have an aspirin."

"Don't worry. I'll live. Just ignore me when I start with the four-letter words again." He grimaced. "Fuckin' navy was good for something."

Stormy trotted to Boomie, put her paws on his thighs, and licked his face.

"God," he muttered, "that's more compassion that I got from either of my first two wives."

Chuck laughed. "Hang in there. Soon as Gabi gets back, I'll go into town and see if I can commandeer an EMT."

"Where'd Gabi go?" Boomie shifted his position slightly, winced.

"She saw two guys go into the wreckage of the grill. She thinks they might be the bad guys she's been searching for."

"Dicey stuff. A chick against a couple of killers." A matter-of-fact statement.

"She's an FBI agent."

"I know, but . . ." Boomie let the words trail off. He closed his eyes, tilted his head back. Beads of perspiration slid down his face. Pain.

Chuck stood, paced to the corner of the generator, and stared in the direction of the Gust Front. All appeared quiet. Was that good or bad? A general sense of unease settled over him. Odd how things never seem to get resolved in the time frame they're expected to. With the twin tornadoes past, the drama should be over.

Yet here he was with an injured cameraman, Gabi possibly on a fool's errand, and the key to a million-dollar payday missing. Stormy brushed against his leg. Chuck looked down.

"Hey, girl. Ya know, if you were Lassie, I could send you after Gabi. Or maybe off to find the SSR. After all, this whole thing started because of you."

Stormy cocked her head at Chuck.

"I mean, you did bring me Metcalf's original proposal after it blew away."

Stormy tensed, growled.

Chuck followed her gaze. A figure emerged from the grill's wreckage, dashed to the SUV, got in, and moved it out of sight behind the pile of debris. Where was Gabi? The other guy? Chuck glanced around for a weapon and spotted a broken piece of wood about the size of a baseball bat. He grabbed it and lit out for the grill, Stormy at his heels.

From behind him, the blare of an auto horn brought him to a halt. He pivoted and saw Sam Townsend's pickup plowing through the debris-strewn parking lot in his direction. Sam pulled up beside Chuck and jumped down from the cab.

"My God," he said, taking in the destruction around him, "this is catastrophic. I knew from monitoring the radar we'd taken a hit, but I didn't expect this." Distress mixed with sadness registered in his eyes. "My place . . . my place is gone. I can't believe it."

"It got hit by a double funnel," Chuck said.

Sam stared at him.

"We got it on film. Well, *had* it on film. I'm not sure what happened to it."

Sam didn't seem to be listening. Instead, he continued to stare at what used to be the Gust Front. After a moment his gaze fell on the chunk of lumber in Chuck's hand.

"What the hell?" he said.

"I think there's trouble up there," Chuck answered, using the makeshift weapon to point at the wrecked grill. "A couple of guys went in there after the storm. Gabi went after them."

Sam appeared to have trouble digesting the information. "Gabi? The lady who's traveling with you? Why her? What the fuck's going on, Chuck?"

"She's FBI."

"Jesus, I feel like I just came in in the middle of a movie."

"Sorry, no time to fill you in. I think she might be in trouble."

GABI, SPRAWLED IN the dust and debris of the Gust Front Grill, opened her eyes, searching for the thing she'd seen—well, thought she'd seen—before being blindsided by a blow to the back of her head. Maybe it hadn't been real. Perhaps a hallucination, an optical illusion triggered by the meds. She could only pray. But she knew otherwise.

Her head felt as though it had been split by an ax. But fear overcame the pain. No, not fear: absolute piss-in-your-pants terror. She attempted to move, but her body wouldn't respond. It was as if she were trapped in a nightmare, alive and functioning but unable to flee the monster. She felt for her handgun, moving her arms sluggishly, patting the floor for the weapon. Gone.

A small sound to her right drew her attention—something displacing the broken glass and shattered plaster coating the floor. Something slithering. Something large and heavy.

Her heart rate exploded, thundering like a jackhammer. She turned and witnessed an apparition from hell, wishing she were dead. The vision, forked tongue flickering, came at her. The jaws of its huge, flat, triangular head yawned open revealing bandsaw rows of backward-facing fangs. Hypodermics. Behind the head, a massive brown- and yellow-patterned body, as thick as the trunk of a pine tree, propelled the creature forward in a corkscrew death-glide.

CHUCK AND SAM went rigid as a scream rent the air. Female. From the direction of the Gust Front. Not a scream for help, but one of pure terror. Chuck had always thought of one's hair standing on end as a cliché, but his hair stood on end. A chill ran up the back of his neck. Nothing clichéd about it at all.

"Oh, no," Sam said, his voice almost a whisper, as if he'd received news of the death of a friend.

"What?" Chuck said

"She's met Monty." He took off in a sprint toward the rear of the crumpled grill.

Chuck followed. "Monty's real?" The question came out amid breathless gasps.

"Very."

"Will he hurt her?"

"Monty is a 22-foot Burmese python. He hasn't eaten in three weeks."

Stormy, barking, dashed after them.

"A snake? Monty's a snake?"

Chuck stumbled over a tangle of shredded boards and roofing, fell, got up, and sprinted in pursuit of Sam.

They reached the rear of the grill. Fifty yards from them, a black SUV with a heavy-duty nylon tow strap attached to something in the wreckage labored to pull it out. The driver spotted Chuck and Sam and pointed a pistol at them through an open window. He squeezed off a round. The slug zinged off a bent and dented steel storage tank.

The two men dived for cover behind a large section of someone's roof—debris from town.

"Jesus," Sam said, "I haven't been shot at since 'Nam."

"Well, it's a first for me," Chuck responded, barely able to speak.

Stormy crouched with them, her tail wagging, not understanding the gravity of the situation.

Sam peeked over the upended chunk of roofing. "Bastards got my safe."

The SUV's driver fired another shot.

"Where's the snake and nape when you need it?" Sam muttered.

Chuck stared at him.

"War talk. In 'Nam when we got in trouble, we waited for the Zoomies to bail us out with Snakeye bombs and napalm."

"I don't think we have that option here. What the hell do we do?" Chuck considered the black irony of his situation. He'd just cheated death from an EF-5 tornado, but now was about to be murdered.

Sam laid a steady hand on him. "Nothing. Relax. The guy isn't going to hit us with a handgun at this distance from a moving vehicle. He's just keeping us away."

"We need to get to Gabi."

"I know, I know. Just let these guys haul away the safe first."

Chuck chanced a glance over the makeshift barrier shielding him and Sam.

The SUV, its engine yowling with high revs, yanked the safe free of the Gust Front's wreckage and dragged it through the twisted metal and wood littering the ground.

"What on earth do those bozos think they're going to do with it?" Chuck asked.

"It's not that heavy. Once they get it out of the debris field, the two of them probably can hoist it into the vehicle."

The SUV, encountering revetments of twisted rubble, made only slow progress. Sam stood and watched. No more shots rang out.

"Okay," he said after several moments, "let's go get the lady." He dashed toward the grill.

Chuck, Stormy trotting beside him, followed, dreading what they might find.

GABI HAD HAD TIME only to raise her arm in a futile defensive maneuver before the snake lunged, sinking rows of razor-honed teeth into her forearm. The pain hit with excruciating force. She screamed, felt lightheaded, and tumbled into a nightmare abyss of unconsciousness.

She came to, but had no idea how much time had elapsed since she'd passed out. Searing pain radiated from her arm. Unbearable. She attempted to scream, but could push only a faltering breath of soundless air from her lungs. The snake, still locked onto her with its serrated teeth, had managed to wrap several coils of it huge, scaly body around her torso, squeezing with massive force.

What is this thing? What do they do? She attempted to remember . . . and did. Simultaneously, a paralyzing dart of horror blasted into her gut. A constrictor. This monster is a constrictor. It squeezes its prey to death, then eats it. Or maybe even begins its meal before whatever it attacked dies.

Frantic, she squirmed and quivered, fighting for her existence, or at least for another handful of breaths. But each time she moved, the reptile responded with increased crushing power; each time she exhaled, the helix tightened.

Eventually, all she could to was sip oxygen in tiny, silent gasps. She slipped toward unconsciousness again, willing it to come, praying for God to let her die oblivious to the method. Her prayer hovered unanswered. She remained aware, but only in a distorted, foggy, pain-wracked sense. She went limp. Suffocating. Her life being squeezed from her centimeter by centimeter, the powerful embrace of her killer relentless. A rib cracked. She whimpered.

Her heart fluttered. *Yes, stop. Please stop beating. Save me.*

The tenets of her religion taught of peace in death. Yet in hers there was none; only horror. An image of her parents floated past, just out of reach. A likeness of Chuck circled above, twisting, drifting, hazy.

Is Chuck here? She willed her eyes to open and focus. Not Chuck. Just the snake.

How many beats of her heart did she have left? How many shallow inhalations?

I know I can count them.

One.

Two.

Three eluded her.

Chapter Twenty-nine

**SUNDAY, MAY 11
LATE AFTERNOON**

STORMY, LEAPING over fallen timbers and squirming through narrow openings in the layered debris, was first to reach Gabi and the python. She halted abruptly and loosed a fusillade of furious barks.

Chuck and Sam clambered into the room behind her. Stormy mock-charged the huge snake several times, but the creature remained unfazed by the presence of the dog. It merely did a half roll with Gabi, kicking up dust and tiny pieces of glass and wood as it attempted to distance itself from the dog, a nuisance, not a threat.

At the sight of the reptile wrapped around Gabi, blood streaming down her arm from where the snake had locked onto her, bile rose in Chuck's esophagus. He gagged on it, choking it back, forcing himself not to vomit. His stomach knotted. A storm surge of revulsion, fear, and shock rippled through his body, momentarily paralyzing him.

Sam stumbled toward Gabi, knelt, and, ignoring the snake, felt for her pulse. He looked back at Chuck. "She's almost gone," he said.

Chuck, breaking from his paralysis, threw himself on the snake, hammering at it with his fists. He might as well have been an ant attacking an elephant. The python responded by tightening its coils around Gabi. Chuck glanced at her—limp and motionless, her eyes rolled back in her head.

"Damn it, do something," Chuck screamed at Sam. Stormy, frightened by the fury in her master's voice, backpedaled.

Chuck realized the futility of his assault, but in that futility found new determination to save Gabi. Past his initial shock, he willed himself to find a solution. He glanced around the wreckage, searching for Gabi's gun. Not there. Something else then, a weapon of any sort. A piece of wood, a shard of glass, a metal shaft. He scanned the debris. All candidates either too large or too small.

What else? Snakes are cold blooded. He stood. "Ice? Have you got ice, Sam? We can bury the snake in it. Maybe render its muscles useless."

Now Sam seemed frozen, unable to think or take action. He stood over Gabi, gaping at the horrific scene, not moving, not responding to Chuck entreaties.

Chuck rose, gripped Sam by the shoulders, shook. "Ice, Sam? Where's the kitchen? We need ice." His words rang with desperation.

Sam stared back, vacuous.

"Godammit, Sam, come back to me." Chuck slapped his friend.

Sam raised his hand to his cheek, felt where Chuck had struck him. "Why ice?" The words barely came out.

"To kill the snake."

"Kill Monty?"

"He's killing Gabi," Chuck bellowed.

Sam took a step back. "Ice?"

"Jesus, yes. Snakes are cold—"

"Yeah, yeah, yeah." Sam seemed suddenly endowed with new life, as though he'd been away on a trip, perhaps back to the horrors of Vietnam, but had abruptly returned home. "No, not ice."

"Yes, Sam, yes."

"No. Stop thinking like a scientist. Start thinking like a warrior. Follow me." He turned, dropped to his knees and scrambled underneath a tumble of crumpled and splintered wood.

Chuck hesitated, then followed. Stormy remained and resumed her angry barking at the python.

A quick crawl brought Chuck and Sam into the remains of the Gust Front's kitchen. Water sprayed from broken pipes. Pots and pans littered the floor. Several commercial-sized ovens and dishwashers lay broken and bent under piles of wreckage.

Sam, now frantic, pawed through the debris until he uncovered a large cabinet. He yanked open several drawers and found what he was looking for. "Here," he yelled.

He extended a large carving knife to Chuck. Came out with a meat cleaver for himself.

The two men plowed back into the charnel room. Sam launched himself at the snake, swinging the cleaver at the midpoint of the reptile, the portion not wrapped around Gabi. Chuck targeted a point just behind the creature's head and plunged the knife into it, precise and determined with his aim to avoid injuring Gabi.

The snake twitched, but refused to release its meal.

Sam swung the meat cutter again and again. Chuck withdrew the knife and drove it deep into the reptile repeatedly, twisting and turning the weapon each time. The python suddenly released its grip on Gabi and lunged at Chuck, rolling Gabi over as it did so.

Chuck stumbled backward, away from the snake's charge, dropping the knife.

At the opposite end of the snake, Sam wielded the cleaver in a final, vicious motion, severing the rear ten feet of the reptile from the remainder of its body. The massive tail continued to twitch and flex as though it possessed a life of its own. Only a minimum of blood appeared, oozing from the pink innards and muscles of the python.

The snake unwound one of its coils from Gabi and lunged repeatedly at Chuck, who scooted backward on his butt, away from the creature as it came after him, jaws gaping, wide open enough room to consume his head.

Stormy, emboldened, resumed her own offensive, attempting to sink her teeth into the reptile's neck where Chuck had opened a jagged wound. Stormy would attack, nip, back off, then make another run. She punctuated her attack with aggressive barks. Then, too slow. The snake turned and propelled itself in a blur of motion at the dog, catching a paw as she tried to retreat. Stormy wailed in pain as the python dragged her across the room.

Sam, clever still in hand, fell headlong on the reptile, slashing at the massive gash Chuck had carved out. Monty released Stormy and turned on its keeper, locking its teeth onto his hip. Sam screamed but continued his onslaught. Chop. Chop. Chop.

Chuck could see Sam's energy flagging, but he refused to relent. Then at last, success. The gargantuan body, at least the portion still attached to the head, fell away from it. But the snake's jaws still held Sam in a death grip.

Now two parts of the python twitched and squirmed, one on the floor, the other still wound around Gabi. The reptile's head remained glued to Sam.

"Get this son of a bitch off me," he screamed.

Chuck recovered the carving knife, jammed it into the snake's nose, and twisted. At last, the head fell away from Sam's hip, plopped onto the floor, and remained there, mouth agape, its beady eyes staring at nothing.

"Monty, you turncoat bastard," Sam yelled.

"A little help here," Chuck demanded. He pried at the dead coils encircling Gabi, the muscles spasmodically contracting and relaxing. The pungent odor of the snake's innards, human blood, and body fluids filled the room.

Sam joined Chuck in his effort to free Gabi of the snake's spasming body. Stormy lay in a far corner of the room, licking her bloody paw and whimpering.

"Hang on, Storms," Chuck said. "You'll be okay."

The two men worked rapidly, at last freeing Gabi. Chuck pulled her away from the carnage of the battle and laid her on a spot of the floor brushed clear of debris. She appeared lifeless, not moving or breathing. Chuck's eyes misted as he positioned himself to perform CPR. He'd at least learned rudimentary first aid when he ran Thunder Road Tours.

He placed the heel of his right hand on the center of Gabi's chest and laid his other hand on top. He interlaced his fingers and went to work, pushing straight down, hard and fast. Press. Press. Press. One hundred times per minute. Even faster for the first 20 seconds. *Need to get oxygen to her brain.*

"Sam," he said, "do you have an AED in here? Maybe we can shock her heart back to life." Press, press, press. No stopping.

"I used to. It may be buried in all this shit."

"Look for it."

Chuck persisted with CPR. Blood seeped from the wounds in Gabi's forearm, and she remained unresponsive. Stormy continued to whimper, more softly now.

Ty burst into the room. "Oh, my God! Holy shit! What happened in here?"

Chuck looked up, but kept working on Gabi's chest. "Little bit of a mess, isn't it?"

Ty pointed at the snake . . . snake parts. "What the hell is that thing?"

"It was a python. It got Gabi."

Ty's eyes widened, something dawning on him. "That's not even funny. Monty Python?" He spotted Stormy and knelt beside her. "You, too, girl?" He reached for her paw, but Stormy pulled back and growled.

Metcalf appeared. "We got back here as soon as we could. We found Boomie. He said you guys—" He stopped in mid-sentence, apparently stunned by the scene. He whirled. "Ziggy," he yelled, "get a Steadicam in here."

Ty went for Metcalf, grabbed him by the collar. "Out, you

motherfucker. If I see a camera anywhere near here, you'll need a proctologist to remove it from your butt." Spittle from Ty's mouth sprayed into Metcalf's face.

He spun Metcalf around and gave him a shove, propelling him into a stack of debris. Metcalf righted himself and started to say something, but didn't; instead, he stumbled out of the wrecked room, muttering inaudibly.

Ty squatted next to Chuck. "How is she?"

Chuck looked at his son but couldn't speak, his eyes welling with incipient tears. He could only shake his head. He continued CPR.

"She needs mouth-to-mouth, too," Ty said. "I learned that much from hanging around army medics. Let me help." He tilted Gabi's head back, positioning her for rescue breaths. He checked for a pulse, looked at Chuck, and shook his head.

Sam reappeared. "I couldn't find the defibrillator," he said, discouragement threading his voice. "The place where we kept it is . . . gone."

Ty placed his hand on Chuck's shoulder. "Dad, let me take over the compressions. You do the breathing for Gabi. I'll do 30 compressions, then you do two breaths. Okay?"

Tears tracked down Chuck's face, like drops sliding down a picture window on a rainy afternoon. Tears for Gabi. Tears because his son had just called him Dad. He nodded, and moved aside, allowing Ty to take over.

Ty, counting, pressed down 30 times. "Now, two breaths," he said to Chuck. "Pinch her nose shut. Cover her mouth with yours and blow."

Chuck followed instructions, gave Gabi two strong breaths. Ty resumed compressions.

They continued the cycle for several minutes, then switched positions.

As Ty waited to give Gabi mouth-to-mouth, he pointed at Sam's bloody hip. "Snake get you, too?"

"Nailed just about everyone except for your dad."

Ty gave Gabi her breaths, then pulled out his cell and punched in three numbers. "We need help," he said when someone answered. He listened, then spoke again. "Hear me good. Don't give me this 'we're kinda busy' bullshit. I fucking know that. Get medics to the Gust Front Grill now. I've got a patient in cardiac arrest, another losing blood, and a third down with a severe injury near the auxiliary generator. I don't normally make threats, miss, but unless help arrives within three minutes, I'll make it a personal crusade to make sure you never hold another dispatch job in your life." He disconnected the call.

"Okay, Dad, switch again," Ty said. "I'll take over the compressions."

Once more they traded tasks.

"Tell me what happened in here," Ty said.

Chuck explained. The brief version.

Ty listened, then said, "Those SOBs cold-cocked Gabi, set the snake on her, then drug Sam's safe outta here?"

Chuck nodded, then gave Gabi more breaths. This time she responded, opening her eyes and staring at him, drawing a shallow breath. "Stealin' kisses?" she said, the words more akin to tiny gasps than speech. Chuck started to answer, but she lapsed back into unconsciousness, slipping away from him, sea foam on an outgoing tide.

"We almost had her," Ty said. "Can't quit now." He resumed the compressions.

Chuck held his head close to Gabi's. "Come back," he whispered, "come back."

Moments later, Chuck and his son switched positions again.

Chuck pushed against Gabi's chest, relentless in his work, refusing to let her go. He wouldn't lose another person on his watch. Especially her. "No, no, no." He mouthed the words in cadence with his compressions. Sweat mingled with his tears, blurring his vision almost to opaqueness.

He persisted in his efforts. His shoulders grew weary, matching his spirit, but he rejected even a fleeting notion of quitting. He'd found a groove, a rhythm, in his compressions and kept at it. He thought once again that Gabi's eyes fluttered, but wasn't sure.

He snapped his head up as the sound of moving and shifting debris punched through the wreckage. Two EMTs scrambled into the room, Ty guiding them.

"We got her, sir," one of them said. He dropped to his knees beside Chuck and uncased a portable defibrillator. The other withdrew an Ambu bag, a hand-operated resuscitator, from his kit. Chuck moved out of the way and let them take over.

He watched as they worked, pumping air into her lungs with the Ambu bag, slitting her blouse, waiting for the AED to analyze her heart rate, shocking her, waiting, another shock,

then . . . a definite fluttering of her eyelids, a moan, a breath!

Chuck tilted his head toward the ceiling and let his tears flow.

"I think she's gonna make it, Dad," Ty said, resting his hand on Chuck's shoulder.

Sam startled them. "Hey," he said, "feel kinda floaty." He lowered himself into a sitting position on the floor.

Ty went to him. "You're losing blood." He tore off his shirt and gave it to Sam. "Press this against your wound."

"Could use a Dust-off about now." His eyes went glassy.

"I know, I know. Help is here. Hang in there."

"Thanks," Sam whispered.

"Tell me, where'd those bastards go, the ones who got your safe?"

"Out back," Sam said, his words slightly slurred, "dragging the safe across the parking lot with their SUV. Probably going to try to get it clear of the wreckage, then lift it into their vehicle."

"Damned if I'll let them."

"Don't worry about them. It's not worth the—"

"I'll just run a quick recon," Ty said.

"Ty, wait," Chuck said.

"I know what I'm doing, Dad. You stay here with Sam and Gabi." Ty left.

"Chuck." Sam's voice, faint.

Chuck knelt by him. "What? The medics are here, you know. You'll be okay now."

Sam extended an arm toward Chuck, rested his hand on his thigh. "Those are bad people out there. Better give your son some parental guidance. He's a good man, Chuck. Nobody else needs to get hurt."

Chuck shot a glance at Gabi. Her chest rose and fell rhythmically. One of the EMTs busied himself attending to her damaged forearm. Chuck looked back at Sam. "Yeah, he is a good man. I'm on my way." He stood and called to the med techs, pointing at Sam.

The one who had used the AED responded. "Don't worry, we'll take care of him."

"And there's a third guy down outside, by the generator."

"Got it."

Chuck darted from the destroyed building.

In the parking lot, he found Ty crouched behind a pile of wreckage and squatted beside him. "What's up?" he asked.

"Gabi okay?" Ty held his gaze straight ahead, watching the individuals near the black SUV.

"I think so. The medics got her breathing again."

"Ya did good, Dad."

"You, too—" He paused a beat, then spoke the word for which he'd been waiting clearance—"son."

"We still got a problem here," Ty said. "Those SOBs got the safe and are trying to get it into their SUV."

Chuck peeked over the top of the debris stack. About 150 yards away and slightly downhill in a broad gully relatively clear of wreckage, two men stood next to Sam's safe, preparing, it appeared, to hoist it into the rear of their vehicle.

"I assume you called 911," Chuck said. "Again."

"Yeah. Different dispatcher. Same response: We're pretty much tied up at the moment. I let it go. This really isn't a life or death situation like what we had with Gabi."

"Yeah. But these guys are probably murderers."

"In any other situation, I'm sure the response would have been immediate." Ty took another quick look at the two men and ducked back down. "You don't suppose your buddy Sam has a weapon stowed away someplace, do you?"

"Probably. But we'd never find it now."

"Well, shit. We're in deep doo-doo then."

Chuck found an opening in the pile of wreckage that permitted him to watch the bad guys without exposing himself. They seemed to be carrying on an animated discussion. One of them, the taller and slimmer of the two, kept glancing in the direction of Chuck and Ty, obviously aware of the surveillance. The other, squat and powerfully built, fanned a hand in front of his face as though warding off a foul odor.

Chuck scanned the area around their GMC. His gaze fell on a puddle of water adjacent to a badly damaged outbuilding not far from the vehicle. He watched the puddle intently for several moments, then tapped Ty on the shoulder. "See that?" he said, and pointed.

Ty, too, studied the small pool of accumulated rainwater. "Ah, yes. Bubbles." He kept his voice low. "A ruptured feeder line, I'll bet."

"Think we can bait them into self-immolation?"

Ty smiled. "You bet."

"Any ideas?"

"Yep. I can draw their fire."

"Something safer than that."

"No, really. I got pretty good at that stuff in Afghanistan. Besides, if all they've got is a handgun, they haven't got a prayer at this range."

Before Chuck could object, Ty stepped out from the behind their cover and took off in crouching run toward the black SUV. A short dash brought him to the shelter of another heap of wreckage.

The taller thug reacted. He withdrew a pistol, probably Gabi's, from the waistband of his pants and sprinted for cover behind the SUV. Taking aim at Ty's position, he steadied the weapon on the vehicle's hood. The other man squatted beside him.

Ty ran a visual recon of the area around him. He signaled Chuck of his intent to make a lateral move, a dash to a low mound of rubble about 30 feet to his left.

Chuck nodded his understanding. A ripple of moral ambivalence for what was about to happen swept over him, but quickly dissipated. He had no sympathy for the two criminals, degenerates who had just fed a woman to a python, quite likely had murdered others, and were preparing to open up on his son with a .40-caliber handgun.

Ty gave Chuck a thumbs-up, stood and sprinted into the open, feinting briefly in the direction of the gunman. The man fired. Ty crumpled and sprawled onto the debris-laden Tarmac. He lay there, grasping his thigh.

"Shit," he screamed. "I don't fucking believe it. The bastard hit me."

Chuck gaped, stunned as their ad hoc plan came apart at the seams.

Chapter Thirty

SUNDAY, MAY 11
EARLY EVENING

THE GUNMAN broke cover and started up the slight incline toward Ty.

Chuck performed a quick analysis, a flash recap of his thought process. That had to be natural gas bubbling up through the puddle. Why else would that guy have been fanning his nose. A small puff of wind confirmed his hypothesis. He caught a whiff of rotten eggs.

If at first you don't succeed . . . Surely the guy with the gun can't get lucky twice.

Chuck stood, made no effort to conceal himself, and strode directly toward the gunman and Ty. He spread his arms, palms up, on either side of his body: Hit me if you can.

The guy raised his gun and fired. Chuck saw the muzzle flash, never heard the shot, only an ear-splitting thunder clap. He tumbled backward as the blast wave from the explosion blew over him.

He landed on his back and found himself staring upward into a cloud-dappled sky. He raised himself on one elbow and looked down the gentle slope into a roiling cauldron of fire. The black SUV hadn't exploded, but sat consumed in flames. The gunman lay face down several yards from the blazing vehicle, the back of his shirt on fire.

Chuck struggled to his feet and ran to Ty.

"I'm okay," Ty said, his hand clamped over a bloody pant leg. He flicked his head toward the fireball. "Better check on those guys, but be careful. Watch out for weapons."

One of the EMTs who had worked on Gabi darted toward Chuck and Ty. He knelt by Ty, glanced at the burning SUV. "What the hell happened?" he asked.

"Gas explosion," Chuck said. "Those guys ripped off a safe from the grill. They were trying to get away, fired a couple of shots at us and hit Ty. But they didn't know, or forgot, they were standing next to a natural gas leak. Boom!"

"They?" the EMT asked, opening his trauma bag. "There's only one body down there."

Chuck, who'd been squatting next to the EMT, stood and surveyed the scene. The gunman hadn't moved. His partner had vanished. Chuck had a pretty good idea why. Not even a firefighter in a Nomex suit could have survived the gas-fed inferno that now roared less than a hundred yards from him.

Out of compassion, not rational thought, he scrambled toward the prone man whose shirt had been completely consumed by flames. The victim lay motionless, arms spread on the ground, one hand still gripping a pistol. Chuck kicked it away and bent to grab the man's wrists. The heat from the fireball licked at his face, on the verge of searing it. The man's naked back, a blistered mix of crimson and charcoal, forced Chuck to avert his gaze.

The man moaned, loud and long, as Chuck dragged him away from the inferno. Then words: "Raleigh," he said. "My brother. My brother." He lapsed into whimpering.

Chuck continued to tug the injured man. "I didn't see anybody else," he said. "But I'll look. Gotta get you away from the fire." Chuck knew that the man's brother likely hadn't survived the blast and ensuing blaze.

"Raleigh," the man sobbed.

"Okay, okay, take it easy now," Chuck said, feeling almost sorry for a human being who moments ago had fired shots at him and Ty, sicced a reptile on Gabi, and in all likelihood had murdered several people. But the operative word was "almost." In truth, Chuck couldn't make the transition from hatred to agape love in the blink of an eye merely because flesh was peeling off a man's body.

DRIFTING SMOKE, from both the fires in town and the burning SUV, turned the setting sun into a dull orange, a glowing orb tarnished by death and destruction. The keening sirens of emergency vehicles filled the growing dusk.

An EMT stood next to Chuck in the wasteland that had once served as the parking lot of the Gust Front Grill. The red flashing lights of an EMT truck stabbed through the haze, adding to the eeriness of the fading light.

"We'll transport the lady and the burn victim to Bartlesville," the medical technician said. "There's a small hospital in Pawhuska, but it's already full, so Bartlesville is our next best option. It's about 25 miles east. The burned man will probably end up in Tulsa or Ok City."

"And eventually in prison, I hope," Chuck added.

"I understand he's a criminal, but he's in no shape to pull any shenanigans at the moment. There'll be law enforcement officials waiting for us in Bartlesville."

Chuck nodded. "And the other injured folks?"

"They're less seriously hurt. The gentleman with the gunshot wound—your son, I'm told—will be fine." The EMT patted Chuck on his shoulder, a "don't worry" gesture. "Another ambulance will be along shortly to transport him and the other gentleman to Bartlesville, too."

"How's the other guy?"

"The one by the generator? Concussion and broken shoulder, but he'll be okay."

"And the body?" The charred remains of what presumably was the bad guy's brother had been discovered a few feet from the blackened and still smoldering frame of the SUV.

"We'll have to get a coroner out here first. They'll arrange for transport to a morgue."

"What about the snake bite victims? I mean I know the thing wasn't poisonous, but—"

"Massive doses of antibiotics. For the puppy, too. She'll need to see a vet." The medic glanced toward his vehicle. "Well, look, we gotta get rollin'. Good luck." He extended his hand to Chuck.

"Thanks for all you did," Chuck said, shaking the medic's hand. "Thanks for patching up my face, too." He tapped a large bandage taped to his cheek. "You guys are the greatest."

"I tell you what, sir, it's not often we get gunshot victim, a burn victim, a concussion victim, and the victim of a snake attack all in one call." A thin smile, not quite a grin, crept across his face.

Chuck patted him on the back. "Go," he said. "I suspect this is a day you'll never forget."

"Not a chance," the EMT answered, and clambered into the truck. The vehicle pulled away, the driver steering carefully through the debris field.

The strobing lights disappeared into the haze. Chuck stood and watched, noting the irony of the event. Gabi and the object of her pursuit, both badly injured, being carted off to a hospital together. A tactical draw, but a strategic victory for Gabi. Chuck closed his eyes and uttered a brief, silent prayer for her.

Sam, his stovepipe hat accordioned to half its former height and missing the decorative feather, joined Chuck. Together they walked toward the generator where Boomie and Ty awaited transportation to Bartlesville.

"How's your hip?" Chuck asked.

"Hurts like hell," Sam answered. "Next time I'll use a German shepherd as a guard."

"Your safe—you think it survived the fire?"

"Probably." He stifled a laugh.

Chuck stopped walking. "What's funny? Something about the safe?"

"The robbers would have been really pissed if they'd been able to break into it."

"You mean there was no money in it?"

Sam shook his head. "Not much. Only enough to meet a couple of months' payroll."

"So the story about your fortune was just a folk tale?"

"Not exactly."

"Come on, Sam. We've been friends for a long time. No more secrets, not after today. Okay?"

"Okay." Sam paused and massaged his hip, then continued. "The only thing those guys would have found in that safe—besides a few thousand bucks—was matted straw and chicken bones."

"What . . . ?" Chuck couldn't formulate a question.

"Monty used to hang out in there. He generally had free run of the office area, crawled around in the attic mostly. But he liked to curl up in the safe once in a while. Mainly after a chicken dinner. I usually kept the door open for him, but I shut it before I left this morning."

"So there never was much money in there?"

"Oh, there was a lot of money in there. Once. A few million, in fact. But I got a wild hair up my ass when the stock market tanked in 2008, took all the cash and bought securities—everything and anything that looked like a bargain."

"Smart Indian." Chuck clapped Sam on the shoulder. "Rich Indian now."

"Just upholding the Osage legend."

In the middle distance, Metcalf's team picked its way through the wreckage that layered the parking lot, searching for the Panavision, or more precisely, its SSR, the solid state recorder harboring the images of the twin tornadoes. Million-dollar images.

"Hey," Boomie said as Chuck and Sam approached. A greeting, not a shout. He still sat with his back against the generator.

"Feeling better?" Chuck asked.

"A bit. The medics gave me a shot of something. Just waiting for our ride to the hospital now."

"Any luck on the SSR?"

"Not yet. Still looking."

Next to Boomie, Stormy, her paw bandaged by one of the EMTs who seemed to have had a way with animals, lay with her head resting on Ty's lap. Ty had dozed off.

"You were gonna tell me about double tornadoes," Boomie said. "How the hell does something like that happen?"

Chuck looked out at the people combing the debris for the SSR. He wondered if he shouldn't be out there with them. After all, it was his payday they were searching for.

Boomie evidently sensed his ambivalence. "Just a short answer," he said, "then you can help the searchers. I'd like to know what the hell almost killed me."

"Short answer then. First, a primer on supercells. A supercell is a thunderstorm that contains a mesocyclone, a deep rotating updraft that can spawn tornadoes. Mesocyclones can persist for hours. Tornadoes themselves are more transient—forming, maturing, dissipating, then repeating the cycle, often in just a matter of minutes."

Boomie shifted his position slightly, but held his gaze on Chuck. "Okay, if I've got this straight, a tornado forms within a mesocyclone, which forms within a thunderstorm. Kind of like a circulation within a circulation within a thunderstorm."

"Yes," Chuck said. "And sometimes you'll get a mesocyclone that spins out a new tornado even before the old one has completely croaked. So occasionally you might see a thin, rope-like twister, a dying one, right beside a more robust tornado that's just beginning to blossom."

"I think I see where you're going with this," Boomie said. "I'll bet you're going to tell me that on very rare occasions a new twister will form and mature even before the old one gets a stake driven through its heart."

Chuck nodded. "So what you can end up with is what we saw: two full-blown tornadoes side-by-side. And you're right, it's extremely rare. Not only that, when it does occur, you can probably put a stopwatch on its longevity. Like I said, the last twin monsters photographed were almost 50 years ago . . . until today."

"And the evidence got blown away," Boomie said, his words laced in exasperation. "Get out there and help them find that damned recorder."

Chuck didn't need any further exhortations to join the search. He, accompanied by Sam, strode through the litter toward Metcalf, who seemed to be coordinating the effort.

"Anything?" Chuck asked when he reached Metcalf.

"Chuckie," he said, "what kind of a dumbass question is that? Has one goddamned thing turned out right on this expedition? I mean think about it. Our vehicles are beat to shit, one virtually DOA in Tulsa thanks to a buffalo stampede—how often has that happened on a tornado chase? A million-dollar Panavision got turned into scrap metal. A second one is MIA. One of my cinematographers almost got swept into the Land of Oz. Your lady friend, who turns out to be a Fed—" he rolled his eyes "—just about became a full-course meal for a snake. And, oh yeah, you created a crispy critter in a gas explosion. Your kid got shot. And your puppy and Injun bud got chomped on by a Python named Monty. Jesus, that's hilarious. And ridiculous. And absurd. A comic tragedy. No. We haven't found the frigging camera. Or the recorder." He waved the two men off. Dismissive.

As Chuck and Sam walked away, Metcalf muttered in a stage whisper, "Please, God, take me now."

Ziggy motioned for Chuck and Sam to move to the periphery of the search group, toward the southern end of the parking lot.

"Should have brought a flashlight," Chuck said.

Sam agreed. "It'll be dark in 15 or 20 minutes."

After 25 minutes, Metcalf called off the search. "We really don't have a clue where that thing might have ended up, do we?" he said. "It could be in Kansas, right? Or Arkansas?"

Sam gestured at the wreckage surrounding them. "Or you could have walked by it a dozen times this afternoon without spotting it in all this shit. We'll hit it another lick tomorrow. Start early in the morning when the sun angle is low. Great contrast for tracking."

"Okay, Tonto," Metcalf said. "I'll let *you* lead the hunt tomorrow. This is your land. Just steer us clear of buffalo herds and snakes. Heap big wampum if you find the SSR." He raised his voice and addressed the assemblage. "Everybody back here at sunup tomorrow. Red Ryder and Little Beaver here are going to lead us to the Happy Hunting Ground for digital movie cameras."

Sam's jaw tightened. Chuck laid a hand on his shoulder and whispered into his ear. "Don't take it personally," he said. "He's an equal opportunity offender."

"So I've noticed."

The group dispersed. Ty and Boomie had been picked up, leaving Stormy to fend for herself. Now she limped behind Chuck and Sam as they headed to Sam's truck.

"I've got a friend in Pawhuska," Sam said. "We can stay there tonight."

They rode in silence, Chuck allowing his thoughts to drift toward despair as he stared out the side window into the darkness. He had to be realistic. The odds against recovering the SSR were prohibitive. It wasn't beyond the realm of possibility the thing really had been swept into another state.

Yes, he had to be realistic. In all likelihood he was about to end up back where he'd started, subsisting in a cheesy apartment in Norman. Only this time without even a minimum-wage job. It seemed the weather gods had once again conspired against him. He issued an audible sigh, his breath fogging the window.

"Sometimes it's a long road home," Sam said.

"I don't have a home."

"That's why the road is sometimes long."

Sam flicked his headlights on high beam, illuminating the deserted highway.

"You seem to be the eternal optimist, Sam."

"No, it's just that I've been there before, after I got back from 'Nam. It took me a long time to find myself. To find the road. To find home. Sometimes I still get lost. You'll be fine."

"Everything hinges on finding the footage Boomie shot."

"It doesn't, actually. But I know you don't believe that now. Anyhow, I think we might find it."

"Yeah?"

"I might have a dream."

Chuck stared at him. "A dream?" Sam's face, tinted in the glow of the dashboard lights, appeared almost abstractionist.

Sam glanced over at Chuck. "Indian stuff. Ask me in the morning."

Chapter Thirty-one

MONDAY, MAY 12

CHUCK AND SAM stood at the edge of the Gust Front's parking lot, watching the sun lift into an azure sky, a firmament free of clouds, free of threat. An antithesis to the previous day. Chuck turned up the collar on his wool jacket to ward off a chill galloping over the plains on a gusty northwest wind. The gusts bore the lingering stench of destruction, an odor of charred structural remains.

Stormy sat next to the two men, seemingly reluctant to take off on one of her usual early- morning galavants. Perhaps she'd been traumatized by the snake attack, or maybe she was just confused by the acres of debris.

"I had a dream last night," Sam said.

"And?" Chuck said.

"I was back in 'Nam."

Chuck waited for Sam to continue.

"Waiting for a Dustoff to land in a stand of elephant grass to ferry the wounded to a field hospital. The Gooks were shooting at the chopper. We returned fire. Drove the Slopes off. But it was too late, the Medevac had left, called to another mission. The Gooks came back, started dropping mortar rounds into our position. Bad situation. Under attack. Lots of wounded. No help."

Sam paused, raised a hand to shield his eyes from the rising sun.

"A mortar round exploded right in front of me. Almost blinded me. I thought we were goners."

"Sam," Chuck said, "this was a dream or something that actually happened to you?"

"Yes."

Chuck reached down and petted Stormy and waited for Sam to continue, wondering what all of this might have to do with Indian lore and finding the SSR.

"In 'Nam, a flight of gunships escorted the Dustoff back to the LZ and bailed our asses out. In my dream, an Indian pony burst out of the tall grass and galloped through our position. It cut a swath through the grass that we were able to follow to safety . . . into an old Michelin rubber plantation. To a stand of trees where we were able to defend ourselves."

"You guys didn't know about the plantation?"

"There was no plantation. Only in my dream."

"Sorry. Forgot."

"Anyhow, I woke up this morning, after the dream, thinking about prairie grass and horses and where your recorder might be. What the dream told me."

"You believe in that stuff?"

"The Indian part of me does, not the soldier in me. That part only thinks about death."

Metcalf's Lincoln and the camera truck pulled into the lot. Metcalf, a new Greek fisherman's cap pulled low over his eyes to ward of the low-angle sun, strode to Chuck and Sam. "Okay, chief," he said to Sam, "where do we look?"

Sam squinted at him. "How about the Little Big Horn?"

Metcalf brushed his fingers through his beard. "Sorry," he said. "Where do we look, Mr. Townsend?" He put sarcastic emphasis on "Mr. Townsend."

"I suggest you and your team go through the debris covering the parking lot again. Yesterday, everyone was tired and stressed out, and the light was failing. Today we're rested, the light is great and we've got the whole day ahead of us. Be methodical and thorough. Dig through everything. Like I said yesterday, you might have walked right by the camera or recorder a dozen times without realizing it."

"What about you and Chaz?"

"We're going to take my truck and check the grasslands around the lot, just in case the thing got blown out onto the prairie."

"Or farther," Chuck added. Dejection riddled his words.

"We'll find it," Sam responded. "Let's go." He spoke to Metcalf: "Call Chuck's cell if you find anything."

"Like that's gonna happen," Metcalf mumbled. He motioned for his crew to follow him into the center of the parking lot.

Chuck lifted Stormy into the bed of Sam's pickup, then climbed into the cab beside Sam. "What are we really looking for?" he asked as Sam steered the truck into prairie.

Sam shrugged. "A horse. Maybe a trail through the prairie grass. A rubber plantation."

"Jesus." Chuck sank down into his seat. He fixed his gaze on the floorboard, not the grassland.

Sam chuckled. "I'm kidding about the rubber plantation. Look, only half of me is Osage. The other half is like you. Rational. Let's give it an hour or two. Who knows . . ."

Chuck didn't respond. He didn't believe in mystical guidance from dreams, but on the other hand, the hours spent searching yesterday had proved fruitless.

"Okay?" Sam asked.

"No more than two hours."

The prairie grass, lush and green from the recent storms, lay semi-flattened in the bright dawn. Debris—strips of insulation, shingles, sheets of aluminum, all manner of wastepaper—coated the rolling landscape to the near horizon. The litter appeared less dense than that which layered the area immediately surrounding the Gust Front, but . . . they could search for days and never find the SSR. Chuck shook his head. There seemed no hope. Only another defeat.

He and Sam rode in silence for the better part of half an hour.

"Sam, this is ridiculous," Chuck finally blurted. "I don't mean to offend—"

"There," Sam said. He pointed dead ahead of the pickup.

Chuck lowered the sun visor to shield his eyes. "What's that?"

"Wild horse. Usually they run in herds. This one seems to be alone." Sam gunned the engine. The truck lurched forward. The horse wheeled and galloped toward a low rise.

Chuck gripped the grab bar above the door as the pickup bounced and hopped over the grassland in pursuit of the horse.

"Christ. Easy, Sam. You're gonna break your truck."

"Don't wanna lose the horse."

"It's just a horse, damn it."

"You think?"

Chuck didn't answer.

The horse reached the ridge and slowed his pace, allowing Sam to close the gap. The animal trotted down the opposite slope as Sam reached the peak of the rise.

"Well, shit," Sam said, looking down the slope. He stopped the truck.

The horse had led them to his herd, not the Panavision, not the

SSR.

"So much for Indian lore," Chuck said. But he had to admit he was more disappointed than angered. He had, in fact, held out just a smidgen of hope that Sam's vision would bear fruit.

"Get out and look around," Sam said.

"Sam—"

"Humor me."

Chuck dismounted, told Stormy to stay put. "You can't help out here, girl. You need to rest that paw. We'll get you to a vet this afternoon." Stormy whimpered, but remained in the bed of the truck.

Chuck and Sam tramped around in the grass for almost an hour before Sam raised the white flag. "Well, there's nothing here," he said.

"Lots of horse pucky." Chuck examined the bottom of his left shoe. "That's not a metaphor."

"Kind of what you'd expect, I guess. From real horses. Not dream horses. Sorry, partner." He rested a hand on Chuck's shoulder.

"I was kind of hoping—"

"I know you were. So was I. Maybe I'm more soldier than Indian."

Chuck's cell rang. He answered.

"Well, Chazaroo, your Injun bud knew what he was talking about after all," Metcalf said. "We found the Panavision and the SSR in the parking lot. They were under a big pile of wreckage from the motel. But we got 'em! How about that shit?"

Chuck turned to Sam. He couldn't help it, the words came tumbling out: "I'm a millionaire, Sam. A fucking millionaire. Can you believe it?" Elation swept over him. An emotion that had been matched only twice in his life: by the birth of his son and the birth of his daughter.

Sam high-fived him.

"We'll be back in 30 minutes, Jerry," Chuck yelled into the phone. "Hang on."

"Hey, Chucky," Metcalf said, "before you wet your pants in excitement, let me correct one thing. You ain't a millionaire. See ya back here." He hung up.

The buoyancy that had filled Chuck mere seconds ago exploded from him like air bursting from a pinpricked balloon.

Chapter Thirty-two

MONDAY, MAY 12

CHUCK AND SAM rolled into the debris-shrouded parking lot of the Gust Front Grill a half hour after receiving Metcalf's call. Metcalf, in an animated discussion with Willie Weston and Ziggy, stood near his Navigator.

Chuck dismounted from Sam's pickup and marched toward Metcalf, who greeted him with a forced smile. Willie and Ziggy stared at the ground, as though examining their shadows.

"What the hell did you mean, Jerry, I'm not a millionaire?" Chuck snapped. "We had a deal. You gave me a one-day extension. I delivered. I found your supertwister."

"You did."

"So what's the problem? You gonna try to claim it wasn't an EF-4 or -5 that caused all this." He gestured at the wreckage surrounding them, at the flattened grill, the destroyed town.

"No."

"You're just gonna stiff me then, you son of a bitch?"

No longer smiling, Metcalf stepped closer to Chuck. "Watch your mouth, Chuckie. I'm not a guy who welches on deals. But we never had one." His voice rumbled with an undertone of menace.

"We shook hands on it."

"I said—and I remember my words precisely—I'd give you an extra 24 hours."

"So?"

"So I never said I'd extend the contract. The million-dollar incentive expired on Saturday."

"I'll get a lawyer. I'll fight this in court." Chuck attempted to sound resolute, but effeteness strangled his retort. He knew he'd just been shoved off a cliff.

The smile returned to Metcalf's face. "Sure you will, Chaz. Outside of the fact you don't have a pot to piss in, the only *signed* document you can produce is the original contract, the one that gave you 14 days to earn your prize. Day 15 didn't count."

Chuck clenched his fist, measuring the distance to Metcalf's smile. *Enough is enough from this asshole.* He cocked his arm and fired an uppercut at his tormentor's chin.

Sam, suddenly beside Chuck, blocked the punch. "Don't."

Chuck, chest heaving, stared at his friend.

"He'll have you arrested for battery," Sam said, gently pushing Chuck's arm down. "Don't give the bastard any more to gloat over than he's already got."

"Jesus, Sam . . ." But no more words came. He'd been gutted by Metcalf, like a trout freshly yanked from a mountain stream. His legs went wobbly and he sank to his butt on a pile of debris.

Willie stepped forward, confronted Metcalf. "Come on, Jerry. The guy delivered. We got some of the best footage of a twister ever shot. That alone—"

"Back off, Willie. Let me handle the business end of things. You stick to directing." Metcalf turned to Chuck. "Hollywood is a dog-eat-dog world, Chuckie. Nothing personal."

"It's actually pretty damn personal. You screwed me." Chuck stared straight ahead, not at Metcalf.

"I wish Monty were here," Sam said. "He'd take care of things."

"Yeah." Dejection smothered Chuck . He'd taken a long journey, from doubt to resurrection, from defeat to victory, from dream to reality. But in the end, it had all been an illusion. There was no pot of gold at the end of the rainbow. He should have known that.

Sam rested a hand on Chuck's shoulder. "A wise man once said, 'In a fight between you and the world, back the world'."

"Osage wisdom?"

"No. Franz Kafka." Sam extended his hand to Chuck. "Come on. Let's blow this joint."

"Where to?"

"There are some people in a Bartlesville hospital that would probably like to see you," Sam said. He pulled Chuck to his feet.

Metcalf tipped his cap to Chuck and Sam as he climbed into his SUV. "Maybe next time, gentlemen."

Sam gave him the finger.

Willie approached Chuck. "Sorry," he said. "This just isn't right. The trouble is, legally, the bastard is on solid ground. Morally, that's another story. I hope you don't judge everyone in the business by him."

Chuck shrugged. Drained.

Ziggy remained near Metcalf's Lincoln. He looked in Chuck's direction, shook his head slightly, his dreadlocks swinging like grandfather clock pendulums, and mouthed, "Sorry, man."

"Come on you guys," Metcalf yelled at Willie and Ziggy. "Let's get out of cowpuke country and back to civilization." He gunned the engine.

Stormy limped to Chuck, stood on her hind legs, and licked his hand.

CHUCK ENTERED GABI'S room at the Jane Phillips Medical Center in Bartlesville. Her eyes closed, she stirred uneasily as the door clicked shut behind Chuck. A monitor tracking her blood pressure and other vital signs beeped softly. Inserted in her right hand, an IV drip, presumably an antibiotic of some sort, went about its work silently.

He sat in a chair next to her bed. Contrasted against her ebony hair, her face, washed of color, appeared even paler than it likely was. After a moment, she opened her eyes and offered a weak smile. "My hero," she said, her words slightly slurred.

He placed his hand on top of her unencumbered one, but didn't respond, afraid he'd blubber.

"The doctors told me you and Ty, but you especially, performed CPR on me for quite a while until the EMTs got there with their little shock machine and squeezy thing."

"It's called a Ambu bag."

"Whatever. My point is, if you save a life, you're forever responsible for it," she said, her voice almost a whisper. "Think you're up to the job?"

He gathered himself, checked his emotions. "Probably not."

"Why not? I'm not going to be a vegetable, you know." Her voice remained soft. "It's a funny thing to say, but luckily, that damned snake—" she shuddered "—squeezed me so hard it stopped my heart before I suffocated. If I'd suffocated—you know, no oxygen to the brain—you'd probably have a turnip for a girlfriend." She stopped talking, seemingly exhausted by her effort.

"A lot of pain?" Chuck asked.

"I think I'm stuffed full of pain killers. Hey, at least my migraine is gone." She managed a fragile laugh.

A nurse entered the room and checked the monitor, writing

something on a clipboard. She bent over Gabi. "How ya doin', honey? Can I get you anything? Water? Something to eat?"

"Ribs."

"You that hungry?"

"No. *New* ribs. For me."

The nurse patted Gabi's head. "I know, darlin'. Those'll take a while to mend. Sorry. Not much we can do for 'em. Well, the doc will be along shortly to talk to you. Okay?"

Gabi nodded. The nurse left.

"Hey," Gabi said, a thought seeming to strike her, "did you find the recorder? The images of the tornado?"

"Yes."

She smiled, more robustly this time, then winced. "Chuck, that's great."

"Not really."

"Why? I thought—"

"Metcalf screwed me." He explained.

"That son-of-a-bitch," Gabi said after he'd finished. The words came out strong, surprising Chuck. "We've got a lot of lawyers in the Bureau. Let me see what—"

"It's okay, Gabi. All I've got is a handshake on my side. Worthless. The only thing that matters legally is the contract I signed. It says time ran out on me Saturday, not Sunday."

"Yeah," she whispered, and closed her eyes. "I'm sorry." She squeezed his hand with surprising strength.

"I need to be going, Gabi. Ty's being released today. Gotta get him back to Ok City; and Stormy to a vet."

She opened her eyes and continued to grip his hand. Her voice remained subdued. "Remember, you're responsible for me now."

"Okay," he said. He bent over and kissed her on the lips, knowing a broke, jobless, middle-aged man couldn't effectively be responsible for much of anything.

"I expect you back here tomorrow," she said, a sweetness coating her words. She released his hand.

He nodded, noncommittal, and slipped from the room. In the hallway, head down, he trudged toward the main entrance. What had he accomplished the last two weeks? Won the battle, lost the war? Pretty much. He'd led the film crew to the greatest tornado ever filmed . . . and came away empty-handed. He'd fallen for a woman . . . but had nothing to offer her. He'd perhaps closed, slightly, the breach that separated him and his son . . . but couldn't deliver on his promise of financial restitution. And he still hadn't come to grips with exactly where he stood with Ty. Or God.

Was he, Chuck, being tested as Abraham had been with Isaac? Must he leave Ty on the mountain, a sacrifice? Did the answers lie in the Bible bound in strict conservative armor? Or in modern-day 21st-century science? Some people, Chuck knew, like his father, seemed to find clear-cut, black and white answers in the Bible. But the real world existed in shades of gray.

Behind the main information desk of the hospital lay a chapel. Chuck stepped into it, found it unoccupied, and seated himself in a pew. The confusion over how to address his relationship with Ty continued to unsettle him. The chasm between them seemed have narrowed over the past two weeks, but could it be bridged completely? What was right? How do you balance the pejorative terminology about homosexuality in the Bible with the inherent desire to love your children unconditionally?

He bowed his head and prayed, hoping to find guidance in the silence of the sanctuary.

He emerged a short time later and found Ty and Sam waiting for him in the lobby. Ty wore slightly worn golf shorts, flip flops, a tee shirt adorned with a big red O U, and a heavy bandage around his left thigh.

"Nice threads," Chuck said.

"Nordstrom was closed. Goodwill was open. At least they found me a University of Oregon shirt."

Chuck laughed. "O U? No, I think you're a Sooner now. How are you feeling?"

"Like I've been shot in the leg. Ironic isn't it? Not a scratch in Afghanistan, then I get a Purple Heart in Oklahoma?"

"Not much logic to life, is there?" Chuck said.

"Yeah. I guess we both should know that by now."

Sam interrupted the conversation. "Take your time, you two. I'm gonna mosey off and get the truck. I think Stormy might be getting kind of lonely. I'll meet you at the front entrance." He tipped his still-mashed top hat and strode off.

Ty inclined his head toward the chapel. "So, did you find any answers in there?" He spoke softly, not challenging his father.

"Not really. I just ended up with more questions. My conversations with God usually turn out to be pretty one-sided."

Shoulder-to-shoulder, father and son strolled toward the entrance. Outside, the brilliant late-afternoon sun reflected like tiny supernovas off the windshields of the vehicles crowded into the parking lot. A steady flow of people, both entering and leaving the facility, suggested the hospital was busier than usual. The traffic, Chuck guessed, consisted mainly of visitors seeking out victims of the previous day's tornadoes.

"Maybe," Ty said, "the answers lie within you. God probably wants you to find them for yourself. Not in some booming voice from heaven."

"Or even a quiet voice."

They walked in silence for a few moments, then Ty said, "So, where do I stand, Dad?"

Chuck stopped and touched his son on the shoulder. "When was the last time I hugged you?"

Ty turned to face him. "I don't remember. Years ago."

Chuck reached out and pulled Ty to him. "This is the answer I found within me." He wrapped his arms tightly around Ty, embracing him with the fierceness of a tacit request for forgiveness.

Ty responded with a bear hug. "Dad," was all he said, a catch in his throat.

"I love you, Son."

"That's all I ever wanted to hear," he responded, the words broken.

They released each other. Through the mist in his eyes, Chuck could see a watery redness in his son's.

They resumed their walk and reached the front entrance. Sam hadn't yet arrived.

"You're still wrestling with God and the Bible on this, aren't you?" Ty said.

"No."

"No? What's changed?"

"I remembered a passage from one of Paul's letters to the church of Corinth. "And now these three remain: faith, hope, and love."" He looked directly into his son's eyes. ""But the greatest of these is love.""

"Good ol' Paul."

"Yeah, I know. He comes down pretty hard on 'men . . . inflamed with lust for one another' in Romans."

"So where does that leave you?"

Chuck looked out at the circular drive fronting the entrance. "Sam's here."

Ty didn't move. "Dad."

Chuck turned to face his son.

"I asked where that leaves you."

"It leaves me," Chuck said, his voice firm and unwavering, "with immense love for my son. Is he a sinner? The answer is I really don't know and I really don't care."

"Dangerous for a Christian."

"I'm comfortable letting God sort it out."

"I think He'll be okay with that," Ty said. A brightness shined in his eyes that Chuck hadn't seen before.

"Something else, Son." Chuck's throat constricted.

"Yes?"

"Forgive me? I tossed you into a black hole ten years ago. That was unconscionable—"

"Dad." Ty held a finger to his lips, signaling Chuck to stop talking. "Don't beat yourself up. I acted like a shithead, too. So let's just toss those years into a memory shredder and start over. Father and son. Okay?"

"Okay." A beautiful word, but he barely got it out.

Sam honked the horn of his pickup. Stormy stuck her head out the passenger side window and barked. Chuck laid his arm across Ty's shoulders and they exited the hospital together, plunging into the intense radiance of the late-day sun.

Far away, low on the horizon, the alabaster anvil of a supercell fanned out over the flat Oklahoma landscape.

Epilogue

TUESDAY, AUGUST 19

CHUCK GRIPPED the sweating beer can, tipped it to his lips, and took a long swallow. He sat on the front steps of his Norman apartment, Stormy beside him, watching the sun lift into a cloudless sky. The heat already bordered on enervating. The fifteenth consecutive day of 100-degree temperatures seemed a slam dunk. At least the RedHawks were on the road; he wouldn't have to suffer through another steamy evening pointing people to their seats at the ballpark.

His neighbor's door opened. A man bent to retrieve the morning paper. *"Buenos días, señor* Chuck."

Without turning toward the man, Chuck raised his beer in greeting and said, *"¿Cómo estás,* Pedro?"

"Ricardo," the man said. *"Estoy bien, gracias."* He shut the door.

"Sorry," Chuck said, too late, "I know how it is when a guy can't even get your name right." He ruffled Stormy's fur and belched softly.

He continued his monologue. "Should be another action-packed day, Storms. Maybe we can walk to the Cowboy Corral and see if we can bum you another bone or two. Sorry I can't afford Science Diet or Iams or something."

Stormy cocked her head at Chuck and woofed softly.

"You're a good listener, gal. Glad I got somebody to talk to." He brought the beer to his mouth, drained the can, and tossed it into the dead bushes fronting his apartment. He remained seated, chin resting in his hands, watching the traffic on the main road. A black Lincoln Navigator turned into the apartment's parking lot.

"Looks just like that weasel Metcalf's SUV, doesn't it, Storms? Well, don't worry, girl. That shyster is a million miles from here, out of our lives."

Stormy stood, stiffened, and stared at the approaching vehicle. She took a step forward, issued a warning growl.

Chuck tracked the SUV, too. It pulled to a stop in front of his apartment. The door opened and the driver stepped out.

"Well, shit," Chuck said. He spat the words.

"Good to see you, too, Chuckie," Metcalf said. He strode toward Chuck, extended his hand.

Chuck ignored it and remained seated.

"Mind if I sit?" Metcalf said.

"I do."

Stormy, growling intermittently, remained at Chuck's side.

"Well, okay then. I understand." Metcalf's strange attire—shorts, hiking boots, Greek fisherman's cap—hadn't changed since Chuck first met him, four months ago. "Maybe you got another beer?"

"No."

Metcalf folded his arms across his chest and placed one foot on the step between Chuck and Stormy. "You kinda gotta understand my position, too. If I'd shelled out a million bucks on a handshake with no contractual authority, my bosses would have been roasting my ass over a barbecue pit in Malibu right now. I woulda been dead meat. Or more likely, having a beer for breakfast someplace, just like you."

"But you aren't."

Metcalf shrugged. "Life's unfair."

"Thanks. I hadn't figured that out."

The door to the apartment next door opened again and three children spilled out, giggling and calling for Stormy. Stormy barked and ran after them as they darted down the sidewalk in the direction of a nearby playground.

Metcalf plunked himself down on the spot vacated by Stormy.

"By all means, have a seat," Chuck said.

"How's your son?" Metcalf asked.

"We talk every week. He invited me out to spend a week on the Oregon coast with him."

"That's a beautiful place in the summer."

"I'll never know. I'm broke." He turned to look directly at Metcalf. "Some guy screwed me out of a million bucks."

"Maybe you just aren't a very astute businessman, Chuckie."

"Goddamnit, Jerry, my name is Chuck."

Metcalf appeared unfazed by Chuck's outburst. "How about the FBI chick, still see her?"

Chuck moved his gaze from Metcalf and stared at the ground. "She called a few times. We went out for coffee once or twice, but . . ." His words and thoughts trailed off.

"But what? She's hot for you, man. Everybody on the hunt could see that."

"But what?" Chuck snapped. "But what?" His voice rose. "In case you hadn't noticed, jerkoff, I'm an unemployed, broken down, middle-aged loser. I have a beer for breakfast—as you noted—and scintillating conversations with my dog. A night out is a Coke and a hot dog at a RedHawks game."

"Feeling sorry for yourself will probably fix that." Metcalf examined the bottom of his hiking boot. "I think I stepped in something."

"No. That's just you, Jerry."

A chuckle rumbled out of Metcalf's belly. "Hey," he said, "how about your Injun friend on the buffalo range? How's he doing?"

"Sam's rebuilding," Chuck mumbled. "He'll be fine. At least his money didn't burn up in the gas explosion."

"Yeah, that reminds me. What happened to the guy that shot at you and fed your lady friend to the snake, he in prison?"

"Recovering from his burns. His trial starts next month. He'll probably ride the needle to his final reward."

"That could take years, I'll bet."

The siren of an emergency vehicle wailed in the distance.

Metcalf cupped a hand behind his ear. "Ah, sounds just like that last day of the Great Hunt, doesn't it?"

Chuck moved his gaze back to Metcalf. "What's with you, Jerry? You didn't come all the way to Oklahoma to reminisce about old times. Maybe you just wanted to poke a stick in my eye again? Get your kicks pouring salt into an open wound?"

"Damn hot here. How can anybody live in a place like this?"

Waves of heat rippled off the parking lot. "Maybe you've been sentenced to hell and just haven't figured it out yet," Chuck said without humor.

"Possibly."

The men sat quietly for several moments.

Metcalf broke the silence. "The movie isn't going to be made."

Chuck let the words sink in before he spoke. "After all we went through? After you got some of the greatest tornado footage ever shot? After your cameraman was almost killed?" He shook his head in disbelief. "What the hell, Jerry?"

Metcalf shrugged. "That's Hollywood. The producers found a different horse to back."

"Meaning?"

"A better story."

"So the twin tornadoes will never see the light of a silver screen?"

"Maybe, maybe not."

"Damn it. Quit talking in riddles." Stormy trotted back from her foray with the neighbor's kids, sniffed Metcalf's shoe, and sat by Chuck.

Metcalf shifted slightly, reaching into a pocket of his cargo shorts, and pulled out a folded set of papers. He extended it to Chuck. "It's a contract. Read it over."

"A contract? A contract for what?" Chuck didn't accept the papers.

"Your services."

Chuck laughed. "Been there, done that. No thanks."

"Here's the deal, Chaz . . . Chuck. When I told the producers about our storm safari, you know, with all its little Alice-in-Wonderland misadventures—a buffalo stampede, killer EMTs, a lady FBI agent, a snake the size of Rhode Island, a shootout at the OK Corral—they were all over it. That's our movie, they said. Forget about *The Okies*." He offered the contract again.

Chuck refused it.

"At least look at it."

Chuck sighed, accepted the papers and leafed through them. Finished, he handed them back to Metcalf.

"Well?" Metcalf said. "It's a half-million-dollar deal." A tinge of anger clung to his words. "For the rights to your story. For you to act as technical advisor."

"Fool me once, shame on you. Fool me twice . . ."

"Have a lawyer look it over."

"I can't afford one."

"Jesus, Chuck."

"Okay, then. Let's go back to where we started. One million bucks."

"I'm sorry I suggested you weren't a very good businessman. Look, I'll level with you. I'm authorized to go to $800,000. That's it. That's as high as I can go."

"Too bad. I think it would have made a great movie, too." Chuck stood, brushed off his pants and turned to enter his apartment.

"Come on, man," Metcalf pleaded. "I'm hamstrung here."

"Take the other $200,000 out of *your* pocket." Chuck opened the door. Stormy squeezed past him and rushed into the coolness of the interior.

"Okay, okay. Hold on a minute. Invite me in."

Chuck stood aside and motioned for Metcalf to enter.

Metcalf did. He took a moment to look around. "Jesus, what a dump."

"It's how you end up when you get screwed by someone you thought you could trust."

Metcalf smiled. "I'm not the devil." He placed the contract on the kitchen table, pulled out a pen, and made some notations on the papers. "You win. One million dollars." He slid the documents to Chuck. "All I need is your signature."

"I think I'll take your advice and have a lawyer look it over."

"If it will speed things along, here's an incentive." Metcalf retrieved his wallet, extracted a check and handed it to Chuck.

Chuck took it, stared at it, found himself unable to swallow. "$250,000?"

"Down payment. The next quarter when we start production. The final half upon completion of the film."

"Shit. You knew all along we'd end up at a million. I should have asked for more."

"Probably."

Stormy growled, then barked and pounced at a roach as it ran across the kitchen floor.

THAT EVENING, CHUCK sat at his customary table beneath the neon sign advertising BEEF, BEER and BANJOS at The Cowboy Corral.

Daisy approached. "Hey, hon. Good to see ya. Ya usually don't wander in until Friday evening."

"Special day."

"Yeah? Well, ya want something special?" Curly red hair framing a big smile, she leaned in close to Chuck, perhaps hoping he'd catch a whiff of her perfume. But that hope, if it was there, disappeared in short order, swallowed by the resident aromas of grilled steaks and spilled beer.

"Bring me a Black Jack on the rocks. And you can get a couple of filets going on the grill."

"Two?" She gave Chuck a suspicious squint.

"I'm meeting someone."

"Oh. A lady?" A hint of a frown shadowed her face.

"Get my Black Jack, Daisy. Please."

Gabi arrived ten minutes later and took a seat across from Chuck. "So, boyfriend. I thought maybe I'd been black-listed. It's been so long since—"

"Ever been to Oregon?" Chuck asked.

"That's somewhere near Alaska, isn't it?"

"Not that close."

"You aren't proposing a romantic weekend getaway are you?" She fluttered her eyelashes in mock flirtation. She looked good, fully recovered from the trauma of the snake attack. A form-fitting white blouse offset her dark complexion, revealing the fullness of her breasts and triggering a yearning in Chuck he thought had died.

"More like a romantic week. Ty tells me there's a really nice little town on the coast called Manzanita. He's rented a house there the first week of September."

She reached across the table and took his hand. A smile, like a sunrise over a still pond, lit her face. "Tell me what happened," she whispered.

"I will. Oregon?"

"Do they have pythons there?"

"No."

"Supercells?"

"No."

"When do we leave?"

Glossary

AED Automated External Defibrillator

AMBU BAG a hand-operated resuscitator

ANVIL the flat, anvil-like—or in more modern terms, ironing-board shaped—top of a well-developed thunderstorm

ATV All-Terrain Vehicle

BNSF a railway company (originally the Burlington Northern and Santa Fe Railway)

BOUNCING BETTY an anti-personnel mine that pops about three feet into the air prior to detonating

CAP a layer of warm air aloft (usually around 2000 to 10,000 feet) that tends to suppress thunderstorm development; also known as a "capping inversion"

CAPE Convective Available Potential Energy—a measure of the energy, or instability, on tap for thunderstorm development; the higher the CAPE, the stronger any storms are likely to be

CHARLIE slang for Viet Cong soldiers (Vietnam War)

CIN Convective Inhibition—thermodynamic factors limiting or precluding thunderstorm development, usually due to a cap (see above)

CONVECTION vertical motion of air caused by the tendency of warmer air to rise and cooler air to sink; thunderstorms are driven by convection

CORE PUNCHING driving into the center, or core, of a large thunderstorm where the visibility is restricted; extremely dangerous if the storm harbors a tornado

CUMULONIMBUS a large, billowing cumulus cloud; usually a thunderstorm cloud

CUMULUS a convective cloud with a puffy, cotton ball-like top and flat base

DOA Dead On Arrival

DOWNDRAFT the down rush of cool air from a thunderstorm

DRYLINE the boundary between humid tropical air from the Gulf of Mexico and dry continental air from the Interior West; usually develops over the southern portions of the High Plains

DUSTOFF a medical evacuation helicopter (Vietnam War)

EMT Emergency Medical Technician

GENESIS Panavision's premier digital motion picture camera

GPS Global Positioning System

HABOOB a strong wind, usually due to a thunderstorm downdraft, causing a duststorm or sandstorm (Arabic origin)

HAIL ROAR the sound of large hail stones aloft colliding with one another; also, the sound of large hail striking objects on the surface at some distance

HELICITY the sum of shear in a vertical column of air; or, more simply, the amount of "twist" in a column of air

HIGH-RESOLUTION RAPID REFRESH MODEL (HRRR) an experimental, real-time, hourly-updated model; useful for short-range thunderstorm forecasting

LZ Landing Zone (military)

MESOCYCLONE the rotating updraft, usually one to ten miles in diameter, within a strong thunderstorm

MIA Missing In Action (military)

MOTHERSHIP a perfectly symmetric supercell with a wall cloud that looks like an alien spaceship

OVERSHOOTING TOP the domelike protrusion above a thunderstorm anvil; indicative of a powerful updraft

PDS Particularly Dangerous Situation; term used by SPC (see below) to describe situations in which long-lived and unusually violent tornadoes are possible

SPC Storm Prediction Center; the National Weather Service agency responsible for issuing tornado and severe thunderstorm outlooks and watches; local National Weather Service Offices issue warnings

SSR Solid State Recorder

STEADICAM a stabilizing system, like a harness, for movie cameras when hand-held

STRATOSPHERE the higher region of the atmosphere beginning at roughly 6 to 10 miles above the earth's surface

SUPERCELL the most violent and least common of thunderstorms;

it's characterized by a deep, persistent, rotating updraft called a mesocyclone

TAIL CLOUD a cloud band, often laminar and tube-shaped, attached to a wall cloud and reflective of strong inflow into a supercell

TORNADO SIGNATURE the Doppler radar indication of a strong mesocyclone within a thunderstorm and therefore a high probability of a tornado—see TVS; sometimes accompanied by a hook-shaped precipitation echo

TORNADO WARNING means a tornado is or may be imminent (based on actual sightings or Doppler radar indications); local National Weather Service Offices issue warnings

TORNADO WATCH means conditions are favorable for tornadoes to form within the next few hours; SPC outlines geographical areas where such conditions exist

TREXIMET a migraine medication; a combination of sumatriptan and naproxen sodium

TVS Tornado Vortex Signature; a Doppler radar algorithm that suggests the presence of a strong mesocyclone within a thunderstorm and therefore a high probability of a tornado (in more technical terms, based on how Doppler radar works, a TVS is a small, tight couplet of strong winds toward the radar immediately adjacent to strong winds away from the radar)

VORTICITY the measure of local atmospheric rotation around a vertical axis

WALL CLOUD a low, rotating cloud mass beneath the base of a strong thunderstorm, usually a supercell; often precedes tornado formation

WEDGE TORNADO a tornado that appears as a massive black triangle with its apex on the ground; a true wedge should be as wide at the ground as it is tall (measured from the cloud base)

WIND SHEAR the local variation of wind speed and direction along a vertical axis

XM short for XM Satellite Radio

ZOOMIES slang for Air Force personnel, especially fighter pilots

Author's Note

While Supercell is a work of fiction, several of the scenes in the book were inspired by a tornado chase I went on with Silver Lining Tours (www.silverliningtours.com) in 2012.

Specifically, the pursuit of the supercell from Levelland, Texas, toward Lubbock by the brothers Clarence and Raleigh was based on a chase I participated in. The big difference was that in the novel, the cell spun out a destructive twister. Although the storm I pursued with Silver Lining was big and black and mean, it didn't drop a tornado. It did, however, coat the ground with a blanket of hail several inches deep. It left the roads on the south side of Lubbock looking as if it they'd been smacked by a High Plains blizzard.

Another scene inspired by the chase I was on was the one in which Chuck leads the film crew into a hailstorm along the Red River in Texas, then seeks shelter from the storm's massive hail stones in a car wash. Silver Lining Tours ran an intercept on a big hailstorm in the same area and also hunkered down in a car wash. But the storm we tracked weakened and the hail core lumbered by just north of us, so we never witnessed the giant chunks of ice depicted in the novel.

I learned a lot about supercells on the chase, mainly drawing on the vast knowledge of Silver Lining Tours gracious co-owner, Roger Hill, and one of the tour's veteran guides, Tom Howley. Tom, a retired dentist, provided invaluable input not only to the novel's chase episodes, but also to the emergency medical care scenes. Happily, Tom turned out to be a first-rate literary critic, too, and helped me smooth out the book's rough first draft.

Several other people also read through the initial draft and offered immensely helpful feedback: Dave Spiegler, a longtime friend and American Meteorological Society Fellow; Gary Schwartz, a friend and avid reader who knows his job *isn't* to tell me what a great book I've written—quite the opposite, and because of that I've become a better writer; and Jeanie Pantelakis, my literary agent, who goes the extra mile for me—most agents don't want to see your work until it's spit shined, but Jeanie actually *participates* in the spit-shining.

My critique group at Peerless Book Store in Alpharetta, Georgia, suffered through countless readings of raggedy-ass, fresh-off-the-press chapters, and helped make them better. My special thanks to the regulars: John Sheffield, John Tabellione, Mark All and Valerie Connors.

John House, an urgent care physician and fellow novelist, vetted my emergency medical care scenes.

Greg Forbes, "Storm-meister Greg," The Weather Channel's severe weather expert and a former co-worker, answered a multitude of questions I had about severe thunderstorms and tornadoes. He also examined some of the technical explanations presented in the book, including the Glossary, and made sure they were on track. If I stepped on my meteorological poncho anyplace, it was my fault, not Greg's.

A couple of excellent books helped me fill in my (lack of) knowledge of storm chasing and tornadoes. *Tornado Alley—Monster Storms of the Great Plains,* by Howard B. Bluestein, offers a well written, relatively technical look at supercells and tornadoes. *Storm Chasing Handbook (Second Edition),* by Tim Vasquez, proved a wonderful, practical guide for storm chasers . . . and novelists.

About the Author

H. W. "Buzz" Bernard is the bestselling author of EYEWALL, PLAGUE and now, SUPERCELL.

EYEWALL, his debut novel, became a number-one best seller on Amazon's Kindle. Buzz is a native Oregonian and attended the University of Washington in Seattle where he earned a degree in atmospheric science and studied creative writing. He's currently vice president of the Southeastern Writers Association.

He lives in Roswell, Georgia, near Atlanta, with his wife, Christina, and over-active Shih-Tzu, Stormy. If you'd like to learn more about Buzz you can go to his Website: buzzbernard.com; or his author page on Facebook: H. W. "Buzz" Bernard.

CPSIA information can be obtained at www.ICGtesting.com
Printed in the USA
LVOW08s2101271013

358796LV00004B/23/P